ISBN 978-0-483-31137-4
PIBN 10063976

This book is a reproduction of an important historical work. Forgotten Books uses
state-of-the-art technology to digitally reconstruct the work, preserving the original format
whilst repairing imperfections present in the aged copy. In rare cases, an imperfection in
the original, such as a blemish or missing page, may be replicated in our edition. We do,
however, repair the vast majority of imperfections successfully; any imperfections that
remain are intentionally left to preserve the state of such historical works.

Terence O'Rourke

Gentleman Adventurer

By

Louis Joseph Vance
Author of "The Brass Bowl," etc.

New York
Grosset & Dunlap
Publishers

Preface

AS originally compiled, this history appeared serially under the titles of "O'Rourke, Gentleman Adventurer," and "The Further Adventures of O'Rourke," in *The Popular Magazine*, New York: to Messrs. Street and Smith, the owners and publishers of which, thanks are due for their courtesy in permitting this reproduction.

In welding together the many adventures in the career of this Irish gentleman, with a view to their appearance in this present form, the author found both convenient and advisable the omission of certain passages, the addition of some new material, as well as other minor changes in the text. It is hoped that these alterations will meet with the approval of the friends of Colonel O'Rourke: to whom his biographer wishes to offer his gratitude for their appreciation.

L. J. V.

New York, April, 1905.

Contents

❦

PART FIRST

The Empire of Illusion

Contents

❦

PART SECOND

The Long Trail

The Empire of Illusion

CHAPTER I

HE IS ROWELED OF THE SPUR OF NECESSITY

MADAME THÉRÈSE was of a heavy build — round and stout and comfortable-looking; nevertheless she possessed a temper. The vicious bang of the door behind her was evidence of that sufficient unto O'Rourke, even if he had not the memory of her recent words to remind him of the fact.

He drew a long and disconsolate face, standing in the precise center of what he called his "compartment" — it was six feet one way by nine another, and boasted of but one window, set in a slanting roof. His mobile and sympathetic lips drooped dolefully at the corners; his expressive brows puckered wofully over the bridge of his nose; and even the nose itself was crinkling with dismay. Madame's words still rang in his ears, even as the sound of her descending footsteps was still distinctly audible — and Madame Thérèse was by then on the fifth flight down, the second up from the street.

"The rent!" she had shrilled tempestuously. "The rent, m'sieur, must be paid by to-morrow morning! Otherwise—"

O'Rourke sighed from the bottom of his heart. "Faith, yes!" he said plaintively. "Otherwise . . . Oh, sure!" He frowned at the cracks in the floor, and with one forefinger tentatively caressed a light stubble of beard on his square chin.

But presently it occurred to him that care had been responsible for the death of the domestic cat. He smiled faintly, apprehensively, as though half afraid that a smile would hurt; finding the experiment painless he prolonged it, grinning broadly.

Below stairs, the last echoing thump of Madame's feet was to be heard. O'Rourke lifted his shoulders together, sighed, chuckled, and anathematized his landlady.

"*Brrrrr!*" cried O'Rourke, with a flirt of his hand in the general direction of the *conciergerie*. "*Brrrrrp!* And may the Old Boy fly away with ye!"

He turned to the window, dismissing his troubles with a second shrug of his broad shoulders, and, leaning his elbows on the sills and himself perilously far out over the eaves, stared earnestly at a window in the attic of the house that stood just behind O'Rourke's *hôtel*. But it proved vacant.

O'Rourke pursed his lips and whistled persuasively. "Faith, darlint," said he, and as earnestly as though he really expected to be heard, "'tis no more than a glimpse of your red cheeks and bright eyes that I'm needing to put the heart into me. Will ye not come, — only for one little minute?"

He whistled again, more piercingly. There was no response; the little dormer window, where a black-eyed and red-cheeked little seamstress ordinarily sat of a morning, sewing industriously — but not too industriously to be altogether unaware of the infatuated Irishman's burning glances — remained desolately empty.

"Oh, well!" conceded O'Rourke, in the end. "If 'tis obstinate ye are, me dear, sure and that only proves ye a true daughter of Mother Eve!"

[2]

And he swung a chair up to the window and sat down, cocking his feet upon the sill. A pipe lay convenient to his hand — a small and intensely black clay; unconsciously O'Rourke's fingers wandered towards it. They clasped with loving tenderness about the bowl, while the fingers of his other hand explored his coat pocket for a match. That found, the Irishman discovered a fresh beauty in the brilliant morning — a beauty but enhanced by the clouds of blue-gray incense that floated between him and the open casement.

By degrees, however, his smile faded. Not always was it possible for O'Rourke to laugh in the teeth of his adversities.

His gaze wandered far out from the open window and over the billowy sea of Parisian roofs that lay steaming in a bath of May sunshine.

The morning was one clear and brilliant, following on the heels of a day of scourging rain. Paris was happy; her face was washed, and she had on a clean pinafore dashed with the perfume of the spring things that were budding in her gardens. O'Rourke alone, perhaps, was out of tune with the universal spirit of contentment.

Now, good reasons why a man may be out of sorts in a Parisian springtide are few and far between; but they exist; O'Rourke had brought his with him when he had moved upon the capital on the edge of the winter, just vanished; and thereafter he had eaten and slept, moved and had his being in their company, enduring them with what patience he might — which was not overmuch, in truth. But now he was especially wistful and uneasy in his actions.

His supply of ready cash was not alarmingly low; it was non-existent — one all-sufficient reason for the disquietude of his soul.

Again, city life irked the man, who was of a nature tran-

[3]

sient, delaying under one roof no longer than was unavoidable — happiest, indeed, with no more than the wide sky for his bed canopy, the soft stars for his night lamps.

Finally, for some months O'Rourke had been kicking the heels of him about the pavements of civilization, devoutly praying for a war of magnitude; but in answer to his prayers no war had been vouchsafed unto him.

The broad world drowsed, sluggish, at peace with its neighbors -- save in a corner of Afghanistan, where the British Empire was hurling army corps after army corps at the devoted heads of an insignificant, bewildered tribe of hillmen who had presumed to call their souls their own — knowing no better.

But the tempest in that particular teapot had slight attractions for O'Rourke, sincere seeker after distraction and destruction that he was. He felt rather sorry for the hill tribe who at the same time were beginning to feel rather more than sorry for themselves, and to wish that they hadn't done so.

The Irishman, however, positively refused to fight with, if he did not care to fight against, England. So there was, in his own disconsolate phrasing, nothing doing at all, at all.

And now the *concierge* was insisting upon the payment of that overdue rent. Plainly, something must be contrived, and that with expedition.

O'Rourke swore, yawned, stretched widely. He removed his feet from the window sill, and arose.

"I'll do it," he said aloud. "Faith, 'tis like pulling teeth — but I'll do it. I despise the necessity. *Conspuez* the necessity! *A bas* the necessity!"

At the foot of the bed stood his sole personal property — a small, iron-bound trunk, aged and disreputable to the eye, sown broadcast with the labels of hotels, railways and steam-ships.

O'Rourke went to it with a deep and heartfelt sigh, un-locked it, and for a space delved into its tumbled contents, eventually emerging flushed and triumphant from his search, with a watch in his hand — a watch of fine gold, richly chased, and studded with gems.

He shook his head, gazing upon it, and sighed deeply.

Long since the timepiece had been presented to O'Rourke by the grateful president of a South American republic, in recognition of the Irish adventurer's services as a captain-general under that republic's flag. It was so stated in an inscription within the case.

O'Rourke treasured it lovingly, as he treasured the por-trait of his mother, his love for the land of his nativity, the parting smile of his last sweetheart. He treasured it as he valued his honorable discharge from the Foreign Legion, the sword he had won in Cuba, and the captain's commission he had once held under the Grecian flag.

But — the rent!

He slammed his hat upon his head, the watch into his pocket, and the door behind him; he was going to call upon his "aunt in Montmartre."

When he returned he was minus the timepiece, but able to reinstate himself in the *concierge's* graces. Indeed, as she signed the receipt, the lady declared that she had always known in her soul that monsieur was an honorable gentleman.

O'Rourke accepted the honeyed words sourly, disgruntled to the extreme. He had a residue of a very few francs: actual hardship was but staved off for several days. Never-theless, he had indulged himself in the luxury of a complete file of the day's papers.

[5]

Back in his little room again he read them all, thoroughly, even with eagerness; read the foreign news first, then the native, the scandal, the advertisements — even the editorials.

He found that England had completed her subjugation of the hill tribes, and incidentally the education of her rawest troops. On the horizon no war cloud threatened — unless in one spot.

From a meager paragraph, eked out by his knowledge of Central American politics, O'Rourke gleaned a ray of hope: trouble boded on the Isthmus of Panama. But that was indeed far from Paris.

He put aside his pipe and the last sheet, and glowered longingly across the roofs to the western sky line.

What his eyes rested upon, he saw not; mentally he was imaging to himself, scenting, even feeling the heat haze that lowers above that narrow ribbon of swamp, rock-spined, which lies obdurate between two oceans.

On his businesses of the moment he had crossed the isthmus several times. He had warred in its vicinity. He knew it very well indeed, and were there to be ructions there he desired greatly to be in and a part of them — to grip the hilt of a sword, to hold a horse between his thighs, to sweat and swelter, to toil and to suffer, to fight — above all, to fight —!

Clearly the obvious course of action was to go — to stand not on the order of his going, but to go at once.

O'Rourke started from his chair, with some half-formulated notion of proceeding directly to the Gare du Nord, and taking train for Havre; thence, he would engage passage *via* the French line to New York, thence, by coasting steamer to Aspinwall.

The route mapped itself plain to his imagination; the way was simple, very; there was but one complication. Realizing which O'Rourke sat down again, and cursed bitterly, if fluently.

"The divvle!" he murmured in disgust. "Now, if I hadn't been so enthusiastic for paying me rent —"

He produced his fortune and contemplated it with a disgusted glare: five silver francs and a centime or two, glittering bright in the rays of the declining sun.

"Why, sure," he mused, "'tis not enough to buy the dinner for a little bird — and 'tis meself that's no small bird!"

Now, how may a man by taking thought increase five francs one or two or three hundred fold?

At nightfall he concluded to give it up, the problem looming unsolvable. There seemed to be no answer to it, and O'Rourke was considering himself a much abused person with no friend to call his own the wide world 'round, barring —

"Paz!" he cried suddenly. "And why did I not think of Paz before, will ye be telling me?"

He sat silent for some time, wrapped in thought, as in a mantle.

"Likely am I to go hungry, the night," he admitted at length, ruefully; "but I'll dine in style or not at all."

Incontinently, he began to bustle about the narrow room — how he had grown to hate its mean confines of late! — preparing to go out.

He started by shaving his lean cheeks, indelibly sunburned, very closely; then he wriggled into the one immaculate shirt his wardrobe boasted, brushed with care and donned his evening clothes and an inverness; and completed his adornment with gloves and shoes of the sleekest — both of which he had been hoarding all the winter against just such an emergency.

[7]

When through he indulged in a moment's approving inspection in his mirror, and nodded with satisfaction because of the transformation he had brought about in his personal appearance.

"I'll say this for ye, Terence, me lad," he volunteered: "that when ye are of the mind to take trouble with yourself, 'tis the bould, dashing creature ye are!"

And he chuckled light-heartedly at his own conceit, extinguishing the lamp and locking his door.

Yet he had no more than hinted at the irrefutable truth, for he was by no means ill-favored by nature: a man tall and broad beyond the average, with square shoulders and a full chest, with lean yet muscular flanks and long and sinewy limbs, well-knit and well set-up. His countenance was dark, — as has been indicated, the hall mark of a veteran campaigner — but nevertheless of a versatile mobility, and illuminated with eyes of warm gray, steadfast yet alert, swift to mirror the play of his emotional and passionate nature, bespeaking good-humor, an easy temper and — ordinarily at least — a habit of optimism.

For the rest he carried himself with confidence and assurance, as fits well upon an Irish gentleman — was he not "the O'Rourke"? — but without any aggressiveness. He was ready of wit, quick of tongue, tolerant of disposition: a citizen of the wide world, seasoned, sure of himself, young.

He descended the stairs with spirit, passed out before the *conciergerie* with an air. Madame Thérèse, the vigilant, observed and admired, regretting the harsh terms she had applied to her lodger, earlier in the day. "He gives the *hôtel* distinction," she murmured; and resolved mentally that in the future she would accord this splendid young person more consideration.

[8]

Now, it so came about that Madame Thérèse was not afforded the opportunity of putting in effect that good resolution for many and many a long day; the turn of affairs presently precluded Colonel O'Rourke's return to his little room. Which, however, was not greatly to his dissatisfaction.

But at the moment, O'Rourke himself had no more apprehension of this than had she. He was, in point of fact, anticipating an early return and a penniless to-morrow. The prospect did not tend to lighten his mood.

In the street he turned and cocked a — momentarily — jaundiced eye up at the towering, smudged, gloomy façade of the lodging house.

"'Tis no palace ye are," he apostrophized it, hating it consumedly; "'tis no gilded cage ye are, for a bird of me brilliant plumage. But 'tis needs must whin the divvle drives, I've heard — and if wishes were motors, this beggar would ride!" And then, "Faith, 'tis damnable — no less!" he declared with a short laugh. "To think of me, the O'Rourke, in all me fine feathers, that can't so much as afford the price of a *fiacre!*"

CHAPTER II

THE house of Paz fronts upon the Boulevard Roche-chouart — which is not the worst street in Paris, morally, though near it — and wears the dismayed, ingenuous expression of a perfectly innocent house which suddenly finds itself rooted in a neighborhood which is — well, *not* perfectly innocent. In other words, the house managed by Monsieur Paz is something of a hypocrite among houses; in sober reality it is no better than it ought to be, or even not so good.

A high, pale yellow façade is broken by orderly rows of windows that are always blank and sleepy-looking; never is a light visible from within, and for a very good reason: they are fitted with an ingenious device which allows for ventilation, but does not permit a single ray of light to escape to the street.

It was somewhat after eight o'clock in the evening that O'Rourke approached, having traversed the width of Paris in order to reach the place.

In previous, more prosperous days he had known the house of Paz rather intimately — too well, at times, for the good of his own interests. But of late, in his lowly estate, he had neither cared nor dared to pass its portals; which are not for the impecunious.

At present, however, he had a use for it, and was relying both upon his former acquaintance therein and his generally affluent appearance to procure for him admittance to its charmed precincts — something none too easy to a stranger without credentials.

He neared it, I say, and with some trepidation, becoming to a man of emotions who is going to stake his all on a single throw, — which was what O'Rourke proposed to do, — eying the exterior aspect of the place with a wonder as to what changes might have occurred within, in the few years that he had been a stranger to its walls.

While yet some distance away he observed the door opening with circumspection. For a single second the figure of a departing patron was outlined in the light; then the doors swung to, swiftly and noiselessly.

O'Rourke remarked, without great interest, that it was a young man who was leaving so early in the night; a man who stood hesitant at the foot of the steps, glancing up and down the street irresolutely, as one who knows not whither to go.

In a moment, however, he seemed to have made up his mind, and started off toward O'Rourke, walking briskly, but without any spring in his step, holding his head high, his shoulders back. There was a suggestion of the military in his bearing.

As he passed, O'Rourke noted the tightly compressed lips, the hopeless, lack-luster eyes of the man.

"Cleaned out — poor chap!" he sympathized.

Simultaneously the doors open again, briefly; a second man emerged, ran hastily down the steps, and started up the street as though in pursuit of the first.

This man was of an uncommon and distinguished appearance; large and heavily built, yet lithe and active; with a fat-cheeked face, bearded sparsely; thick lips showing red through the dark hair; a thin, chiseled nose set between eyes pouched, yet bright and kindly, the whole surmounted by a forehead high and well modeled — a type of Gallic intellectuality, in short.

He swung past the Irishman hurriedly, intent upon his chase, but favored him with a searching scrutiny — which O'Rourke returned with composure, if not with impudent interest.

But the evening was yet young, and there was nothing in the encounter to particularly engage his fancy; he dismissed it from his mind, and turned into the house of Paz.

He knocked peculiarly: the familiar signal of old. A minute passed, and then a panel in the door slid back, exposing a small grating, behind which was the withered face of the *concierge*, with a background of dim, religious light.

"O'Rourke," announced the Irishman, languidly, turning his face to the window for identification.

That was scarcely needed. His name was a magic one; the *concierge* knew, and had a welcome for one who had been so liberal in the matter of gratuities in days gone by. The doors swung wide.

"M'sieur le Colonel O'Rourke!" murmured the *concierge*, bowing respectfully.

O'Rourke returned the greeting and passed in, with the guilty feeling of a trespasser. He disposed of his inverness and hat, and ascended the stairway directly to the second floor.

Here was one huge room, in floor space the width and depth of the building, infinitely gorgeous in decoration, shimmering with light reflected from gold leaf, from polished wood and marble.

Around the walls were chairs and small refreshment tables; the floor was covered with rugs of heavy pile, well-nigh invaluable, the walls with paintings of note and distinction.

Beyond reasonable doubt Monsieur Paz was prosperous, who could provide such a *salle* for the entertainment of his patrons.

But in the center of the room was the main attraction — that lodestone which drew the interest of the initiated with a fascination as irresistible as the magnetic pole holds for the needle: an enormous table topped with green cloth whereon was limned a diagram of many numbered spaces and colors.

And in the center of the table, under the electric chandelier, was a sunken basin of ebony, at whose bottom was a wheel of thirty-seven sections, alternately red and black, each numbered from 0 to 36: the roulette wheel.

O'Rourke slid unostentatiously into a vacant seat at the extreme end of the table. A man at his elbow looked up with passing curiosity, but immediately averted his gaze; otherwise the Irishman attracted no attention. For a few minutes he sat idle, watching the play, the players, the croupier presiding over the wheel — a figure that fascinated his imagination: a man vulture-like with his frigid impassivity, mathematically marvelous in the swiftness, the unerring accuracy of his mental computations as he paid out the winnings or raked in the losings.

He stood, imperturbable, watching the board with vigilant, tired eyes, his bald head shining like glass under the sagging electric sunburst. From time to time he opened his wicked old mouth, and croaked dismally the winning number and color, whether odd or even. Followed the ring of coin and the monotonous injunction:

"*Messieurs, faites vos jeux!*"

The *salle* was very still, save for the sound of the spinning ivory ball, the click of the wheel, the cries of the croupier.

To O'Rourke, new from the freshness of the spring air, the atmosphere was stifling and depressing — hot, fetid, lifeless though charged with the hopes and fears of those absorbed men who clustered around the board, sowing its painted face with coin and bills, hanging breathlessly on the words of the croupier, as he relentlessly garnered the harvest of lost illusions.

The Irishman was not yet ready to bet, having counted on the room being more crowded, forgetful of the early hour. He had but one play to make, the lowest the house permitted — five francs, — and it was so insignificant a sum that the man felt some embarrassment about offering it, fearing that it might attract sneering comment. In a crowd it might have passed, especially if he lost — as, in all likelihood, he would.

He summoned an attendant and ordered a cigar — "on the house" — to make time; and while he was waiting, eyed the man opposite him, at the farther end of the table.

The latter was young, weary and worried, if his facial expression went for aught; he played feverishly, scattering gold pieces over the cloth — as often as not, probably, betting against himself. His face was flushed, for he had been drinking more than could have been good for his judgment; and O'Rourke fancied he recognized in him the youthful lieutenant of a cavalry troop then quartered near Paris.

Abruptly a man flung into the room, as if in anger; at the door he paused to collect himself, scanning each player narrowly, and finally chose a seat near the lieutenant.

"Hello!" thought O'Rourke. "So you're back so soon! I wonder — well, none of me business, I suppose."

It was the man with the beard whom he had noticed leaving the gambling house in such apparent haste, and not so very long since.

The attendant returning with the cigar, the Irishman lit it leisurely, and sat puffing with an enjoyment heightened by the fact that he had been deprived of the luxury of cigars for some weeks.

Presently he turned his attention to the board, and acted a little farce for his own self-satisfaction.

With the air of a man of means, who merely desires to while away an idle hour — win or lose — O'Rourke thrust his hand into his breast pocket and produced a small wallet, tolerably plump and opulent-looking — a result due to ingenious stuffing with paper of no value.

He weighed it in his palm, seeming to debate with himself, then deliberately returned it to the pocket. His manner spoke plainly to the observer — were there one: "No; I'll risk but a trifle of change."

Abstractedly he thrust his fingers into his waistcoat pocket and brought out the said change; to his utter surprise it turned out to be no more than five silver francs!

But finally he made up his mind to play that utterly insignificant sum.

At that moment the ball rattled, was silent. There was an instant's strained silence. The wheel stopped.

"*Vingt-quatre,*" remarked the dispassionate croupier; "*noir, pair et passe!*"

He poised his rake, overlooking the great board.

The young lieutenant arose suddenly, knocking over his chair; he stood swaying for a moment, his fingers beating a nervous tattoo upon the edge of the board; he was pale, his face hollow-seeming and hopeless in the strong illumination. Others looked at him incuriously. He put his hand to his lips, almost apologetically, essayed what might have been intended for a defiant smile, turned, and moved uncertainly

toward the staircase as one who gropes his way in darkness
— a ruined man.

"*Messieurs, faites vos jeux!*"

O'Rourke hardly heard the words; he was wondering at
the bearded man, who was prompt in following the defeated
gamester.

"'Like to know what's *your* game," muttered O'Rourke.

Simultaneously, without actually thinking what he was
doing, he placed his five francs on the cloth. When he
looked he saw that they stood upon the nearest space, the
36. He puckered his lips together, thinking what a pitiful
little pile they made.

"'Tis the fool I am!" he admitted, wishing that he might
withdraw. But the ball merely mocked him, as the wheel
slackened speed, with its "*whrr-rup-tup-tup!*"

"A fool —" he began again.

But it seemed that he had won!

"'Tis not true!" he cried exultantly, yet almost incredu-
lous. But he accepted the one hundred and eighty francs
without a murmur, cast them recklessly upon the black, and
multiplied the sum by two, and by blind luck.

Then, with his heart in his mouth — it was all or nothing
with him now — he allowed his winnings to remain upon
the black; which again came up, making seven hundred
and twenty francs to his credit.

"'Tis outrageous," he insisted gaily. "Will I be making
it, now?"

Fifteen hundred francs was the mark he had set himself to
attain; that much he needed to carry him to Panama; it was
to be that or nothing at all. He divided his winnings, re-
serving half, scattering the remainder about the numbers,
hope high in his heart.

He lost. He played and won again. And again. He reached the mark, passed it, asked himself if he should not stop, now, when the gods were favoring him. . . .

He need not have asked; by no means could he have stopped; for the gambling fever was as fire in his veins. He played on, and on, and on. He won fabulously, with few reverses; lived for a time in a heaven of wealth, upborne by the fluttering, golden wings of chance — and, at length, awoke as from a dream, to find himself staring at an empty spot on the board before him — the place where temporarily his riches had rested ere they took unto themselves wings and vanished.

Not a single franc remained to him. He had lost.

"Gone?" he muttered blankly. "Faith, I didn't think—" He became aware that he was being watched, though indifferently; in particular the man with the beard was observing him with interest, having now for a third time returned.

O'Rourke yawned nonchalantly, suddenly on his mettle; he was not willing to let them see that he cared.

"Five francs," he thought, arising; "small price for a night's entertainment. Sure, I got the worth of me money, in excitement."

He looked at the clock; to his amazement the hands in-indicated two in the morning. Now the room was half deserted, the attendants gaping discreetly behind their hands. A few earnest devotees still clustered about the table, winning or losing in a blaze of febrile haste.

The ball clattered hollowly; the tones of the croupier only were the same:

"*Onze! Noir, impair et manque!*" and "*Messieurs, faites vos jeux!*"—as though it were an epitaph,—as it too often is.

And when he left the room, O'Rourke marked that the bearded man was pushing back his chair and arising.

CHAPTER III

HE DECIDES THAT BEGGARS SHOULD RIDE

O'ROURKE found the night air soft and balmy, humid but refreshing. He walked with great, limb-stretching strides, throwing back his shoulders and expanding his chest — bathing his lungs, so to speak, with the cleansing atmosphere.

His way led him straight across the city, a walk of no slight distance to his lodgings; but he made a détour to prolong it, to give the exercise an opportunity to clear his brain and steady his nerves — unstrung as they were, from his recent excitement, as from the action of an opiate.

It was later than he began to think; for he could not immediately believe that time had flown so rapidly in the house of Paz. Only the almost deserted streets in which his footsteps echoed loud and lonely, the quietness that lay upon the city, the repose of the gendarmes on the corners, brought home to him the wee smallness of the hour.

He was not sleepy — anything but that; he was very much awake — and yet he was dreaming, holding a "*post-mortem*" (as he termed it) on his luck and misfortunes of the night, and planning toward his future; or rather, he was striving to solve the riddle of his future, drear and uncompromisingly blank as it then loomed, to his imagination.

For the present — it came to him as a distinct shock — he was exceedingly hungry, and, through his own folly, found himself without the wherewithal to satisfy that young and healthy appetite.

But he told himself that he, an old campaigner who had known keen privation in his time, could stave off starvation by reefing in his belt. "A light stomach makes a light conscience," was the aphorism from which he was seeking consolation when he noticed that he was being followed.

Quick, determined footsteps were sounding in the street behind him.

"Is it possible," he inquired aloud, "that me friend with the Vandyke beard is after me, with his nefarious designs, now? I've half a mind to stop and let him interview me."

He glanced over his shoulder; the man behind was passing under a light about a block distant; O'Rourke judged that he was a heavy, bulky man, with a beard.

"The same!" he cried, pleased as a child with a toy, with the strangeness of the affair. "Faith, now, I'll be giving him a run for his money."

He mended his pace, lengthening his stride; but the other proved obstinate, and was not to be shaken off. For some time O'Rourke could tell by the sound that the distance between them was neither increasing nor decreasing; and then he began to puzzle his head about the pursuer's motive.

The man had dogged two men, at least, besides O'Rourke himself, from the gambling house; and each had been, or had seemed to be, broken in fortune, and therefore likely to be more or less desperate, and ready to seize upon any chance to recoup.

What then had this fellow to offer ruined gamesters? O'Rourke wondered. His inquisitiveness made his feet to lag, for he was now determined to find out; and he cast about for an excuse to halt altogether, finding it in the half of a cold cigar upon which he had unconsciously been chewing.

He felt in his pocket for a match, and stopped to strike

it under one of the gloomy arches of the Rue de Rivoli. His man came up rapidly. O'Rourke dallied with the match, pretending an interest in the odd aspect of the almost desolate street, so generally populous.

"Monsieur —"

He jumped, by premeditation, and looked around. The man with the beard stood by his side, breathing heavily. O'Rourke eyed him gravely.

"The top of the morning to ye, sir," he said courteously; "and what can I have the pleasure of doing for ye, may I ask?"

The other recovered his breath in gasps, begging for time with an uplifted, expressive hand. He bowed ponderously; and O'Rourke made him a graceful leg, his eyes twinkling with amusement; after all the Irishman was no more than a boy at heart, fun-loving, and just then resolved to extract what entertainment he might from the Frenchman.

"Monsieur, I have a favor to ask —"

"A thousand, if ye will!"

The man was quick-witted; he saw that he was being trifled with, and expressed his resentment by the gathering of his heavy brows and a significant pause. At length, however, "Monsieur has been unfortunate," he suggested coldly.

"In what way?" demanded O'Rourke, on his dignity in an instant.

"At roulette," returned the other. "I presume that monsieur is not —" He hesitated.

"Not what, if ye please?"

"Rich, let us say; monsieur feels his losses of to-night —"

"He does? And may I ask how monsieur knows so much about me private affairs?"

"I was watching —"

[20]

"Ye were!"

The other flushed, yet persisted: "Not precisely. One moment — I will explain —"

"Very well," O'Rourke consented ominously.

"Perhaps you are in need of money? Now, I am —"

He got no further; that was a bald impertinence to an O'Rourke, even if to a penniless one; and the destitute adventurer, made thus to realize how desperately he was in reality in need of money, was not pleased.

"That," he broke in placidly, "is none of your damned business!"

"What!"

A deeper shade of red mantled the face of the Frenchman. He stepped back, but, when the Irishman would have passed on, barred the way.

"Will monsieur please to repeat those words?" he requested, with ceremony.

"I will," returned O'Rourke hotly; and obliged. "Now," he concluded, "ye are at liberty to — get — out — of — me — way, sir!"

"But — you have insulted me!"

"Eh?" O'Rourke laughed shortly. "Impossible," he sneered.

"Monsieur! I insist! My card!" He flourished a bit of pasteboard in O'Rourke's face. "For this you shall afford me satisfaction!"

"Angry little one!" jeered O'Rourke. Now thoroughly aroused, he seized the card and tore it into a dozen scraps, without even looking at it.

"I'll afford ye no satisfaction," he drawled exasperatingly, "but — if ye don't remove yourself from me path, faith, I'll step on ye!"

[21]

Quivering with rage, the Frenchman began to draw off his gloves. O'Rourke divined what he purposed. He paled slightly, and his mouth became a hard, straight line as he warned the aggressor.

"Be careful, ye whelp! If ye strike me, I'll —"

The gloves were flicked smartly across his lips, instantly demolishing whatever barriers of self-restraint he had for a check upon his temper. He swore, his eyes blazing, and his arm shot out. The Frenchman received the full impact of the blow upon his cheek, and — subsided.

Standing over the prostrate body, O'Rourke glanced up and down the street; it seemed very still, quite dark, almost deserted. Only upon a distant corner he made out the figure of a man leaning negligently against a lamp-post; he might prove to be a gendarme, but, so far, apparently, his attention had not been attracted to the affair.

O'Rourke's primal impulse was to pass on, and leave his adversary to his fate; but the retaliating blow had cooled his anger by several degrees. On second thought, the Irishman decided to play the good Samaritan — which was egregious folly. His man was sitting up, by then, rubbing ruefully his cheek; O'Rourke gave him a generous hand and assisted him to his feet.

"I trust," he said, "that ye are not severely injured —"

"*Canaille!*" rasped the Frenchman, sullenly, dusting his coat; and he drove home the epithet with a venomous threat.

O'Rourke laughed at him.

"Aha," he cried, "then ye've not had enough? Do I understand that ye want another dose of the same?"

Silently the man picked up his hat from the gutter, knocked it into shape, and rubbed it against his sleeve in fatuous effort to restore some of its pristine brilliancy.

[22]

"If ye are quite through with me," continued the Irishman, "I'll go to the devil in me own way, without your interference. And, monsieur, a word in your ear! Attend to your own affairs in the future, if ye would avoid —"

The man with the beard cursed audibly, gritted his teeth and clinched his hands; but when he spoke it was coolly enough.

"I have not done with you, *canaille*," he said. "You will do well, indeed, to go on, for I intend to hand you over to a gendarme."

"The divvle ye say!"

O'Rourke found that he was addressing the back of the man, who was making hastily toward the figure under the distant lamp-post. "That looks," he debated, "as if he meant business! Faith, 'tis meself that will take his advice — this once!"

Accordingly he started off in the opposite direction, in leisurely fashion; he was not inclined to believe that the Frenchman would really carry out his threat of arrest. Nevertheless, he kept his ears open, nor was he greatly surprised when presently, as he debouched into the Place de la Concorde, he heard mingled with shouts the sound of two pairs of running feet in the street behind him.

"Why, the pup!" he exclaimed, deeply disgusted, and stopped, more than half inclined to face and thrash both the representative of the law and the impertinent civilian. But he quickly abandoned that alluring prospect; it was entirely too fraught with the risk of spending a night in custody — something that he desired not in the least.

By then, the sounds of pursuit were nearing rapidly. Already the gendarme had caught sight of his figure, and was yelling frantically at him to halt and surrender.

"This won't do, at all, at all," reflected O'Rourke, and

himself began to run, cursing his hotheadedness for the predicament into which it had led him.

A sleepy cabby woke up, startled by the unusual disturbance, and added his yelps to those of the policeman and the much-abused Frenchman. Others joined in the chorus. A belated street gamin shrieked with joy, and attached himself to the chase. His example was followed by others. O'Rourke began to be very, very regretful for his precipitancy.

He doubled and turned into the Champs Élysées, hounded by a growing, howling mob. It seemed to him that men sprang from the earth itself to help run him down; and the sensation was most unpleasant. He began to sprint madly, his inverness flapping behind him like the wings of some huge, misshapen bird of night. He dug elbows in ribs, clenched his teeth, and threw back his head, careful to keep as much as possible in the shadows.

And the mob grew, whooping joyously with interest; from their cries it seemed that they considered O'Rourke an escaping criminal of note.

The Irishman kept himself ever on the alert for some chance of escape — any subterfuge to throw the pursuit off his track; but none appeared. He realized that he was gaining by sheer fleetness of foot, but not for a moment did he imagine that by swiftness he might distance the mob. For a rabble is always fresh, never tiring; the places of those who drop out, exhausted and breathless, are instantly filled by fresh and willing recruits. And in the end the mob gets at the throat of its quarry — if the running be in the open.

O'Rourke knew this entirely too well for the peace of his own mind; therefore, he grasped avidly at the first chance that presented itself, heedless of its consequences.

Drawn up at the curb, a *fiacre* stood with open door. He could see the driver turning on the box to discover the cause of the uproar. That was good, O'Rourke considered; the man, then, was wide awake.

He reached the vehicle and jumped upon the step, shouting to the driver the first address which entered his head:

"To the Gare du Nord! At once! With haste!"

Immediately the *fiacre* was in motion; O'Rourke experienced some difficulty in drawing himself in and closing the door because of the rapidity of the pace. In another moment the horse was leaping forward furiously, under the sting of a merciless lash.

"Bless the intilligent man!" muttered O'Rourke fervently. He felt that he could have kissed the driver for his instant obedience. But at once he was crushed by a paralyzing thought; how, in Heaven's name, was he to pay the hire of the vehicle?

He cursed his luck, and attempted to seat himself — gasped with astonishment, and incontinently stood up again, bumping his head against the roof.

"Madame!" he cried astounded, into the obscurity. 'I' beg —"

The reply was instant and encouraging.

"My pardon is granted, monsieur. Will monsieur be pleased to resume his seat?"

For the other occupant of the *fiacre* was — a woman.

CHAPTER IV

"THE Saints," prayed Terence devoutly, "preserve us all!"

Immediately he felt himself stricken as with a dumbness — fairly stunned. The woman upon whose privacy he had so unceremoniously intruded, composedly and with a pretty grace made a place for him by her side; and he, obedient, but speechless, collapsed into the seat.

It came to him that this must be an exceptionally wonderful manner of woman, who could accept his rude invasion with such unruffled calmness; and he had noted that her voice was not only absolutely unmoved, but most marvelously sweet to hear.

The *fiacre* whirled on as though the devil himself were at the whip (thought O'Rourke). It rocked from side to side, perilously upon one or two or three wheels — never safely upon four; it sheered about corners, scraping the curbs barely.

Conversation became obviously impossible under such circumstances; O'Rourke recognized the necessity of explanations, but found that he must perforce be silent; and, for that matter, he was rather grateful for the chance to get his breath and collect his scattered wits.

So he abandoned as hopeless the task of framing up some plausible excuse for his conduct, as well as that of accounting to himself for the extreme placidity with which his fair neighbor had welcomed him; and, consistently with his character,

[26]

he at once became the more intensely occupied with an attempt to discover the identity of the woman.

But he was baffled in that. The street lamps, reeling like telegraph poles past the windows of a moving train, illuminated but fitfully the interior of the *fiacre*, and he could see but little, strain his eyes as he might.

His companion, the woman — or girl, rather; for the youthfulness of her seemed impressed upon the impetuous and impressionable Irishman by his mere propinquity with her — made no effort, for the time being, to break the silence. O'Rourke was moved to marvel much thereat. Was she accustomed to such nocturnal escapades that she could take them as a matter of course? Or was she strangely lacking that birthright of her sex — the curiosity of the eternal feminine?

She nestled closely in her corner, with her head slightly averted, gazing out through the window. Evidently she was in evening dress, and that of the richest; a light opera cloak of some shimmering fabric wrapped soft folds about her. Her arms, gloved in white, were extended languidly before her, while her hands — very bewitchingly small, O'Rourke considered them — lay clasped in her lap. Beneath the edge of the cloak a silken slipper showed, pressing firmly upon the floor as a brace against the sudden lurchings of the *fiacre* — and surely the foot therein was preposterously tiny!

By now the cries of the rabble had died in the distance, and the speed of the vehicle slackened; presently it was bowling over a broad, brightly lighted boulevard at quite a respectable pace; and within the vehicle the darkness became less opaque.

The Irishman boldly followed up his inspection; but the woman was not aware of it — or, if she were, disregarded it, or — again — was not ill-pleased. And truly that admiration which glowed within O'Rourke's eyes was not unprovoked.

Against the dark background her profile stood in clear, ivory-like relief, clean cut and distinguished as a cameo — and perilously beautiful; her full lips were parted in the slightest of smiles, her eyes were deep, warm shadows, the massed waves of her hair uncovered, exquisitely coiffured · · · "Faith!" sighed the Irishman. "'Tis a great lady she is, and I . . ." He was, notwithstanding his self-depreciation, conscious of considerable satisfaction in the knowledge that he was attired properly, as a gentleman; but, "Oh, Lord!" he groaned in spirit. "What will she be doing with me when she finds me out?"

For it was appealing to him as very delightful — this adventure upon which he had stumbled — even though he had not a single sou to give the driver. That O'Rourke was young has been mentioned; he was also ardent and gallant; and it was to his blandishments of tongue that he was trusting to extricate him gracefully from his predicament.

But — did he honestly desire to be extricated? Not — he answered himself with suspicious instantaneousness — if it was to deprive him of the charming companionship which was his, for the moment; not if it left him still hungry for a peep within the cloak of mystery that shrouded the affair.

He made a closer inventory of the *fiacre;* it was rather elegant in appointment — no mere public conveyance, that is to be picked up on any corner; all of which confirmed his suspicions that this was a woman of rank and pedigree.

And when he ventured a more timid glance, sideways, it was to find her eying him with an inscrutable amusement.

"Mademoiselle," he faltered clumsily, "I — I — faith! if ye'll but pardon me again —"

She looked away at once — perhaps to ignore his eyes, which were pleading his cause far more eloquently than were his lips.

"Monsieur," she pronounced graciously, "is impetuous; but possibly that is no great fault."

"But — but, indeed, I must apologize —"

"Surely that is not necessary, monsieur; it is understood." She paused. "You were long in coming, indeed; I had grown quite weary with waiting. But since you did arrive, eventually, and in time, all is well — let us hope. As for the delay, that was the fault of Monsieur Chambret — not yours."

O'Rourke stared almost rudely, transfixed with amazement, incapable of understanding a single word. What did she mean, anyway?

"Me soul!" he whispered to himself. "Am I in Paris of to-day — of me day — or is this the Paris of Dumas and of Balzac?"

But he received no direct answer; the girl waited a moment, then, since he did not reply, proceeded, laughing lightly.

"At first, I'll confess, the sudden burst of noise in the street alarmed me, monsieur. And when you appeared at the door, I half fancied you the wrong person — perhaps a criminal fleeing from the gendarmes."

"And what reassured ye, mademoiselle?" he stammered blankly.

"The password, of course; that set all right."

"The password!" he echoed stupidly.

"Naturally; yes, monsieur!" She elevated her brows in delicate inquiry. "'To the Gare du Nord,' you cried; and by that I knew at once that you were sent by Monsieur Chambret."

Beauty and mystery combined were befuddling the Irish-man sadly; when she ceased, looking to him for an answer, he strove to recall her words.

"Monsieur Chambret?" he iterated vaguely. Then, to himself, in a flash of comprehension: "The password, 'To the Gare du Nord'!"

"*Mais oui!*" she cried, impatiently tapping the floor with the little slipper. "Chambret — who else? Oh!" She sat forward abruptly, her eyes wide with dismay. "You *must* be from Monsieur Chambret? There *cannot* have been any mistake?"

For a second O'Rourke was tempted to try to brazen it out; to lie, to invent, to make her believe him indeed from this "Monsieur Chambret." But to his credit be it, the thought was no sooner conceived than abandoned. Some-how, he felt that he might not lie to this woman and retain his self-respect.

Not that alone, but now that he could see more clearly her eyes, he fancied that he perceived evidences of mental an-guish in their sweet depths; she seemed to have been counting dearly on his being the man she had expected. No — he must be frank with her.

"I fear," he admitted sadly, "that there *is* a mistake, mademoiselle. In truth, I'm not from your friend; ye were right when ye fancied me a fugitive. I *was* running away — to avoid arrest for an offense that was not wholly mine: I had been strongly provoked. I saw the *fiacre*, supposed it empty, of course, jumped in . . . Ye understand? Believe me, I sincerely regret deceiving ye, mademoiselle, even un-intentionally."

He waited, but she made no answer; she had drawn away from him as far as the *fiacre* would permit, and now sat watching his face with an expression which he failed to fathom. It was not of anger, he knew instinctively; it was no fear of him, nor yet acute disappointment; if anything, he could have fancied her look one informed with a subtle speculation, a mental calculation. But as to what?

That was the stumbling-block. He gave it up.

"If I can be of any service in return —?" he floundered in his desperation. "But I must again humbly sue for pardon, mademoiselle. I will no longer —"

The man's accustomed glibness of tongue seemed to have forsaken him most inopportunely; he saw that it was a thankless task to try to set himself right. What cared she for his protestations, his apologies?

And in such case he could do no more than act — get out of her sight, leave her to her disappointment. He reached toward the trap in the roof, intending to attract the driver's attention and alight.

But it appeared that this was not a night upon which even a headstrong O'Rourke could carry to a successful conclusion any particular one of his determinations. For, as he started up, the girl stirred, and put a hand upon his arm, with a gesture that was almost an appeal.

He halted, looking down.

"One moment, monsieur," she begged. "I — I — perhaps you might be willing to —" She hesitated, torn with doubts of the man, total stranger that he was to her.

"To make amends?" he broke in eagerly. "To be of service to ye, mademoiselle? If I can, command me — to the uttermost —"

"Then . . ." She sat back again, but half satisfied that she was acting wisely; her eyes narrowed as she pondered him; O'Rourke felt that her gaze pierced him through and through.

She frowned in her perplexity — and was thereby the more enchanting.

"Thank you," she concluded, at length. "Possibly — who can tell? — you may serve me as well as he whom I had expected."

"Only too gladly, mademoiselle!" he cried with unfeigned enthusiasm.

She nodded affirmatively, patting her lips with her fan — lost upon the instant in meditation, doubting, yet half convinced of the wiseness of her course.

O'Rourke waited uneasily, afire with impatience, fearful lest she should change her mind. Eventually, she mused aloud — more to herself than to the stranger.

"You are honest, I believe, monsieur," said she softly; "you would not lie to me. Who knows? You might prove the very man we need, and — and, oh, monsieur, our need is great!"

"But try me!" he pleaded abjectly.

"Thank you, monsieur — I will," she told him, a smile lightening the gravity of her mood.

And the *fiacre* came to a halt.

CHAPTER V

"Our destination, monsieur," the girl indicated briefly, with a dainty little nod of her head.

Half stupefied, the Irishman managed to get himself — somehow — out of the vehicle. Wholly fascinated, he made haste to turn and assist the woman to alight; for a moment her gloved hand rested in his broad palm — her hand, warm, soft, fragile . . . ! But, almost immediately, it was gone; O'Rourke found himself bowing reverently, and, he felt, idiotically, over space. He recovered himself, and followed the girl, his eyes aglow with a new, clear light.

Their *fiacre* had halted before a certain impressive mansion on a broad boulevard — a *hôtel* familiar to the Irishman in a way, and yet nameless to him. Rather than mansion, the building might be termed a palace, so huge, so impressive it bulked in the night. Seemingly a fête of some sort was in progress within; the windows shone with soft radiance, faint strains of music filtered through the open entrance, at either side of which stood stolid servants in gorgeous livery after the English fashion.

From the doors, down the steps to the curb, ran a carpet under an awning. The girl tripped nonchalantly up the steps, as one knowing well the place, and gave a whispered word or two coldly to a footman who bowed with a respect which struck the Irishman as exaggerated.

They passed through an elaborate vestibule banked with

plants, its atmosphere heady with the fragrance of flowers, and so into a great hallway where other servants relieved the newcomers of their wraps.

Before them a doorway arched, giving upon a ballroom, whence a flood of sound leaped out to greet them: laughter of women and the heavier voices of men; scraping of fiddles and of feet in time to the music; the swish of skirts, the blare of a French horn.

Mademoiselle had accepted the arm of the Irishman; they moved toward the ballroom, but before entering she turned toward him, speaking confidentially, yet with an assumption of lightness.

"You are to converse with me, monsieur, lightly, if you please, as though we were lifelong friends. I shall chatter — oh, positively! — and you must answer me in kind. It — it is essential, monsieur."

He bowed, attempting an easy smile, which failed utterly; for a regally attired personage at the doorway demanded the honor of announcing the late guests. And O'Rourke had not the least clew to his mademoiselle's identity! He colored, stammered, hating the servant rabidly for what he considered his cold, suspicious eye.

Yet he need not have shown confusion, had he but guessed. He managed to mouthe his name — "Colonel O'Rourke" — and the servant turned to the ballroom, raising a stentorian voice:

"Madame la Princess de Grandlieu! Monsieur —"

His own name followed, but was lost to O'Rourke in the thunder of his companion's title. And the châteaux of romance which he had been busy erecting *en Espagne* fell, crashing about his astounded ears.

A princess! And, if that did not place "mademoiselle"

[34]

far beyond his reach — he, a mere Irish adventurer! — she was also "madame" — married!

"Monsieur!" the voice of the woman came to his ears through the daze of his reverie; and it was a-thrill with dismay. "Monsieur, for the love of Heaven do not look so wrathful! You — why, you are ruining our play; you must, *must* pay attention to me —"

With an effort he contrived to gain some control of his emotions; he schooled himself to bend an attentive ear towards the woman, and to smile lightly the while they chatted of inconsequential matters, slowly threading a way down the length of the *salon*, through a whirling maze of dancing couples: all of which floated vaguely before O'Rourke's eyes, a blur of women's gleaming, rounded shoulders, of coruscant jewels and fugitive flashes of color, all spotted with the severe black-and-white costumes of men. They ran the gantlet of a thousand pairs of curious eyes, whose searching and impertinent scrutiny O'Rourke keenly felt, and as keenly longed to return.

They were making, he found, for the far end of the room — towards a wall of glass through which peeped green, growing plants. And there, in the conservatory, the princess presently left the adventurer.

"You will await me here," she instructed him, "that I may know where to find you when the time comes. In ten minutes, then, Colonel O'Rourke!"

She smiled graciously. He was gripping himself strongly, in order that he might answer her with some semblance of coherency; and he blushed in his embarrassment, finding himself slow to recover — very boyish looking, young and handsome.

Madame la Princesse turned away, smiling inscrutably,

and left him. He strolled about for a few moments, then seated himself upon a bench in full view of the room he had just quitted. For ten long minutes he waited, as tranquilly as he might; which is as much as to say that he was restless to the extreme and vibrant with curiosity.

For fifteen minutes or so longer he wriggled on the seat of uncertainty, wondering if he was being played with, — made a fool of. A thought struck him like a shot: was she detaining him while sending for the police?

The essential idiocy of that conjecture became evident within a few minutes. The princess was but proving her inborn, feminine method of measuring time; she returned at last — flushed and breathless, more bewitching than he had imagined her, who had not ere this seen her in a good light.

"Come, Colonel O'Rourke, if you please."

He was instantly at her side, offering his arm. She seemed to hesitate the merest fraction of a second, then lightly placed her fingers upon his sleeve, where they rested, flower-like. The man gazed upon them with all his soul in his eyes. His hand trembled to seize them — oh, already he was far gone! But the manner of Madame la Princesse kept him within bounds; its temperature was perceptibly lower than formerly.

For her part, she was choosing to ignore what he could not conceal — the devotion which her personality had so suddenly inspired in the breast of the young Irishman.

They re-entered the ballroom; now it was half deserted, and a facile way lay open to them on the floor that had been so crowded.

By an almost imperceptible pressure upon his arm the princess guided him across the room, and into a *salon* that was quite deserted.

"It is late," she said, half in explanation, half to keep the man's mind on matters other than herself; "in a quarter of an hour the fête will be a thing of the past, monsieur."

"And the guests all departed on their various ways," he said — merely to make talk.

She favored him with a sidelong glance. "Not all," she returned, with a meaning which he failed to grasp, and stopped before a closed door, of which she handed him the key. He opened in silence, and they passed into a large room and gloomy, furnished rather elaborately as a library and study, its walls lined with shelves of books.

In the center of the room stood a great desk of mahogany, upon which rested a drop-light with a green shade that flooded the desk itself with yellow radiance, leaving the rest of the apartment in shadow.

The princess marched with determination to the farther side of the desk and there seated herself.

"The door, monsieur," she said imperiously: "you will lock it."

Wondering, he did her bidding; then stood with his back to it, instinctively in the pose of an orderly awaiting the command of a superior officer — shoulders back, head up, eyes level, feet together, hands at sides.

She noted the attitude, and relented a trifle from her frigid mood. "That Colonel O'Rourke is a soldier is self-evident," she said. "Be seated, monsieur," — motioning to a chair on the opposite side of the desk.

Again he obeyed in silence; for, in truth, he feared to trust his tongue.

The woman lowered her lashes, drawing off her gloves slowly, as though lost in deepest meditation. As a matter of fact she was planning her campaign for the subjugating of this adventurer; at present, he was impossible — too earnest, too willing to serve, too fervent for comfort.

For a time she did not speak, and the room was very quiet. If she watched him, O'Rourke was unable to make certain of it; for the upper half of her face was in deep shadow. Only her arms, bared, showed very white and rounded; O'Rourke might not keep his gaze from them.

But she found a way to bring him to his senses. Suddenly she leaned forward, and turned the shade of the lamp so that its glare fell full upon the Irishman's face; her gaze then became direct; and, resting her elbows upon the table, lacing her fingers and cradling her chin upon the backs of her hands, the girl boldly challenged him.

"Colonel O'Rourke," she said deliberately — at once to the point; "you are to consider that this is a matter of business, purely."

He flushed, drew himself bolt upright.

"Pardon!" he murmured stiffly.

"Granted, monsieur," she replied briskly. "And now, before we implicate ourselves, let us become acquainted. You, I already know, I believe."

"Yes, madame?"

"There was a man of whom I have heard, of the name of O'Rourke, who served as a colonel in the Foreign Legion in the Soudan, for a number of years."

"The same, madame," he said — not ·without a touch of pride in his tones.

"He received the decoration of the Legion of Honor, I believe? For gallantry?"

"They called it such, madame."

He turned aside the lapel of his coal; she nodded, her eyes

brightening as she glimpsed the scrap of ribbon and the pen-
dent silver star.

"I begin to think that chance has been very kind to me,
Colonel O'Rourke," she said, less coolly.

"Possibly, madame."

"You have seen other service, monsieur?"

"Yes —"

"For 'Cuba Libre,' I believe?"

"But the list is a long one," he expostulated laughingly.

"For so young a man — so gallant a soldier!"

"Oh, madame!" he deprecated.

"You are," she changed the subject, "pledged to no cause,
monsieur?"

"To yours alone, madame."

She thanked him with a glance. He was amply rewarded.
After an instant of hesitation, she proceeded bluntly:

"You, I presume, know who I am?"

"Madame la Princesse —" he began.

"I do not mean that," she interrupted; "but before my
marriage —?"

"No —" he dubitated.

This seemed to gratify her.

"That is good, then — you do not know me, really," she
concluded. "You do not even know where you are?"

"No more than in Paris," he laughed.

"Oh, that is good, indeed! Then I may talk freely —
although I must ask that you consider every word confidential. I rely upon your honor —"

"Believe me, ye may."

"Then — to business."

Heretofore she had been studying his features intently;
what character she had read therein must have been reassur-

ing to the girl, for at once she discarded the constraint which she had imposed upon their conversation, and plunged *in medias res*.

"Colonel O'Rourke," she began slowly, as if choosing each phrase with care, "I have a brother — a very young man: younger even than I. His wealth is great, and he is — very regrettably weak, easily influenced by others, wild, wilful, impatient of restraint, dissipated. His associates are not such as one might wish. But let that pass. You comprehend?"

"Perfectly, madame."

"Some time ago — recently, in fact — he conceived a harebrained scheme, a mad adventure — I cannot tell you how insane! I believe it fraught with the gravest danger to him, monsieur. I have sought to dissuade him, to no effect. At the same time I discovered by accident that it would further the interests of — certain of his companions to have him out of the way — dead, in fact. I questioned my brother closely; he admitted, in the end, that it was proposed to him — this scheme — by those same persons. I made inquiries, secretly, and satisfied myself that not one of my brother's so-called friends was anything more or less than a parasite. For years they have been bleeding him systematically, for their own pockets. And now, not content with what they have stolen from him, they want his fortune *in toto*. In short, he consorts with sycophants of the most servile, treacherous type."

She paused, drawing her long white gloves thoughtfully through her hands, eying O'Rourke abstractedly beneath her level brows; the Irishman's gaze assured her of his sympathy.

"Proceed, madame," he said gently.

"To-night, monsieur — this morning, rather —" she

smiled — "my brother gives this rout to cover a conference with the instigators of the scheme. It — it must certainly be of an unlawful nature, monsieur, else they would not meet so secretly, with such caution. Even now certain of the guests are assembled in another room of this, my brother's house, conspiring with him. To-morrow, possibly — in a few days at the latest — my brother will start upon this-— this expedition, let us call it. For my part I cannot believe that he will return alive. I fear for him — fear greatly. But I have obtained his consent to something for which I have fought ever since I found that he would not give up his project; he has agreed to take with him one man, whom I am to select, to give him high place in his councils, and — what is more important — to keep his identity as my agent a secret from the other parties interested.

"I had but twelve hours to find the man I needed. He must be a soldier, courageous, loyal, capable of leading men. I knew no such man. I consulted with the one being in the world whom I can trust — a family friend of long standing, one Monsieur Chambret. I — I — monsieur, I cannot trust my husband; he is allied with these false friends of my brother!"

O'Rourke started, afire with generous indignation; she cautioned him to silence with a gesture.

"One moment. I am not through, if you please. . . . Monsieur Chambret was equally at a loss for a suitable man. He did what he could. This evening he came to me, offering a last hope, saying that he knew of a place where men of spirit who were not overly prosperous might be expected to congregate. I was to take my carriage, and wait at a certain spot in the Champs Élysées. He was to bring or send the man, should he find him. If the gentleman came alone he would make himself known to me by the password — which you know.

"So — apparently Monsieur Chambret failed in his mission. The rest you know. You came — and now that I know you, Colonel O'Rourke, I thank —"

"Madame!" cried the Irishman arising.

She, too, stood up; her glance met his, and seemed deeply to penetrate his mind. As if satisfied, impulsively she flung out a hand towards him. O'Rourke clasped it in both his own. He felt himself unable to speak; for the moment mere words were valueless.

But beneath his glance the woman colored; her regard of him did not waver; the earnestness of her purpose blinded her to the danger of encouraging that grand amoreux, Terence O'Rourke. Her eyes shone softly and it may have been that her breathing was a trifle hurried.

"Monsieur," she cried, "I — I love my brother. I would save him from — from himself. Will you, then, enter my service — go with him and guard him, stand at his side and by his back, shielding him against assassination or — or worse? Will you, can you bring yourself to do this thing for me, whom you do not know, and for my brother, whom you will dislike?"

"For ye, madame!" he declared. "To the ends of the earth, if need be!"

He felt the pressure of her fingers on his own, significant of her gratitude. O'Rourke bent over the little hand, raising it to his lips. . . .

There was a knock on the door. The woman released her hand, swiftly, with an air of alarm.

"Quick!" she cried. "The key, monsieur! This will be Monsieur Chambret!"

CHAPTER VI

HE DRAWS ONE CARD

O'ROURKE fumbled in his pocket desperately, his fingers on that key all the time; but he did not want to give it up, he did not care to see Monsieur Chambret — not just yet. A dozen pretexts to escape the meeting, to prolong the interview, flashed through his brain in a brief moment; but none that he dared use.

Meanwhile, the rosy palm of his princess was outstretched to receive the key, and she was eying him with no great favor, biting her lip with impatience, because of his dalliance. In the end O'Rourke had to surrender both the key and all hope of delaying the introduction.

Madame la Princesse, with an audible sigh of relief, swept over to the door. O'Rourke remained, standing, at the side of the desk. Perhaps it was entirely by accident that his elbow touched the edge of the lamp shade, and replaced it in its former position; perhaps he made the adjustment in his preoccupation; perhaps — not.

At all events, that was what immediately happened, before the princess had time to get that door open; and then the line of the light cut sharply across the lower part of O'Rourke's shirt bosom, as he stood there, leaving the upper portion of his body — his face, in particular — deeply shadowed.

He turned toward the door in uneasy expectancy.

Now it was at last open; the princess stood to one side, her hand on the knob, bowing mockingly and with a laugh.

"Welcome, monsieur!" she cried. "But you are late."

"I was delayed."

"But just in time, as it is," added the girl.

The newcomer nodded moodily, hesitating at the door, looking from the princess to the man with whom she had been closeted, and back again — as one with the right to demand an explanation.

The princess was prompt to give it.

"Monsieur Adolph Chambret," she said ceremoniously: "my new-found friend and our ally in this affair, Monsieur the Colonel O'Rourke, Chevalier of the Legion of Honor!"

Both men bowed, O'Rourke deeply, Chambret with a trace of hauteur and without removing a remarkably penetrating gaze from the countenance of the Irishman.

"You see, *I* have succeeded!" continued the princess triumphantly. "The hour grew late — I judged that you had failed, monsieur."

"You were right," assented Chambret — still eying the Irishman. "I failed lamentably."

He breathed rapidly as he spoke, his face red as with unaccustomed exertion, and his clothing — impeccable evening dress — somewhat disordered and dusty.

He was a man largely framed, and a trifle overweight, carrying himself well, with a suggestion of activity and quickness in his bearing; his face showed intellectuality of a high order — and an uncertain temper; he was bearded, full-cheeked; and one of his cheeks bore the red stamp of a recent blow.

Remarking, for the first time, his disheveled appearance, the girl inquired concerning its cause. "You have had an accident, monsieur?" she asked solicitously.

"Nothing of moment," he replied carelessly: "an en-

[44]

counter with a loafer of the streets, who attempted to assault me."

"And — and — ?" she suggested.

"It was nothing — nothing, madame," he returned with ease. "I was forced to call a gendarme, and give the fellow in charge, to be rid of him. He will spend the night in prison, which may improve his manners," he added.

His veiled meaning was quite unintelligible to O'Rourke, who drew his breath sharply, otherwise exhibiting no emotion at the Frenchman's remarkable account of the affair.

"Me faith!" he chuckled to himself. "So I've been arrested, have I? Good! That lets me out. He neither recognizes nor suspects me!"

A clock in the library chimed softly, twice. Upon the sound the princess turned, and looked at the dial.

"Half-past three!" she cried. "So late! Indeed, we are just in time, messieurs. I have no time to waste explaining to you, Monsieur Chambret, how remarkably Colonel O'Rourke was sent to me in my need," she continued. "I go at once to my brother and his — *council!* I will return for you in — say, ten minutes at the most."

She courtesied gaily to the two men, and left the room.

To O'Rourke it seemed as though the study, bereft of her presence, acquired an entirely new and uncomfortable atmosphere. He inspired harshly again — half a sigh, half in expectation of what might follow.

Chambret, bowing reverently at the door as the princess passed out, straightened himself, almost with a jerk, and shut it sharply. He stood for a moment as if lost in thought, then wheeled about, and came down the room deliberately, slowly removing his gloves, his gaze again full upon the face of the Irishman.

As for the latter, he appreciated the fact that it was a ticklish moment for him, an encounter fraught with peril. His only course was to face the man down, to defy him, to rely upon his effrontery — if it so happened that Chambret had indeed recognized him.

He was not long to be left in doubt, — if he did honestly doubt.

Deliberately, Chambret approached the table, halting by its edge, not a yard distant from the Irishman, his brow black with rage, his eyes scintillating with hate. Abruptly he brought his gloves down, with a sharp slap, upon the polished wood.

"So, *canaille!*" he said sharply.

"What?" demanded O'Rourke audaciously. His manner said plainly enough, "Is it possible? Can I believe me ears? What *does* he mean?"

Chambret quickly swung up the shade of the lamp, nodding in satisfaction as the glare disclosed the lineaments of the Irishman.

"I thought so," he said. "I was not mistaken."

O'Rourke dropped languidly, easily, into the chair, swinging a careless leg over one of its arms.

"Upon me word!" he mused aloud. "What is he driving at now, d'ye think? Is the man mad?"

Chambret's attitude was a puzzle to him. If the man had immediately identified him, why had he not been denounced to the princess at once? Why this delay, this playing to the gallery for melodramatic effect?

"Of course," he admitted, "the man's a Frenchman; 'tis not in the likes of him to miss a chance of showing off. But nobody's watching him now, save me. What for is he waiting?"

However, he **was** yet to become acquainted with Monsieur Adolph Chambret. That gentleman took his full time, carefully mapping out his plan of action behind that high, thinking forehead of his, as carefully subduing his anger — or, rather, keeping his finger upon the gage of it, that it might not get beyond his control.

"You are wondering what I propose to do with you, monsieur?" he queried at length, in a temperate, even tone.

"Faith, I was wondering what I'd have to do to ye, to make ye keep quiet," amended O'Rourke, abandoning all pretense.

The Frenchman moved impatiently. "You are presumptuous, monsieur," he said.

"I'm the very divvle of a fellow," admitted O'Rourke with engaging candor. "We'll take all the personalities for granted, if ye please, Monsieur Chambret. But as to business —"

"I am debating whether or not to hand you over to the gendarmes."

"Ye harbored that identical delusion a while ago, I believe. Don't bother with it; 'tis not so, really."

"And what is to prevent me, may I ask?"

"The answer, monsieur," returned O'Rourke, unruffled, "is — meself. Do ye connect with that?"

Chambret's eyes blazed; but still he held his temper in leash.

"May I inquire how you elbowed your way in here?"

"'Tis easy enough; I've no objection to telling ye. Ye called your policeman — I ran. Ye pursued — I saw the open door of madame's *fiacre*, thought it empty, jumped in, telling the driver to go to the Gare du Nord. He went — bless him! — as though every gendarme in Paris was after him."

"And —"

"And so I became acquainted with madame; she knew me, it seems,— knew me record, — and asked me to join her in this affair. I agreed."

"You know — everything, then, monsieur?"

"Sure I do, me boy. And now, what are ye going to do about it?"

"Nothing," announced Chambret coolly, seating himself in the chair which the princess had vacated. "Nothing at all."

He directed a level stare at O'Rourke, who sat up and faced him suddenly.

"I'll be damned!" the Irishman prophesied admiringly. "D'ye mean it?"

"I do, most certainly."

"Why?" gasped O'Rourke, astonished.

"Because we need you, monsieur. More particularly, because madame needs you. My personal feelings must — wait, I presume."

"Upon me word, I'm disposed to apologize to ye!"

"You forget that there is no apology for a blow. I shall expect my satisfaction upon your return."

"Faith, ye can have it then — or now," O'Rourke fired up. "I'll say this to ye, for your own good: The next time ye see that a man's broke, don't throw it in his face. 'Tis worse than a red rag to a bull."

"An error of judgment, perhaps," agreed Chambret, thoughtfully.

"But as for your satisfaction — I'll permit no man to outdo me in generosity, sir; I'm at your service when ye please."

Chambret put his hand to his face; upon his cheek the red weal blazed. His brows darkened ominously; and he glanced from O'Rourke to the clock.

"We have time," he debated, "to settle our little affair before the return of madame."

"What d'ye mean, monsieur?" asked O'Rourke, wide-eyed.

"I'll take you at your word," concluded Chambret, arising suddenly. "You shall give me satisfaction now."

"The divvle ye say!"

O'Rourke, too, got upon his feet.

"Precisely. We can fight here as comfortably as anywhere. The room was designed for absolute quiet; the walls are sound proof."

"Faith!" cried the Irishman. "D'ye mean we're to duel with pistols — here?"

"Just so, monsieur."

"But — the weapons?"

Chambret pulled open a drawer of the desk, peered within and removed from it a revolver.

"This," he indicated.

"But that's only one!"

"All that will be necessary, monsieur. We will let the cards decide." He took from another drawer a deck of playing cards — new.

"We will deal, monsieur," he continued, "one to me, one to you, card by card. He who receives the ace of spades — You comprehend?"

"Suicide, d'ye mean?"

"No. The unlucky one of us to stand at the farther end of the room; the other to remain here with the revolver, to count three, aim and fire instantly. Are you agreeable?"

O'Rourke whistled his admiration — an emotion not, however, untinged with perturbation.

"Ye have your nerve with ye, if ye are in earnest," he

protested. "Let's see, this is your proposition: First, we play an innocent game of cards; then one of us commits a murder? Is that it? Well — since ye are the one to propose it, I'm your man. Deal on, monsieur!"

Chambret nodded coldly, stripped the deck and shuffled with care, O'Rourke watching him narrowly. Finally Chambret was satisfied, took up the deck and drew off the top card.

"One moment, monsieur!" interposed O'Rourke. "There's a man of me race that has said, 'Trust every man, but cut the cards.' Faith, I'm thinking that's good advice."

The Frenchman ground an imprecation between his teeth, and slammed the deck upon the desk. O'Rourke cut them with care.

"Proceed," he consented calmly.

Trembling with anger, Chambret dealt: a card to himself first — the nine of hearts; a card to O'Rourke —

The Irishman felt the room swimming about him; he clutched the arms of his chair with a grip of agony, his gaze transfixed upon the card before him: the ace of spades.

He heard Chambret laughing lightly, saw the gleam of his white teeth in the lamplight, and staggered to his feet.

"Very well," he heard himself saying, as with another's voice, distantly. "'Tis the fortune of war. Proceed, monsieur."

He was aware that he walked, but as one dreaming, to the farther end of the apartment; he remembers turning and facing Chambret; he recalls folding his arms and reminding himself to hold his head high; but the heart of him was like water. He waited there what seemed an interminable time, while Chambret, grinning malevolently, tested the revolver, assuring himself that it was properly loaded.

And then his grimace faded; O'Rourke saw the weapon slowly swinging at the man's side; and he head a voice ringing through the room, reverberating upon his tympanums like the thunders of the Day of Judgment.

"*One — two —*"

The arm ceased to sway; in a moment it would arise, Chambret would fire; O'Rourke even fancied that he heard the beginning of the fatal monosyllable:

"*Th —*"

He closed his eyes — only to open them again immediately, as the voice of madame the princess sounded, following upon the sudden opening of the door:

"*Messieurs!*"

Chambret's half-raised arm fell. O'Rourke steadied himself with a hand against the wall; a dim mist swam before his eyes, seemingly almost palpable. Through it the voices of madame and Chambret came to him with odd and unfamiliar intonations.

"Monsieur Chambret! What is this?"

"A test of marksmanship, merely, madame. I am exhibiting my skill to Monsieur le Colonel O'Rourke; you will observe he holds a card in his hand."

O'Rourke clenched his teeth and so forced himself to a state of thought wherein he was capable of intelligent action. Chambret's concluding words were ringing in his ears; he glanced at his hand, saw that indeed he was holding the fatal ace of spades — which he must have picked up and retained unconsciously. He glanced at the woman, at Chambret; the latter stood stern and implacable; in his eyes O'Rourke read murder.

He divined the man's purpose to turn the farcical situation into a tragedy; but within him the instinct of self-preservation seemed dormant — or bound and helpless, enchained by the tenets of that thing called "honor."

Mechanically O'Rourke raised his arm, holding the card in his hand, a little to one side.

Chambret again took deliberate aim. The princess started forward with a cry of protest.

She was too late; Monsieur Chambret had fired.

CHAPTER VII

HE CONSIDERS THE GREAT SCHEME

BANDIED back and forth by the four walls of the study the report crashed and echoed, reverberating, like a peal of thunder. When it died out, there was absolute silence for a space, during which all three actors of the litte drama stood almost as though stricken motionless.

O'Rourke saw Chambret slowly lower the revolver, the whites of his eyes gleaming in the lamplight; while from the muzzle of the weapon a thin, grayish spiral of smoke trickled up to join the heavier, pungent cloud that hovered near the ceiling. He saw Madame la Princesse standing, swaying ever so slightly, her hands clasped before her, her lips a-quiver with mute inquiry, her eyes, horror filled, fixed upon his face.

Chambret stepped back and cast the revolver upon the desk, whereon it fell with a heavy thud, shattering the silence and quickening the tableau simultaneously.

Madame started toward O'Rourke with a low cry.

"A good shot!" said the latter composedly. "A very good shot, Monsieur Chambret; for which pray accept me congratulations."

He held out the card in a hand that was steadiness itself.

"Observe, madame," he said unperturbed, "the bullet penetrated the precise center of the ace — and in this half light!"

She was near enough to him now to snatch the card from his fingers, not rudely but in an agony of suspense. Holding it up to the light she verified his statement; and he saw that her own hand was shaking.

A vague sense of triumph caused him to look toward Chambret; who bowed ironically.

"But — but you are not injured, monsieur?"

It was the princess who addressed him; O'Rourke dared to smile at her — a smile that was at once bright with his consciousness of his triumph, and itself a triumph of dissimulation.

"Not in the least," he hastened to reassure her; "Monsieur Chambret is too skilful a shot to have chanced a mistake."

"You are satisfied as to my skill, then, monsieur?" inquired Chambret.

"Quite — and shall be so for a long time to come." He remembered his rôle in the deception which they were united in practising upon madame, and laughed again. "I yield the point, monsieur," he added, "and likewise the palm. Ye are a finer shot than I, be long odds."

But it is a question as to whether or not they were successful in deceiving the princess; the glance that she shifted from the one to the other was filled with dubiety.

She felt instinctively, perhaps, that here was something deeper than appeared upon the surface; but she might not probe it courteously nor with any propriety, since both seemed to desire her to believe that the affair had been nothing more than a test of Monsieur Chambret's mastery of the weapon.

"In the future, messieurs," she announced frowning, "I trust that you will confine your exhibitions to more appropriate hours and localities. Moreover, I do not like it. At best it is dangerous and proves little. Colonel O'Rourke, your arm."

She gathered up the train of her evening gown, and moved

away with the Irishman; who by now was so far recovered that he could not repress his elation. This, he felt, was in some way a distinct triumph over his saturnine rival; for as such he already chose to consider Chambret. And he ventured to turn and wink roguishly at the Frenchman as they left the room.

As for Chambret, it seemed that he was not bidden to the conference with the brother of Madame la Princesse; they left him staring glumly at the floor and twisting his mustache, in a mood that seemed far from one of self-satisfaction.

"Now, 'tis strange to me," volunteered O'Rourke, "that the shot startled no one — the servants, or your brother and his guests."

"The servants," explained madame, "are trained to ignore the unusual in this house; besides, their presence is not desired above stairs at this hour. As for my brother, he is closeted with his friends in another wing of the building."

Thereafter she lapsed into a meditation, from which he made no attempt to rouse her; he kept the corner of his eye upon her fair, finely modeled head that was bowed so near to his shoulder; and he recalled jubilantly the look of keen anxiety that had been hers when she had fancied him wounded. To be able to think of that, and to be in her company, O'Rourke felt, were happiness enough for him — enough and far beyond his deserts.

Thus quietly they traversed a series of broad, dimly lighted corridors, meeting no one; but, after some time, his princess stopped with O'Rourke outside a certain door.

"Monsieur," she said softly, nor raised her eyes, "it is here that I leave you to return to my home. Within this door you will meet my brother, Monsieur Lemercier; my husband, Monsieur le Prince de Grandlieu, and — and others. You may — I fancy you will — find them uncongenial; I could almost hope that you would. I can only trust that you will be able to endure them, monsieur. You know what I — I expect of you; and will presently learn what other duties will be yours to perform. I think I may rely upon you to play your part."

"Madame," he returned lightly, yet with earnestness underlying his tone, "I realize that I am, in a way, a forlorn hope. But ye may trust me."

"I believe so," she said soberly. "I shall not — may not see you again for some time. You — you will —?"

"I will do all that ye wish me to, madame, so far as lies in me power — and a trifle further, perhaps."

She smiled, amused by the gallant boast, and gave him her hand.

"Then," she breathed, — "then, good-night, my friend."

"Madame!" cried O'Rourke.

For the tenth part of a second her fingers rested in his, then were withdrawn. He sighed; but she merely turned and knocked gently upon the panels.

Almost immediately the door was opened; a man peered out, and, recognizing the princess, emerged, closing the door behind him.

"Oh, it's you, Beatrix," he greeted her languidly.

"Yes, Leopold. I have brought you the gentleman of whom I spoke: Colonel O'Rourke, Chevalier of the Legion of Honor, once of the Foreign Legion in the Soudan — my brother, Monsieur Leopold Lemercier."

The young man turned to O'Rourke, offering his hand with a ready, feebly good-humored smile.

"Colonel O'Rourke!" he cried, with a vapid laugh. "The very man! I'm glad to meet you, monsieur; I have heard of you before."

"The divvle!" thought O'Rourke. "And, by that token, I've heard of ye — ye little scamp!" But aloud he returned the greeting blandly.

"Thank you, Beatrix," continued Lemercier. "And —"

"I am going home," she replied. "Good-night, messieurs. Monsieur le Colonel O'Rourke, *au revoir*."

Lemercier, rather than at once returning with O'Rourke to his companions, lingered until his sister was out of ear-shot, with the manner of one who has something on his mind.

He was very youthful in appearance,— a mere slip of a boy, attired a trifle too exquisitely in the positive extreme of the fashion. No force of character was to be seen charted upon his smooth, lineless countenance — just then somewhat flushed; though whether from alcohol or excitement, O'Rourke could not determine.

His eyes, which were small, were of a vague and indefinite gray, his hair light, of a neutral tint, and inclined to fall across his forehead in a stringy bang. His mouth was weak, lacking character, his nose a smooth arch, conveying no impression of mental strength. As a rule, he kept his hands uneasily in his pockets; at other times they were constantly busy with some object — his watch chain, or the heavy, gem-encrusted rings with which his slight fingers were laden.

O'Rourke was inclined to take his measure thoroughly, not only because of the strange and interesting manner in which they had been thrown together, but also because "*le petit Lemercier*" was a national character of France — or the national laughing stock.

For some years this weakling, the enormously wealthy son of a rich chocolate manufacturer recently deceased, had kept Paris agape with his harebrained pranks, his sybaritic entertainments, his lavish disbursement of the money which he had inherited.

Rumor had it that already, in the four years that had elapsed since he had come into his fortune, he had not only expended all of his income, huge as that was known to be, but had made serious inroads upon his capital.

This was undoubtedly due to his incapacity and dissipation; "the little Lemercier" maintained constantly a circle of scheming flatterers and panderers, who had always some fresh scheme ready to assist in the separation of the young fool from his money.

And now that he knew whom he was to protect, O'Rourke felt as if a blindfolding bandage had suddenly dropped from his eyes; not only did he realize that the fears of Madame la Princesse for the welfare of *le petit* Lemercier were well grounded, but he had no difficulty in identifying that lady with the young girl, who, fresh from the seclusion of a convent, had been persuaded by this same brother, Leopold, to contract a marriage with Prince Felix, the debauched head of the insignificant and impoverished principality of Grandlieu.

He recalled quite distinctly the sensation that marriage had created, a year or so back; as well as the public indignation and sympathy for the ignorant and unsophisticated girl who had given her hand and her immense fortune into the keeping of the most notorious *roué* in Europe.

A sudden rage welled in O'Rourke's heart, as he thought of this, and a faint disgust stirred him as he gazed upon this enfeebled, weak-eyed, self-complacent stripling who was negatively responsible for the degradation of his sister.

But *le petit* Lemercier put an end to the meditations of the Irishman.

"One moment, monsieur, before we enter," he stipulated. "You understand what circumstances have induced me to accede to Beatrix's absurd notion? Well," he went on, without waiting for a reply, "it *is* absurd, anyway; and, just to keep my word with her, I've had to tell them inside that I've known you for a long time, and sent for you on purpose for the work in hand. I couldn't insult my friends by telling them the real reason why I'm employing you."

"Very well," assented O'Rourke, between his teeth, his blood seeming to boil in resentment of the assumption of superiority with which *le petit* Lemercier was treating him.

"Yes, monsieur; since that's understood, and you won't be making **any** blunders, we'll go inside, if you please."

He turned the handle of the door, and his back insolently to O'Rourke, and stalked stiffly into the room; the Irishman swallowed his rage at the other's impertinence, and followed.

The room which he entered was almost a duplicate of the one wherein he had conferred with his princess, save that it was somewhat smaller, and, instead of the desk, a huge table occupied the center of the floor.

Round it were ranged armchairs, wherein lounged four men, who rose at the entrance of the stranger.

Lemercier marched to the head of the table, and sat down.

"Messieurs," he said, with a negligent flirt of his white, pudgy hand, "you will permit me to introduce Monsieur le Colonel O'Rourke, of the Foreign Legion — the gentleman of whom I have spoken, as the future commander-in-chief of the imperial army. Colonel O'Rourke, I have the honor to make you known to Monsieur le Prince de Grandlieu, and Messieurs Valliant, Mouchon, and D'Ervy."

The messieurs bowed ceremoniously — and most coldly, apparently resenting this intrusion upon their charmed circle;

on the principle, possibly, of the more birds of prey, the less gorging of each individual crop.

As for O'Rourke, he returned their greetings with scarcely less frigidity of manner. He constrained himself to bare civility, but was unable to feign any considerable pleasure because of the association in which he found himself.

Lemercier indicated a chair, into which the Irishman dropped unwillingly; had he followed his own inclinations he would have delayed not one moment ere leaving before he knew more, before pledging himself and his sword to the service of this gathering of blackguards.

But he recognized that he was, as he put it, "in for it"; he had given his word to his princess, and the desire to serve her outweighed his personal tastes in the matter.

Le petit Lemercier invited the Irishman to help himself to the wine and cigars which were set out upon a convenient buffet, then concerned himself no more for the comfort of his guest. He got upon his feet unsteadily — it became momentarily more apparent that he was drinking too deeply for the clearness of his brain — and began to talk in a halting fashion, leaving the half of his sentences unfinished and inconclusive.

But the attention he received was flattering; with the possible exception of the prince, his sycophants hung upon his words with breathless interest. Only O'Rourke permitted his eyes to stray from the face of his host to the countenances of the others, mentally inventorying their characters, cataloguing them for future reference.

Monsieur le Prince de Grandlieu he had not expected to like; what he saw of him did not tend to remove the prejudice — a slim, tall figure of a man, ridiculously padded at every possible point, and corseted so that his figure resembled a woman's more nearly than a man's; he was hatchet-faced and dark, with evasive eyes of a saturnine, sneering cast; impeccable as to dress, an elegant; ostentatiously rakish.

Apparently returning O'Rourke's disdain with interest, he sat slouched in an armchair, airily twirling an end of his black mustache, occasionally eying the intruder with no friendly glance.

As for the others, they were ordinary types of Parisians: Valliant, a heavy, swaggering growth of the boulevards, red-faced and loud-voiced; Mouchon, pasty of complexion, nervous, slinking, and apologetic in manner; D'Ervy, a vice-marked nonenity of Lemercier's grade, pimply, heavy-eyed, ungracious, and vacuous.

Meanwhile, *le petit* Lemercier was talking — rambling on in an aimless, inconsequential fashion, chiefly in praise of his own wonderful sagacities and abilities in planning an enterprise which he as yet had not named. Suddenly, however, he broke off, flushed his throat with a glass of champagne; and the conversation took on a complexion which commanded O'Rourke's undivided interest.

"Messieurs," said Lemercier, puffing with importance, "we are assembled on the eve of a movement which will astonish and compel the admiration not only of all Europe, but of the civilized world as well."

He paused, and turned to the Irishman.

"O'Rourke, *mon ami*," he continued, with abrupt familiarity, "these, my comrades, are already intimate with my project. For months we have been planning and perfecting it; latterly we have waited only for you, *mon brave*, a soldier tried and proven, to work with us for glory and for — empire!"

"The divvle ye say!" interjected the disgusted O'Rourke to himself.

"In a week, monsieur, we start upon our expedition. In two weeks or less the Empire of the Sahara will be inaugurated — in a month it will be a fact accomplished."

He gestured toward the wall, and D'Ervy sprang from his chair, to unrol an immense map of Northern Africa which hung thereon. *Lepetit* Lemercier, swelling with pride, went to it and indicated his points as he talked.

"Here," he said, drawing O'Rourke's attention to a spot on the west coast of the continent, "is Cape Bojador. Here, again," moving his finger a foot north upon the coast line, "is Cape Juby. To the north lies Morocco; to the south lie the Spanish Rio de Oro possessions. But between the two capes is unclaimed land. There, messieurs, lies the land that shall be our Empire of the Sahara. There shall we establish and build up a country greater even than our France!"

Valliant rapped his applause upon the table; Mouchon cheered weakly. O'Rourke looked dubious.

"Pardon," he said, "but is not that the coast of the Sahara? Is it not desert land, — waste, arid?"

"Ah, yes, monsieur; that is the general impression. But you shall see what we shall do in this No-man's Land which the grasping English have overlooked, which France disdains, which Spain forgets! In the first place, the land is not arid; to my personal knowledge there is a large and fertile oasis a short distance inland from the coast, in one spot; and beyond doubt there be others."

"Undoubtedly!" affirmed the prince.

"Here, monsieur," Lemercier continued enthusiastically, pointing to an indefinite, ragged line winding inland a little distance below Cape Juby, "is the Wädi Saglat el Hamra — the dry bed of an ancient stream —"

"Dry?" queried O'Rourke, beginning to be interested in spite of himself.

"Now dry, *mon ami;* but wait — wait until we have discovered its former sources, wait until Science has reopened and made them to flow again. Then shall the Wadi Saglat make its majestic way to the ocean — a mighty stream, fertilizing and irrigating the surrounding territory. Moreover, artesian wells shall be sunk wherever practicable; around them oases shall spring to life, rejuvenating the desert. We — *we*, messieurs! — shall be the vanguards of empire, the reclaimers of the waste lands of the world, making the desert to blossom as a garden!

"Cities shall be built, colonists shall flock to us, homes shall be established for thousands of families. The sands of the desert will yield up their gold to us. A port will be established as a terminus for the thousands of desert caravans who now take their goods to the Senegal. Messieurs, the Empire of the Sahara, within two years, shall obtain recognition from the Powers of the world. Within five it shall be a Power itself. And I — *I*, messieurs! — shall be Emperor!" ...

The ardor of *le petit* Lemercier was pitiable, yet infectious; the Irishman found himself listening eagerly.

"There's something in it!" he whispered. "Me faith, I do believe it might be done!" His adventurous spirit kindled, flashing from his eyes. "There'll be fighting," he considered shrewdly.

Lemercier turned to him, breathing quickly with excitement, carried away by his own schoolboy eloquence.

"Colonel O'Rourke," he announced pompously, "you are to be Commander-in-chief of my forces, with the pay of a corps commander of the French Army. Do you accept?"

"Faith," said O'Rourke rising, "I do that. 'Tis a great scheme ye have, monsieur."

He filled him a glass of champagne, turning to the others.

"Messieurs," he said, "I give ye the health of Monsieur Lemercier!"

"No!" interposed the prince, also rising with his glass. "You forget, Colonel O'Rourke. The health we drink is the health of Leopold le Premier, l'Empereur du Sahara!"

He flashed a hinting glance to the others; they, too, rose, with *bravos*, and drank standing.

O'Rourke's gaze fell upon the stripling, wine-flushed and staggering, complacent and conceited — a mere vain child, dreaming of empire as a plaything for his vanity.

And then the eyes of the Irishman turned to the others — the motley, self-centered crew of leeches, who, to this vapid youth of a multi-millionaire, bent "the pregnant hinges of the knee, that thrift might follow fawning."

It nauseated him; he put down his glass, and for a moment watched the cold, calculating, sardonic Prince de Grandlieu, who was, with meaning glances, showing the way to his associates to half madden *le petit* Lemercier with flattery. And the warning of that man's wife, of the princess, recurred to the Irishman. Again disgust stirred him.

"The divvle!" he muttered. "I'm in for it. Sure, there *will* be fighting, or I'm no O'Rourke!"

But his thoughts were concerning themselves with Chambret and Felix of Grandlieu. The more that he had occasion to consider them, at that time, the more thoroughly he became convinced that there would be much fighting ere *he* was done with them.

CHAPTER VIII

THUS it was plotted; and in such wise Colonel Terence O'Rourke came to cast his fortunes with those of that man concerning whom the Parisian boulevards were soon again to be gossiping — the youth who called himself Leopold the First, Emperor of the Sahara.

Their conference lasted into a late hour of the next morning; the conspirators breakfasted together, gathering up the loose ends of their scheme and giving and receiving final suggestions and instructions.

It had been settled that O'Rourke was to be Commander-in-chief, with the title of Lieutenant-General, of the forces presently to be assembled on the west coast of the Sahara Desert.

Monsieur le Prince de Grandlieu was to be chief adviser to his majesty-to-be; when the government was finally organized he was to be Premier.

Monsieur Valliant, who, it appeared, was a member of the French bar, received the appointment of chief justice of the Empire — when it should exist and the administration of justice should become necessary. In the meantime, he was to remain in Paris, and, with the help of associates (whose salaries, be sure, were to come out of the pocket of *le petit* Lemercier), formulate a Code Leopoldan; a judicial system which was expected to combine all the good points of existing legal codes and to contain none of their defects.

[65]

Messieurs Mouchon and D'Ervy were to rejoice respectively in the portfolios of commerce and agriculture — their absolute unfitness for the holding of any office whatsoever being to all appearances their greatest recommendation in the eyes of Lemercier.

It was understood that the two latter gentlemen were to collaborate, at first, in the work of enticing colonists to the promised land; and they also had charge of the purchase of all supplies for the new empire — a sinecure in which O'Rourke shrewdly scented large and gratifying "commissions" for the purses of the two secretaries.

But the Irishman had little time in which to criticise or to pass judgment upon his associates. He was ordered immediately to the south of France for the purpose of recruiting troops.

He had one week for his task; it was the sense of the conclave that forty picked men would be required for the work of annexing the sands of the Sahara, and in the judgment of O'Rourke this number was none too large, if the expedition was to lack that element of *opéra bouffe* which he feared would prove one of its integral parts.

It was characteristic of the adventurer that, little faith as he had, on calm reflection, in the imperial scheme of Monsieur *le petit* Lemercier, he threw himself into his work heart and soul, determined that, should failure come to his employer, it would be through no fault of his.

He sent to his lodgings for a change of clothes, which was brought him while breakfasting. When through he took the first express to Marseilles, having been provided with funds and authorized to draw upon Lemercier should that become necessary.

Once in Marseilles, he set about his work with the systematic energy of a born organizer and old campaigner; he knew his ground thoroughly, had full powers to work as a free agent and to offer liberal inducements, the better to enlist the finest body of men that could be found either within or without the borders of the French Republic.

In such case he felt that success was assured from the start, so far as he personally was concerned; in five days he had his force complete — chiefly composed of seasoned veterans.

Ex-Spahis from the Soudan were there, and swart Turcos — lean, brown, lithe, and wiry little fellows, all of them ready to fight at the drop of a handkerchief; discharged artillery-men and marines of the republic; and, for leaven, a sprinkling of his own countrymen, together with a few adventurous spirits — mercenaries — of other lands: a villainous-looking gang, taken as a whole, fearing God nor man nor devil, fighters born, every mother's son, ready to fight for the highest bidder or for the pure love of battle; but, for the most part of them, brave and loyal to their masters for the time being, to be depended upon in any emergency.

Thirty-nine were they of the rank and file; over whom, as his lieutenant, with the rank of captain, he placed one Daniel Mahone — familiarly known as "Danny": a red-headed chunk of an Irish lad, according to O'Rourke's description, who had been the adventurer's body-servant in days gone by, when O'Rourke had been more prosperous.

Of late, they had been separated by stress of circumstance, which had forced Danny to strike out for the wherewithal to stay his own stomach, since he might no longer depend upon the bounty of the O'Rourke of Castle O'Rourke (under the very shadow of whose walls Danny had been born and brought up).

[67]

Red-headed he certainly was, this Danny, according to all accounts, and hot-headed, too; but cool and temperate in his element, which was time of danger, and no man ever served a master more loyally and devotedly than Danny had served and was destined to serve O'Rourke.

The adventurer had come upon him wandering disconsolately about on the docks of Marseilles, looking — and, it appeared, with ill success — for a berth on a Mediterranean coaster. And the lure of gold had been no more potent than the lure of devotion which brought him back into O'Rourke's service. The master took occasion quietly to congratulate himself upon the acquisition of this invaluable man; nor was his joy premature.

In small batches, the better to excite no comment, the mercenaries of the proposed ''standing army'' were shipped to Las Palmas, with instructions to await their commander in that town. O'Rourke trusted to the moral influence of Danny's temper and ready fists to keep the rabble in order and moderately sober until the time when he himself should go to Las Palmas to take charge, or until the coming of the *Eirene, le petit* Lemercier's colossal private steam yacht.

Upon this vessel, whereon were expected Lemercier, Grandlieu, Mouchon, and D'Ervy, O'Rourke's mercenaries were to embark for Cape Juby and the Wadi Saglat el Hamra, in the neighborhood of which was the rumored oasis that was to form the site of the future capital of the Saharan Empire.

About the first of June the last of his men were despatched to Las Palmas; a day or so later O'Rourke followed them, per packet.

He arrived at the Puerto de la Luz on a simmering night, and at once had himself conveyed to the city of Las Palmas itself.

CHAPTER IX

HE DEMONSTRATES THE USES OF DISCIPLINE

By night Las Palmas much resembles almost any other Spanish colonial city in a semi-tropical land; select at random a city of equal size from any of the Spanish-American countries, transplant it bodily to an island of volcanic origin and with sparse vegetation, and you have Las Palmas of the Gran Canaria.

There is the inevitable plaza, with its despondent garden and its iron railings; there is the inevitable palatial residence of the governor; there are the cafés and restaurants, the municipal band that executes by night, the señoritas with their immense, fanlike tortoise-shell combs and their mantillas, the señors adorned in white ducks and cigarettes, the heat, the languor, the spirit of *mañana* and *dolce far niente*.

The nights are long, warm and sticky, and sickly sweet; the darkness is so soft and so thick as to seem well-nigh palpable; the sky hangs low, and velvety, sewn thick with huge stars.

It was on such a night that O'Rourke arrived. On the way to his hotel he kept his eyes open for members of his corps, but saw none of them.

He was disturbed; Las Palmas is not a metropolis so great that forty fighting men can be set down within its boundaries without creating comment.

Nor is it so puritanical in atmosphere that forty fighting men with graduated thirsts and eruptive dispositions are like to become childlike once under its influence — to content them with a diet of cow's milk and crackers, to sleep and spend their days in the ordinary processes of tourist sightseeing.

O'Rourke knew his men well — that was why he had chosen them; with him at their head he had little fear of trouble, for he was wont to command with a firm hand, and they were accustomed to be commanded by him or by men of his resolute stamp.

But, with Danny alone to keep them in order — Danny himself of a nature none too pacific, and, as they would be bound to consider, merely by chance of favoritism their superior officer — O'Rourke was by no means satisfied that his lambs were being safely shepherded.

Nor was he uneasy without reason.

His carriage rolled through the winding, darksome streets — strangely quiet, thought the perturbed Irishman — swiftly from the boat landing to the Grand Hotel. O'Rourke leaned back in the seat, alertly on the lookout, chewing a cold cigar. But not a sound nor a sight of his command could he discover; he swore softly, bit the cigar in two in his agitation, threw it away, and set his lips in a firm line.

He realized that his work now lay to his hand; and he was promising himself that, should Danny have failed dismally, there would be a new second in command before another sun had time to rise.

The *Eirene* was due to make port about the following noon, if the schedule of *le petit* Lemercier went through without change; by that hour, if O'Rourke was to demonstrate his fitness for his position, peace must obtain among the mercenaries, a united, complete and lamblike corps must be ready to salute its employer.

He alighted from the carriage, in front of the hotel, paid

the driver, surrendered his light luggage to the attendants, and turned to look out over the plaza. Now, the plaza itself was lively enough; the band was playing an explosive Spanish national air; the lights were blazing in the cafés and before the residence of the governor; the crowds were parading, smoking, laughing, chattering, flirting — the walks thronged with the volatile, light-hearted inhabitants taking their constitutionals in the only cool hours of the day.

From the middle of the plaza two men emerged, arm and arm, strolling toward the hotel; two men in the ragged uniforms of Turcos, respectably amusing themselves and — O'Rourke thanked high Heaven — sober!

He waited for them; they approached slowly, suddenly became aware of the military figure of their commander, dropped their arms, stood at attention and saluted.

O'Rourke returned the salute.

"*Bon jour, mes braves!*" he greeted them, endeavoring to show no trace of his worriment. "Where are ye quartered?"

They indicated a side street.

"Your captain?" he inquired.

There was silence for an answer; the two Turcos glanced uneasily from their commander to one another, and hung their heads.

O'Rourke briefly repeated his question. One of the Turcos stepped forward, saluted again, and reported with a military brevity which won O'Rourke's approval, if the tidings he heard were ill.

The two, they asserted, were of the last party to arrive at Las Palmas; they therefore spoke on hearsay knowledge, for the most part. Among the first ten men, whom Danny had accompanied, peace and good feeling had obtained until the arrival of the second detachment of fifteen. The twenty-five

[71]

had, according to good military usage, fraternized; despite Danny's prohibitive orders, they proceeded to take possession of the town.   To this the authorities had made no objection, at first; the five and twenty were not overly well supplied with ready money; a mercenary rarely is so when he enlists; they spent what they had, but it was not enough to fire their martial spirits to the fighting point.

With the coming of the third instalment of legionaries — ten more men — there had been disorder, however (the Turcos regretted to state).   Among them had been one with much money — a Frenchman who had served in the desert.   The Turcos were desolated to admit it, but their comrades had become disgracefully intoxicated.

Captain Mahone had done his utmost to quell the disturbance; one man against thirty-five, however, is at an obvious and undeniable disadvantage.   By the time of the arrival of the last five men he was struggling vainly against fate and overwhelming numbers.

The men were drinking, and anarchy threatened in the peaceful island of Gran Canaria.   The authorities were scared and powerless.

Mahone, almost at his wits' end, had connived with the five and the gendarmes.   Fortunately, the rejoicing ones were unarmed.   That simplified matters considerably.   At the head of his five — with the police politely umpiring the game — he descended upon the roisterers and gave them battle.

The Turcos sighed regretfully; from what they said O'Rourke gathered that it had been a joyous conflict, lasting many hours, fought freely and fairly throughout the many narrow thoroughfares of Las Palmas; it was not often, averred the Turcos ruefully, that one came upon so satisfy-

ing a fight in times of peace. They licked their lips reminiscently, as men who remember a favorite dish.

Fortunately, the day had been for the lawful; one by one at
first, later by twos and threes, finally by squads, the legionaries had been overcome, even to the thirty-fifth man, and
kicked into the *carcel*.

"But Mahone?" demanded O'Rourke.

It was terrible, the Turcos admitted, but by grave misfortune the attire of the Captain Mahone had become disordered
in the *mêlée;* the police had been unwilling to discriminate
between him and his soldiers, saying that one so disreputable
in appearance deserved imprisonment at the least, on general
principles. For two days the captain had been disciplining
his troops in the *carcel*.

O'Rourke laughed, his heart suddenly lightened. They
were by now sober, in such case; and Danny had undoubtedly
succeeded in reducing them to submissiveness. On the mor-
row O'Rourke would go to the governor, pay their fines and
procure their releases.

He tipped the Turcos liberally, ordered them to report to
him in the morning, and went to bed with a lightened heart,
to sleep soundly the night through, and wake with his campaign planned to his satisfaction.

During his breakfast a man entered the dining-room of
the hotel, walked directly to his table and tapped O'Rourke
on the shoulder. The Irishman looked up in surprise, then
jumped to his feet. It was Chambret.

"You here, monsieur?" cried O'Rourke.

"Precisely, monsieur — as a colonist."

"Sit down and join me," the Irishman invited him.

"Thank you, but I have just breakfasted on the yacht."

"The yacht?"

"The *Eirene*, monsieur."

Chambret took a chair and seated himself, smiling pleasantly because of O'Rourke's bewilderment.

"I do not understand," admitted the latter. "The *Eirene?* A colonist? But I thought ye —"

"That I was at odds with the little emperor, monsieur? That I disapproved of his enterprise?" Chambret's mood was of the most friendly, judging from his expression — and that notwithstanding the peculiar circumstances attendant upon the last encounter of the two.

"There you are right, monsieur," he went on. "It's folly — madness. The scheme will never succeed; it spells 'Ruin' for Monsieur Lemercier. Nevertheless—". He hesitated.

"Proceed, if ye please," begged the Irishman, striving to conceal his astonishment, and entirely unable to understand this move of Chambret's.

"Nevertheless, upon reflection I have been led to change my mind. You behold in me, Monsieur O'Rourke, the first colonist of l'Empire du Sahara!"

O'Rourke put down his knife and fork, tipped back in his chair, and accepted the cigar which the Frenchman offered him.

"Chambret," he said slowly, "I'm playing a lone hand in this game. I hardly know what is trumps. Ye know the sole consideration that induced me to draw cards? No? I'll tell ye candidly. 'Tis just what I believe is keeping ye in the affair: the desire to serve Madame la Princesse. So far as meself can judge from the backs of your cards and the way ye play them, that is your motive, also."

He fixed his gaze upon the eyes of the other, which met his regard unflinchingly. "Listen, mine enemy. We have had our differences, ye and I. Let them pass, for the time being;

at the end of this affair we'll balance accounts; I'm thinking that 'tis me own turn now to demand satisfaction, and I'll claim it when the time comes."

"Monsieur will find me ready," interjected Chambret, with composure.

"Very good; but — let it pass, as I've said. At present we two have a mutual object in view, a common quarrel. Let us combine forces. Let us play partners against the pack of 'em. Show me your cards, and I'll show ye mine."

Chambret's answer was instantaneous: a hand proffered O'Rourke.

"The proposition," he said warmly, "would have come from me had it not come from you, monsieur. It was decided upon between madame and myself *en voyage.*"

"What!" O'Rourke colored. "Madame —?"

Chambret laughed lightly. "One moment, monsieur — I begin at the beginning of my account. In the first place, Madame la Princesse has full confidence in you, monsieur, as, you will permit me to add, have I. Nevertheless, it has seemed advisable to us both that you should have reinforcements — backing, I think you term it."

"'Tis that I need," assented O'Rourke.

"For this consideration I went to madame's brother, Leopold, feigned interest in his plans, and offered myself as his first colonist. He was overjoyed — received me with open arms. At the same time, madame decided to accompany Monsieur le Prince, her husband, upon his journey — and insisted, despite his pronounced opposition. This morning, the *Eirene,* bearing us all, made this port. The situation, monsieur, is this: Prince Felix conspires for the death — I speak bluntly — of his brother-in-law. The reason is simple: madame is her brother's heir; Felix already has run through madame's fortune, and counts on enjoying Leopold's when she comes into her inheritance. You comprehend?"

"The hound!" O'Rourke growled between his teeth.

"Precisely. My cards (as you call them, monsieur), consist simply of my skill as a pistol shot, of which you have some knowledge. Monsieur le Prince is a noted duelist; Monsieur le Prince has no liking for me, as you may guess. He will seize the first opportunity of calling me out. In that event the end is a foregone conclusion, I flatter myself."

"It should be," O'Rourke agreed. "Faith, when *we* two fight, monsieur, 'twill be with rapiers."

Chambret bowed courteously. "It is your choice," he assented gravely. "But now, my friend, you understand my position. To follow out your simile, monsieur, will you disclose your own hand?"

"I will that," affirmed O'Rourke. "Come with me, if ye please."

In the *patio* of the hotel his two Turcos were waiting, with their comrades — three grim Spahis. He signed to them to follow, and went out into the plaza with Chambret.

"Monsieur Lemercier sent ye to look me up, I presume?" he inquired of the mystified Frenchman.

"Yes, monsieur. I came ashore to see if you had arrived as yet; and, if you had, with instructions to tell you to bring your command to the yacht at once."

"Monsieur l'Empereur is contemplating no delay, then?" pursued O'Rourke, leading the way across the square to the residence of the governor.

"He is rapt with visions of his future glory," laughed Chambret: "impatient for his scepter and purple raiment."

O'Rourke turned and passed into the *patio* of the government house. Chambret, troubled by his companion's reticence in this time of confidences, put a hand upon his arm.

"But, monsieur," he objected, "this is not reciprocation of my frankness?"

"In half an hour," promised O'Rourke, "then ye shall understand me."

He begged an audience with the governor, stating his business; under the circumstances that harassed official delayed not a moment in according the honor, despite the unholy earliness of the hour for the transaction of business — according to Spanish notions. It was soon settled; upon O'Rourke giving his word of honor that he would immediately take the thirty-five mercenaries out of the island, he was permitted to pay their fines and received an order on the jailer of the *carcel* for their immediate delivery.

Still, accompanied by Chambret and followed by the Turcos and Spahis, he proceeded to the *carcel* itself — a gloomy, shedlike structure, more resembling a pig-pen than a municipal prison in a civilized age.

Their arrival was timed at a critical moment — for the jailer; breakfast, or what passed for it, was being distributed to the prisoners; when still blocks away the ears of O'Rourke and his party were assailed with an indescribable chorus of shrieks, oaths, growlings, and grunts that proclaimed the supreme joy of the incarcerated at the sight of food — or, possibly, other emotions that had been roused by the quality of the meal.

"Me angels," indicated O'Rourke, with a smile.

"Certainly their singing is heavenly," agreed Chambret.

Admitted by the jailer — a surly, low-browed Spaniard, who gave sincere thanks to the entire body celestial for this opportune blessing — they passed into the building. Its center — for it was but an enclosure, open to the sky save around the walls, where a partial roofing served as protection from the elements — they found occupied by a swirling, seething mass of men, from whose throats proceeded the unearthly concert. It was surrounded by a dense cloud of dust; and from its midst there proceeded a veritable eruption of fists, fragments of torn clothing, hats and bones.

Slightly in advance of his companions, O'Rourke halted, his presence for the time being unremarked of the combatants. He watched them in silence for a little while, his lips curving into a grim smile.

Finally, however, raising his walking-stick — a slim wand — he opened his mouth, and let out a stentorian command:

"*Fall in!*"

In the excitement it went unheeded. Again he called, and again:

"*Fall in! Fall in!*"

Gradually his voice carried meaning to the intelligence of the rabble. One turned, saw the motionless, commanding figure of the newcomer; he shrieked the news to his comrades. Others observed. By degrees the tumult died.

At the third command they were quiet, with one accord turning to gape at this rash intruder. Suddenly he was recognized; at the fourth command the trained soldiers sprang to their places as if electrified — one long line of thirty-nine figures stretching across the *patio*.

"Attention!" roared O'Rourke angrily. "Silence in the ranks!"

There was not a whisper to be heard, where had been the uproar of a chaos.

"Captain Mahone?" he demanded.

From around the end of the line appeared the shape of a

man whom O'Rourke entirely failed to recognize at first glance. Presently he placed him. Danny, but Danny well-nigh disintegrated — a Danny clothed in rags and tatters, with two black eyes and a face swollen and misshapen from cuts and bruises. One of his arms hung in a sling; the other he raised to salute.

"Yer honor!" he responded, out of one side of his mouth.

"Be silent!" cried O'Rourke. He walked down the line, sternly examining each man as he passed. They remained stiffly at attention, eyes to the front — soldiers all in the presence of their commander.

O'Rourke returned to the center of the line.

"Danny," he inquired, "how did this come about?"

"Yer honor — faith! Gineral O'Rourke, I mane — 'tis the forchunes av war-r, sor. Wan av the prisoners had a wad av money, sor, an' wid this an' wid that trick 'twas himself that conthrived to get liquor smuggled into th' place ivery noight. As f'r meself, sor, I've been thryin' to lick thim into shape for yez. Some av them I've licked twice over, but it does no good, sor."

"That will do. Who is this wealthy volunteer?"

There was a moment's silence, a hesitation; then slowly a man slouched forward, saluting carelessly. O'Rourke watched him like a cat, his brows contracting.

"Your name?" he asked sharply.

"Soly," responded the fellow insolently.

O'Rourke took thought.

"If I mistake not," he said, "ye came to me in Marseilles with a letter of recommendation from Monsieur le Prince de Grandlieu."

"Monsieur is correct in his surmise."

"Where did ye serve last?"

"In Algiers."

"In the camel corps?"

"Yes."

"A *sans souci?*" thundered O'Rourke, naming that branch of the French service to which criminals and deserters are condemned.

"What of that?"

O'Rourke made no verbal reply. He approached the man, dropping his cane; the fellow must have anticipated what was coming, for he sprang suddenly at O'Rourke, flourishing a knife.

Before he realized what had happened, he was on his back, his wrist held as though in a vise; the knife was wrested from him, and pocketed by O'Rourke.

"Get up!" commanded the Irishman.

The malcontent arose, mumbling guttural threats, brushing the filth of the prison from his clothes. When erect a clenched fist caught him in the mouth, knocking him flat; he arose again, was bowled over again. Finally:

"Are ye satisfied, *canaille?*" snarled O'Rourke.

The man drew himself up, saluted.

"*Oui, mon commandant!*" he said clearly.

O'Rourke turned to the motionless line; not one man had moved to the aid of his comrade.

"Are there any more of ye, *mes enfants,*" he inquired, sweetly, "who desire to taste of me discipline?"

The answer was an unanimous shout.

"*Non, monsieur le commandant!*"

"Ye are ready to follow me, at me command?"

The shout swelled to a roar.

"To the death, monsieur!"

"Very well. Captain Mahone, form your men in fours,

and march them to the landing. Let no man dare to fall out on the way!"

Danny wheeled about, raised his hand and issued the command. In ten ranks of four men each, the lines tramped out of the prison. O'Rourke watched in grim quiet, his eyes testifying to his satisfaction as to the qualities of his "children."

"Spirited, ye see," he told Chambret, as they left. "Those, monsieur, are me cards!" he added.

The Frenchman nodded. "You play with a full hand, monsieur," he said; "thirty-nine cards — all trumps!"

CHAPTER X

IN the northwest a drift of inky smoke trailed just above the horizon; otherwise there was no sign of man nor of life on the sea, save for the *Eirene*, fighting forward on her way thrilling with the vibration of the screws, panting hoarsely, ramming her keen nose into the sullen, strong swells.

On her decks men clustered like flies wherever a bit of shade was to be had; but men motionless, staring ahead with straining eyes, reluctant to lift a finger — crushed by the oppression of the heat.

Where the sun struck the pitch bubbled in the planks; iron stays and brass fittings were so hot that they blistered the hand that incautiously touched them. The man at the wheel dripped, bathed in perspiration, his thin shirt and light duck trousers sodden with moisture, his face a dull, reddish purple in color. By his side an officer languished, opening his mouth regretfully to deliver low-voiced orders. Everyone, man and master, was sunk deep in a daze of suffering caused by the heat.

Madame la Princesse kept to her stateroom; Mouchon, D'Ervy, the prince, and Chambret lounged listless in the main saloon, hugging the windows for a breath of air; in the chartroom *le petit* Lemercier hung over the table, his eyes glued in fascination upon a map of the adjacent littoral. The captain leaned over his shoulder, poising a pair of compasses to indicate a particular spot on the map.

"If your information is correct, monsieur," he said, "here is the oasis. Here should be the mouth of the Wadi Saglat — and here is the *Eirene*."

"So near?" breathed the visionary. "So near?"

"In two hours, monsieur, we make the coast."

"Yes — yes," responded Lemercier, devouring the map — his future empire! — with his gaze.

Some minutes passed, the captain waiting with his head to one side, his eyes narrowed, as a man that harkens for an expected sound. Presently he was rewarded; the ship seemed to spring to sudden life. There was a commotion upon the decks, the sounds of excited voices crying, "There! there!" to one another; and then the voice of the lookout:

"Land ho!"

Le petit Lemercier wheeled about with a strangled cry of expectation, and rushed from the chartroom, the captain following.

In the saloon, Chambret arose, startled for the moment. "Cape Juby at last, messieurs!" he cried.

Monsieur le Prince turned upon him a cold, malicious eye. "Monsieur is excitable," he observed, sneering offensively.

Chambret fought down his resentment of the personality; he had agreed with O'Rourke not to permit the prince to quarrel with him, as yet.

"Possibly," he admitted at last, placidly. " I go on deck to observe the fringe of the new empire," he added.

Prince Felix yawned and stretched himself.

"Monsieur is at liberty to go whither he lists," he remarked, with the same air of insolence.

"Without obtaining permission from Monsieur le Prince?" inquired Chambret respectfully. "For that, many thanks."

He met Prince Felix's gaze with one so steadfast that the

roué-duelist drooped his lashes; whereupon Chambret, with a short laugh, went on deck.

As he emerged from the companionway he met O'Rourke, walking forward.

The Irishman was dressed for his coming part; there would be an immediate landing, as all guessed from a knowledge of the impatient nature of *le petit* Lemercier, and O'Rourke would be expected to head the army of occupation. He was, therefore, attired in khaki, with a pith helmet and puttees of the same dust-colored material; on his shoulders were the straps bearing the insignia of his rank, and by his side a light sword; a leathern holster hung at his belt, holding a revolver of respectable size.

Thus attired he looked uncommonly comfortable and even at peace with the heat; the light green lining of his helmet threw over his brow a pale, cool tint that added to the general effect, and aroused Chambret's humorously expressed jealousy.

"If monsieur will consent to become an officer of the army," retorted the Irishman, "he may wear one of these beautiful uniforms."

"It is gay and tempting," admitted Chambret. "Does your offer include the accouterments?" he added, glancing at the revolver.

"All," returned the Irishman imperturbably.

"I've a great mind to accept," said Chambret. "I desire to wear one of those pretty popguns that you affect, monsieur."

"It would adorn ye."

"And add immeasurably to my peace of mind."

O'Rourke raised his brows in inquiry. "Monsieur le Prince?" he asked, in a low tone, nodding significantly toward the companionway.

[84]

"More offensive than ever," said Chambret. "How you manage to endure his insinuative insults is more that I can comprehend in you, monsieur, whom I know for a man of spirit."

"Thank you; 'tis meself that's all of that," agreed O'Rourke readily. "But for the present I'm cold-bloodedly biding me time. 'Tis sure to come."

"And —"

"And from the moment Monsieur le Prince attempts any funny business ashore, Chambret, he will begin to lose prestige. In fact," he drawled, "I think I may state that he will be the most astonished princeling that ever journeyed to Africa."

"I do not comprehend —"

"Wait — wait, *mon ami.*"

Laughing confidently, O'Rourke went forward, accompanied by Chambret.

Lemercier was hanging over the bows, the captain by his side; O'Rourke drew Chambret's attention to him.

"Drunk with imperial glory," he commented; "a sad sight!"

He entered the wheel house familiarly, and returned at once with a pair of binoculars. Chambret had already climbed to the bridge; O'Rourke joined him, adjusted the glasses, and began to sweep the nearing coast line with a painstaking attention.

Time and again he scanned its visible configuration with the glasses; at length, sighing as though with relief, he turned them over to Chambret. The latter, who had marked O'Rourke's intent scrutiny with wonder, focussed the binoculars to his own eyes eagerly, and imitated his companion's use of them. When he put them down, "There is nothing?" he said inquiringly.

"Nothing," affirmed O'Rourke, "save sand and heat and silence, so far as one can tell. Praises be to the saints if it is so in truth!" he added piously.

"What do you mean, monsieur? What did you fear to encounter in this uninhabitable desert?"

"Tawareks," answered O'Rourke briefly.

"Tawareks? What be they, monsieur — bird or beast, or —?"

"Devils," the Irishman indicated sententiously; "devils in human guise, me dear Chambret."

The Frenchman frowned, perplexed.

"I do not comprehend."

"Ye've never heard of the Tawareks, monsieur? 'The masked pirates of the desert,' as your press terms them? The natives that made ye more trouble in the Soudan — around about Timbuctu — than any others?"

Chambret shook his head doubtfully. "I remember hearing of the fighting thereabouts," he admitted; "but, believe me, monsieur, to me the name of one tribe of blacks means no more than that of another."

"Tawareks," O'Rourke objected, "are no niggers. They are the lords of the desert — inhabitants of the Sahara proper — a branch of the Berbers: perhaps the root-stock of the Berber family tree — for they're almost white. They infest the caravan routes; in a word, they're pirates, and rule the country with a rod of iron. Not a caravan gets safely through their territory without paying tribute in the shape of toll money to the Tawareks. They are — divvles incarnate, no less!"

"And you fear them here, monsieur?"

"Much. Why else should I have insisted on a force of forty fighting men, rather than the original ten which Monsieur le Prince suggested?"

Chambret pursed his lips and shrugged his shoulders.

"I will join your army, monsieur," he volunteered pres-ently, "and wear one of your pretty uniforms — and the revolver."

"Ye will be welcome," said O'Rourke simply, again as-suming the glasses. After a second reassuring inspection he nevertheless called Danny and issued to him orders concern-ing the arms and ammunition of the troopers.

The *Eirene* plowed on toward the coast; gradually it loomed before her bows until its outlines were easily to be discerned with the unaided eye — a long, low border of shelv-ing beach that was tossed back from the sea in yellow sand hills, irregular, studded with clumps of stunted grass: hills that stretched away inland to the eastern horizon in a broken perspective of rounded forms, sweltering beneath the sky of brass and its unblinking sun, lonely, desolate and barren — a monstrous bald place upon the poll of the earth. Not a sign of life was there; naught but sand and silence and the sun. Its effect of solitude seemed overpowering. Not even a bird of prey hung poised in the saffron sky; for here was nought to prey upon.

Those of the ship's company who were to land — that is, all save the complement of the yacht — watched the scene unceasingly, and with increasing perturbation. Surely, they said one to another, it was inconceivable that man could win him a foothold in this place of barrenness. They turned their eyes to *le petit* Lemercier, some of the more outspoken grumbling, fomenting mutiny among their fellows. Was he to take them there, to pen them in the solitude of that land without shade or water? Did he dream of this?

Even Lemercier himself was disturbed; the rosy visions that had been his, faded. For an instant he was perilously near

[87]

to disillusionment, near to turning back and abandoning his project.

This land loomed so different from what he had been led to expect, from the empire in embryo his wishful imagination had pictured to him. Had he been deceived — or had he been merely self-deceived? Should he persist? Would his plans bear fruit?

Thus he vacillated; and would probably have acknowledged defeat ere giving battle with this wilderness but for Monsieur le Prince de Grandlieu.

Instinctively, the latter had dreaded the effect of Lemercier's first sight of the land he had come to conquer. Now he was ever at his dupe's elbow, an evil genius whispering encouragement in his ear.

"Irrigation! Ah, but wait, *mon ami*, and observe what irrigation shall accomplish here! The oasis? We have been misled; our information was erroneous. Beyond doubt it exists, either here or hereabouts. The makers of maps are prone to mistakes. Let us go on, down the coast —" and so forth.

Lemercier's mood changed under the stimulus of his mentor's encouraging words. His brow cleared; he straightened his slight form, throwing back his shoulders proudly, frowning at the desert.

He had come to fight it. So — he would fight it! And he would conquer it, — conquer or die in the attempt.

By his order, for hours the *Eirene* shaped her course southwards, down the coast. By degrees almost imperceptible, the latter changed in aspect; the dunes became higher, more solid appearing to the eye, the lay of the country more rough and rugged.

At about four o'clock in the afternoon the yacht rounded a

point, to come suddenly upon what seemed to be, at first glance, a broad bay and a natural harbor.

The captain of the vessel was the first to discover its true nature; after a hasty inspection of the chart, he announced:

"The mouth of the Wadi Saglat."

"A river!" cried Lemercier triumphantly.

"A dead river," amended the captain; "its mouth forms an estuary of a kind. There should be anchorage here."

"But the oasis?"

At this moment Prince Felix entered the chartroom.

"The lookout," he said, "reports a large clump of trees a considerable distance inland."

Lemercier danced with excitement, shrilling out orders; Monsieur le Prince watched him with an amusement tempered with disdain — which, however, he took care to hide.

When the ship was brought to a stop within the mouth of the Wadi, the anchor was dropped and the surmise of the captain proved correct; a good holding was there.

Boats were lowered, and the troops piled into them, Monsieur *le petit* Lemercier in the foremost, standing at the prow with the pose of the heroic leader of an invading army, a pith helmet in his hand, his hair, the color of tow, tossed back in strings from his narrow forehead, his head high, eyes fixed, lips mechanically smiling — an object, in short, of derision to the more light-minded members of his expedition, of pity to all.

O'Rourke followed, in the second boat, with a portion of his command. He was the second to step ashore, and at that opportunely to catch the arm of the impetuous Lemercier and save him a fall in the sands.

For this Frenchman who would be emperor, in his overwhelming desire to set foot upon the lands he designed for empire, was over-hasty in jumping ashore. He slipped, stumbled, plunged forward with wildly grasping hands.

"An omen!" he whimpered, turning toward O'Rourke, when by his aid he had regained balance. His countenance had lost its proud smile; he seemed a very child to O'Rourke — a child frightened by the darkness or by an old woman's tale. His lip trembled, his eyes were filled with dread as with tears; he quivered with a sort of terror.

"An omen!" he repeated piteously. "An inauspicious omen!"

"Nonsense!" derided O'Rourke, moved by sudden compassion for the child. "Monsieur stumbled, it is true: the way to empire is not smooth. But he did not fall; he stands firmly on his feet. . . . I would ask monsieur not to forget by whose hand," he added, with meaning, yet laughing.

Lemercier brightened.

"I shall not forget, *mon ami*," he promised.

"The memory of monarchs is short," O'Rourke reminded himself, lest the promise should make him over-sanguine of the future.

Other boats followed, discharging their occupants, and returned to the *Eirene* for more; within a short time the toiling sailors at the oars had landed the expedition in its entirety.

So far there had been no demonstration.

Now Lemercier stood surrounded by his associates and friends — by no means to be confused. On the one hand, were Madame la Princesse — charming, beautiful, and distinguished, and utterly out of place in her Parisian summer gown — with O'Rourke and Chambret; on the other, Prince Felix, D'Ervy, Mouchon; and behind them all, in double rank, the forty troops commanded by Danny — all now neat and soldierly of appearance in khaki uniforms, all armed with Mausers, bayonets, revolvers.

Mouchon, bearing the jacketed standard of the new empire, offered it to Lemercier, judging that the time was ripe. *Le petit* Lemercier, however, was of a different mind.

"Not here," he decided: "not upon the seashore; I am not inclined to imitate King Canute. Let us go inland — to the oasis."

And the procession moved off, plodding desperately in the hollows of the dunes, guided by men who climbed the hills to report the way.

But it seemed that it was farther than their leader had calculated; he himself grew weary of the tiresome journey, and when O'Rourke moved up to his side, and suggested that it would be impossible to reach the oasis before dark, he halted immediately.

"Mouchon!" he called. "Give me the flag. At least it shall be unfurled in the sun's rays."

They stood in the center of a natural depression, something like a square half mile in area, almost level, bounded by silent and forbidding hills of sand.

Again the little company arranged itself in anticipation of the ceremony. Lemercier took the standard and unwrapped its waterproof covering. He stepped to the fore of the assemblage, raising his shrill, nasal voice.

"In the name of the progress of God's civilization," he announced, "I, Leopold, do declare this country mine by the right of discovery; and I name it the Empire of the Sahara!"

There was a moment's silence; Leopold had been schooled to his part. He sank upon one knee and bowed his head, appearing to invite the blessing of the Deity upon his empire.

Then, abruptly, as though moved by springs, he leapt to his feet and unfurled the standard.

It fluttered, in the breeze created by his own rapid motions, from side to side — a purple flag, fringed with gold, with three golden bees embroidered upon it in a triangular arrangement, in the center of which was the Emperor's initial — "L." The last crimson rays of the dying sun lit it up brightly.

From the group about the emperor a feeble cheer arose; then Danny rose to the occasion.

"Cheer, ye tarriers!" he growled in an undertone, raising his sword aloft and waving it. "Yelp, ye scuts, as though ye believed in him yerselves! Prisint ar-rms!" he roared. "Now, byes, wan, two, three —"

The soldiery, grinning, filled the little valley with their shouts.

" *Vive l'Empereur !* "

"Again!"

" *Vive l'Empereur !* "

"Wance again, la-ads! Now —"

For a third time they gave *le petit* Lemercier a crashing cheer; it thundered from their throats and — was lost. That silence which lay upon the hills, lifeless, dull, empty even of echoes, fell upon and crushed the uproar to nothingness.

But, for all that, the noise, the spirit of the words cried in his name, was meat and drink to *le petit* Lemercier, and a joy to the soul of him. He raised his head, regally, smiling, and began a speech.

"Messieurs!" he cried pompously. "I —" His voice died to a whisper in his throat; his flush paled; he collapsed suddenly from the statue of an emperor to that of a frightened child. "General O'Rourke —" he faltered, with a frightened gesture.

The eyes of the company followed the direction of his gaze.

Abruptly, noiselessly, the summits of the surrounding hills had become peopled; out of the wilderness its men had sprung to look upon this man who dared declare himself their ruler.

O'Rourke cast his eyes about the whole circumference of the little valley; on every hilltop he saw men, seated silently upon the back of camels, watching, it seemed, sardonically the trumpery show beneath them: men of giant figures and of lordly bearing, clothed for the most part in flowing white burnooses, with headdresses of white. Each bore upon his hip, as a cavalryman carries his carbine, a long rifle; and each was masked with black below his eyes.

For a full minute the tableau held: the forlorn little company in the valley, motionless with astonishment, transfixed with a chill of fear; the spectators upon the dunes, gazing grimly down — quiet and sinister, bulking against the darkling sky like some portentous army of ghosts.

O'Rourke was the first to recover; he realized that the time was brief for that which must be accomplished. Already the sun was down; there would be a few fleeting moments of twilight, then the sudden, swooping desert night.

"Tawareks!" he shouted. "The masked Tawareks! Men, form a square! Danny, run back and see if the way to the boats be clear; if not, we'll have to fight through them!" He turned to his princess. "Madame," he said gently, "there will be but one place for ye — the center of the square. We fight for our lives now, and against odds!"

And he drew his breath sharply, mindful of the two long miles that lay between them and the boats.

CHAPTER XI

IN an instant the little valley was the scene of confusion; for a frantic moment men were running hither and thither, apparently aimlessly, weaving in and out amongst their comrades — shouting, screaming, cursing aloud.

Danny, obedient to the order of O'Rourke, shouted to his men, commanding them to form a square similar to that used by British infantry when repelling attacks.

In the center of the square would be placed all those who might be counted upon to act as non-combatants in event of a possible mêlée between the landing party and the rightful lords of the desert — the Tawareks. These would be, probably, Madame la Princesse de Grandlieu, her husband, Prince Felix, together with Mouchon and D'Ervy and Monsieur Lemercier himself — Leopold the First, Emperor of the Sahara.

O'Rourke seized the arm of the princess, near to whom he had been standing, in a grasp whose roughness might only be condoned in view of his anxiety to get her quickly to the place of most safety. She did not resist; she did not even seem to resent his action. In her eyes, upturned to his, O'Rourke caught a look — even in that moment of terror and confusion — which he never forgot, which he was to treasure jealously for the rest of his days — a look of confidence, commingled (he dared hope) with an emotion deeper, stronger. In the deepening twilight they shone like clear,

dark pools of night, lit with a light from within. Small
wonder that the headstrong Irishman was conscious of his
leaping heart, or that he lost himself momentarily in their
depths.

But the voice of Chambret brought them both to reason —
Chambret, who had been no less instant to the side of the
princess. He shouted something in a tone tinged with impatient worriment. O'Rourke heard and turned, shaking
his head like a man restive under the influence of a dream.

"Chambret!" he cried. "Thank God! Ye're armed?
Then take her, man, and — and guard her as ye would your
life. Madame," he murmured, "ye will pardon me — me
seeming roughness. I — I was —"

"I understand, monsieur," she said quietly, still with her
gaze upon his eyes; "you are needed elsewhere. Monsieur
Chambret, your arm, if you please. I shall not run away,
that you need clutch me so rudely!"

O'Rourke was gone. Chambret stared at the face of the
woman in deepest chagrin. Did not the excuse the Irishman
had claimed apply to him, to Chambret, also? He had however, no time for protest. Immediately they found themselves surrounded by a pushing mob of men, which presently
resolved itself into an orderly square, ten men to a side, en-
closing the civilians and the pseudo-emperor.

O'Rourke took command, unsheathing his sword and
drawing his revolver.

"Fix bayonets!" he cried.

There was a heavy thudding as the Mausers grounded
upon the sand, and there followed the rattle of steel. In another moment the square bristled like a hedgehog, with the
long, curved blades outturned upon the end of each firearm.

So far O'Rourke's attention had been directed solely to

getting the command in a state of defense against the expected attack; now he turned his eyes to the enemy. Among
them there was noticeable no confusion, no trace of excitement; still they sat motionless atop their camels, gazing steadfastly down into the gathering shadows of the valley, where
the intruders were running frantically to and fro, making
much ûnseemly noise.

Still the lords of the desert sat stolid and imperturbable,
ranged about the summits of the surrounding dunes, unawed by the hostile preparations, awe-inspiring in their impassivity, their light-hued burnooses looming against the cool
violet sky line, themselves as imperturbable as so many car-
rion birds waiting for their prey to die ere descending upon
the tempting carcasses.

In the valley the little company was watching them breathlessly. O'Rourke grasped at a flying hope that their intent
might be, after all, pacific; it brought a sigh of anticipated
relief to his throat.

Hurriedly he unswung his field glasses and turned them·
toward the rear — in the direction from which the landing
party had come. They covered the figure of Danny, who
was still bravely running back to see if the way to the boats
were clear.

Already the man had covered more than a quarter of a
mile from the square and was pushing on, regardless of the
danger he neared at every step; for, although it seemed that
the bulk of the Tawareks had massed themselves to the north
and east of the square, with a few to the south, yet two were
waiting upon their camels at no great distance from the depression between two western sandhills by which the party
had entered this valley.

For a moment or two, O'Rourke watched Danny flounder·

and struggle forward through the cumbering, loose sand that clogged his feet.

"I was rattled — a fool to send him!" muttered the Irishman remorsefully. "'Wish I might call him back before 'tis too late! He can tell little in this darkness, and he's running into almost certain — Ah!"

A rifle's crack rang sharp in the hush; the Tawarek nearest Danny had fired. His long weapon spat a yard of flame that showed crimson and gold against the dusk. Danny plunged forward, falling upon his knees.

From the square rose a cry of horror that changed abruptly to a yelp of rage from the stricken man's comrades. They fingered the triggers of their Mausers nervously, looking to O'Rourke for an order to fire.

He shook his head, then again put the glasses to his eyes.

"Not yet," he cried. "There's a chance that we may get through without bloodshed if we hold our fire!"

"Without bloodshed!" echoed Chambret. "When they've murdered him —"

"He's not murdered!" declared O'Rourke. "I don't believe he's hit, even. See, he's up again!"

This was true. It seemed possible that Danny had stumbled and fallen, rather than that he had been shot. He was even then rising, slowly and with evident effort; and he turned, looking back irresolutely, as though undecided whether or not to push on.

O'Rourke raised his voice, shouting with all the strength of his lungs.

"Come back, Danny!" he roared. "Back!"

Reluctant to retreat in the face of his foes, possibly, the man continued to hesitate. O'Rourke, in an undertone, cursed him for his stupidity. He observed that Danny had

[97]

drawn a revolver and was looking from one to another of the Tawareks. "The infernal daredivvle!" murmured O'Rourke, conscious of a slight constriction in his throat. For he loved the boy as only an Irishman can love a loyal servant.

But he was right; Danny's action, which he had been prompted to take by the instinct of self-preservation alone, was folly, being open to misinterpretation by the Tawareks. One — he who had fired — called aloud to his companion: an odd, thin, wailing cry, the first that had come from the impassive natives. It shrilled uncannily in the ears of the foreigners.

And it produced an immediate effect, sealing the fate of Danny. The second Tawarek swung his rifle to his shoulder, and fired.

Danny staggered and cursed the fellow — the syllables indistinguishable because of the distance. He seemed to try to raise his weapon and return the fire, but his arm would not move from his side. He took a step or two forward, faltering, and then, amid a breathless silence, reeled and fell prone.

O'Rourke was swept off his feet in a gust of rage.

"Fire!" he thundered. "Fire!"

A lean ex-Spahi was the first to respond — a sharpshooter he had been in the French Army. Hardly had the command passed O'Rourke's lips than, with his Mauser still at his hip, this fellow fired.

The rifle snapped venomously, like the crack of a black-snake whip. The Tawarek who had been the last to fire lurched in the saddle, dropping his rifle, and slid listlessly forward upon the neck of his camel.

Then night came as a dark mantle cast upon the face of the earth — night, deep and softly black, the invading party's worst enemy, since it left them lost in the midst of desolate sandhills, without guide or notion as to their where-abouts.

Bright stars leaped suddenly from the vault of heaven, casting a pale bluish illumination upon the desert; a cold wind sprang from nowhere and chilled the foreigners to the bone.

One volley was fired, almost unanimously, upon the heels of the Spahi's wonderful shot. Had it been as effective as it seemed to be, things would have been well indeed with the little party; for when the vapor had cleared the dunes were bare and lifeless again — the Tawareks had disappeared.

"Forward!" shouted O'Rourke. "To the boats!"

Upon the word, the command began to move toward the seashore and the *Eirene* — or as nearly in that direction as it might guess. The square formation was preserved, as was the silence, the men alertly awaiting the expected attack and with keen eyes searching the dunes for sign or sound of the enemy.

None appeared, save now and then the red tongue of flame from the top of a sandhill and the dull report of a rifle; for the most part the shots were poorly aimed, flying high above the heads of the foreigners. Nevertheless, they were irritating, galling to the ready fighters who asked nothing better than a chance to stand up and shoot and be shot at by an enemy who dared fight in the open.

"Aim at the flashes!" O'Rourke told them, and this advice they followed, but with what result they knew not.

For the Tawareks did not cry aloud their hurts, sustained they any; they fought with deadly purpose and in utter silence, these men born to and bred in the eternal silence of the desert. And continually they maintained a fire that seemed to come from every point of the compass, and minute by minute grew more acute and galling.

Those primal shots which had whistled harmlessly over the invaders' heads were followed by others less inaccurate, as the Tawareks improved their range of their enemies. Bullets began to plow up the sand at the toes of the retreating soldiers; and one was hit hard and dropped his rifle to stanch the flow of blood from his chest.

Another screamed shrilly and reeled about, to fall with his face to the sea — stone dead: a Turco that. A third groaned at the loss of a finger nipped off by a flying bullet.

By now they were come up with the prostrate figure of Danny. O'Rourke dropped the command for a moment to lean over this countryman of his and to feel of his heart; it was still beating, and the man moaned and stirred beneath O'Rourke's touch. He called two of the soldiers and bade them carry their wounded captain to the rear as gently and as expeditiously as they might; then turned his mind to the problem at hand.

Rapidly the situation was becoming desperate; two more men were out of the fighting — one with a bullet through his brain, another with a shattered forearm. Massed as they were, they formed a conspicuous mark, a dark blur upon the starlit sands, a bold target for the Tawareks; while the latter kept themselves carefully in concealment.

With each second a spurt of fire would belch from a black clump of sand grass on a hilltop; and never twice from the same tuft. The foreigners fired valiantly at the flashes; but it is doubtful if their bullets did more than to disturb the sands.

O'Rourke thought quickly, as quickly came to his decision. It appeared that their present mode of retreat was untenable, their pace slow, their eventual escape to the boats problematical. Meanwhile, Madame la Princesse was in the gravest danger; the men who shielded her were falling right and left; it was but a question of minutes ere she would no longer have protection even from their bodies.

"Chambret!" O'Rourke shouted; and the answer of the Frenchman came clear above the din of the firing:

"Here and safe, monsieur!"

O'Rourke made his way to the Frenchman's side.

"Take madame and ten men — the nearest ten — and make for the boats. If ye reach the yacht, send up rockets to guide us to the coast. We'll stay and hold these devils off to cover your retreat."

He turned to find *le petit* Lemercier at his elbow — a pale, fear-stricken thing, shaken with tremblings.

"Monsieur," advised O'Rourke, "it is your duty to us all to go with madame and Monsieur Chambret."

"*Non, monsieur!*" he cried shrilly. "I stay and fight — here with my men! There is a weapon for me? I fight!"

"Bully for ye!" O'Rourke found time to mutter as he moved away. "Ye've more sand in ye than I thought, me lad!" The next moment he had mounted a convenient dune and was directing the retreat. "Scatter!" he told the men at the top of his voice. "Scatter — ten yards between each man. Lie down and fire from the hilltops, behind the clumps of grass. In open order — *deploy!*"

A cheerful yelp greeted his words; the men obeyed, burrowing into the sands like rabbits. Chambret's contingent had already started for the rear, swelled in numbers to some twenty strong, including the wounded, Mouchon, D'Ervy, and Prince Felix; they made way rapidly, and were unmolested. For the tactics adopted by O'Rourke — quick-witted soldier that he was, who had been instant to learn his lesson from the Tawareks and to copy their mode of guerrilla warfare — had stopped the advance of the natives.

The foreigners spread out, fanwise, completely covering the way to the coast. They fired, and now with more effect, for the Tawareks, recklessly brave, were forced to expose themselves more or less in order to determine the movements of their antagonists.

Between shots the invaders would drop back a few yards, then again seek the convenient shelter of a dune and wait for the silhouette of a Tawarek turban above the sky line as a mark for their bullets. The Mausers kept up a continual chatter, fast and furious as the drum of a machine gun, and now and then neighbor would call to neighbor a jeering comment that was a delight to the soul of O'Rourke, for it showed him that he had chosen his men wisely — men who could laugh in the heat of battle.

He cheered them on himself, with the rifle of one of the fallen hugged close to his cheek; but now he found he had a double duty to perform — not alone to command but also to watch over the new-fledged emperor, by whose side the Irishman hung tenaciously.

As for *le petit* Lemercier, he was proving himself more of a man than any would have credited him with being; he laughed hysterically for the most part, it is true; but he kept his Mauser hot and the sands spraying up from the Tawarek's sheltering dunes. And to him, also, the heart of the Irishman warmed, as it always did to a ready fighter.

Thus they fought on steadily, as steadily falling back; to O'Rourke it seemed as though the way were endless, and more than once he feared that they were going rather inland than toward the coast; but in the end the hiss and detonation of a rocket behind him proved that he had not erred in trusting to instinct.

He turned to watch the sputtering arc of sparks that lingered in the rocket's trail, and saw it flare and spread almost directly above his head. He cheered aloud, shouting to his comrades the glad news that they were within appreciable yards of the shore.

In their turn, they cheered breathlessly; and simultaneously the fire of the Tawareks dwindled to a perceptible extent. A second rocket screamed its way to the skies and burst aloft with a deafening roar — a wrecking rocket, that.

From the Tawareks came their first human utterances — a chorus of fearful shrieks; they fired no longer. A third rocket swept inland, exploding in their neighborhood; they shrieked again, and their fire died out completely.

The battle of the sandhills was over.

O'Rourke, breathing a blessing upon the saints who had preserved him, checked the now almost automatic firing of the fledgling emperor and hurried him back to the beach; they burst from among the dunes and into sight of the yacht in company with others of the fighters.

Their fellows arrived momentarily, to throw themselves down on the wet sands and pant out their exhaustion. O'Rourke counted them as they came on and estimated a full roster — that is to say, none had fallen since his adoption of Tawarek strategy.

Between the yacht and the shore, boats were plying. The captain of the vessel had waked to his duty, and now rapid-fire guns coughed, and Gatlings jabbered, sending a storm of missiles over the heads of those on the beach, to fall far inland about the ears of the fleeing natives.

O'Rourke sat him down upon the sands and produced a cigar, which he trimmed with careful nicety and lit.

"Your majesty," he told *le petit* Lemercier, "the Empire

of the Sahara has been baptized indeed, this night — and with blood."

But his majesty the Emperor Leopold only stared vacantly at his general. His majesty's eyes looked dull, as though he were dazed by a swift blow, and his teeth chattered — but whether from fear or from the biting night wind of the desert, O'Rourke could not say.

CHAPTER XII

WITHIN fifteen minutes after the return of O'Rourke to the beach, all were aboard the *Eirene*, and over the sandhills reigned a silence as profound as though they had not been the scene of a furious skirmish half an hour before.

The commander of the yacht deemed it advisable to keep up a peppering of the desert with the machine guns at intervals throughout the night, but O'Rourke decided against this measure.

"Ye'll hear no more of the Tawareks," he told Lemercier confidently — "for a while, at least. I rather fancy we've taught them a lesson that they will not be quick to forget. But the morning will decide that; then we can go ashore and look over the battle-ground." He laughed, as a tried soldier might, at his dignifying of the conflict with the name of battle.

"For the rest of the night," he continued, "'twill be sufficient to arm the watch and keep them on the lookout. Also, 'twould be advisable to continue the use of the searchlight; 'twill do no manner of harm, and may do good. The rockets frightened them; the searchlight may keep up the good work."

"Convey my orders to that effect to the captain," responded *le petit* Lemercier, who had by now recovered from his fright. "In half an hour, monsieur, I shall expect you to attend a council of war in the saloon."

"I'll be wid yez, your majesty," promised O'Rourke,

himself still gay — laughing as a man will, half-intoxicated with the wine of war. "Faith," he told himself, "'tis O'Rourke who is not sorry that he's here!"

But perhaps the light he had seen in the eyes of Madame la Princesse had somewhat to do with his self-satisfaction.

He saw the captain, and later hurried off to the sick ward to see primarily what could be done for Danny; afterwards he was concerned for the other wounded.

Two dead and eight wounded were the casualties which had been sustained by the little army of occupation. Four men had been wounded but slightly, among them the man Soly, whom O'Rourke had disciplined at Las Palmas; a bullet had plowed a furrow across his shoulder, which proved painful, but not serious.

Of the four others, however, one was expected to die — an ex-Spahi, whose chest had been torn open; one other must wear his arm in splints, for a time, perforce of a shattered forearm, and another would have to lie upon his back for weeks pending the healing of a hole in his lungs.

As for Danny, the poor fellow was unconscious; the shot of the Tawarek had taken effect in the back of his head, near the base of his brain — perilously near.

O'Rourke cursed himself for his stupidity, not only in ordering the man into certain danger, but for another more serious oversight; he, upon whom had devolved the bulk of the military preparations, had neglected securing the services of a surgeon.

But, like most veterans, he had some slight knowledge, himself, of the treatment of wounds and the care of the wounded; and with the assistance of Chambret — always willing to do what he termed "his possible" — and of the yacht's medicine chest, which happened by good ch be well stocked, the Irishman was able to accomplish much toward alleviating the sufferings of the stricken.

Two of them he relieved of lodged bullets; and concerning the remainder his mind was at rest with the double exception of Danny and the man with the torn chest. For them he knew not what to do; Danny's wound was so close upon the delicate regions of the brain that he dared not probe for the bullet; and the other was beyond help.

He told Chambret this, turning a face to the Frenchman that was lined deep with his mental trouble and with sorrow for the plight of his countryman.

"In sober truth," he declared, "I don't know what the divvle to do for them. 'Tis meself that's no angel to soothe their agonies."

Chambret, who had watched with growing admiration the Irishman as he moved about attending to the sufferers with a sympathy that seemed almost womanly and with hands as soft and gentle as a child's, smiled sadly, and shook his head.

"You have my sympathy, *mon ami*," he assured him; "but the fatal mistake lay in not bringing a surgeon."

"Faith, then," cried O'Rourke, "we'll just have to go for one!"

"*Comment?*" demanded Chambret, wondering if O'Rourke was out of his senses to suggest obtaining a surgeon's services in that howling wilderness.

"I say," repeated O'Rourke, "that these men shall have proper attention. If Monsieur l'Empereur" — he sneered slightly — "is to found his empire in the hearts of his servants he'll be obliged to turn the *Eirene* back to Las Palmas."

Chambret whistled.

"I prophesy trouble, monsieur, if that is the advice you will give his majesty."

"Me soul! Trouble? If he denies me, 'tis himself who'll have all the trouble he desires!"

Again the Frenchman made a sign of dissent.

"It will not be his majesty who will deny you, but —" he shrugged his shoulders expressively.

"Monsieur le Prince?"

"You have said it, monsieur."

The Irishman snapped his fingers angrily.

"That for the whelp!" he declared.

"You do not fear him?"

"Fear — *him? Mon ami*, ye do not know me."

"You are a bold man, monsieur, to think of defying his highness."

"I suppose he will think so," said O'Rourke shortly, preparing to leave the sick bay. "But, come, Monsieur Chambret. Ye attend the conference?"

"If you seriously purpose to advance your proposition, monsieur, wild horses would not serve to keep me away."

The Frenchman joined arms with O'Rourke, laughing.

"A bold man!" he repeated. "Bold, indeed, to brave the displeasure of Monsieur le Prince, Felix de Grandlieu! I have told you that he is a noted duelist?"

"A noted coward, Chambret!" O'Rourke muttered an impolite Anglo-Saxon epithet that appealed to him as highly applicable to the character of Prince Felix. "If he does me the honor," he growled, "of calling me out, I'll take all the pleasure in life in blowing his ugly head off his shoulders."

Again Chambret laughed.

"Decidedly, monsieur," he said lightly, "when we come to settle *our* affair I must be on my guard!"

"Our affair! I thought ye had forgotten that."

"*Non, monsieur;* the blow I can forgive you, now

know you. But there are other things." He paused meaningly.

O'Rourke disengaged his arm.

"As to what?" he demanded sharply.

"As to — madame."

It was O'Rourke's turn to whistle. "Lies the wind that
way, d'ye tell me? There, indeed, have we cause for dis-
agreement, *mon ami!*"

"All in good time," returned Chambret patiently; "wait
until this chimera of empire is dissipated. Then, by the
grace of God, I shall balance accounts with monsieur. For
the present, we are — what you say? — partners."

"Faith, 'tis yourself has a queer way of showing it!"

They were now on deck, walking aft toward the main
saloon. The yacht was as silent as a dream ship, with but
the faintest of lapping under her quarters as she rose and
fell upon the tide. They ceased their conversation, suddenly, under the spell of the night's beauty; and that was
supreme, resplendent with the multitude of high, clear, wonderful stars that cluster above the desert; a black night and
cold — nipping cold as are all nights upon the Sahara.

Upon the shore the long, deliberate surge of the Atlantic
broke monotonously, beating prolonged rolls that merged
with and became a part of the stillness; only the occasional
hiss and splutter of the searchlight in the bows actually disturbed the quiet as its fierce, white, glaring lance wheeled and
veered out over the desert or darted skywards, clearly defined
in the dust-laden air, like a sword of wrath trembling over
the heads of the Tawareks.

Here and there one of the watch leaned idly upon the rail,
his carbine ready to his hand, his eyes fixed undeviatingly
upon the shore line; and presently the two, the Gaul and the

Celt, united in war and divided in love, came upon *le petit* Lemercier himself, standing by the rail, and talking in low tones with his familiar dæmon, Monsieur le Prince.

He looked around and nodded as they approached, continuing his conversation in a somewhat higher pitch, as a man will when improvising talk to cover some awkward contretemps.

O'Rourke remarked this, and nodded significantly to Chambret, whose eyes likewise showed his comprehension of the situation — that Monsieur le Prince had been caught in the act of poisoning the mind of the emperor against one or both of the allies.

"Here," invented the Lemercier, "will be our harbor — widened and deepened by dredging. Here, also, we will build long quays of stone and iron out into the ocean, making it an ideal port for the desert caravans, who shall here bring their gums, their ivory, their gold and rich stuffs, and here obtain their supplies, sold them at cost by a paternal government."

"Here, by all means," echoed the intriguing prince.

"And now, messieurs," continued the emperor, turning, "to our conference, since you are ready."

He looked toward O'Rourke, or rather toward the place where O'Rourke had been; but his lieutenant-general was gone, running up the deck as though fear itself were treading close upon his heels.

Chambret stood staring after him with mouth agape; in his surprise the emperor took a couple of steps after the hurrying man, then halted, amazed.

He saw the Irishman leap suddenly and fall upon the shoulders of one of the watch, whose carbine promptly slipped from his grasp, and splashed in the waters of the harbor.

"Not that, ye damn fool!" he cried. "D'ye want to ruin us all?"

The man squirmed, spluttering with surprise, choking with explanations. Lemercier arrived just in time to place a staying hand upon the infuriated Irishman's arm, and to secure the release of the hapless sentry.

"What are you about, monsieur?" he demanded angrily.

"About?" roared the Irishman. "Look ye there! And this fool would have killed him had I not happened to see him raise his gun!"

His majesty glanced in the direction the Irishman had indicated; he noticed that the searchlight was holding steady, unswerving; and there, upon the beach, in the center of the disk of illumination, was the figure of a Tawarek, standing alone, erect, motionless, wrapped about with a burnoose of crimson and gold, masked in black to his eyes, disdainful and dignified despite the nature of his errand.

In one hand, outstretched, he bore a long lance; a cloth of white dangled from its tip.

"A flag of truce!" cried O'Rourke. "He has come as an envoy to make peace with ye, Monsieur l'Empereur! And this — this blockhead would have spoiled it all!"

"I will have no dealings with him," announced *le petit* Lemercier, haughtily turning his shoulder to O'Rourke. "Let the man fire."

"Your majesty," protested O'Rourke, "that is madness—"

"They attacked us," persisted the emperor coldly.

"They rule the desert," expostulated the Irishman. "Ye were speaking of opening a port for the caravan trade. Without the cooperation of these desert pirates ye will gain nothing; if they oppose ye they will never permit one caravan to pass into your territories!"

[111]

"That is so," counseled Monsieur le Prince. "The advice of Monsieur le Colonel is good, your majesty."

"Very well," *le petit* Lemercier gave in, regretfully; "have him aboard, then, and see what he wants."

He swung upon his heel, and went into the saloon, apparently highly offended by this disputation of his wishes. But the Irishman was too elated by the victory to care aught for *le petit* Lemercier's humor. He turned to the sentry, and caught him by the shoulders.

"When ye've served under me another minute, me boy," he told the man, "ye'll know better than to fire without orders. What's that ye say?"

"Monsieur," declared the man, "I have served long with the camel corps in Algeria. Our orders were to shoot a Tawarek on sight."

"Well, then, there's some excuse for ye. But in the future be careful. Now, go and find me a man who speaks the language of these devils."

The soldier saluted, and went off hurriedly, glad to escape further reprimand. As he did so, the man Soly slipped forward, out of the obscurity of the night, and saluted.

"Monsieur," he said humbly, avoiding O'Rourke's eye, "I was passing and heard what you desired."

"Well?"

"I speak Tamahak — the language of the Tawareks, *mon général.*"

"Very well. Hail that fellow and find out what he wants."

The former member of the *sans souci* went to the rail and cupped his hands about his mouth; the next moment a thin, wailing cry, nearly the counterpart of that which had been the signal for the shooting of Danny, trembled upon the stillness.

The Tawarek moved slightly — for the first time since **he** had appeared upon the beach; he waved his lance, making the flag of truce flutter, and answered the call. Again Soly hailed him, and again he replied.

"Well? Well?" demanded O'Rourke impatiently.

"He says that he is come to arrange peace," interpreted the man; "that you are to send a boat to bring him aboard."

"The nerve of him!" muttered O'Rourke.

Nervetheless, he gave orders to have the boat lowered and manned by a heavily armed crew; at the same time he directed that the deck guns should be trained upon the shore.

"Tell him," he ordered Soly, "that we will send for **him,** but that at the first sign of treachery we'll blow him into eternity!"

Soly complied readily, but the Tawarek preserved a dignified silence.

While the boat was making for the shore the Irishman ordered that the searchlight should sweep the surrounding desert, following its path with his binoculars; they showed to him no further sign of the enemy — naught, in fact, save that solitary, gorgeous figure, waiting patiently upon **the** beach.

CHAPTER XIII

PRESENTLY, the boat scraped and bumped against the side; the first to ascend was Soly, the second the Tawarek.

O'Rourke was awaiting him at the head of the gangway, respectfully, as befitted the welcomer of a man of rank and place in his country — as the Irishman suspected the visitor to be. To none else than a head man, he considered, would such an errand be intrusted — a matter which affected the interests of a whole tribe.

Nor was he wrong, as he realized when the Tawarek stalked past him without deigning him a glance or a word. The man Soly himself had jumped at once to the threshold of the saloon door, where he stood at attention, his keen eyes furtively alternating between the faces of the Irishman, the native envoy and those in the interior of the cabin.

To him, evidently content to recognize in the man who spoke his native Tamahak his only friend, the Tawarek went direct, and when the soldier stepped to one side, accepted the implied invitation and entered the saloon.

O'Rourke followed, — himself a large man, but dwarfed for the moment by the huge stature of the enormous Tawarek.

Fully six feet six inches in height (a tallness not unusual among his kin, however), and broad and heavy in proportion, he stood with his shoulders well back and proudly, as became a free lord of the Sahara, one who neither bows the knee nor pays tribute to any man — as are the Tawareks all, even the most beggarly of them.

His burnoose was richly embroidered with gold, and of the finest silken mesh, heavily lined for a protection against the cold of the desert nights. This he presently threw aside, disclosing a costume of yellow silk over a shirt and baggy trousers ending somewhat below the knee, both of white; across his shoulders and about his waist ran a sash belt, into which were stuck handily heavy cavalry revolvers of a now obsolete type, but for all that deadly weapons in competent hands.

For a headdress he wore a turban of white, with a flap of black silk hanging down across his forehead to his brows; and sharply across the middle of his face was a second cloth; the two leaving but his eyes and a portion of the bridge of his nose visible. But those eyes were keen, straightforward, quick; deeply set and wrinkled about with that network of fine lines which comes from steady gazing over plains glaring in the full of the noonday sun.

O'Rourke stepped to his side; for a moment the two men stood, eying one another with respect, — men, both of them, of giant build and free carriage, in contrast striking to the others in the saloon: to the weaklings, Mouchon and D'Ervy; to Monsieur le Prince, padded, emaciated: to the weary-eyed Lemercier, posing himself with an assumption of the dignity that should become an emperor, — perhaps really believing in his heart that he wore the majesty of men born to rule. Only Chambret approached either O'Rourke or the Tawarek in size or dignity of address; and Chambret was discreetly effacing himself, as far as possible from the center of the group.

After a brief interchange of glances, the Tawarek bowed

his head slightly, in lordly salutation of O'Rourke, acknowledging the one man whom he had failed to look down. The Irishman smiled, and motioned towards a chair, which the Tawarek accepted with suspicions that were evidenced by the excess of precautions he took in seating himself.

So far, no words had passed. Soly had entered upon a gesture from O'Rourke, and stood at one side, leering, ready when called upon to play his rôle of interpreter.

A blaze of electric light was in the cabin; the Tawarek blinked in its glare, then set himself to study the faces of these men who were invading his land — the land sacred to him by the rights of occupation dating back into the fogs of antiquity.

His sharp, bold eyes flitted from face to face, challenging, reading, rejecting with disdain all save O'Rourke and Chambret. In the end it was to O'Rourke that he turned and addressed himself in a few words of Tamahak, his voice low and pleasantly modulated, his words deferentially spoken.

To Lemercier O'Rourke looked. "Your majesty," he said, keeping straight and serious the mouth that always was tempted to twitch at the corners when he used the title which Leopold had arrogated unto himself: "your majesty, 'tis meself that's had some experience with these men in the Soudan, as ye know. Have I your permission to treat with him?"

"Yes," granted Lemercier graciously.

"What does he say, Soly?" inquired the Irishman, turning to the guest.

The soldier interpreted: "He says that he is Ibeni, chieftain of all the Tawareks hereabouts. He says, monsieur, that if harm comes to him his people will rally in force and sweep your dead bodies into the sea."

"The hell he does!" commented the Irishman, without moving a muscle of his face for the Tawarek to read. "Tell him that he is as safe here as in his own camp."

Soly interpreted again; the Tawarek replied at length.

"He says, *mon général*, that he desires to know who you may be, what your purpose here, how long you intend to stay; and by what right you invade the lands of the Tawareks without arranging to pay tribute to the tribe."

"Tell him," replied O'Rourke, "that we are Frenchmen by birth, for the most part, subjects by inclination of Leopold Premier, l'Empereur du Sahara."

"Tell him that we come to make oases in the desert by digging wells, that we purpose to build up here a land as fertile as the Soudan or Senegal, and to establish a port for the trade of caravans and ships. Tell him that we shall stay as long as the sun hangs in the sky; and as for tribute, tell him to go to — No," he interrupted himself laughingly; "don't tell him that. Your majesty" — turning to *le petit* Lemercier — "for the sake of peace, let me advise that ye pay the tribute demanded by this man. I promise ye that it will not be large."

Lemercier coughed, hesitated, glanced at his mentor, Monsieur le Prince. The latter's expression negatived the proposition decidedly.

"No tribute," announced the emperor.

"If Monsieur the Prince will permit me to disagree," disputed O'Rourke suavely; "he is in the wrong. The United States Government, your majesty, pays the Indians for the lands it takes from them. We have to consider that these Tawareks regard the Sahara as their land as jealously as the American Indians held theirs. What tribute he exacts will amount to little in Monsieur l'Empereur's estimation, but it will insure peace, and it will insure the unmolested passage of caravans through the territory of the Empire of the Sahara. I presume your majesty does not contemplate a chicken-hearted withdrawing of his hand at this late day?"

"Most certainly not," declared Lemercier, flushing under the sting in the Irishman's irony.

"And I am sure that Monsieur le Prince does not wish a repetition of this evening's excitement. Let me promise ye, messieurs, that if tribute be not paid to these men, pirates though they be, each day will see a duplicate of the skirmish of to-day. Ye will need regiments, messieurs, rather than tens, of men, if this is to be your method of conquering —"

"Enough," interrupted *le petit* Lemercier — avoiding the eyes of Monsieur le Prince, however; "tell him that we will pay in reason."

"Ask him how much," O'Rourke instructed Soly, who had meanwhile been steadily translating to the Tawarek.

"One thousand francs in gold yearly," was the reply; "for that he assures you safety and freedom from molestation from his or other tribes."

"We will pay it," said Lemercier, smiling at the insignificance of the sum.

O'Rourke could not repress a triumphant glance at Monsieur le Prince.

"Your majesty has the gold handy, I have no doubt?" he suggested.

"Get it, D'Ervy," commanded his majesty.

That individual went upon his errand, returning with the money in a canvas bag; it was handed the Tawarek, who accepted as his by right, and placed it in a fold of his burnoose.

With a few more words he rose as if to go.

"He places the countryside at your disposal, messieurs,"
interpreted the man Soly; "he says that, in the morning, he
and his men will be far from the oasis El Kebr, as he calls it.
He bids you good-evening, intrusting you to the care of
Allah."

"One moment," O'Rourke told him; "inform Monsieur
Ibeni, or whatever his name is, that in token of our good-will
we wish to make him a little present."

He drew from his holster a revolver of the latest type — a
quick-firing, hair-trigger, hammerless forty-four caliber.
The eyes of the masked chieftain glistened covetously as they
fell upon this weapon whose range and worth his tribe had
cause to bear in mind.

With one movement of his arm O'Rourke swung the
weapon above his head, pointing it through the open sky-
light, and pulled the trigger. The six shots rang as one prolonged report.

In an instant the ship was in an uproar; the men came
running from their quarters; Soly, by O'Rourke's orders, reassured them, motioning them back from the companionway.

Even Madame la Princesse had been startled; she opened
the door of her stateroom and stepped into the saloon, pale
and tight-lipped with anxiety.

O'Rourke was apprised of her entrance by the eyes of the
Tawarek, who, it may be, had never before seen a woman of
civilization — though there is little likelihood of that. But
certainly he had never looked upon a woman more fair nor
one more sweetly beautiful. Her experience of the evening
had set its mark transiently upon her face, ringing her eyes
with dark circles that served but to accentuate their loveliness. And the glance of the Tawarek lightened and grew
more bold as it fell upon her.

She moved slowly toward the group about the native.

"Messieurs," she said, a bit unsteadily, looking from face to face, "is — is there anything amiss?"

"Only me folly, madame," replied the Irishman bowing gallantly; "'tis meself that should have remembered the shots would alarm ye. I crave madame's pardon. I was but demonstrating the beauties of this revolver to monsieur the Tawarek; I fired it for that purpose and for another — to prevent his using it if perchance he were inclined to be treacherous ere leaving us. Soly, find a box of cartridges for this gentleman."

He broke the weapon at the cylinder, ejecting the still vaporing cartridges, whipped a silk handkerchief through the barrel, and handed the revolver to the Tawarek.

Soly returned with the cartridges; the chieftain accepting both with words of gratitude. His mask concealed whatever facial expression he may have had, and it was only from his eyes that they might guess something of his emotions; for his gaze had not left madame since she had appeared in the saloon. Even as he took his leave, which he did with a scant bow to O'Rourke and a total ignoring of the remainder of the party, he continued to watch Madame la Princesse until he had reached the foot of the companionway, when he turned, made her a low obeisance, and vanished, accompanied by O'Rourke.

The commander-in-chief was occupied on deck for several minutes, seeing the Tawarek over the side, and watching the boat on its journey to and from the beach. He then had the men dismissed from their places at the guns, and before returning to the saloon he sent away the man, Soly, to his quarters, and said a low word to three grave Turcos. These nodded comprehension, and placed them-

selves at no great distance from the saloon companionway.

When he rejoined the council, his princess had left the
saloon for her stateroom; chairs were drawn up around the
central table, champagne was being served by the steward
and partaken of by Monsieur l'Empereur, Monsieur le Prince,
D'Ervy, and Mouchon. Chambret sat some distance apart,
thoughtfully consuming a cigarette.

Lemercier looked up and indicated a chair; his attitude
was not one of great welcome for the commander-in-chief
of his forces, however; it was momentarily becoming more
evident to the Irishman that in his own case Prince Felix had
been successful in his attempt to turn *le petit* Lemercier's
favor to displeasure.

For the present, however, he was disposed to pass this over.
He had planned his battle; in his mind he had already won
it. It remained but for matters to come to an issue between
himself and Prince Felix.

"We were saying, monsieur," said Monsieur le Prince
languidly to O'Rourke, "that, since our little affair with
your friends, the Tawareks, is settled, our next move
should be to address a note to the Powers, proclaiming
the sovereignty of Leopold as the first Emperor of the
Sahara."

"To the contrary," objected O'Rourke; "your first move
is to establish your base, to found your capital city; then to
encourage or in some way to procure a respectable coloniza-
tion. An empire of some forty population is an absurdity
on the face of it. Do ye seriously expect the Powers to
recognize such a comic opera affair?"

There fell a moment's silence; Monsieur le Prince was anything but pleased; the look he gave the Irishman was evidence

enough of the esteem in which he held him. But O'Rourke only smiled benignly upon the prime minister.

As for his majesty, Leopold, his face had lengthened with disappointment; shallow though he was, yet he had occasional glimmerings of common sense, even as he exhibited occasional flashes of spirit. He could but recognize the justice of O'Rourke's pronouncement; and he was not alone fain to bow to superior wisdom, but also generous enough to acknowledge it. Therefore he ignored the black looks of Monsieur le Prince and agreed with the Irishman.

"Another thing," propounded the latter: "Your first duty, your majesty, is not to your empire. 'Tis to humanity. Two of those who fought for ye this day lie wounded unto death in the sick bay; they need immediate attention from a skilled surgeon if their lives are to be saved. Las Palmas is not so distant that ye cannot spare time to go there," he concluded. "I make so bold as to advise an early start — this very night, in fact."

This was the opening that Monsieur le Prince had been awaiting. He interrupted Lemercier's reply.

"They were paid to take the risk," he said coldly; "let them die. We cannot permit ourselves to be put back for a matter so slight."

"Your majesty," broke in Chambret, "I have been in the sick bay; I can bear witness to the urgency —"

"One moment." Prince Felix fixed his gaze, sardonic and cruel, upon Chambret. "May I inquire, your majesty, when this conceited upstart became a member of your council, entitled to a voice therein?"

O'Rourke motioned the furious Chambret to silence.

"I will save his majesty the trouble of answering ye, Monsieur le Prince," he said calmly. "Monsieur Chambret to-day was appointed me aide, me second in command, and me successor in event of any misfortune of mine. As such, he is entitled to all rights as a member of the council."

"Appointments are not valid unless ratified by the council," objected Prince Felix, choking down his rage.

"It is not legal under your code, perhaps, monsieur," admitted O'Rourke fairly. "Ye will recall, however, that the Empire of the Sahara has no code as yet. The appointment is made by me, by me authority, and will stand, I warn ye, monsieur, whatever your objections!"

Monsieur le Prince rose slowly from his chair, toying with his wineglass.

"Monsieur," he drawled, his eyes narrowing, his white teeth showing through his snarl, "your words verge perilously upon insolence."

"If that be insolence," retorted O'Rourke sweetly, "ye can make the most of it! . . . Be careful, monsieur! If ye throw that glass at me, I'll have ye put in irons!"

"Canaille!"

O'Rourke moved to one side, quickly; the wineglass shattered to a thousand fragments upon the wall behind him.

"Ye fool!" he cried, almost laughing. Now he had his man where he wanted him; he turned towards the companion-way and whistled.

Upon that signal the three Turcos entered, and dashed down the steps, to halt at the bottom and salute O'Rourke.

"Arrest that man!" he told them, indicating Monsieur le Prince.

Lemercier, who had seemed stunned by the sudden turn of affairs, jumped to his feet with a cry of protest; but before it had passed his lips Prince Felix was helpless between two Turcos, a third at his back pinioning his arms.

[123]

"O'Rourke —" began *le petit* Lemercier, his face white with wrath.

"Leave me alone, your majesty. Men, hold him. If he struggles overmuch — ye know how to discourage him."

Prince Felix leaped forward furiously; and the yell, compounded of rage and pain, that burst from his lips as the Turcos hauled him back, attested to the truth in O'Rourke's suggestion.

"You will suffer for this!" Monsieur le Prince shrieked.

"Oh, I hear ye."

Lemercier sprang before O'Rourke, gesticulating wildly, trembling with his anger and excitement.

"Monsieur," he spluttered, "I demand an explanation. I insist that Prince Felix be released at once."

"Tell them so, then," said O'Rourke calmly.

Lemercier turned to the Turcos reluctantly. "I command you to release him!" he quavered.

The Turcos remained motionless, watching O'Rourke; his majesty repeated his demand, with no more result. He wheeled again upon O'Rourke.

"What do you mean?" he cried. "This is rebellion — this is —"

"I mean this," said O'Rourke slowly, his eyes shining: "I mean that *I* am master here, and that I brook no interference. I mean that 'tis the O'Rourke who holds the balance of power, for the men are serving me first, yourself next, monsieur. They take me commands while I live; for they know me, and that I stand by them. One moment more — let me finish. I mean that I am in your pay, your majesty, for the express purpose of making ye an emperor; 'tis meself that believes it can be done, with square, honest dealing; I believe that your scheme is practicable — though Monsieur le Prince does not in the black heart of him. And I mean, further, that I am going to do my damnedest, monsieur, to put ye on a throne, in spite of the hostility of Monsieur le Prince, who would make of ye the laughing-stock of Europe, and who eventually would kill ye to enjoy your fortune be inheritance. I'll do it, furthermore, in spite of the conspiracies of Messieurs Mouchon and D'Ervy, his tools." He paused for breath, then raised his voice again:

"We're south of Gibraltar, messieurs, and in this land every man is his own law! Here, for the time being, I am the law, your majesty. And, if ye show a disposition to turn back from your enterprise, monsieur—for now me own honor and reputation are at stake—by God! I'll make ye an emperor in spite of yourself!"

He paused, breathless with his own vehemence, looking in triumph at the group before him; at Monsieur le Prince, who, while well-nigh frothing at the mouth with rage, was yet unable to free himself; at Mouchon and D'Ervy, who had drawn back, panic-stricken; at Chambret, his face glowing with delight; at the impassive Turcos; finally, at his majesty.

Leopold was staring blankly at him, like one dreaming; he passed his hand over his eyes, dazedly, as one who wakens suddenly, when O'Rourke had made an end to his speech.

With the shadow of disillusionment fading, with the light of hope and faith again dawning upon his face, he watched the Irishman intently, as though striving to read his inmost thoughts. And by some intuitive power he must have been convinced of the honest purpose of O'Rourke; or else what common sense he had must have told him that there was but one course now open — to trust the adventurer.

Abruptly he stepped forward, and seized the hand of

O'Rourke. "Monsieur," he said simply, "I take you at your word — and shall hold you to it."

O'Rourke smiled his thanks. "You'll not regret it," said he; then, to the Turcos: "Release monsieur."

For he felt that he was safe now — that he had broken the sway of the favorite, Monsieur le Prince, Felix de Grandlieu.

CHAPTER XIV

HE ACTS BY THE CODE

An irregular oval in form, in extent about three acres, the oasis, El Kebr, flourished around three wells.

Probably these had been sunk in ancient times, before the records of man, when this desert of the Sahara had been a fertile land, well-watered and luxuriant of vegetation, supporting an immense population. The age-old masonry about their curbs attested to the truth of this surmise, and might have afforded interesting material for the antiquarian.

From the wells it radiated — the oasis — a wilderness of green growing things, interspersed with the slim, towering boles of a grove of date palms; but the sands were ever insidiously creeping, creeping in toward the water; year by year the acreage of verdure was diminishing, and, left to nature, it was only a question of time ere the desert would hold full sway, even to the lips of the life-giving wells, which, too, were doomed to be choked and lost.

But for the present it sufficed for the purposes of Monsieur l'Empereur, Leopold le Premier. It was settled upon by him to be the site of his capital city of the future — Troya, as he already called it in the fervor of his magnificent imagination.

O'Rourke came to El Kebr, early in the following dawn, at the head of a party of reconnaissance. It was apparent that the Tawarek, Ibeni, had kept faith in regard to his departure with his men; satisfied he undoubtedly had been to

have extorted tribute money from the invaders, after sustain-
ing at their hands a putative defeat; and there was nought to
be gained by lingering in the vicinity — unless it were a gratification of his curiosity.

On the route to the oasis, however, no sign of a Tawarek
had been seen by O'Rourke's command; and it was there
only that the natives had left traces of their camp about the
wells.

O'Rourke returned to the *Eirene*, and reported, advising
his majesty that there was in his judgment no cause to fear
another attack. Preparations were accordingly put forward
with all haste toward the landing of provisions, the tents, and
varied paraphernalia with which the yacht had been laden
with a view to making existence in the desert endurable.

For it had been decided at a protracted session of the council (which was suddenly subservient to the will of O'Rourke)
that Lemercier and his party would not return to Las Palmas
with the yacht; they were to land and make a settlement —
in a way as proof of their good intentions: a first definite move
toward the establishment of the Empire of the Sahara.

Even Madame la Princesse was determined to stay by the
side of her brother, and positively refused to put herself out
of possible danger by returning to Europe, as she had been
urged to do by the party.

Chambret alone was to go with the wounded, intrusted
also with other commissions than that of seeing Danny and
his fellows safely in hospital.

Portable houses had been bought in large numbers by
Lemercier before starting upon his expedition; they should
by that time have arrived at Las Palmas, if the contractors
had kept their words about shipment.

These Chambret was to see stowed aboard the *Eirene,*

and he was furthermore to enlist a force of workingmen, as many as he might be able to engage, to come to the oasis — masons, builders, carpenters, plasterers, and others of kindred crafts.

These were, primarily of course, needed for the building of the city of Troya; later, Monsieur l'Empereur hoped he might be able to induce them to stay and become colonists.

Since early dawn the men had been busy lightening the yacht of its stores; it was slow business, for the vessel could not get near inshore, and all transportation had to be accomplished by means of boats and a couple of portable catamaran rafts.

It was eleven in the evening, or later, as O'Rourke sat in his tent in the oasis, having one final talk with the Frenchman, Chambret; the *Eirene* was to sail as soon as the last of the cargo was ashore, but her captain estimated that that would not be until two in the morning at the earliest.

Chambret, therefore, had plenty of time at his disposal.

"And Danny?" O'Rourke was asking him, for the Frenchman had just returned from the vessel.

"In the same condition — comatose," replied Chambret; "but his temperature is lower; I don't think you need fear for him. If he holds as he is until we reach Las Palmas, he'll pull through all right."

"'Tis the delay that worries me," put in O'Rourke. "I had to consent to it, ye know; I couldn't make me newly asserted rule too dictatorial to start with."

"No," laughed Chambret.

He rose and walked to the front of the tent, drawing back the flap and looking out; and the Irishman joined him.

"'Tis a thriving settlement we have, monsieur," he suggested.

Near at hand was the elaborate *marquee* of Monsieur l'Empereur, glowing with light. By its side stood another, almost as imposing a tent, which had been erected for the use of Madame la Princesse alone. Farther removed were others — tents for Monsieur le Prince, for Mouchon and D'Ervy (whom O'Rourke could hit upon no plausible excuse for banishing), as well as for the soldiery and the servants.

As the two stood watching, a corporal's guard of soldiers marched past under one whom O'Rourke had appointed a petty officer, until such time as he should get his organization perfected.

"Going to change the sentries," remarked O'Rourke. "'Tis near midnight. Faith," he yawned wearily, "a long day it has been for me!"

"You've posted a guard, then?"

"All around the edge of the oasis. I don't trust monsieur, the Tawarek, any farther than I can see him. From as much as I observed of Ibeni, or whatever his name is, he's a chap that is likely to keep his word; but we'll take care to hold him at his distance, anyway."

"And Monsieur le Prince?"

"Oh — fudge!" cried O'Rourke good-humoredly. "Does the man still worry ye? Why, monsieur, he's down and out — a wind bag perforated."

"Don't be too sure. He is —"

As Chambret spoke he let the tent flap fall, and turned back to his chair. O'Rourke remained standing, his hands clasped behind him, laughing at Chambret's fears. Abruptly he chopped the laugh off short.

A shot rang through the camp.

O'Rourke wheeled about.

"Tawareks — so soon!" he cried.

But Chambret suddenly seized him by the arm, pulling him away from the door of the tent. At the same time he stooped over and extinguished the lamp with a swift twist of the wick.

"Not so fast!" he cried. "Do you seek death, *mon ami?*"

"What the divvle —?" demanded O'Rourke.

"That was no Tawarek shot, monsieur. It was a Mauser."

Enlightenment began to dawn in the Irishman's eyes.

"D'ye mean —?"

"Monsieur le Prince? Certainly — who else? Observe, monsieur!"

He indicated two dark holes in the white wall of the tent, seemingly on a direct line with the position of O'Rourke's head as he had been standing when the shot was fired.

"Assassination!" gasped the Irishman.

"Ah, Monsieur le Prince bears a grudge, be sure!" Chambret laughed shortly. "Had you stepped forth then the assassin would have shot again. You can thank me for saving your life. No matter — I shall claim it some day," he added.

"Faith!" said O'Rourke absently. "I'll try to give ye a run for your money, *mon ami.*" He paused, thinking, for a moment. "Come," he said sharply; and hurriedly he left the tent.

Without there was confusion and a running to arms. O'Rourke desired to humor this for the present, having no mind to disclose his suspicions as to the man who had fired the shot. Giving orders to warn the pickets to redoubled vigilance he made a round of them in person, accompanied by Chambret; and finally returned to the guard tent.

A Spahi was there — a tall, gangling, bronzed fellow, who

had known the desert since childhood; an Algerian of European parentage. O'Rourke called to him.

"Find the man Soly," he said softly, in the Spahi's ear, "and bring him to me at once. Don't make any fuss — but shoot him like a dog if he resists. Also, bring me his arms."

His Spahi saluted, and walked carelessly away, with the air of one on no pressing errand. O'Rourke watched him out of sight, into the shadows of the palms, with an approving nod. "A good man, that; I'll remember him."

He returned to his tent, entered and relit the lamp. Chambret protested against this heedless courting of danger, but the Irishman remained obdurate. "No more trouble tonight," he insisted.

Within ten minutes the Spahi had returned, Soly in his charge; he scratched upon the canvas wall, and upon receiving permission entered. His prisoner preceded him, with an alacrity that might have been accounted for by a revolver, half concealed, in the Spahi's hand.

O'Rourke placed himself behind his table; his own revolver lay upon it, and he fingered it nervously, looking Soly over with a placid brow. But when he spoke, he first addressed the Spahi.

"Can ye keep a quiet tongue in your head, me man?" he asked.

The Spahi saluted. "Yes, *mon général*."

"See that you do — lieutenant."

The Spahi flushed with pleasure; O'Rourke silenced his thanks with a gesture.

"Where did ye find this man?" he asked briskly.

"In his tent, monsieur."

"What was he doing?"

"Cleaning a rifle, monsieur."

"His own?"

"*Non*, monsieur — one belonging to his tentmate."

"So!" O'Rourke paused; his eyes, resting upon the ex-member of the "condemned corps," grew flintlike — hard and cold. ' So,'" he repeated thoughtfully; then, sharply: "Ye try to assassinate me with your comrade's rifle, do ye?"

"*Non, monsieur le général —*"

The words died on Soly's lips; he was gazing with deep interest into the muzzle of O'Rourke's revolver.

"Tell the truth, ye whelp," thundered the Irishman, "or I'll brain ye! Now — ye shot at me just now?"

Soly hesitated.

"*Oui*," he admitted at last, sullenly.

"Good. Why?"

Soly was silent.

"I give ye two minutes to tell the truth, the whole truth, and nothing but the truth. At whose instance did ye attempt to assassinate me?"

Soly threw back his head defiantly; but the muzzle of the revolver still held his attention. It was inflexible. Moreover, the watch of Chambret lay ticking under the Irishman's eye.

"One minute!" O'Rourke announced. Later: "And a half."

"Monsieur le Prince," Soly blurted desperately.

"Ah! Thank ye. Lieutenant, take this man, and guard him for the night."

The Spahi saluted, wheeled about, and deftly pinioned the wrists of Soly. They left O'Rourke's presence in the closest intimacy.

O'Rourke put his elbows upon the table, and bowed his

[133]

head in his hands, thinking deeply. Thus he remained for some monotonous minutes, considering the case of Monsieur le Prince. At length he stood up.

"He must leave on the yacht to-night, Chambret," he decided aloud.

There came no reply. Chambret was gone. O'Rourke looked about the tent stupidly. "What the divvle —!" he muttered. A flash of comprehension illuminated his intelligence. He cursed to himself softly, caught up his revolver and sword belt, and ran out. It was but a step to the tent of Monsieur le Prince. He had reached it in an instant, and was scratching on the canvas. Receiving no reply he drew aside the flap, and peered within, to discover it empty.

O'Rourke swore again irritably.

"Divvle take the hot-headed Frenchman!" he cried. "For why does he want to treat me so?"

He dashed up the line of tents to one which had been allotted to Mouchon and D'Ervy; he had a very distinct notion as to what Chambret was about, and it pleased him not at all. Arriving, he did not stand upon ceremony, but burst in upon a scene that at once confirmed his fears.

Three men were in the tent: Mouchon, Chambret, and Monsieur le Prince. The latter was standing, facing and addressing Chambret. Mouchon had backed against the wall of the tent; his eyes were wide with fright.

As the Irishman entered, Prince Felix said a word or two, low-toned and tense — worried them between his teeth, like an ill-dispositioned cur, and flung them at Chambret insultingly.

Chambret laughed softly. "Thank you, monsieur. That precisely is what I sought."

His hand moved more swiftly than thought; the slap rang

like a pistol shot. One cheek of Monsieur le Prince suddenly paled, then flushed scarlet with the imprint of Chambret's fingers. He gasped, thrust his hand swiftly into his breast pocket, and sprang for Chambret's throat, flourishing a blade that glittered in the lamplight. But he brought up abruptly, and recovered his senses, with his nose to the muzzle of O'Rourke's revolver.

Monsieur le Prince's eyes ranged furiously from the Irishman to his own compatriot. He put up the knife with a swagger. "Ah," said he; "a conspiracy, I see, messieurs."

"Exactly," drawled O'Rourke. "Just as much so as yours with Soly."

Prince Felix stepped back, with a little cry of rage.

"The man lies!" he gasped.

"Of what is monsieur accused, that he should defend himself?" inquired O'Rourke politely.

Monsieur le Prince was caught. He darted a furious glance at O'Rourke, biting his lip.

"Well," he said doggedly, "what do you purpose doing about it?"

"This is my affair," interposed Chambret. "Monsieur has insulted me? Will you fight — dog?"

"A duel?" The eyes of Monsieur le Prince expressed unbounded amazement.

"Yes."

"Ah!" cried the prince. "You afford me that chance, eh?"

"No," Chambret coldly negatived.

"But, as the challenged party, I shall choose swords."

"Very well; I am agreeable."

O'Rourke turned to the terrified Mouchon.

"Ye there!" he cried sternly. "Go to the tent of your master, and fetch his case of rapiers."

The prince's eyes sought Mouchon's; they exchanged a glance of understanding, which O'Rourke was at no trouble to interpret.

"And," he added, as Mouchon prepared to leave the tent, "mind ye, monsieur, if ye breathe one word of this to any soul ere I give ye leave, I'll shoot ye on sight!"

Mouchon bowed, and sidled through the flap; no further communication passed between him and his master. Indeed, so potent was the Irishman's threat that the little Frenchman was back almost before they considered he had had time to accomplish the half of his journey.

Chambret looked at his watch. "Twelve-thirty," he announced calmly. ' I have just enough leeway to attend to Monsieur le Prince."

"Monsieur Mouchon will no doubt be glad to act as his second," said the Irishman; "I, of course, act for ye, me friend. To avoid a possible mistake, however, about our place of meeting, it would be well for Monsieur Mouchon to accompany ye, Chambret; I will give Monsieur le Prince the pleasure of me own company. Now, go, gentlemen. We will follow at a discreet interval."

When they were alone, Monsieur le Prince threw himself into a chair with a grim laugh — indeed, it was more like a snarl. "It is already decided, this duel," he told O'Rourke familiarly; "your principal walks in a dead man's shoes. Now, had it been you, monsieur, I would be less easy in my mind. But Chambret! He knows naught of the sword."

"Do ye believe it?" queried O'Rourke incredulously. "And yet, d'ye know, I've a premonition that ye die to-night, monsieur."

CHAPTER XV

HE IS ASTONISHED

A FAINT moon, late rising, lighted them on their way as they left the borders of the oasis and made in the direction of the *Eirene*. As they progressed, it rose and gained in power. By the time they had arrived at the agreed place of meeting with Chambret and Mouchon, it was flooding the desert with a clear, cold radiance that served for the purpose at hand as well as would have served the light of day — better, indeed, since now there was no suffocating heat, but rather such tingling cold as rouses a man to activity.

Such preparations as they made were simple; Chambret and Monsieur le Prince removed their coats. O'Rourke tested the foils, and allowed Mouchon the choice. A level place was discovered, some twenty yards or so from the line of travel between the oasis and the yacht, and screened by dunes from observation; the sand was not so soft as to clog seriously the feet of the combatants.

They took their places — Chambret, cold, pale, and silent; Monsieur le Prince, blustering and confident. O'Rourke stepped aside.

"Are ye ready, messieurs? Proceed!" he said.

The prince brought his heels together and the hilt of his rapier to his chin in a superb salute. "*Au revoir*, Monsieur Chambret," he said mockingly. "I shall find you in hell, when my time comes."

"*Au revoir*," responded Chambret, saluting with an

awkwardness that showed his lack of skill with the weapon he handled. "On the contrary, Monsieur le Prince, when I have slain you I intend to lead a virtuous life. There is no danger of our meeting in the hereafter."

Monsieur le Prince chuckled, supremely disdainful of the prowess of an opponent admittedly an absolute ignoramus with the sword. He brought himself with one swift movement to the guard.

Their blades clashed in the moonlight, glimmering, singing, glinting fire.

To the onlookers it appeared that Chambret was forcing the attack. He seemed to throw himself almost bodily upon Monsieur le Prince, as a desperate man might, utterly careless of the outcome. The end came abruptly, unexpectedly; Monsieur le Prince fell. Chambret staggered back, two-thirds of his blade missing.

Mouchon flung himself forward with a cry, half of despair, half of terror, falling upon his knees by the side of the prostrate man, pawing him frantically, muttering to himself, calling the man's name aloud. Presently he looked up, a queer expression in his eyes, his hand dabbled with blood showing black in the silvery moonlight.

"He is dead, messieurs — quite dead," he stated simply.

The word seemed to rouse Chambret as from a stupor; he withdrew his hand from his eyes, and with a gesture of finality cast from him the hilt of the rapier with its stump of broken blade.

O'Rourke wrung his hand, congratulating.

"How did ye manage it?" he demanded joyously. "Faith, the heart of me was in me mouth, and that dry with fear for ye!"

"I don't know," said Chambret dully. "I was assured

that this would be the end, from the first, despite my inexperience. I'm told that a novice is the most dangerous of opponents, as a rule."

"Faith," cried the Irishman, "I owe ye a debt of gratitude that grows like a rolling snowball. And, *mon ami*," he added thoughtfully, "I'm thinking that when we fight 'twill be with snowballs. I know nothing else that ye cannot best me with."

It was three o'clock in the morning when O'Rourke returned to the oasis, side by side with the Frenchman, Mouchon. At the door of the latter's tent he stopped and looked around.

There was none within hearing distance. O'Rourke lifted the flap of the tent and glanced in; on a cot he made out the dim form of D'Ervy, snoring in a stupor begotten of the champagne he had swilled with Monsieur l'Empereur an hour gone.

"Mouchon," said the Irishman, "one moment. If ye let slip one word of what has passed this night, to D'Ervy or to Monsieur l'Empereur, until I give ye permission — I fancy I need not warn ye what will happen. As for Monsieur le Prince, he decided suddenly last night to return to Las Palmas with Chambret. There was little time for *adieux*. We accompanied him to the yacht. That is all ye are to know."

Mouchon nodded with compressed lips, staring at him with frightened eyes; he was very much in awe of this Irishman, whose word to him was now as law.

"Very well, monsieur," he acceded plaintively.

The Irishman sought his cot; he lay down fully dressed, too weary to compose himself properly for his slumbers. What he needed, must have, was rest — no matter how, nor when, nor where. Sleep, oblivion — he desired it as he hoped for salvation.

But it appeared that he could not sleep. The night was old, the moon in her glory; a pale, intense light filtered down through the overhanging date palms, and lit up the interior of the tent, sharply defining its every object with black shadow.

O'Rourke closed his eyes obstinately. It seemed as though his mental vision insisted upon repeating with maddening exactness the look that had been upon the face of Monsieur le Prince — that was: who was Monsieur le Prince no longer.

They had buried him in a shallow ditch in a grave dug in the sands of the desert by Mouchon, with a spade which the Irishman had succeeded in obtaining from the yacht without exciting comment. They had placed him on his side, with his face to the sea, looking away from the woman whom he had wronged, away from the man he had deluded and enticed into this futile scheme for empire. And yet the Irishman felt that he himself lay under the gaze of those dead eyes, miles distant though they were.

It appeared that he had nerves; the eyes haunted him. He cursed the habit of dueling, cursed himself for having permitted the fight to take place, for being an accessory before a fact of murder — justifiable murder in the eyes of men; but, nevertheless, plain murder.

And yet he was glad — that he might not honestly deny; he was glad that Monsieur le Prince was gone to his final accounting; glad that it was not by his hand; glad that the affair had freed from bonds that were worse than galling the woman upon whom O'Rourke's every thought was now centered; glad that he was now free to think of her without dishonoring her by the thought of loving her — another man's wife.

He tossed upon his cot, that creaked and added to his sleeplessness. He imagined something pregnant in the air —-something foreboding trouble and disaster. He could not sleep. Once he thought a cry fell upon his ears — a slender, wailing moan; and he rose, and went to the door to look out.

But then the tramping of feet as the guards made their rounds reassured him, and again he lay down.

In time — but it was very long indeed — he slept; uneasily, it is true, but sleep of a sort, temporary unconsciousness that robbed him of his carking thoughts, and thus proved grateful.

And yet it was little more than a mockery of rest; he was permitted no more than a brief hour's nap. A hand shaking him by the shoulder roused him.

He found himself sitting up on the edge of the cot, rubbing his eyes, striving vainly to collect wits that seemed reluctant to return from their wool-gathering. His head ached with the weariness that possessed him, and he felt that his eyes were sore and red-rimmed — though that might be partly due to gazing over the desert glare.

His shoulder ached from the grip of the man who had wakened him; he looked up, saw that it was a Turco, and grinned drowsily. "Me soul, Mahmud!" he muttered stupidly. "Ye have the divvle of a strong hand. What are ye waking me for, at this ungodly hour, can ye tell me?" he added wrathfully, beginning to come to his senses.

"Pardon, *mon général*," replied the man respectfully. "We judged it best to let you know at once."

"What?" He was on his feet now, staring at the Turco with clear understanding that something had gone desperately amiss while he had slept. "What? What's wrong, man? Speak up!"

Mahmud had hesitated, fearful of his general's just anger. Now he stiffened himself against the coming storm.

"There has been evil work this night, *mon général,*" he reported. "Three men have been slain, and one is missing."

"Three slain? One gone? Who? Speak out, man; or I'll —"

"Monsieur recalls that a Spahi came to his tent with the Frenchman, Soly, last night? That Spahi was one Abdullah; he is dead — his throat has been slit. Also the Frenchman is gone. Also two pickets, Ali, of the Turcos, and a Frenchman, Rayet, have been slain, with daggers, on their posts."

O'Rourke was buckling on his sword and looking to the loading of his revolver.

"Which posts?" he demanded sternly.

"Those two at the southernmost end of this oasis, *mon général* —"

"And what the divvle, can ye tell me, were the rest of ye doing while this was going on?"

The storm had broken; Mahmud endured in piteous silence; when occasion afforded he fled as from the wrath of the Judgment Day.

As for O'Rourke, he went out, and calling a guard of soldiers made a round of the posts. It proved true, as Mahmud had said; not only was the Spahi, Abdullah, foully murdered, but also the two outposts on that edge of the oasis which was most distant from the camp.

And Soly gone! Here was food for consideration. Whither had he escaped? Not upon the yacht, O'Rourke was certain; for he himself had been the last to leave that vessel before she had sailed. Moreover, he felt assured that the murder of Abdullah would have been discovered quickly had it occurred before his return to the camp; he remembered distinctly having seen the men moving about Abdullah's tent while he was bidding good-night to Mouchon.

No; it had taken place since he had lain down to sleep. He recalled with a start that cry which he had heard while half asleep, and, hearing, had attributed to his imagination.

So — where was Soly?

Not in the oasis, for that had been beaten thoroughly; not a hiding-place therein had been overlooked — not a hole large enough to conceal a rabbit. The search had gone on by his orders while he was making the rounds of the pickets; he was satisfied as to its thoroughness.

It was about five o'clock, at the hour of the windy dusk that foretells dawn upon the desert. O'Rourke lingered near the dead body of one of the unfortunate sentries, looking out to the eastern horizon where a pale and opalescent light was growing steadily.

Was Soly out there? And if so, where? What did he purpose, how might he hope to exist, without food or water or camels?

His eye was caught by the flutter of a white thing, far out on the sands. He walked slowly out to see, without actually attaching much importance to the matter. It was idle curiosity that led him — that alone. And yet when he at last came to it and stopped, it was with an exclamation of direst dismay.

He stooped suddenly, trembling with an uncontrollable agitation, and put forth his fingers. They closed about the white object; he brought it close to his eyes, as if doubting much its reality; for surely he must be dreaming!

It was a handkerchief — a mere bit of sheer linen, for

the most part lacework and embroidery. It was real; he could feel and see it, he dared no longer doubt the evidence of his senses, and yet the initial in the corner struck terror to his heart.

Suddenly, he found himself running back to the oasis, his heart in his throat. He dashed past his escort, thrusting them from his path with frantic strength; and they looked first at his face, drawn and haggard with straining eyes — the face of a madman — and then to one another, shaking their heads gravely.

It was not until he had reached the door of Monsieur l'Empereur's tent that he paused — not then, in fact, for he rushed on in, regardless of the etiquette that hedges about the sanctified persons of monarchs, and caught the sleeping Lemercier roughly, dragging him from his bed.

"Monsieur," he commanded rudely, "get up and dress yourself."

"What — what's trouble, O'Rourke? *Eh-yah!* Br-r-r, but it's cold."

"Monsieur," cried the exasperated O'Rourke, "I give ye two minutes to dress yourself and to go to the tent of Madame la Princesse, to see if she is there. Ye are her brother, and alone dare enter."

The Lemercier opened his eyes.

"What?" he stammered.

Briefly — curtly, in truth — O'Rourke related the events of the morning hours. He had scarce need to finish, to tell what he feared. At the sight of the handkerchief and upon his telling where he had found it, *le petit* Lemercier was struggling into his clothes.

Together they ran to the *marquee* of madame. Lemercier, standing outside, raised his voice and yelped for his sister;

then, that unavailing, went within and found — precisely what they had feared.

Madame was gone.

Soly was gone.

Whither?

There was but one answer: The desert.

Somewhere out there in the fastnesses of that great, silent, sterile waste, whereon the sun was just beginning to cast a crimson flush, were madame and her abductor, Soly.

There was no time for arguing over the mystery of the affair, for trying to fit a reason to the whys and wherefores of the former *sans souci's* mad conduct. The conclusion was irrefutable that he had kidnaped madame, for some occult reason of his own.

O'Rourke did not stop to analyze the case. Upon *le petit* Lemercier's frightened report he whirled about and snatched a Mauser from one of his troopers. Then, calling to the others to follow, he made off at the top of his speed for the spot where he had found the linen handkerchief.

Once there he knelt, and scrutinized the ground painstakingly; and it seemed to him that he could discern faint traces of the footsteps of three people. But why three? Had Soly a confederate in the camp, as yet undetected?

He rose and walked on as rapidly as he might and still maintain his scrutiny of the trail. Here the surface was rather hard packed than merely soft, shifting sands; in some places the wind had covered the traces of footsteps thoroughly with a thin film of sand; but still he would come upon them a little farther on, trending always to the southward.

And he pressed ever on, the troopers at his heels exchanging muttered speculations as to the sanity of their commander.

Something like a half a mile to the south of the oasis, El

Kebr, lay the dry river bed called the Wadi Saglat; this O'Rourke had forgotten completely; the rolling face of the desert had deceived him, leading him to the very brink of the gully before he saw it. He stumbled, slipped and rolled to the bottom — some twenty feet — in a smother of sand and pebbles.

He got up, shook himself, and set his jaw with commingled determination and despair. Here it was absolutely an impossibility to trace footprints.

He turned half-heartedly to the east, towards the interior, and passed along the bed of the gully for a matter of about twenty feet. And then he stopped suddenly — brought to a halt by a shot.

A puff of gas ascended above a rock a little ways ahead, and he saw the helmet of one of his own troopers dodge down behind it. Instantaneously a bullet shaved his cheek closely, and buried itself deep in the wall of the gully.

With a cry of relief, O'Rourke sprang forward, hope high in his heart. He swung around the corner of the rock and covered with the Mauser the figure of Soly — Soly recumbent upon one elbow, clutching his rifle with feeble fingers, lying in a welter of his own blood.

The man looked up sullenly, and growled faintly.

"Go on!" he said. "Shoot me; I haven't long to live, anyway, monsieur."

O'Rourke wrenched the Mauser from the man's grip and knelt beside him; the rest of the searching party came up and stood about, wondering aloud.

"Ye are right!" exclaimed the Irishman, rising after a diagnosis of the fellow's wound. "Ye have about an hour to live. Ye have been bleeding for some time?"

"About two hours, monsieur." The man shuddered.

"I'm faint, or I would have potted you, sure. But I wasn't shooting at monsieur; I thought you were that damned Tawarek."

"Who? Speak up, man; or I'll throttle ye."

"Will you?" said the fellow, leering hideously. "And what will monsieur be learning then about madame? Let me tell the story my own way, or I'll not tell it at all. First — brandy."

A Spahi produced a flask and gave it to the wounded man, who drank greedily, with great gulps, and seemed revived somewhat. Life, however, was but flickering; he was mortally injured, with three gaping bullet holes through his body.

He sighed with satisfaction: "Ah-h!" smacking his lips over the liquor, and began to talk jeeringly, vaingloriously: a fearful and sickening spectacle, with the death pallor on his face, and the intense, pitiless sun beating full upon him.

"Ah-h, messieurs! I wish that Monsieur le Prince were here to listen. It would do him good — that devil! It was such a pretty scheme, messieurs, and we took you all in — only it miscarried at the finish. Listen. Monsieur le Prince sent for me in Paris. He knew me of old; many's the dirty little trick I've turned for him. I'll say this for him, though, he always paid handsomely. Well, he sent for me, and told me he wanted me to enlist with you. You recall that he gave me a letter of recommendation to you, describing me as an honorable old soldier of the republic? He told me what he wanted, and we cooked up the plot. It was very simple. . . .

"Among you all I was the only one, monsieur, who understood Tamahak. That I discovered while we were in that pig-sty of a prison at Las Palmas. It was first planned that I should escape from the encampment here and go to the Tawareks with our offer. But they saved us the trouble. That night — last night — when was it? — that Ibeni came aboard we played the farce to perfection, messieurs, right under your very noses. I was interpreting to you just what you wanted to hear, and you were gobbling it down greedily. More brandy!"

He got it, slobbering over the flask greedily, leering without shame or fear of a just God. O'Rourke was patient perforce, forbearing to press the wretch for fear he would turn stubborn and refuse to talk; the fellow knew it, and taunted them — in the face of death.

"Let's see — where was I? Oh, the Tawarek. I was telling him what Monsieur le Prince desired of him, and he was setting his price, bargaining over it while you thought he was treating for peace. Monsieur le Prince wanted your sou-centime fool of an emperor kidnaped, put out of the way, and was willing to pay for it. As things stood, Monsieur Lemercier paid for it himself. Eh — a good joke, messieurs? . . . We arranged it all — under your very noses — you, so wise and righteous! When Ibeni left it was all arranged that he was to come to the camp on the following night, and that I was to meet him and help him overpower Monsieur l'Empereur. Or, if not that night, the first that the simpleton slept ashore."

He paused, drank deep, and proceeded with some difficulty.

"Madame spoiled it — she with her beauty. Monsieur le Prince well-nigh spoiled it, paying me to shoot at your shadow. How I missed I never could tell; you should be dead now, Irish pig that you are! But I missed, and you were sharp enough to catch me; and so I had to cut the throat of your Spahi, What's-his-name. A difficult job, let me tell you, to do noiselessly. However — I did it. Me, I am clever! . . . Then I went out to meet Monsieur Ibeni. He was waiting here in the gully with three camels: one for Monsieur l'Empereur, one for himself, one for me. I whistled the signal, low, but he heard and came and helped finish your pickets.

"But then there was trouble. He was going back on his bargain, the treacherous dog! He had seen madame, and preferred to abduct her. I did not understand until he made me, with the revolver which you so kindly gave him, Monsieur O'Rourke. He threatened, and — I gave in, and helped him. But when we got her out here in the gully, messieurs, and madame wept, then my heart turned, and I would have none of the business. I am a fore-damned scoundrel, beyond doubt, and hell will be my portion. But I love the ladies, the pretty dears! Me, I am a Frenchman, and gallant where the sex is concerned. . . . So we quarreled, the Tawarek and I — and he did this to me, you remark. However, I evened up matters with the gentleman, somewhat. I shot one of his camels, and kept him away from the other, so that he had to go away finally afoot, with madame perched atop the other beast — and weeping. I tried to shoot him, too, but he kept away. The other camel is around the bend of the gully up there, messieurs; when the sun came up I had to crawl to this rock for shelter, and leave the brute.

"I trust that you will catch Monsieur Ibeni, and serve him as he served me. Otherwise . . . It has been a great farce, has it not, messieurs? We have all been fooled — myself and Monsieur le Prince and Monsieur Lemercier and madame. All — except the Tawarek, with whom God at least will deal. Ah-h-h!"

Thus blaspheming, he shuddered and died.

By rights, wounded as he was, he should have been dead

before they found him; a magnificent hardihood had sustained him, aided by a desire to be revenged upon the Tawarek, and to laugh at those whom he had hoodwinked.
They buried him without ceremony beneath a pile of rocks
— as fitting a grave, possibly, as he deserved.

As for O'Rourke, he had not waited for the end of the narrative. The man's gestures had told them which direction
the Tawarek had taken with his captive; to the east, up the
gully called the Wadi Saglat. Without an instant's delay
O'Rourke rounded the farther bend in the gully's walls, and
there discovered the camel, hobbled, of which the man Soly
had spoken — a magnificent animal, a racing dromedary,
beyond doubt the flower of the Tawarek's stable. This
O'Rourke knew from former experience with camels in the
Soudan; and than this he had never seen a finer beast, he
told himself.

He tightened its surcingle, unhobbled the beast, blessing
it and keeping out of the way of its curling lips and sharp,
white teeth. When ready, he mounted, and gave the word
to proceed. The dun-colored beast arose by sections —
first the one hind quarter, then the other, then the fore quarters with one sudden, tremendous lurch; O'Rourke shouted
at it a native word of command. It started forward swiftly,
long neck outstretched, up the gully of the Wadi Saglat,
bearing the Irishman into the unknown wilds of the desert.

O'Rourke was without food or water, without protection
from the sun; he had nothing to depend upon but this camel,
his Mauser, and the high, bold heart of him.

But that was light; for he knew that he was going to rescue
madame.

CHAPTER XVI

HE RACES WITH DEATH

THE desert is no level plain; it rolls in vast steppes, with long, wavelike undulations, much like a wind-swept sea miraculously petrified.

Ibeni, the Tawarek, unable to compete with the range of Soly's Mauser, at length gave it up; dawn approached too nearly; he had a long journey to make up the Wadi ere he should dare to show himself upon the surface of the desert.

Swearing copiously with childish rage he emptied at Soly the last cartridges of the revolver which O'Rourke had presented him; and had the vain pleasure of seeing the bullets plow up the sand and ricochet from the sun-baked, rocklike walls of the gully.

Soly replied with a shot that sent up a spurt of dust too near the feet of the Tawarek for comfort; he took up his long rifle and aimed carefully for the head of the dun racer; at least, if he might not have it, the Frenchman should not.

Again his shot fell short; and Soly sent a bullet whose wind nipped the cheek of Ibeni.

Seizing the swaying lanyard of the pack camel the Tawarek retreated hastily another fifty yards; he was out of the range there, and also out of sight of the Frenchman. Moreover, he had but two loads for his rifle, and these he dared not waste. With them gone he would be at the mercy of chance, dependent wholly upon his long knife.

It was cruel to leave his precious racer there, but it seemed that he had no choice; besides, he promised himself he would return at the head of his warriors, regain the dun racer, and wipe the invaders off the face of the desert.

Madame la Princesse was on the back of the pack camel, securely bound, both to prevent her falling and to render futile any attempt at escape she might be minded to make.

Ibeni looked up at her; she was dry-eyed now, had ceased her lamentations, sat deep sunken in despair; she moved her head painfully, looking ever to the rear, in an agony of hope of rescue.

She was very fair to the eyes of the Ibeni; and his eyes glistened. After all, he considered, it was worth the sacrifice of a dun racer to win such a beauty. Indeed, she was worth many racers. He recalled that he had once traded six pack animals, such as madame rode, and a black dromedary, for a girl of the tribe of Oulad-Naïl, who had run away with a lover as soon as occasion offered.

And she had been as nothing — as the stars to the moon — compared with this fair daughter of the Franks.

The sun was mounting; there was naught for it but the weary journey of some twenty miles over the blistering desert to Zamara, the next oasis, where his men were awaiting him. Certainly, it was no great hardship for him to walk that distance — he, Ibeni, who had walked the burning sands since he could toddle.

Thus he contented himself, and, with his hand upon the lanyard of the pack animal, the camel obediently stepped out at a fair pace, Ibeni pattering swiftly by its head.

After some time they left the gully; El Kebr was out of sight by then — only the waving tips of her hundred-foot palms broke the sky line behind them, to the east.

The sun rose, gathering power, and glared down terribly upon the domain over which it held sway, undisputed and indomitable. The hoofs of the camel raised a yellow mist of dust; on its back madame swayed, half-unconscious, cut cruelly by the ropes, in a daze of suffering. The Tawarek drew up his mask until nothing remained but the very narrowest of slits to see through.

Slowly the morning wore on; the pack camel trotted spiritlessly, its master plodding, mute, desperate. The heat grew well-nigh unbearable, beating down fiercely from directly above. The desert shimmered in a saffron sheen of torridity; the sands had become as hot to the touch as clinkers fresh from the pit. Overhead the sky lowered, white hot to the eye, infernally dazzling.

Thus they proceeded for hours that seemed as eons to the suffering woman; she had long ceased to have coherent thought. She had abandoned hope. There was naught for her but endurance and — death by her own hand so soon as she might be able to make an opportunity.

At noon the camel lifted its head and sniffed, then lengthened its stride. Ibeni cried out hoarsely with his parched and dusty lips and throat; for the oasis of Zamara could not be far, now that the camel had scented the water.

Madame heard, but without care or comprehension. There was now only one thing that could rouse her from her lethargy. And that was to come.

Zamara was still afar when the report of a rifle caused the Tawarek to turn his head; at the same moment a spoonful of sand rose from the face of the desert, on the off side of the camel; it sailed almost a yard in the air, feathered and disappeared.

Ibeni blasphemed by all the gods in the Mohammedan

calendar; he reached up to the long rifle which swung at the side of the pack camel.

They were in the middle of a saucer-like depression in the desert. Ahead of them was a league-long grade, behind them a similar one, which they had just covered. And down this latter slope was coming the heat-distorted shape of the dun racer, with a man upon his back — grotesque as a chimera, a full mile behind, yet looming so huge through the haze that it seemed as though Ibeni would be overtaken in another moment.

He loaded the rifle, calling to the camel to halt, waiting patiently for the pursuer to get within range. He was not greatly afraid; for behind, in Zamara, his warriors would soon be hearing the fusillade and sallying out to his rescue. .

The pack camel sheered off to one side; the dun racer came on steadily. Ibeni dropped to his knee, and took aim, resting the long rifle firmly to insure accuracy. Still he waited; still the dun racer neared, growing in size, a huge, splendid target.

A minute passed; now he felt that he might not miss. He fired.

Fruitlessly? For the dun racer continued to approach relentlessly at top speed. He heard the report of a Mauser, and a scream; a quick glance aside showed him that the pack camel had fallen upon its knees, and was threatening to roll upon and crush the woman in its death agony.

That was the last thing his eyes rested upon on earth; O'Rourke fired again, almost at random, risking everything, even the woman he loved, in the necessity of saving her from what was, if not death itself, worse than death.

The Tawarek shrieked piercingly. He sprang suddenly to his feet, throwing out his arms to the brazen sky, as though invoking the aid of Allah. His eyes were glassy; blood trickled from the corners of his mouth. He recognized that he was done for, at last. With one final supreme effort he reeled, faced about and fell with his head to the east, toward Mecca.

O'Rourke did not stop; the dun racer passed the fallen Tawarek with giant, league-consuming strides, and as it did so, to make all things sure, the Irishman sent another bullet into the prone body.

Simultaneously he gave the cry for halt, dropped the rifle and leaped from the back of the racer, while yet at full speed, landing on his feet by the head of the wounded camel.

It was kneeling, swaying from side to side, its long-lashed eyes wide with pain, fast glazing. O'Rourke was by the saddle in one spring; he drew his knife and cut the ropes that bound madame, wrenched her from the back of the pack animal just as it slumped over upon its side, kicking spasmodically in its death struggle.

For a moment he held the woman he loved in his arms — there, with nothing above them but the wide, blazing sky, with nothing about but the seething sands, with none to observe but the well-trained dun racer, that had halted a few feet distant.

She was conscious; by a magnificent demand upon her courage she had staved off the faintness which was clutching at her sentience.

There was a breathless pause, while he collected his faculties for action; hitherto every atom of him had seemed concentrated on the purpose of overtaking madame; now it was with an effort that he remembered the equal necessity of encompassing a return to El Kebr.

Perhaps it was an outside influence that finally brought him to active knowledge of what he must do. Faint, far-sounding shots were to be heard, followed by a chorus of yells — Tawarek yells, from the warriors of the dead leader, coming out from the oasis of Zamara to the rescue.

Intuitively the Irishman divined their source. He shuddered with despair. They had but one camel.

He forced himself to realize that, at whatever cost, madame must be saved, and hastily bearing her in his arms, as though she had been a feather, to the dun-colored dromedary, bade the animal to kneel, and placed madame upon its saddle, fastening her there with the straps provided for the purpose.

Their plight was desperate; the woman did not remonstrate, recognizing the futility of argument with the Irishman, showing her appreciation of his character by not wasting time with useless protestations. She knew full well that he was going to risk his life for her, and that he would do it, willy-nilly; it would but expose him to a greater danger to dispute the matter.

But in her eyes he read his reward.

The dun racer rose at the command; with trembling fingers O'Rourke transferred the lanyard from its headstall to the surcingle, making a sort of loop, which fell to the level of his elbow. Beyond the rim of the saucer-like depression the shouts of the oncoming Tawareks were now perceptibly louder.

Silently the man handed his Mauser to the woman; as silently she took and bound it to the saddle.

The Irishman slipped his arm through the loop, and ordered the animal to go on.

It started off slowly, unwilling to leave the nearer oasis; O'Rourke wasted strength in urging it on. Momentarily the Tawareks were gaining; soon they would be at the head of the rise. He shouted furiously at the beast. Eventually it began to move briskly, gathered impetus, and was going at racing speed, the Irishman running by its side, half pulled along by the loop from the surcingle.

In the beginning he managed fairly well. But the long slope to the rim of the saucer made fearful demands upon the reserve of air that he held in his great chest. He reached the rim, crossed it half fainting, getting his breath hardly.

Beyond it was not so bad; there was a grateful downward grade, along which he sprang, carried partly by his own momentum; the speed of the dromedary became terrific. It was excited by the commotion in the rear; evidently the Tawareks had come upon the body of their dead leader, Ibeni. Long, wailing howls conquered the silence itself, overpowering as that was, filling the void between heaven and earth with nerve-racking, long-drawn wails of lamentation and grief and rage, punctuated with ominous rifle shots.

These acted upon the dun racer as a stimulant; it lowered its long, scrawny neck until it seemed that its head almost touched the sands, and stretched out its slim, knobby legs, rocking from right to left like a ship in a heavy sea, devouring fathoms of the desert at a stride.

Its motion robbed madame of strength; she shut her eyes, struggling with the nausea induced upon the novice by camel riding. Thus she could not see O'Rourke; it was as well.

Two miles they covered, ere his breath began to give out. The hot sands burnt through the soles of his shoes, the sun above seemed to strike into his body piercingly, to the very core of the man. He struggled on: better to die thus than to become a goal for Tawarek bullets. His arm through the loop aided him wonderfully; the dun racer sped fleetly, as though it were not dragging a weary load of man in addition to the burden of the woman.

Somehow, that strange thing termed the second wind came to O'Rourke, at a time when he felt himself in his last extremity, when his lungs ached and burned, when his legs were moving only automatically in obedience to his iron will. This happened when they had put a distance of something like four miles between them and the scene of the tragedy.

He revived a trifle; his head that had been hanging erected itself, he stared out toward El Kebr that he could not have seen had it been within sight, his eyeballs starting from their sockets. For a brief space the strain grew lighter.

He mended his stride, hanging less like a dead weight upon the loop; for a little while it swung loosely upon his arm.

After them came the chase, marked by a pillar of yellow dust raised by the flying hoofs of the camels; it seemed that they gained — the pursuers — for the cloud grew nearer and nearer, larger and larger, and the yells sounded more loudly.

But of these the fugitives were unaware; they had neither thought nor desire to look back. It was nothing to them whether the chase were near or far; there was naught thought of, save to maintain the going, no matter how.

Again the Irishman's head sank; his chin fell and waggled loosely upon his chest; the sun was claiming him for its prey. His mouth gaped open, his tongue protruded, dry as a bone, white-caked with the sand and dust that flew about him in minute particles. His nostrils were distended to their utmost, straining in the dry and superheated air.

He lost the sense of motion in his legs, — nearly lost consciousness. For some time the desert had been rising and falling; now it reeled dizzily about him, swirling like a maelstrom in a blood-red flood. His heart labored mightily, beating with trip-hammer blows upon the walls of his chest;

and his lungs were like twin crucibles brimming with molten metal.

An inquisition could have devised no torture more sublime; practically the man was already dead; only that something which was death-defying in his make-up, that determination almost superhuman, held him upon his feet, and kept those digging into the sand and spurning it to the rear, in time to the rocking of the dun racer.

Before them, after many ages had crashed on into infinity, loomed the green walls of El Kebr. Behind, the Tawareks had drawn so nigh that they were encouraged to take pot-shots that flew wide and far because of the staggering pace of their own camels; the which made aiming impossible, a hit a miracle.

But of all this neither of the fugitives comprehended aught; the woman had passed into a merciful unconsciousness and had slipped forward in her fastenings upon the saddle of the dromedary, jerking back and forth and from side to side, mechanically, with a flaccid and puppet-like motion horribly suggestive of a lifeless thing.

O'Rourke plunged still on, as automatically, knowing nothing, more than anything else imaginable resembling a dead man mocking the action of the living. His eyes stood wide open and seemed to glare downwards at the streaking desert sands—that were not sands but fire solidified, even as the air was not atmosphere, but fire pure and immaculate; but the staring eyeballs were fixed and sightless, spheres of exquisite pain in their sockets, caked like his tongue with the impalpable sand drift of the desert. His ears were filled with a thundering that rolled ever louder and stronger and more maddening. The color of his face had gone from ruddy bronze to scarlet, from scarlet to purple, and from purple had merged into the dense black hue of congestion; on his temples the great, swollen veins stood out like black cords, distended and throbbing almost to the bursting point; and presently from his nostrils there trickled slowly a sluggish, dark hemorrhage.

Yet they racked on, pursuers and pursued, the hunters and the hunted, the quick and the dead — a nightmare-like vision of a dead man fleeing with his beloved from a ruthless and vengeful mob of fiends; all in that day of brass and fire.

*   *   *   *   *   *   *   *

Alarmed by the crackling of the Tawarek rifles, the imperial guard of Leopold le Premier, l'Empereur du Sahara, suddenly emerged in force and checked the pursuit.

But when they picked up the corpse-like body of O'Rourke and bore him back into the cool recesses of the oasis, they quite failed to recognize their leader; nor, possibly, would they ever have done so, save by processes of deduction — for he was quite unrecognizable — had not Madame la Princesse revived sufficiently to breathe to her brother a fragmentary account of the manner of her rescue.

CHAPTER XVII

HE HAS WON THE RACE

THROUGHOUT the afternoon the Tawareks hung about El Kebr, keeping well out in the desert, beyond the farthest range of the invaders' firearms. They circled the oasis, warily, on the alert, from time to time giving tongue to fierce cries — signals, apparently, from one to another.

The little garrison of the oasis was left without an actual leader; *le petit* Lemercier, of course, was nominally the head of his empire, but without some more resolute nature to fall back upon in times of stress, lacking at his elbow some man of decided character, whether for good or for evil — such as O'Rourke, or Chambret, or even Monsieur le Prince — Leopold was invertebrate, vacillating, fearful alike of stepping forward or back.

Mouchon and his co-loiterer, D'Ervy, were naturally neither soldiers nor such men as O'Rourke's tried troopers could take orders from and retain their own self-respect. In such case the conduct of the soldiers devolved upon their own heads; and to their credit be it said that they behaved as true fighting men — went about their business as coolly and composedly as though O'Rourke himself were directing their movements.

By mutual consent they selected one man to act as their captain until O'Rourke should recover. This fellow, the Turco, Mahmud — he who had awakened the Irishman with news of murder — had served for years on the Algerian frontier, part of the time with the camel corps. He was cool-headed and clear-sighted — a man skilled in the ways of the desert, and acquainted with Tawarek methods of warfare.

Mahmud ordered affairs precisely as though he had been discharging the wishes of O'Rourke. He posted the pickets, charging them to increased vigilance throughout the day as well as during the night — though that were scarcely necessary, with the fate of their comrades ever in the minds of the men.

Drowsily the afternoon wore out its long, hot hours — hours punctuated by the cries of the far-swooping natives, by the calls of the pickets, and by an occasional bitter *snap!* as a Mauser cracked warning to some too ambitious or too daring Tawarek.

Madame had recovered; after a short interview with the nerveless and indifferent emperor — who stuck to his tent and to his champagne that was cooled by lowering the bottles to the bottom of the wells — Princess Beatrix had the unconscious Irishman conveyed to her own *marquee*, where, with the solitary assistance of a Spahi, she tended O'Rourke faithfully, doing what she might to restore his life to the man who had so nearly given it up to save her own.

But it seemed that there was not much she could do; and the fear that what she contrived for his comfort was all too inadequate struck into the heart of madame terribly — as nothing, not even the unhappiness of her married life, not even the almost maternal love she bore her scapegrace brother, had ever stirred her.

O'Rourke lay motionless as a log, scarce breathing for a time; he had passed into a coma of utter exhaustion. The sluggish blood seemed hardly to stir in his arteries; his pulse

that for a time had boomed fiercely now crawled haltingly —
as slow, as imperceptible as the shifting of the desert sands.
His breath was so casual, his respiration so slight as to be
almost inaudible; he had run himself dry, and not an atom
of moisture stood out upon his fevered body. His face remained the color of that imperial purple which Leopold saw
in his dreams.

They — the dainty and refined princess, and the swart,
rough-soldier, together — labored over the Irishman inces-
santly, bathing him with the cool water from the wells, forcing
swallows of water down his throat — his throat that had so
swollen that he had almost died of strangulation.

But still his temperature continued so high that to touch
his flesh was like putting a finger upon a heated stove; still he
breathed so faintly as merely to dim the mirror which the
princess held to his lips; still his blood seemed to stagnate
in his veins.

In the end, indeed, it was to the Spahi that the credit for
saving him must be given. The man, inured to the desert
suns, remembered somewhat of the proper treatment for heat
exhaustion, according to desert tradition. He left madame
suddenly, without a word, and returned with Mahmud.
Mahmud eyed the Irishman narrowly, then turned and went
to the tent of Mouchon.

He stalked in without ceremony. Mouchon, lying listless
upon his cot, jumped up, angry at the intrusion.

"What does this mean?" he demanded furiously.

"Monsieur," responded the Turco roughly, and to the
point, "indulges in opium. I have seen it."

"You lie —"

"Monsieur le General lies at the point of death. Opium
may save him. Give it me, monsieur."

"I have none —"

"Monsieur!"

Mahmud caught the little Frenchman by the back of the neck and shook him as a terrier does a rat.

"The opium!" he demanded, releasing Mouchon.

A third appeal was not necessary. The frightened fellow produced his little phial of white tablets. Mahmud saluted ceremoniously and left, returning to the tent of the princess.

Respectfully he requested her to withdraw, and to allow him and the Spahi time to operate on O'Rourke. She refused calmly, and he acquiesced as calmly and accepted her assistance in the dosing of O'Rourke with morphine and in something that was a worse trial to the nerves of the delicate woman — blood letting. A vein was opened in O'Rourke's arm; it saved his life.

Evening brought with it a breeze — the cold breeze that springs up, unaccountably, out of the sands. It helped. By nine in the evening O'Rourke was breathing more freely; he was perspiring slightly; his temperature was lower, his face of a color more nearly normal.

At midnight the woman was shivering with the cold; O'Rourke, at whose side she sat, was aflame with fever — but perspiring. He was saved.

Towards morning he moved for the first time since he had fallen at the end of his terrific run; he stirred, moaned, shut his mouth, opened his eyes — they were staring horribly — and began to babble.

The ripple of the words, born of his febrile hallucinations and of the action of the opium upon his overstrained brain, was as music to the soul of madame. For a little while she bowed her head upon her arms and wept for happiness.

He has Won the Race

As for the Spahi, he rose and left the tent. His work was done; thereafter madame was competent. And, moreover, with instinctive delicacy, this son of the desert did not wish to be present when O'Rourke should come to his right senses. He was not of a strongly intuitive nature, that Spahi; but he could hazard a shrewd guess how matters stood with the heart of Madame la Princesse.

Presently, however, the tears of madame ceased. She began to listen to the words that fluttered between the clenched teeth of O'Rourke. For an hour she harkened — breathless — sometimes with her hand gripping hard above her heart as if to still its tumult in her bosom, at times more calmly, yet always with a great joy shining in her eyes.

Towards dawn there came a lull; the Irishman seemed again deep in stupor. But this was not a dangerous condition; it has become more rest than coma; he was recuperating.

"I dare leave him for a moment," considered Princess Beatrix.

She rose slowly and went to the door of the tent, looking over her shoulder at each step, reluctant to leave him even for a second. And yet — she *must* know. And the man lay quiescent as a child, breathing evenly as an infant by its mother's side.

She drew aside the flap of the tent, and stepped out.

It was barely the verge of that breathing twilight that precedes the dawn. The oasis was silent and dark; not a sound came to her ears to indicate that a soul moved within its borders. Only in her brother's tent a faint light glimmered, only at the edge of the date grove a dim palpitation of dusk seemed to be trembling, as if hesitant to intrude upon the immense sanctity of the night.

She paused, looked back again, listening, then hurriedly fled to the *marquee* of Monsieur l'Empereur. By the door a form stepped to her side and saluted — a sentry.

She gasped with surprise — so suddenly had he come upon her.

"Who are you?" she demanded.

"A guard for Monsieur l'Empereur, madame."

"By whose order?"

"His own."

"And there was no sentry ordered for me?" she asked bitterly.

The sentry was silent for a moment; then:

"Monsieur l'Empereur gave no order, madame. Possibly he knew that there was no need — that each man of us would lay down his life for madame — or for Monsieur le General O'Rourke."

"Possibly," she responded sharply, aware of the implied criticism of her brother's selfishness that had been in her question as much as in the sentry's reply. "Awake monsieur," she commanded. "Tell him I must speak to him. Then — go to the tent of Monsieur Mouchon and inform him that his presence is desired here."

Two minutes later Mouchon, staggering, rubbing his eyes, entered the *marquee* of *le petit* Lemercier. He was at once confronted by madame.

Lemercier, himself blinking with sleep, was sitting on the edge of his cot, striving to appear at ease.

"Monsieur," demanded the woman in a tone that instantly wakened both of the drowsy men, "I insist upon the truth."

"What truth, madame?" asked Mouchon, opening wide his eyes.

"The truth, monsieur! I warn you not to trifle with me!

[166]

I understand that you accompanied Monsieur le Prince" — Mouchon started — "to the *Eirene*, last night?"

"That is so, madame."

"Who accompanied you?"

"Monsieur Chambret and the Irish adventurer —"

"You mean Monsieur O'Rourke? Then name him so. He is more of a man than either of you, messieurs, who sneer at him — 'adventurer'! What happened? Tell me!" she insisted imperiously.

"Nothing, madame. Monsieur le Prince decided to go to Las Palmas —"

"And went — *where?* Come, the truth!"

Mouchon read determination in her attitude; he dared not resist her. He could not evade the answer, and yet . . .

"Monsieur O'Rourke told me not to tell on peril of my life," he murmured abjectly.

"Nevertheless, you had best tell me all. What happened?"

She stamped her foot. *Le petit* Lemercier, suddenly comprehending the drift of her inquiries, nodded approvingly.

"Speak up, Mouchon!" he encouraged his courtier.

Mouchon might not delay; he was a man of no stability, as has been indicated; he capitulated gracefully. In a few vivid words he outlined the tragedy that had made madame a widow — strong words they were, picturing the duel sharply, for the soul of the little Frenchman, or what served him for a soul, had been deeply moved by the horror of the thing.

He paused at the end. Lemercier, on his feet, staring blankly, dazed by the unexpectedness of the news, stupefied by the loss of the man who had been his constant mentor — Lemercier seemed to see the body on the sands, with Mou-

chon digging a narrow trench beside it, with Chambret
and O'Rourke conversing amiably aside — for it was as
hardened murderers that Mouchon had imaged them in his
narrative.

"The assassins!" cried Lemercier, first to find his tongue.

But madame had slipped to the floor; again she was sob-
bing, her face covered with her hands — weeping such tears
as the condemned criminal weeps when unexpectedly par-
doned.

Mouchon did not comprehend. He looked from madame,
the reality of whose emotion he might not question, to Lemercier. Mouchon knew that there had been little affection
between madame and Prince Felix; and he fancied· that the
time was ripe for a move to ingratiate himself into the place
the dead blackguard had left vacant in the graces of Leopold.
He raised his eyebrows and shrugged his shoulders, in humorous deprecation of madame's attitude.

"This is truly touching —" he began.

Then *le petit* Lemercier was guilty of the manliest act of
his life. His hand fell smartly across Mouchon's mouth.

"You puppy!" he cried. "Get out!"

Mouchon, his face flaming with resentment, hastily left the
marquee. Lemercier sank into a chair, gazing at nothing,
strangely conscious of a sensation as of relief — as though
shackles had been struck from his wrists.

There followed a long silence, broken only at first by
madame's subdued sigh — then suddenly shattered by the
report of a rifle.

Another followed — and another — barking Mausers all;
but in between the shots there rang faint echoes from afar.

"The Tawareks — attacking!" cried Lemercier, his face
the hue of ashes.

Madame was already beyond the reach of his voice, hastening toward her *marquee*. Something had told her what to fear.

And her fears were justified. The *marquee* was empty; the cot whereon O'Rourke had reposed stood unoccupied.

CHAPTER XVIII

HE FINDS HIMSELF IN DEEP WATERS

HE had been lying motionless, deep down in the silent depths of an ocean of recuperative unconsciousness; complete inertia had been numbing his every faculty; he had slept the sleep that follows a prolonged struggle with death — slumbers which should have lasted for hours.

Yet to him the crack of that first Mauser had been like the crack of a whiplash to a drowsy horse. The second report had not sounded ere he was on his feet — reeling, it is true, but nevertheless standing. Automatically the man's hand went across his eyes, to brush away the cobwebs of slumber. Mechanically he looked about him, but saw nothing; he was not thinking: a single idea possessed him to the exclusion of all else. His exhausted vitality rallied to his support in the work he had to do; but his weary brain had strength to comprehend but one thing. He did not understand that he was in Madame la Princesse's *marquee*, so he did not wonder at the manner of his coming there. He did not know that he was too weak to move about alone, so he did not hesitate to exert himself.

Simply that he was called upon to help repulse an attack by the Tawareks — that was his whole and only thought.

It naturally followed that there was naught to be done but to obey the duty call; and he responded, if mechanically.

In an instant he was outside the *marquee*, staggering toward the nearest edge of the oasis. Somewhere he blundered into the figure of a man who clapped his arms about O'Rourke. This was Mahmud, but O'Rourke did not know it. He was being hindered — that was all. And he threw the Turco from him as though he had been a mere child.

The Turco glimpsed the outlines of his face in the darkness, and gasped with astonishment. Again he caught the Irishman by the arm.

"But, my general —!" he expostulated.

He was brushed aside like a feather. O'Rourke took a step forward, then instinctively understood that he was unarmed. He returned to Mahmud.

"Bring me a gun," he said dully.

"But, my general —"

"Bring me a gun!"

His tone was lifeless, yet charged with something terribly menacing, to the Turco's imagination. Mahmud gasped and trembled; this being whom he had thought man must be either god or devil; otherwise he could not have moved from his cot.

Mahmud called upon Allah. O'Rourke raised his hand slowly.

"Bring me a gun!" he reiterated, in the same dead monotone.

A soldier passed on the run, carrying his Mauser at the trail. Mahmud leaped after and wrested the weapon from him. The man was naturally angry; he disputed at the top of his voice.

Mahmud pointed simply at the waiting figure of O'Rourke, whose eyes were fixed upon them with a stony, threatening expression. The soldier almost collapsed.

"*Allah!*" he cried.

"Find another rifle," whispered the awed Mahmud, "and

follow him. He is more than man. There will be fighting now."

Mahmud's eyes glittered strangely; he scented the supernatural, and divined that there would be battle and bloodshed, indeed, where this god — or demon unchained — would fight.

He left the gaping soldier and stuck close to the heels of O'Rourke. Presently he broke into a dog trot, the better to keep up with his general. In a moment an idea presented itself, seeming good to Mahmud. It would be well to propitiate this being. "Here, master," he muttered reverently, pressing his revolver into the hand of the Irishman.

O'Rourke accepted without a word and hastened on. They were nearing the edge of the oasis. In front of them a French ex-artilleryman lay prone upon the ground, behind a little hill of sand he had heaped up for himself, and fired out into the vibrating dusk. The flashes of his shots were keen crimson and gold in the half light.

At his shoulder O'Rourke stopped, peering out over the face of the desert. Afar he saw a tongue of flame leap out; the report followed, with the whine of a bullet clipping along very near to them.

O'Rourke swung the Mauser to his cheek and pulled the trigger, aiming for the spot where the flash had been. Perhaps the Tawarek took the hint and moved on; but for some time there were no more shots from behind that sandhill. O'Rourke turned to the ex-artilleryman.

"Ye are overbold, *mon ami*," he said, with a flicker of smile. "I advise that ye retreat to the shelter of the trees."

The Frenchman recognized the leader, swore with amazement, and obeyed hastily. Mahmud followed O'Rourke. Together the two made a circuit of the picket line, warning the men to fall back and screen themselves with the trunks of date palms. In every case the trooper obeyed with a celerity that was heightened by his supreme surprise that a man who should be dead by rights was contrarily walking, talking and commanding.

Mahmud once ventured an explanation.

"I posted these men out here, master," he murmured deferentially, "that they might the better watch the desert."

"Ye did right, under the circumstances; but now the situation is altered. We must protect every man — we shall need them all."

"Truly," muttered Mahmud to himself, "this is prophecy! Truly we shall see great fighting before nightfall."

Inspired or not, O'Rourke was speaking simple truth; they were to need every man ere long. Their little force had been sadly decimated of late; there remained in and about the oasis scarcely thirty fighting men. And as to the number of Tawareks — who could tell? They might easily outnumber the invaders ten to one, each inspired by rabid ferocity and the desire to avenge the death of the leader whom O'Rourke had slain.

Why they had held off so long, was the question. To Mahmud's mind there was only one answer; they had been awaiting reinforcements from an oasis more distant than Zamara, with whose aid they expected to exterminate the French party to the last man.

Under cover of the night, too, they had improved their position; as was evidenced by the nearer line of fire, they had pushed daringly in toward the oasis, taking up sheltered posts on dunes that brought them within easy range of the invaders.

In event of a combined attack from any one quarter, the

foreigners were doomed; O'Rourke dared not draw off a single man from a single picket to help repel the Tawareks. And had he been able to do so, as he justly considered, what were thirty men against three hundred or more? They would be mowed down like grain before a scythe, were they not crushed by sheer superior force of numbers.

Indeed, he recognized the situation as sufficiently desperate to call for heroic measures; what such measures were to be he could not determine.

He ordered Mahmud, peremptorily, to pick out the tallest palm tree in the grove, and to climb it to the top, whence he would be able to command a wide view of the surrounding desert; the better to survey which O'Rourke told the man to fetch the fieldglasses from his tent.

Mahmud complied with all haste; while he was away, O'Rourke again made the rounds of the pickets, finding two dead.

And the fire of the Tawareks was being kept up with fiendish persistency. Once or twice he fancied that they were steadily drawing closer in upon the oasis, undaunted by the equally persistent and probably more effective rifle practice of his own men.

By now, the brain of the Irishman was clearing; some store of reserve force within the man had been tapped; an unsuspected supply of nervous energy was urging him on. He stood erect, without tremor; he thought quickly and to the point, finding no difficulty in commanding his mental powers; he spoke steadily and sharply, issuing his orders with his accustomed *élan*.

Small wonder, then, that Mahmud reverenced and feared him as a war deity — whether celestially or infernally inspired. Small wonder that the men sprang with alacrity to execute his commands; and small wonder that Madame la Princesse, when at last she found him standing absorbed and intent by the side of a sharpshooter, forbore to interfere.

She could not understand, but she knew that now expostulation would prove as vain as it would have been on the previous day when he had prepared to start upon his marvelous race.

Almost timidly she crept to his side, and tentatively she touched his sleeve; and abstracted as the man was, he knew the featherweight of her fingers on his arm and found time to revel in the thrill of it. Nevertheless, it was with a countenance informed with concern that he turned to greet her. For they stood directly exposed to the fire of the Tawareks.

"Madame!" he cried. "Why, this is madness! Ye should be — back there" — indicating the center of the camp.

"As well one place as another, monsieur," she said, as brightly as she might. "There is no security here. Only a moment ago" — her expression saddened — "Monsieur d'Ervy was struck down in his tent by a stray bullet."

"Struck?" he demanded. "Where? Killed?"

She nodded affirmatively.

Mahmud approached to report, saluting.

"Well?" inquired O'Rourke impatiently.

"The desert is alive with Tawareks, master."

"Yes, yes; I knew that. Where are they concentrating?"

"To the north and the east, monsieur. To the west — along the way to the coast — they are very few."

O'Rourke nodded. "So I thought. Listen —"

Madame could hear, above the din of firing, an endless series of the peculiar wailing calls which she had come to know so well as essentially characteristic of the Tawareks.

"They have been signaling to one another for half an

hour," explained O'Rourke. "I inferred that they were massing for a direct attack at some one point. It is to come from the west then, d'ye think, Mahmud?"

"Yes, master."

"Very well; we will disappoint them for a little while, madame."

"How?"

"By leaving the oasis."

"But that is certain death."

"Not so certain as though we concluded to stay here and die like rats in a trap, one by one picked off by their fire or crushed out by an overwhelming charge. No, madame; their object is to force us to the coast,— to sweep us into the sea. And we had best precede them. Out there," he went on, "we can stand them off better than here, as we did once before. And there is always the hope that the *Eirene* may have returned."

"At least, that is our only hope, monsieur," she corrected, smiling bravely.

"Yes, madame," he conceded with gravity. "Mahmud," — his tone changed to one of command, — "concentrate all the men at a point opposite the way to the sea — all, that is, except a dozen or less who shall scatter here, on the east, and keep up a fire till the last moment, for appearances' sake. Be quick!"

But already the Turco was gone.

"Madame," asserted O'Rourke, turning to the woman, "ye are brave?"

"I do not fear death, monsieur."

"And — and ye will obey?"

She looked steadfastly and deep into the eyes of him.

"In all things, monsieur," she said softly, "and forever."

"Madame!" He was dazed by her manner; he could **not** credit the evidence of his senses as to the tenderness of her tone, as to the light that glowed in her eyes.

No; he told himself his wish had been father to his thought. He had misunderstood. He looked away.

"Listen," he said rapidly; "this is me plan: At the mouth of the Wadi Saglat, madame, there lies beached one of the catamaran rafts which the *Eirene* left behind her when she sailed. It will accommodate six at the most. We shall make for that; if we gain it, ye will go aboard with Monsieur l'Empereur and Mouchon. There is a sail,— maybe a breeze."

"But as for you, monsieur?" she demanded.

"I remain with me men to cover your retreat. No—don't dispute. 'Tis the only way."

She bowed her head, apparently yielding; but in her heart she was determined implacably that she would not desert this man who offered so debonnairely to lay down his life for her.

O'Rourke stepped to the western edge of the oasis; from the indications of the Tawarek fire he made little doubt but that practically all of the enemy's forces were massing in the east, as Mahmud had reported. Already his own men were gathering and making ready for the dash to the sea.

The adventurer found himself worried with a vague uneasiness unconnected with the desperate situation that menaced his comrades and the woman he loved. It was not that he was himself frightened, or that he feared death: death was his ultimate portion, a soldier's inevitable fate; he was prepared to accept it uncomplainingly, when it should come. But there seemed to be something awry with the day; its very atmosphere hung motionless, lifeless, indefinitely depressing. It struck him that the heat seemed more sultry even **than** usual.

He strove to shake off this oppressive influence; for a little while he was very busy, his mind distracted with the business of training in a position to repel the expected attack the two gatlings with which the expedition was provided. But when that had been attended to he became again conscious of the ominous foreboding in the air; the day was gravid with portents of terror.

Frowning, he stared out into the east. For a moment he saw nothing amiss; the desert stretched away, as always a sea of sand, desolate, saffron and a-quiver with the oblique rays of the rising sun. Here and there little puff balls of smoke would rise — white clouds no bigger than a man's hand — tremble and dissipate; their appearance followed at an interval by the far, spiteful crack of a native rifle.

Only, he felt as though a copper-colored film had been bound across his eyes; he saw all things as through a tinted glass, yellow. The day seemed to have turned darksome at the dawn. And the silence was almost terrible, more impressive than ever it had been, with a sense of a tangible presence, mute, invisible, threatening. In its profound immensity, the rattle of shots was like the shrill piping of a child's voice in the roar of a hurricane.

But he had no time for conjecture. Mahmud returned to his side, reporting that all was prepared for the sally out to the coast. O'Rourke nodded sternly in his preoccupation.

"Rejoin the party immediately," he ordered. "Place Madame la Princesse and Monsieur l'Empereur in the middle of the square. Then await my coming with these others."

To the south and north the firing of the natives had dwindled out and died completely. Such, too, was the case in the west; where it was hardly noticeable. Only in the east it seemed redoubled, concentrated, fiendishly accurate. On the borders of the oasis the troopers lay at length, hugging the stocks of their Mausers to their lean cheeks, firing doggedly, waiting. They had their instructions as to action in the apprehended event, and were impatient.

Presently, and with startling abruptness, the fire of the Tawareks ceased entirely; beyond the nearest rises of the desert a dead and ominous silence reigned, unbroken.

The jaundiced light of day became more intense, seeming to grow imperceptibly more opaque. In the east a white feather of cloud hung trembling on the horizon.

"Cease firing!"

At O'Rourke's command the troopers obeyed. "Reload!" he told them, and: "Fall back to the guns!" They did so in silence, casting sullen glances over their shoulders at the vast, vacant, terrible desert.

O'Rourke himself reloaded his Mauser, looking to his revolvers, and followed them to the gatlings.

A single shot rang out in the stillness, with the effect of a tocsin heralding a massacre.

In another instant the enemy was in sight, advancing upon the oasis in battle array, afoot and on camelback, at a quick trot, their white burnooses flapping out behind them, wing-like, glistening in the sun. They seemed well-generaled; not a cry rang out, not a man paused to kneel and fire; they came on steadily and silently, implacably determined, as if assured of their absolute irresistibility—a gorgeous array in their many-hued garments, with the sunlight glinting off their arms and the trappings of their camels: a sight to strike terror into hearts less veteran than those of O'Rourke and his men.

Turning, the Irishman sent his voice booming across the oasis, to the other party.

"Forward!" he cried.

In reply, Mahmud's echo told him that his word was heard.

And now the Tawareks were very near, coming on swiftly. They were not dreaming of the rapid-fire guns, which as yet had not been made use of for lack of a target sufficiently important.

O'Rourke waited; his heart hot within him, determined to even somewhat his long score with the men of the desert. He waited — while the men tugged impatiently at his leash. Then —

"*Fire!*"

With one accord the gatlings began to chatter shrilly; they had been accurately trained upon the advancing host; the pelting rain of leaden death swept along their line, mowing it down mercilessly. The Tawareks shrieked rage and dismay, calling upon Allah; they tried to return the fire promiscuously from their rifles.

And the gatlings jabbered on. But the Tawareks were in overwhelming force and invincible. Their enormous losses were disregarded; the huge, terrible swaths in their line were refilled eagerly by others, keen for death and the heavenly houris who attend upon the souls of those of the true faith who fall in battle.

When they were too near, and then only, O'Rourke gave up the fight. He issued the order to abandon the gatlings, which were simultaneously effectually dismantled; the dozen men gathered up their Mausers and swung in at his heels.

For a moment or two there had been firing to the west. This now was silenced. O'Rourke and his command emerged from the shade of the date palms to see the last man of the leading party slinking over the top of a sandhill, his rifle at trail. It was Mahmud, who turned, waved a hand and waited.

A short, quick dash under the broiling sun brought O'Rourke to his side.

"Here there were only six or eight, master," reported Mahmud. "We put to flight such as we did not slay."

"Good," breathed O'Rourke. "And now for it!"

He tightened his belt and gave the command for the double-quick; the forward party heard and mended their pace. In the rear the Tawareks were just bursting through the oasis, howling.

Despite the fact that the foreigners had the start, the Tawareks gained. Halfway to the sea O'Rourke was forced to pause and deploy his men to the right and left, to check the advance; it succeeded momentarily, but as he stood upon a dune top and surveyed the thin fringe of prone figures that were firing, rising, retreating swiftly, and dropping to fire again, his heart sank within him; not twenty men remained of them all.

And fully two miles were yet to be put behind them ere they gained the sea.

Very soberly they fought the distance out, selling each yard dearly, getting their pound of Tawarek flesh for each foot of the ground they yielded; but it was the fighting of men fore-damned, viciously determined to sell their lives to the highest bidder only.

They got their price — but also they paid it. While still a mile from the shore, but ten men remained to O'Rourke; and as he counted them two dropped out — one slain outright with a bullet through his head, another, knowing himself mortally wounded, slipping a shoe from one foot, and

with his toe upon the trigger of his rifle forestalling a lingering death by Tawarek torture.

It was useless; O'Rourke glanced behind him, to the coast.
Madame, Lemercier, Mouchon were vanished. They might
now make a dash for the sea, he considered, and his voice
rang with the command.

The men obeyed hastily, but the Tawareks were now so
near, their fire so deadly, that four were slain as they rose to
join their commander; and now another went down; three
only closed with O'Rourke for the run to the sea.

They hugged their rifles jealously, setting their jaws with
fixed determination to make the coast. The sun's heat
beat upon their defenseless heads with sardonic intensity;
below their feet the sands broiled and reeled. They ran on,
staggering, for many minutes that seemed like hours.

Presently, and to the astonishment of all, they gained the
coast; presently they stood upon the highest sandhill, pausing
to look back ere throwing themselves down to the sea.

O'Rourke saw the little catamaran raft lying half afloat;
madame sat upon it, a revolver in her hand; on the beach
Lemercier and the craven Mouchon sulked, eying the woman
doggedly.

He guessed the situation — that the two had tried to push
off and leave him and his men to their fate, but that madame
had nullified their selfish purpose with her weapon and her
own dauntless loyalty.

But there was no space for consideration of that; it was
enough that Lemercier and Mouchon had failed in their
design. Another thing interested O'Rourke far more: the
Tawareks had given up the pursuit.

Why?

His three remaining troopers had flung down the shelving

hillside to the beach, but O'Rourke lingered, shading his eyes and gazing inland.

In the east and south the horizon had vanished. To the zenith the firmament was discolored, shading from a dense and impenetrable black near the horizon to a thin and translucent copper hue overhead, where the sun hung like a pallid disk; and abruptly that was blotted out.

Out of the heart of the desert there came a long, shrill wail of fear from the Tawareks; and close upon that sound a sighing moan swept shuddering through all the world. A puff of foul, hot wind, like the breath of a smelting furnace, smote the cheek of the Irishman; it was as if he had been touched by flame.

A swirl of air formed afar on the desert; and another, and another — brown wraiths of dust, whirling like mad dervishes, sweeping seawards with the speed of locomotives. Behind them loomed what seemed a wall of night, solid, invincible, annihilating all that stood in its path. It swept westwards, wrapped in thunderings, devouring the earth. El Kebr, that oasis which was sometime the site of Troya, the Magnificent-to-be, vanished, was blotted out as by the hand of God.

The sandstorm advanced with incredible rapidity; O'Rourke, suddenly conscious that he was delaying escape, imperiling the lives of his comrades, by thus lingering, withdrew his fascinated gaze and prepared to descend to the waiting catamaran. And at once he became aware that he stood not alone; a man's figure loomed beside his own. He stared, and, despite the gathering gloom, discovered the features of *le petit* Lemercier, — the face of Leopold le Premier, l'Empereur du Sahara.

The little man was quivering with fright, yet shaken with a

more overpowering emotion. Despair was furrowed deep in his flabby, pallid cheeks; and tears traced tiny rivulets through the dust and grime with which his countenance was soiled. He stood with drooping head, his arms slack at his sides, staring with lifeless and lack-luster eyes at the demolition of his empire of illusion.

Suddenly he fell upon his knees, stretching forth suppliant arms towards the lost oasis.

O'Rourke stooped and bent an ear to the man's lips. He caught the echo of an exceeding bitter cry:

"*My empire!*"

And the heart of O'Rourke was moved to pity, for he now knew that this little Frenchman had actually believed in himself and his mad scheme.

O'Rourke caught the man by the arm and lifted him to his feet without ceremony. And yet solemnly, almost sadly, he said:

"An end to empire, Monsieur l'Empereur!"

A vedette of wind from the storm that was now perilously near struck them both, hurling them from the head of the dune. They floundered a moment on the beach, then managed to creep aboard the raft.

A soldier shoved them off, and himself clambered aboard. A shred of sail was set, the gale caught upon it and the catamaran was hurled seawards.

Immediately O'Rourke crumpled into unconsciousness; the moment the strain of responsibility was lifted from his shoulders, the moment they were in the care of Providence, the Irishman yielded to the demands of an overstrained constitution.

Hours passed blankly. When he awakened, it was to find

the face of the woman that he loved bending over him —
bent maddeningly near to his own countenance, so that he
might feel the caress of her breath upon his cheek, might
catch the elusive perfume of her hair.

"Where are we?" he asked.

A splash of saline spray wetted his face, by way of an answer; he turned his head away for an instant and glanced
about them: the catamaran tossed wildly on the bosom of a
wind-scourged sea. But at once his gaze went back to the
woman. After a while she bent her head more near, smiling
with divine tenderness, and kissed him upon the lips — there
before her brother, in the sight of Mouchon and the three
troopers.

"The *Eirene* is sighted," she murmured. "We are saved
— dear heart."

He sighed, resting his head in the hollow of her arm — her
arm that had served as its pillow for weary hours.

"'Tis a dream," he told her. "A dream, and I'll believe
no word of it, sweetheart. . . . But, my faith, 'tis a heavenly
sweet dream!"

PART SECOND

The Long Trail

CHAPTER I

THE CAFÉ DE LA PAIX

A T ten in the evening of a certain day in the early spring the stout m'sieur was sitting and sedately sipping his bock, at a sidewalk table on the Boulevard Capucines side of the Café de la Paix.

So he had been sitting — a gentleman of medium height, heavily built, with active, searching eyes, a rounded breadth of forehead and a closely clipped beard of the Van Dyck persuasion — for seven consecutive nights.

At one minute past ten of the clock, the stout m'sieur was on his feet, showing evidences of mental excitement, as he peered out into the boulevard parade, apparently endeavoring to satisfy himself as to the identity of a certain passing individual.

And François, the waiter who had attended the stout m'sieur for a full week, put his hand discreetly to his mouth, and observed to Jean, who stood near by:

"At last, m'sieur has discovered his friend!" Adding, to himself alone: "Now I shall have word for Monsieur le Prince!"

A second later, the stout m'sieur's voice was to be heard.

"O'Rourke!" he cried, and again: "O'Rourke, *mon ami!*"

Curious glances were turned upon him, not only by the

[187]

moving throng upon the sidewalk, but also by the other patrons of the café. The stout m'sieur heeded them not. Rather,
he gesticulated violently with his cane, and called again.

To his infinite satisfaction, his hail carried to the ears for
which it was pitched. Out of the mob a man came shoul-
dering his way and looking about him with uncertainty. A
tall man he was, noticeable for a length of limb which seemed
great yet was strictly proportioned to the remainder of his
huge bulk, moving with the unstudied grace that appertains
unto great strength and bodily vigor.

He caught sight of the stout m'sieur and a broad, glad grin
overspread his countenance — a face clean-shaven and
burned darkly by tropic suns, with a nose and a slightly
lengthened upper lip that betokened Celtic parentage; a face
in all attractive, broadly modeled, mobile, and made luminous
by eyes of gray, steadfast yet alert.

"Chambret, be all that's lucky!" he cried joyously. "Faith,
'twas no more than the minute gone that I was wishing I
might see ye!"

He came up to Chambret's table, and the two shook hands,
gravely, after the English fashion, eying each the other to see
what changes the years might have wrought in his personal
appearance.

"I, too," said Chambret, "was wishing that I might see
you. My friend, I give you my word that I have waited here,
watching for one O'Rourke for a solid week.

"Is it so, indeed?" O'Rourke sat down, favoring the
Frenchman with a sharply inquiring glance. "And for why
did ye not come to me lodgings? Such as they are," he
deprecated, with a transient thought of how little he should
care to have another intrude upon the bare, mean room he
called his home.

"Where was I to find you, *mon ami?* I knew not, and so waited here."

"A sure gamble," approved O'Rourke, looking out upon the ever-changing, kaleidoscopic pageant upon the sidewalks, where, it seemed, all Paris was promenading itself. "If one sits here long enough," explained the Irishman, "sure he'll see every one in the wide world that's worth the seeing — as a better man than I said long ago."

"It is so," agreed Chambret.

He summoned a waiter for O'Rourke's order; and that important duty attended to, turned to find the Irishman's eyes fixed upon him soberly, the while he caressed his clean, firm chin.

Chambret returned the other's regard, with interest; smilingly they considered one another. Knowing each other well, these two had little need for evasiveness of word or deed; there will be slight constraint between men who have, as had Chambret and O'Rourke, fought back to back, shoulder to shoulder, and — for the matter of that — face to face.

The Frenchman voiced the common conclusion. "Unchanged, I see," said he, with a light laugh.

"Unchanged — even as yourself, Chambret."

"The same wild Irishman?"

"Faith, yes!" returned O'Rourke. He continued to smile, but there was in his tone a note of bitterness — an echo of his thoughts, which were darksome enough.

"The same!" he told himself. "Ay—there's truth for ye, O'Rourke! — the same wild Irishman, the same improvident ne'er-do-well, good for naught in all the world but a fight — and growing rusty, like an old sword, for want of exercise!"

"And ye, *mon ami?*" he asked aloud. "How wags the world with ye?"

"As ever — indifferently well. I am fortunate in a way."

"Ye may well say that!"

Was there envy in the man's tone, or discontent? Chambret remarked the undernote, and was quick to divine what had evoked it. He had a comprehending eye that had not been slow to note the contrast between them. For it was great: Chambret, the sleek, faultlessly groomed gentleman of Paris, contented in his knowledge of an assured income from the *rentes;* O'Rourke, light of heart, but lean from a precarious living, at ease and courteous, but shabby, with a threadbare collar to his carefully brushed coat, and a roughly trimmed fringe, sawlike, edging his spotless cuff.

"You are — what do you say? — hard up?" queried Chambret bluntly.

O'Rourke caught his eye, with a glimmer of humorous deprecation. What need to ask? he seemed to say. Gravely he inspected the end of the commendable panetela, which he was enjoying by the grace of Chambret; and he puffed upon it furiously, twinkling upon his friend through a pillar of smoke.

"'Tis nothing new, at all, at all," he sighed.

Chambret frowned. "How long?" he demanded. "Why have you not called upon me, *mon ami*, if you were in need?"

"Sure, 'twas nothing as bad as that. I — I am worrying along. There'll be a war soon, I'm hoping, and then the world will remember O'Rourke."

"Who will give the world additional cause to remember him," said Chambret, in the accents of firm conviction. "But why?" he cried abruptly, changing to puzzled protest. "*Mon ami*, you are an incomprehensible. If you would, you might be living the life of ease, husband to one of the richest and most charming women in France; Beatrix, Princesse —"

"*Sssh!*" O'Rourke warned him.

"Ah, monsieur, but I am desolated to have hurt you!" said Chambret contritely; for he had at once recognized the pain that sprang to new life in the Irishman's eyes.

"No matter at all, Chambret. Sure, 'tis always with me." O'Rourke laughed, but hollowly. "'Tis not in the O'Rourke to be forgetting her highness — nor do I wish to, to be frank wid ye. Faith . . ." He forgot to finish his thought and lapsed into a dreamy silence, staring into the smoke rings. His face was turned away for the moment, but one fancied that he saw again the eyes of Madame la Princesse.

"But why, then —" persisted Chambret.

"Have ye not stated it, yourself — the reason why the thing's impossible, me friend? The wealthiest woman in all France, since the death of that poor fool, her brother! Is she to be mating with a penniless Irish adventurer, a — a fortune-hunter? Faith, then, 'twill not be with the O'Rourke that she does it!"

"But I thought —" Chambret persisted.

"That I loved her? Faith, ye were right, there, old friend! 'Tis me life I'd be giving for her sweet sake, any time at all 'tis necessary — or convenient." He chuckled shortly, then shook his head with decision. "No more," he said: "'tis over and done with — me dream vanished. Please God, 'tis the O'Rourke here who will be going back to her some one of these fine mornings, with a pocketful of money and a heart that . . . If she'll wait so long, which I misdoubt. 'Tis not in woman's nature to live loveless, though Heaven forfend that I should breathe a whisper against her faith and constancy!"

He glared at Chambret wrathfully, as though he suspected

that gentleman of having subtly aspersed those qualities in the woman he loved; then softened. "Have ye news of her?"

"No word," replied Chambret. "You know that she retired to the Principality of Grandlieu, after little Leopold's death? She was reported to have left for a tour of Europe, shortly afterwards, but I am certain that she did not come to Paris. Indeed, it is uncertain where she may be."

"She is her own mistress," said O'Rourke doggedly thoughtful.

"She is adorable, *mon ami*," sighed Chambret. "I have good cause to remember how charming she is." He grimaced and tapped O'Rourke on the shoulder nearest him. "Eh, monsieur?" he asked meaningly.

O'Rourke smiled. "Faith!" he declared. "I had almost forgotten that hole ye put in me, when we settled our little differences, ye fire-eater!"

"I have not forgotten, my friend," returned Chambret seriously. "Nor shall I ever forget your gallantry. To have fired in the air, as you did, after having been wounded by your antagonist —!"

"Hush! Not another word will I listen to! Would ye have me shoot down a man I love as a brother? What d'ye think —?"

"Ah, monsieur, but it was a gallant deed! . . . I'll say no more, if you insist, *mon Colonel*. But Madame la Princesse? You have heard from her yourself?"

"Not a line," said O'Rourke gloomily. "Not that I had any right to expect so much," he defended his beloved, instantly. "But 'twas in our agreement that, if she needed me, she was to send for me. I mind . . ."

He broke off abruptly and sat staring moodily into the upcurling spirals of cigar smoke. Chambret forbore to disturb him. Presently O'Rourke took up the thread of his thoughts aloud.

"I mind the night I left ye all," he said. "'Twas while the *Eirene* still lay at Marseilles, — the day afther ye had drilled this hole in me. . . . We were standing in the bows, madame and I, looking at the moonlight painting a path across the sea to Algiers. . . . Faith! she was that lovely I clean forgot meself. Before I knew what I was about, I had been speaking the matter of ten minutes, and she knew it all. . . . And there was no one at all to see, so she was in me arms. . . . Faith! I dunno why I am telling ye all this."

"Continue, my friend. If you had told her of your love, why, then, did you go — as I remember you went — that very night?"

"'Twas me pride — not alone for meself, but for her! Who was I to be making love to the sweetest woman in the wide world? . . . Anyway, 'twas then it was decided upon betwixt herself and me."

"What was — ?"

"That I was to go forth and seek me fortune and come back to claim her when I could do so without hurting her in the eyes of the world. I had a gold sovereign in me pocket, and I took it out and broke it with me two hands and gave her the half of it. . . . She kissed the other half and I put it away to remember her by. . . . She was to sind it me when she needed me. . . . And then I was making so bold as to kiss her hand, but she would not let me. . . . And I left her there and dropped down over the side, with all the world reeling and no thought at all in me but of her white, sweet face in the moonlight, and the touch of her lips upon me own! . . . Two months later I was in India, seeking me fortune. And I'm still doing that."

[193]

He dismissed the subject abruptly, with a gesture of finality. "Ye were saying," he asked, "that ye had been seeking me? For why? Can the O'Rourke be serving a friend in any way?"

"You are unemployed?"

"True for ye, Chambret. Ye have said it."

"Will you accept —"

"*Mon ami*," O'Rourke stated explicitly, "I'll do anything — anything in the whole world that's clean and honorable, saving it's handling a pen. That I will not do for any living man; upon me worrd, sor, niver!"

Chambret chuckled his appreciation of this declaration. "I suspected as much," he said. "But — this is no clerical work, I promise you."

"Then, I'm your man. Proceed."

"Let us presume a hypothetical case."

O'Rourke bent forward, the better to lose no word of the Frenchman's.

"Be all means," he encouraged him.

"But," Chambret paused to stipulate, "it is a thing understood between us, as friends, that should I make use of the actual name of a person or place, it will be considered as purely part of the hypothesis?"

"Most assuredly!"

"Good, monsieur. I proceed. Let us suppose, then, that there is, within one thousand miles of our Paris, a grand duchy called Lützelburg —"

"The name sounds familiar," interrupted O'Rourke, with suspicion.

"Purely a supposititious duchy," corrected Chambret gravely.

"Sure, yes," — as solemnly.

"That being understood, let us imagine that the late Duke Henri, of Lützelburg, is survived by a widow, the dowager duchess, and a son, heir to the ducal throne — *petit* Duke Jehan, a child of seven years. You follow me? Also, by his younger brother, Prince Georges of Lützelburg, a — a most damnably conscienceless scoundrel!" Chambret exploded, bringing his fist down upon the table with force sufficient to cause the glasses to dance.

"Softly, *mon ami!*" cautioned O'Rourke. "I gather ye are not be way of liking Monsieur le Prince?"

"I — I do not like him, as you say. But, to get on: Lützelburg lies — you know where." Abandoning all pretense of imagining the duchy, Chambret waved his hand definitely to the northwest. O'Rourke nodded assent.

"The capital city, of course, centers about the Castle of Lützelburg. The duchy is an independent State maintaining its own army — one regiment — its customs house, sending its representatives to the Powers. You know all that? It is a rich little State; a comfortable berth for its ruler. Duke Henri preserved its integrity, added to its resources, leaving it a fat legacy to his little son. Had he died without issue, Georges would have succeeded to the ducal throne — and to the control of the treasury. Naturally the scoundrel covets what is not his, now. He goes further. He has gone — far, very far, *mon ami.*"

O'Rourke moved his chair nearer, becoming interested. "Gone far, ye say? And what has the black-hearted divvle been up to, bad cess to him?" he asked with a chuckle.

"He has kidnaped little Duke Jehan, *mon ami.*"

"Kidnaped!" The Irishman sat back gasping. "Faith, what does he think he is, now — a robber baron?" he demanded indignantly — this man of strong emotions, easily

[195]

inflamed in the cause of a friend. "Tell me how he has gone about it, and what ye want me to do."

"There is but little to tell, O'Rourke. This is the most that we know for a certainty: that Duke Jehan has disappeared. Georges — the blackguard! — even dares offer a reward to the man who can furnish a clew to the child's whereabouts. In the nature of things, the reward will never be claimed by a Lützelburger; for Georges, now, is the head and forefront of the government, holding, practically, power of life and death over every soul in the duchy. It is this that we fear: that he will do a hurt to the child."

"Why," interposed O'Rourke, "has he not already done it — put him out of his way?"

"Because, my friend, he values him too highly, as an asset toward his purposes. Prince Georges wishes to marry Madame la Duchesse, the child's mother — a woman wealthy in her own right. He has suggested to her that, should she consent to marry him, his own interests would then be more involved, that he would perhaps take a greater interest in the pursuit of the malefactors. You see?"

"Faith, and I do." O'Rourke tipped back in his chair, grinning impartially at Chambret. "And he would marry the duchess? And ye hate the bold blackguard, is it?" he jeered softly.

Chambret flushed under his challenging gaze. He hesitated. "To be plain," he faltered, " to be frank with you, I — I love madame."

"And she?" persisted O'Rourke.

Chambret shrugged his shoulders. "Who can say?" he deprecated. "Madame will not. Yet would I serve her. Already have I made myself so obnoxious to the powers that be in Lützelburg that I have been requested to absent my-self from the duchy. Wherefore I turn to you."

But O'Rourke pursued his fancy. "I've heard she is beautiful?" he insinuated.

Again Chambret hesitated; but the eyes of the man glowed warm at the mental picture O'Rourke's suggestion conjured within his brain. "She is — indeed beautiful!" he declared at length; and simultaneously took from his pocket a leather wallet, which, opening, he put upon the table between them.

O'Rourke bent over it curiously. A woman's photograph stared up at him: the portrait of a most wonderful woman, looking out from the picture fearlessly, even regally, under level brows; a woman young, full-lipped, with heavy-lidded eyes that were dark and large, brimming with the wine of life. Which is Love.

O'Rourke had seen that portrait frequently before, as pub-lished in the prints, but now he began to appreciate this great beauty with a more intimate interest.

"Faith!" he sighed, looking up. "I'm more than a little minded to envy ye, Chambret. She is beautiful, me word!" He paused; then, "Ye would have me go to get back the boy, if I can?" he asked.

"That is what little I ask," assented Chambret. "You will be amply rewarded —"

"I'll go, *mon ami*. Rest easy, there; I'll do what ye would call me 'possible,' monsieur, and a little more, and the divvle of a lot more atop of that. If a man can scale the insur-mountable — I'll be himself!"

He offered his hand, and, Chambret accepting, put his five fingers around the Frenchman's with a grip that made the other wince.

"As to the reward —" Chambret ventured again.

"Faith, man, can I do naught for a friend without having gold showered over me? Damn the reward! Tell me your plans, give me the lay of the land, and I'm off be sunrise. But as for reward —"

He rose, taking Chambret's arm in his.

"Come," he suggested, "let us go and sup — at your expense. And then, maybe, I'll be asking ye for the loan av a franc or two to refurbish me wardrobe. 'Tis the divvle av a winter it has been, I'll niver deny. Come. 'Tis meself knows a quiet place."

CHAPTER II

IT was drawing toward the evening of the third day following, when Colonel O'Rourke rounded an elbow in the road
and came, simultaneously, into view of the Inn of the Winged
God, and to a stop.

He was weary and footsore. He was, moreover, thirsty.
Behind him the road stretched long, and white, and hot, and
straight as any string across the Department of the Meurthe-
et-Moselle, back to Longwy, whence he had come afoot.

For, in consideration of the temper of Prince Georges de
Lützelburg, Chambret and O'Rourke had agreed that it
would be the part of prudence for the Irishman to enter the
duchy as unobtrusively as possible; and in his light tweeds,
with the dust of the road white upon his shoes and like a film
upon his clothes, O'Rourke might well have passed for an
English milord upon a walking tour.

To the seeing eye, perhaps, there was about the Irishman a
devil-may-care swing, a free carelessness in the way he put
his best foot forward, a fine spirit in the twirl of his walking
stick, that was hardly to be considered characteristic of that
solemn person, the Englishman, plugging stolidly forward
upon his walking tour as upon a penance self-imposed. But
the similitude was sufficient to impose upon the peasantry of
Lützelburg; and should suffice, barring accidents.

O'Rourke paused, I say, looking forward to the inn, and
then about him, considering the lay of the land. To the

north, he knew, ran the French-Belgian frontier — how far away he might not exactly state; to the west, also, was the line that divides Lützelburg from French territory — again at an indeterminate distance, according to the Irishman's knowledge.

"But it will not be far, now, I'm thinking," he said aloud; "come sundown, 'tis meself that will be out av France — and thin, I'm advising ye, may the devil stand vigil for the soul of his familiar, Monsieur le Prince!"

But for all his boastfulness, the Irishman was by no means easy in his mind as to how he was to accomplish that to which he had set his hand. The plan of action agreed upon between O'Rourke and his friend was distinguished by a considerable latitude as to detail.

O'Rourke was, in short, to do what he could. If he succeeded in freeing the young duke, well and good. If not — and at this consideration Chambret had elevated expressive shoulders. "One does one's possible," he had deprecated; "one can do no more, *mon ami*."

Now, the Irishman was thinking that it behooved him to be on his way without delay, if he cared to reach the city of Lützelburg before nightfall. And yet, this inn before him was one of possibilities interesting to a thirsty man. He stood still, jingling in his pockets the scant store of francs that remained to him of the modest loan which he had consented to accept of the larger sum which Chambret had tried to press upon him.

It stood unobtrusively back from the road, this inn: a gabled building, weather-beaten and ancient-seeming, draped lavishly with green growing vines. Above the lintel of its wide, hospitably yawning doorway swung, creaking in the perfumed airs of the spring afternoon, a battered signboard, whereon a long-dead artist had limned the figure of a little laughing, naked boy, with a bow and a quiver full of arrows, and two downy wings sprouting somewhere near his chubby shoulder-blades.

O'Rourke grinned at the childish god, deciphering the stilted French inscription beneath its feet.

"The Inn of the Winged God," he read aloud. "Sure, 'tis meself that's the superstitious one — a rank believer in signs. I'm taking ye, ye shameless urchin," he apostrophized the god of love, "for a sign that there's — drink within!" He chuckled, thinking: "'Tis here that I'm to meet Chambret, if need be, for consultation. I mind me he said the inn was but a step this side the frontier. Be that token, 'tis himself that should be coming down the road, ere long, galumphing in that red devil-wagon av his."

But the question remained: Was he to pause for refreshment, or to push on despite his great thirst? For it seemed as though all the dust in the road that had not found lodgment upon his body had settled in his throat.

The fluttering of a woman's skirts put a period to his hesitancy; a girl appeared and stood for a moment in the doorway of the Inn of the Winged God, gazing upon the newcomer with steady eyes that were bright beneath level brows. A tall girl, seemingly the taller since slight and supple, she was, and astonishingly good to look upon: slender and darkly beautiful.

Even at a distance O'Rourke could see as much and imagine the rest; and, more, he saw that she wore the peasant dress peculiar to that Department — wore it with an entrancing grace, adorning it herself rather than relying upon it to enhance her charms. A crimson head-dress of some fashion confined her hair; and that same was dark — nay, black. And there was a kerchief about her throat, like snow above the black of a velvet bodice, which, together with her spreading skirt of crimson cloth, was half hidden by a bright expanse of apron. Moreover, that skirt — in keeping with the custom of the neighborhood — was sensibly short; whereby it was made evident that mademoiselle might, if so she willed, boast a foot of quality, an ankle . . .

Promptly O'Rourke's thirst became unbearable, and he advanced a step or two with a purposeful air.

Mademoiselle as promptly disappeared into the gloom of the inner room.

O'Rourke followed her example, finding it cool within and clean, inviting, and tempting to dalliance. There was a great, cold fireplace; and broad, spotless tables, and chairs were ranged about upon a floor of earth hard-packed and neatly sanded. Also, from a farther room came odors of cookery, enchanting first his nose and then all the hungry man that was O'Rourke.

He stalked to the center of the room, half blinded by his sudden transition from the sun glare to this comfortable gloom, and discovered the girl standing with a foot on the` threshold of the adjoining apartment, watching him over her shoulder.

O'Rourke cleared his throat harshly; and "What would m'sieur?" she desired to know.

"That, me dear," said O'Rourke. With his walking stick he indicated one of the row of steins that decorated the chimneypiece. "And, mind ye, full to the brim," he stipulated.

The girl murmured a reply, and went about his bidding. Slowly, with a suggestion of weariness in his manner, O'Rourke went to the back of the room, where he found a little compartment, partitioned off, containing benches and a small table.

On the table he seated himself, sighing with content. A window, open, faced him, giving upon the garden of the inn. Without there was a vista of nodding scarlet hollyhocks, of sunflowers, of hyacinths, and of many homely, old-fashioned blooms growing in orderly luxuriance. A light breeze swept across them, bearing their fragrance in through the casement.

O'Rourke bared his head to it gratefully, and fumbled in his pocket for pipe and tobacco.

"Upon me word," he sighed, "'twill be hard to tear meself away, now!" Nor was he thinking of the girl just then, nor of aught save the homely comfort of the Inn of the Winged God.

He began to smoke, and, smoking, his thoughts wandered into a reverie; so that he sat lost to his surroundings, staring at the hollyhocks and hyacinths — and seeing naught but the eyes of Beatrix, Princesse de Grandlieu.

The girl's step failed to rouse him; he stared on, out of the window, giving her no heed as she waited by his side with the foaming stein.

For her part, she seemed patient enough. He made a gallant figure — this O'Rourke — sitting at ease upon the table. And some such thought may have been in her mind — that his was a figure to fill the eyes of a woman. Her own never left him for many minutes.

She remarked the signs of travel: the dust that lay thick upon his shoulders, and whitened his shoes; the drawn look about the man's eyes; the firm lines about his mouth that told of steadfastness and determination. And she sighed, but very softly.

But an inn maid may not be eying a stranger for hours together; she has her duties to perform. Presently the girl put the stein down with a little crash.

"M'sieur is served," she announced loudly.

O'Rourke came to with a little start. "Thank you, me dear," he said, and buried his nose in the froth. "Faith," he added, lowering the vessel, "'tis like wine — or your eyes, darlint." To prove this, he smiled engagingly into those eyes.

She did not appear to resent the compliment, nor his manner. "M'sieur has traveled far?" she would know, standing with lowered lashes, her slender fingers playing diffidently with a fold of her apron.

"Not so far that I'm blinded to your sweet face," he averred. "But 'tis truth for ye that I've covered many a mile since sunrise."

"M'sieur does not come from these parts?"

"From Paris."

Although she stood with her back to the light, and though O'Rourke could distinguish her features but dimly, yet he saw that her eyes widened; and he smiled secretly at her simplicity.

"From Paris, m'sieur? But *that* is far?"

"Quite far, darlint. But faith, I've no cause for complaint."

"M'sieur means —"? she queried, with naïve bewilderment.

"M'sieur," he assured her gallantly, "means that no journey is long that has mam'selle at the end av it."

"Oh, m'sieur!" — protesting.

"Truth — me word for it." And the magnificent O'Rourke put a franc into her hand. "The change," he proclaimed largely, "ye may keep for yourself, little one. And this — ye may keep for me, if ye will."

"*M'sieur!*"

And though they were deeply shadowed, he could see her

cheeks flaming as she backed away, rubbing the caressed spot with the corner of her apron.

O'Rourke laughed softly, without moving. "Don't be angry with me," he pleaded, but with no evident contrition. "What's in a kiss, me dear? Sure, 'tis no harm at all, at all! And how was I to hold meself back, now, with ye before me, pretty as a picture?"

It pleased her — his ready tongue. That became apparent, though she sought to hide it with a pretense of indignation.

"One would think —" she tried to storm.

"What, now, darlint?"

"One would almost believe m'sieur the Irishman!"

"An Irishman I am, praises be!" cried O'Rourke, forgetting his rôle. "But" — he remembered again — "*the* Irishman; now, who might that be?"

"M'sieur le Colonel O'Rourke!"

"What!" And M'sieur le Colonel O'Rourke got down from the table hastily. "Ye know me?" he demanded.

The girl's astonishment was too plain to be ignored. "It is not that m'sieur is himself M'sieur le Colonel?" she cried, putting a discreet distance between them.

"'Tis just that. And how would ye be knowing me name, if ye please?"

"Why, surely, all know that m'sieur is coming to Lützelburg!" cried the ingenuous mam'selle. "Else why should a guard be stationed at every road crossing the frontier?"

"For what, will ye tell me?"

"For what but to keep m'sieur from entering?"

"As ye say, for what else?" O'Rourke stroked his chin, puzzled, staring at this girl who had such an astonishing fund of information.

"Am I so unpopular, then?" he asked.

"*Non, m'sieur;* it is not that. It is that m'sieur is a friend of M'sieur Chambret, and —"

"Yes, yes, darlint. Go on."

He spoke soothingly, for he desired to know more. But he found it rather annoying that the girl should persist in keeping her back to the light; it was difficult to read her face, through the shadows. He maneuvered to exchange positions with mam'selle, but she seemed intuitively to divine his purpose, and outwitted the man.

"And," she resumed, under encouragement, "M'sieur Chambret is known to love Madame la Duchesse, whom Prince Georges wishes to marry. · It is known to all that M'sieur Chambret was requested to leave Lützelburg. What is more natural than that he should send his friend, the Irish adventurer, to avenge him — to take his place?"

"Yes. That's all very well, me dear; but what bewilders me — more than your own bright eyes, darlint — is: how did ye discover that I was coming here?"

O'Rourke endeavored to speak lightly, but he was biting the lip of him over that epithet, "Irish adventurer"; in which there lurked a flavor that he found distasteful. "'Tis a sweet-smelling reputation I bear in these parts!" he thought ruefully.

"What" — the girl leaned toward O'Rourke, almost whispering; whereby she riveted his attention upon her charms as well as upon her words — "is more natural, m'sieur, than that Prince Georges should set a watch upon M'sieur Chambret?"

"Oh, ho!" said the Irishman. "'Tis meself that begins to see a light. And, me dear," he added sharply, "ye fill me with curiosity. How comes it that ye know so much?"

"It is not unnatural, m'sieur." Her shrug was indescribably significant and altogether delightful. "Have I not a brother in Lützelburg castle, valet to M'sieur le Prince? If a brother drops a word or two, to his sister, now and then, is she to be blamed for his indiscretions?"

"Sure, not!" cried the Irishman emphatically. "Ye are to be thanked, I'm thinking. And where did ye say this precious frontier lay?"

"The line crosses the highway not the quarter of a mile to the south, m'sieur. You will know it when you are stopped by the outpost."

"Very likely, me dear — if so be it I'm stopped."

And as she watched his face, the girl may have thought that possibly he would not be stopped; for there was an expression thereon which boded ill to whomsoever should attempt to hinder the O'Rourke from attending to the business to which he had set himself.

"Mam'selle!" he bowed. "I'm infinitely obliged to ye. Faith, 'tis yourself that has done a great service this day to the O'Rourke — and be that same token 'tis the O'Rourke that hardly knows how to reward ye!"

"But —" she suggested timidly, yet with archness lurking in her tone, "does not M'sieur le Colonel consider that he has amply rewarded me, in advance?" And upon these words she began to scrub her cheek vigorously with her apron.

He threw back his head and laughed; and was still laughing — for she had been too sharp for him — when she rose, with a warning finger upon her lips.

"M'sieur!" — earnestly. "Silence, if you please — for your life's sake!"

"Eh!" cried O'Rourke startled. And then the laugh died in his throat. The girl had turned, and now her profile was

black against the sunny window; and it was most marvelously perfect. O'Rourke's breath came fast as he looked;
for she was surprisingly fair and good to look upon. It was
the first time he had seen her clearly enough to fully comprehend her perfection, and he stood for a moment, without
stirring, or, indeed, coherently thinking. It was not the
nature of this man to neglect a beautiful woman at any time;
he grudged this girl no meed of the admiration that was her
due.

In a moment he felt her fingers soft and warm about his
own; his heart leaped — an Irishman's heart, not fickle, but
inflammable; and then he repressed an exclamation as his
fingers were crushed in a grip so strong and commanding
that it fairly amazed him.

And, "Silence; ah, silence, m'sieur!" the girl begged him,
in a whisper.

Were they observed, then? He turned toward the outer
door, but saw no one. But from the highway there came a
clatter of hoofs.

"Soldiers!" the girl breathed. "Soldiers, m'sieur, from
the frontier post. Let me go. I —"

Almost violently she wrested her hand from his, darting
toward the door with a gesture that warned him back to his
partitioned corner if he valued his incognito.

Halfway across the floor she shrank back with a little cry
of dismay, as the entrance to the Inn of the Winged God was
darkened by two new arrivals.

They swung into the room, laughing together: tall men
both, long and strong of limb, with the bearing of men confident of their place and prowess. O'Rourke, peering
guardedly out from his corner, saw that they were both in
uniform: green and gold tunics above closely fitting breeches

of white, with riding boots of patent leather — the officers' uniform of the ducal army of Lützelburg.

Now, since his coming, the taproom of the Winged God had been gradually darkening as evening drew nigh. Already — O'Rourke was surprised to observe — it was twilight without; now, suddenly, the sun sank behind the purple ridge of the distant mountains, and at once gloom shrouded the room. In it the figures of the two soldiers loomed large and vaguely.

One raised his voice, calling: "Lights!"

The girl murmured something, moving away.

"Lights, girl; lights!"

"I will send some one, messieurs," O'Rourke heard her say.

"Unnecessary, my dear," returned the first speaker. "Come hither, little one. Here is the lamp, and here a match."

Unwillingly, it seemed to the Irishman, the inn maid obeyed, stepping upon a bench and raising her arm to light the single lamp that depended from the ceiling. A match flared in her fingers, illuminating the upturned, intent face.

And O'Rourke caught at his breath again. "Faith!" he said softly, "she is *that* wonderful!"

Some such thought seemed to cross the minds of both the others, at the same moment. One swore delicately — presumably in admiration; his fellow shifted to a killing pose, twirling his mustache — the elder of the pair, evidently, and a man with a striking distinction of carriage.

The girl jumped lightly from the bench and turned away; but she was not yet to be permitted to retire, it seemed.

"Here, girl!" called he who had mouthed the oath.

She turned reluctantly; the glow of the brightening lamp fell about her like a golden aureole.

"Messieurs?" she asked with a certain dignity.

"So," drawled the elder officer, "you are a new maid, I presume?"

"Yes, messieurs," she replied, courtesying low — to hide her confusion, perhaps; for she was crimson under their bold appraisal of her charms.

"Ah! Name, little one?"

"Delphine, messieurs."

"Delphine, eh? A most charming name, for a most charming girl!"

"*Merci*, messieurs!"

She dropped a second humble courtesy. And O'Rourke caught himself fancying that she did so in mockery — though, indeed, such spirit would have assorted strangely with her lowly station.

But as she rose and confronted the men again, the elder took her chin between his thumb and forefinger, roughly twisting her face to the light.

"Strange —" he started to say; but the girl jerked away angrily.

"Pardon, messieurs," she said, "but I would —"

Nor did she finish what was on the tip of her tongue for utterance. For she was turning away, making as though to escape, when this younger man clasped her suddenly about the waist; and before she realized what was toward, he had kissed her squarely.

O'Rourke slid from his table seat, with a little low-toned oath. But for the moment he held himself back. It seemed as though Mademoiselle Delphine was demonstrating her ability to take care of herself.

Her white and rounded arm shot out impetuously, and her five fingers impinged upon the cheek of the younger man with a crack like a pistol shot. He jumped away, with a laughing cry of protest.

"A shrew!" he cried. "A termagant, Prince Georges!"

In another moment she would have been gone, but the elder officer was not to be denied.

"No, just a woman!" he corrected. "A tempestuous maid, to be tamed, Charles! Not so fast, little one!" And he caught her by the arm.

She wheeled upon him furiously, with a threatening hand; but his own closed about her wrist, holding her helpless the while he drew her steadily toward him.

"But one!" he pretended to beg. "But one little kiss, Mistress Delphine!"

"This has gone about far enough, messieurs," O'Rourke interposed, judging it time.

For it is one thing to kiss a pretty girl yourself, and quite another to stand by and watch a stranger kiss her regardless of her will.

So he came down toward the group slowly, with a protesting palm upraised.

But the prince gave him hardly a glance; he was intent upon the business of the moment. "Kick this fellow out, Charles," he cried contemptuously, relaxing nothing of his hold upon the girl. And then, to her: "Come, Mam'selle Delphine, but a single kiss —"

"No!" she cried. "*No*, messieurs!"

There was a terror in her tone that set O'Rourke's blood to boiling. He forgot himself, forgot the danger of his position —that danger of which he had been so lately apprised by the girl herself. He laid a hand upon the fellow's collar, with no attempt at gentleness, and another upon his wrist. A second later the prince was sprawling in the sand upon the floor.

And O'Rourke promptly found himself engaged in defending himself, to the best of his slight ability, from a downward sweep of the younger officer's broadsword.

"Ye damned coward!" the Irishman cried, ablaze with rage.

His walking stick — a stout blackthorn relic of the old country — deflected the blade. The young officer spat a curse at him and struck carelessly again, displaying neither judgment nor skill. O'Rourke caught the blow a second time upon the stick, twisted the blackthorn through the other's guard and rapped him sharply across the knuckles.

"Ye infernal poltroon!" he said furiously. "To attack an unarmed man!"

The sword swept up through the air in a glittering arc, to fall clattering in a far corner. O'Rourke gave it slight heed. There was much to be accomplished ere that sword should strike the earth.

He leaped in upon the younger officer, whirling the blackthorn above his head; the man stepped back, raising his arms as though dazed. The stick descended with force enough to beat down this guard and crash dully upon his skull. He fell — like a log, in fact; and so lay still for a space.

And O'Rourke jumped back upon the instant, and just in time to knock a revolver from the hand of the elder man.

"Ye, too — a coward!" he raged. "Are there no men in this land?"

Simultaneously, in falling, the revolver was discharged. The shot rang loudly in the confines of the taproom walls, but the bullet buried itself harmlessly in the wainscoting. O'Rourke jumped for it and kicked the pistol through the open doorway.

"So much for that!" he cried, darting toward the corner

where the sword of the unconscious man had fallen. "Come, Prince Georges of Lützelburg — princely coward!" he taunted the elder man. "Come — 'tis one to one, now — sword to sword, monsieur! Are ye afraid, or will ye fight — ye scum of the earth?"

He need hardly have asked. Already the prince was upon his feet, and had drawn. O'Rourke's fingers closed upon the hilt of the saber. A thrill ran through him; this was his life to him, to face odds, to have a sword in his hand.

"Good!" he cried joyfully. "*Now*, Monsieur le Prince!"

He met the onslaught with a hasty parry. A cluster of sparks flew from the blades. O'Rourke boldly stepped in to close quarters, his right arm swinging the heavy saber like a feather, his left ending in a clenched hand held tightly to the small of his back.

The room filled with the ringing clangor of the clashing steel. Prince Georges at least was not afraid of personal hurt; he engaged the Irishman closely, cutting and parrying with splendid skill — a wonderful swordsman, a *beau sabreur*, master of his weapon and — master of O'Rourke. The Irishman was quick to realize this. He had met more than his match; the man who opposed him was his equal in weight and length of arm, his equal in defense, his superior in attack. He fought at close quarters, giving not an inch, but rather ever pressing in upon him, hammering down upon his guard a veritable tornado of crashing blows.

O'Rourke reeled and gave ground under the furious onslaught. He leaped away time and again, only to find the prince again upon him, abating no whit of his determined attack. In his eyes O'Rourke read nothing of mercy, naught but a perhaps long dormant blood-lust suddenly roused. He came to an understanding that he was fighting for his life, that this was no mere fencing bout, — no child's play, but deadly earnest. And with his mind's eye he foresaw the outcome.

Well — one can but die. At least Prince Georges should have his fill of fighting; and an Irishman who fights hopelessly fights with all the reckless rage of a rat in a corner.

So O'Rourke fought, there in the taproom of the Inn of the Winged God. He took no risks, ventured nothing of doubtful outcome. If a chance for an attack was to come, he was ready for it, his eye like a cat's alert for an opening for thrust or slashing cut. But if that was to be denied him, he had an impregnable defense, seemingly. He might retreat — and he did, thrice circling the room — but he retreated fighting. And so, fighting, he would fall when his time came.

In one thing only he surpassed the aggressor — in endurance. His outdoor life of the past few days had put him in splendid trim. He battled on, with hardly a hair displaced; whereas Monsieur le Prince pressed his advantage by main will-power, advancing with some difficulty because of the heaving of his broad chest, gasping for air, at times, like a fish out of its element — but ever advancing, ever pressing the Irishman to the utmost.

Thrice they made the circuit of the room, O'Rourke escaping a fall or collision with the tables and chairs seemingly by a sixth sense — an eye in the back of his head that warned him of obstacles that might easily have encompassed his downfall.

He was outgeneraled, too; twice he endeavored to back himself through the outer doorway, and both times the prince got between the Irishman and his sole remaining hope of escape.

And then it narrowed down to a mere contest of endurance

— Monsieur le Prince already tired, and O'Rourke, fast failing, beginning to feel the effects of his day's long tramp.
The room began to whirl dizzily about them both — like a
changing, hazy panorama, wherein O'Rourke was dimly
conscious of pink, gaping faces filling the doorways, and the
round, staring eyes of frightened and awed peasants at the
windows.

And so, possibly, it was as a relief to both when, eventually,
the Irishman managed to get the breadth of a table between
them, and when each was free to pause and gasp for breath
the while they glared one at the other, measuring each his
opponent's staying powers — for to a test of sheer lasting
ability it was now come. The man who should be able to
keep upon his feet the longest — he was to win. And neither
read "quarter" in his enemy's eyes.

As they stood thus, watching one another jealously, out of
the tail of his eye O'Rourke saw the fallen officer — Charles
— stir, and sit upright. He dared not take his attention from
the prince, and yet he was able to note that the younger man
at first stared confusedly, then staggered to his feet, and so
doing, put his hand to his pistol holster.

Opportunely a curious thing occurred. A voice rang
through the room loudly, cheerfully:

"The O'Rourke!" it stated explicitly. "Or Satan himself!"

All three turned, by a common impulse, toward the outer
door. It framed a man entirely at his ease, dressed in the
grotesque arrangement that constitutes an automobiling costume in these days, holding in his left hand the goggle mask
which the driver affects. But in the other hand, level with
his eye, he poised a revolver, the muzzle of which was directly
trained upon him whom Prince Georges had called Charles.

"Chambret!" cried O'Rourke. "Upon me soul, ye're welcome!"

"I thought as much, my friend," replied Chambret. "And I am glad to be in time to — to see fair play, Colonel Charles! May I suggest, monsieur, that you take your hand from the butt of that weapon and stand aside until my friend has settled his little affair with Monsieur le Prince?"

The face of the young officer flushed darkly red; he bit his lip with rage, darting toward Chambret a venomous glance. Yet he stood aside, very obediently, as a wiser man than he might well have done.

"O'Rourke!" then cried Chambret. "Guard, my friend — guard yourself!"

It was time. Monsieur le Prince, sticking at nothing, had edged stealthily around the table. O'Rourke, startled, put himself in a defensive position in the very nick of time. Another moment and Chambret's warning had been vain.

Again they fought, but now less spiritedly; to O'Rourke it seemed as though the contest had degenerated into a mere endeavor to kill time, rather than to dispose of one another. And yet he was acutely conscious that a single misstep would seal his death warrant.

He found time, too, to wonder even a trifle bitterly what had become of Mademoiselle Delphine. It seemed passing strange that he saw naught of her — had missed her ever since he had come to her aid. Surely she had been very well content to leave him to his fate, once he had championed her cause! It was strange, he thought, according to his lights very odd . . .

And so thinking, he became aware that the brief interval seemed to have refreshed Monsieur le Prince more than it had himself.

Georges now seemed possessed of seven devils, all a-thirst for the soul of O'Rourke. He flew at him, abruptly, without the least warning, like a whirlwind. O'Rourke was beaten back a dozen yards in as many seconds. There was no killing time about the present combat — O'Rourke well knew.

And he felt himself steadily failing. Once he slipped and all but went to his knees, and when he recovered was trembling in every limb like an aspen leaf. And, again, he blundered into a chair and sent it crashing to the floor; when it seemed ages ere he managed to disentangle his feet from its rounds — seemed the longer since the sword of Prince Georges quivered over him like the wrath of a just God, relentless and terrible.

He had one last hope — to get himself in a corner, with his back to the wall, and stand Monsieur le Prince off to the bitter end. At least, he prayed he might get in one good blow before — that end. And so he made for the corner nearest him.

In the end he gained it against odds — for Prince Georges divined his purpose and did his utmost to thwart it. But when at last the Irishman had gained this slight advantage, his heart sank within him; Georges closed fearlessly, not keeping at sword's length, as O'Rourke had trusted he might.

O'Rourke was flattened, fairly, against that wall. He fought with desperate cunning, but ever more feebly. "God!" he cried once, between clinched teeth. "Could I but touch him!"

Georges heard, grinning maliciously.

"Never, fortune hunter!" he returned, redoubling his efforts. "You may well pray —"

What else he said O'Rourke never knew, for at that instant

[217]

he felt the wall give to the pressure of his shoulders, and a breath of cool air swept past him.

"A door!" he thought, and, leaping backwards, fell sprawling in utter darkness.

It was indeed a door. As he lay there the Irishman caught a transient glimpse of a woman's head and shoulders outlined against the light, and then the door was closed, and he heard her throw herself bodily against it, with the dull click of a bolt shot home; also a maddened oath, and a terrific blow delivered upon the panels by the sword of Monsieur le Prince.

CHAPTER III

THE NIGHT OF MADNESS

O'ROURKE was prompt to scramble to his feet. He found himself surrounded by a profound blackness. The place wherein he stood was like the very heart of night itself. But for the quick flutter of the breath of the woman who was near him, he was without an inkling as to where he might be.

But for the moment he was content to know that he was with her. He groped in the darkness with a tentative hand, which presently encountered the girl's, and closed upon it; and he started to speak, but she gave him pause.

"Hush, m'sieur!" she breathed. "Hush — and come with me quickly. You have not an instant to —"

Her concluding word was drowned in the report of a pistol. The girl started, with a frightened cry. A roar of cursing filled the room which the O'Rourke, providentially, had just quitted. It subsided suddenly; and then the two heard the cool, incisive accents of Chambret.

"Not so fast, Monsieur le Prince," they heard him say, warningly. "Take it with more *aplomb*, I advise you. Upon my word of honor, you die if you move a finger within ten minutes!"

"And then —?" came the wrathful voice of Georges.

"Then," returned Chambret, delicately ironical, "I shall be pleased to leave you to your — devices — shall we call them? For my part, I shall go on my way in my automobile."

[219]

They heard no more. The girl was already dragging O'Rourke away.

"Ten minutes!" she whispered gratefully.

"'Tis every bit as good as a year, just now," O'Rourke assured her, lightly — more lightly than his emotions warranted, indeed.

"Ah, m'sieur!" she said fearfully. ·

"Whisht, darlint," he cried. "Don't ye be worrying about me now. 'Tis the O'Rourke that can care for his head, Mam'selle Delphine — now that ye've given me a fighting chance."

But she only answered, "Come!" tugging impatiently at his hand; and he was very willing to follow her, even unto the ends of the known world, as long as he might be so led by those warm, soft fingers.

But he grew quite bewildered in the following few minutes. It seemed that they threaded a most curious maze of vacant rooms and sounding galleries, all in total eclipse. And once, for some time, they were passing through what seemed a tunnel, dark and musty, wherein the Irishman, by putting forth his free hand, was able to touch a rough, damp wall of hewn stone.

But at the end of that they came to a doorway, where they halted. The girl evidently produced a key, for she released O'Rourke's hand, and a second later he heard the grating of a rusty lock and then the protests of reluctant hinges.

"And where will this be taking us?" he asked at length.

"To safety, for you, I pray, m'sieur."

"Thank ye, Mam'selle Delphine."

"Quick!" she interrupted impatiently.

A rush of cool air and fresh enveloped them. O'Rourke stepped out after the girl, who turned and swung to the door, relocking it.

They were standing under the open sky of night. Absolute silence lay about them; infinite peace was there, under a multitude of clear, shining stars. The change was so abrupt as to seem momentarily unreal; O'Rourke shook his head, as one would rid his brain of the cobwebs of a dream, then looked about him.

"Where would we be, now, me dear?" he asked.

"Hush!" she cried guardedly, pointing.

His gaze followed the line of her arm, and he discovered that they were standing upon a hillside over across from the Inn of the Winged God. Its doors and windows were flaming yellow against the night; and set square against the illumination of the main entrance, O'Rourke could see the burly bulk of Chambret. Without, in the road, loomed the black and shining mass of a powerful automobile, its motors shaking, its lamps glaring balefully — seeming a living thing, O'Rourke fancied, very like some squat, misshapen nocturnal monster.

But Chambret did not stir; and from that the Irishman knew that his ten minutes was not yet up. Nevertheless, he tightened his hold upon the hilt of the naked saber which he still carried, and started back toward the inn.

The girl caught him by the arm.

"Where are you going?" she demanded.

"Back." O'Rourke looked down upon her in surprise. "Back to my friend. What! Am I, too, a chicken-heart, to leave him there, alone —?"

"M'sieur Chambret," she interrupted, "is master of the situation, M'sieur le Colonel. He can take care of himself."

"You know him?"

"You — you —" For an instant she stammered, at a loss for her answer. "I — I heard you name him, m'sieur," she made shift to say at length.

"Ah, yes. But, for all that, I'm not going to leave him —"

"Too late, m'sieur. See!"

Again she indicated the inn. O'Rourke looked, swearing in his excitement — but under his breath, that she — an inn-maid! — might not be offended.

He saw Chambret, momentarily as he had been — steady and solid as a rock in the doorway. An instant later, he was gone; and from the taproom came a volley of shouts and curses, tempered to faint echoes by the distance.

Promptly the automobile began to move. And as it did the doorway was filled with struggling men. Chambret appeared to stand up in the machine; his revolver spat fire thrice.

The shots were answered without delay, but the machine gathered speed, and swept snorting westwards. Prince Georges and Colonel Charles of the army of Lützelburg were to be seen pursuing it down the road, afoot, peppering the night with futile bullets and filling it with foul vituperation.

Presently they must have realized what feeble figures they were cutting in the eyes of the peasants; for they halted. By then they were near enough for their high and angry tones to be distinguishable to O'Rourke and the girl.

"Back!" they heard Georges cry. "To the horses!"

"But we cannot overtake him, your highness —"

"Fool! The patrol will halt him, and we shall arrive in good time."

As though in answer to Georges' statement, a volley of carbine shots rang sharply from the direction of the frontier, continuing for a full minute, to be followed by a rapid, dying clatter of horses' hoofs.

The Frenchman's automobile had reached the outpost,

had dashed through its surprised resistance, and was gone, on to Lützelburg.

So much Georges surmised — and truly. "The fools!" he cried. "They were not alert without us, Charles. Come — let us get back to the inn. At least we have left to us that cursed Irishman and —"

"If so be it they have not already escaped through the fields," interrupted Charles.

Their voices faded into murmurs as they retreated. The girl tugged at O'Rourke's hand.

"Hurry, m'sieur," she implored.

But O'Rourke was thinking of his comrade and the gantlet he had just run. The reports of the carbines still filled his ears with grim forebodings.

"God send that he was not hit!" he prayed fervently. "A true man, if ever one lived."

"Yes, yes, m'sieur. But come, ah, come!" — with an odd little catch in her voice.

Obediently O'Rourke followed her. They trod for a time upon a little path, worn through the open fields, making toward a stretch of forest that loomed dimly vast and mysterious to the southwards.

"I'm wondering, Mam'selle Delphine," said the Irishman, "how we got out there on the hillside."

"By an underground passage," she explained impatiently. "The inn," she added, "is old; it bore not always as good a reputation as it does now."

"Thank ye," he said. "And since ye can tell me that, can ye not go a bit further and tell me how I am to balance me account with ye, mam'selle?"

"Yes," she replied; "I — I will tell you."

There was a strange hesitation in her speech — as though

some emotion choked her. O'Rourke wondered, as, silently now, since she did not at once make good her words and inform him, he followed her across the fields.

Nor, indeed, did mam'selle of the inn speak again until she had brought the Irishman to the edge of that woodland, and for a moment or two had skirted its depths. Abruptly, she paused, turning toward him and laying a tentative hand upon his arm.

"M'sieur," she said — and again with the little catch in her tone, — "here lies the frontier of France."

"And there — Lützelburg?" he inquired, unawed.

"Yes — beyond the white stone."

The white stone of the boundary was no more than a yard away. "Come!" cried O'Rourke; and in two steps was in Lützelburg.

"Did ye think me the man to hesitate?" he asked wonderingly. "Did ye think I'd draw back me hand — especially after what's passed between meself and that dog, Monsieur le Prince?"

"I did not know," she confessed, looking up into his face. "M'sieur is very bold; for M'sieur le Prince sticks at nothing."

"Faith, the time is nigh when he'll stick at the O'Rourke, I promise ye!" he boasted, with his heart hot within him as he recalled how cowardly had been the attempt upon him.

She smiled a little at his assurance. There spoke the Irishman, she may have been thinking. But her smile was one heavenly to the man.

Allowances may be made for him. He was aged neither in years nor in heart; and the society of a beautiful woman was something for which he had starved during the winter just past. And surely mam'selle's face was very lovely as she held it toward his — pale, glimmering in the starlight, with sweet, deep shadows where her eyes glowed, her lips a bit parted, her breath coming rapidly; and so near to him she stood that it stirred upon his cheek like a soft caress.

And he bent toward her quickly. Quickly, but not so swiftly that she might not escape; which she did with a movement as agile as a squirrel's; thereafter standing a little way from him, and laughing half-heartedly.

"Ah, m'sieur!" she reproached him for his audacity.

"I don't care!" he defied her anger. "Why will ye tempt me, Mam'selle Delphine — ye with your sweet, pretty ways, and that toss av your head that's like an invitation—though I misdoubt ye are meaning the half of it? Am I a man or — or what? — that I should be cold to ye —?"

"Ah, but you are a man, m'sieur, as you have to-night well shown!" she told him desperately. "You were asking what you could do to even our score?"

"Yes, mam'selle."

"Then, monsieur —" And now she drew nearer to him, trustingly, almost pleadingly. "Then, monsieur, you have only to continue what you set out to do — even at the risk of your life. Ah, monsieur, it is much that I ask, but — am I not to be pitied? Indeed, I am mad, quite mad with anxiety. Go, monsieur, if you would serve me — go on and save to me the little duke! Think, monsieur, what they may be doing to my son —"

" *Your* son — Mam'selle Delphine!"

O'Rourke jumped back as though he had been shot, then stood stock-still, transfixed with amazement. "Your son!" he cried again.

"Ah, monsieur, yes. It is true that I deceived you, but at first it was to save you from arrest. I — I am —"

"Madame la Duchesse!" he cried. "Blind fool that I was, not to have guessed it! Pardon, madame!" And he sank upon his knee, carrying her hand to his lips. "Madame!" he muttered humbly. "'Tis the O'Rourke who would go to the ends av the earth to serve ye!"

Was it accident, premeditation — or what more deep — that led the woman's fingers to stray among the soft, dark curls of the man?

"Monsieur, monsieur!" she cried breathlessly. "Rise. I — you — you are very kind to me . . ."

Her voice seemed to fail her. She paused. O'Rourke rose slowly, retaining his hold upon her hand. His mind cast back in rapid retrospect of the events of the day, since his advent at the Inn of the Winged God. It came to him as a flash of lightning, this revelation, making clear much that might otherwise have been thought mysterious. And he knew that she was indeed Madame la Duchesse de Lützelburg, this girl — she seemed no more — this girl whom he suddenly found himself holding in his arms, who sobbed passionately, her face hidden upon his breast.

For that, too, was his portion there in the infinite quietude of the woodland, under the soft-falling radiance of God's stars. How it came to pass neither could have told. Whether it was brought about by some sudden flush of dawning love on her part for this man whom many had loved and were yet to love, or by the tender, impetuous heart of him, whose blood coursed in his veins never so hotly as when for beauty in distress — who shall say?

But one thing was certain — that she lay content in his .... arms for a time. All other things were of no account, even

The Night of Madness

Chambret and Madame la Princesse, Beatrix de Grandlieu. In the perilous sweetness of that moment friendship was forgotten, the love of the man's life lost, engulfed in the love of the moment. The world reeled dizzily about him, and the lips of the grand duchess were sweet as wine to a fainting man.

CHAPTER IV

BUT she first came to her senses, in time, and broke from his arms.

"Ah, monsieur!" she cried. And the face he saw was beautiful, even though stained by tears, though wrung by distress. "But this is madness, madness!" she cried again.

"Sure," he said confusedly, for indeed the world was upside down with him then, "'tis the sweetest madness that ever mortal did know! Faith, me head's awhirl with that same madness, and the heart of me's on fire — ah, madame, madame!"

"No," she cried softly. "No, my — my friend — I — I cannot —" And she put forth a hand to ward off his swift advances.

Somehow the gesture brought reason to him in his madness. He stopped, catching her hand, and for a moment stood with bended head, holding it fast but tenderly.

"Ye are right, madame," he said at length. "I was the madman. 'Tis past now — the seizure. Can ye forgive me — and forget, madame?"

"Monsieur, to forgive is not hard." She smiled dazzlingly through a mist of tears. "To forget — is that so easy?"

But now he had a strong hand upon his self-control. "'Tis not the O'Rourke that will be forgetting, madame," he told her. "But Madame la Grande Duchesse de Lützelburg must forget — and well I know that! Let be! 'Tis past — past —and there's no time to be wasted, I'm thinking, if we are to outwit Georges this night."

"That — that is very true. Thank you, monsieur. You — you are — generous."

She came closer to him, her eyes upon his face. But he looked away from her, sinking his nails deep into his palms to help him remember his place, his duty. Indeed, the man was sorely tried to keep his arms from about the woman again. "Chambret!" he remembered. And that name he repeated, as though it were a talisman against a recurrence of that dear madness. "Beatrix!" he murmured, also, and grew more strong.

"Lead on, madame," he presently told her, his tone dogged.

She may have guessed from that what war waged itself in the bosom of O'Rourke. Her gaze grew very soft and tender as she regarded him. And abruptly she wheeled about upon her heel.

"Come, monsieur," she requested more calmly. "The night is young, but, as you say, there is much to be accomplished."

He followed her on into the fastnesses of the forest, where the night gathered black about them, and he could only guess his way by the glimmer of her white neckerchief flitting before him.

"Where now, madame?" he asked, after a great while; for it began to seem as though they were to walk on thus forever, and O'Rourke was growing weary.

"We are going to the hunting lodge of — of my son, the Grand Duke," she said. And her manner showed what constraint she put upon herself, told of what humiliation of spirit she was undergoing.

"And for why?" he would know.

"It is where I shall change my dress," she said. "I have the keys to the place, and to-day, when it seemed that I must go to warn you of your danger, monsieur —"

"Bless ye for that!" he interjected.

"I bethought me of the lodge. So, with two maids, I went to it by stealth. They do not know now in Lützelburg what has become of their duchess. I disguised myself — as I thought — in the peasant dress, and went alone and on foot to the inn.

"Ye knew the landlord, madame?" he asked, to take her mind from more serious matters.

"I knew him, yes," she told him, "and bribed him to let me take the place of his servant for the day. Monsieur Chambret, of course you understand, had advised me by what road you would enter Lützelburg. Now, it is to bid farewell to Delphine of the inn, monsieur, and become once more the Grand Duchess of Lützelburg."

By then they had come out into a clearing in the woodland. Before them a small building loomed dark and cheerless; not a glimmer of light showed in any of its windows. Nor was a sound to be heard in the clearing, save the soughing of the wind in the boughs overhead.

"By my orders," madame paused to explain, "there are no lights, the better to attract no comment. You will wait for me here, my friend" — she turned toward him timidly — "my dear friend, until I am ready?"

"Faith, yes, madame; what else?"

"I shall not be long," she said. Yet she hesitated at the door of the hunting lodge, smiling at O'Rourke almost apprehensively.

"You — you will not forget —" she faltered.

"Madame," he told her boldly, "I shall never forget Mam'-selle Delphine of the Inn of the Winged God; as to Madame la Grand Duchesse, I have yet to meet her."

"Ah, monsieur, but you *are* generous. Thank you, thank you."

The woman turned, lifted the knocker on the door, and let it fall thrice: presumably a signal agreed upon between her and her companions. The thunder of the metal resounded emptily through the house, but in response there was no other sound. Again she repeated the alarm, and again was doomed to disappointment.

"Why, I do not understand," she cried petulantly. "Surely they understood me; they were to wait."

The Irishman stepped to her side and tried the knob; under his hand it turned, the door opening easily inward upon its hinges. Madame stepped back with a little cry of alarm.

"I do not understand," she reiterated.

"Something frightened them, possibly," O'Rourke reassured her. "One moment. Do ye wait while I strike ye a light."

He crossed the threshold, stepping into blank darkness, and heard the voice of madame.

"The lodge is lighted by electricity," she was telling him from her stand upon the doorsill. "There is a switch on the right-hand wall, near the window."

"Where did you say?" he inquired, groping about blindly.

"I will show you, monsieur."

She came into the room confidently. "Thank goodness!" exclaimed O'Rourke gratefully, fearful for his shins.

He heard her step beside him, and the swish of her skirt as she passed. Abruptly she cried out, as though in protest: "Monsieur, what do you mean?"

At the same moment the door swung to with a thunderous crash, and a blaze of blinding light filled the interior of the hunting lodge of the Grand Duke of Lützelburg.

For the moment O'Rourke could do naught but blink confusedly, being more than half blinded by the sudden plunge from utter darkness into that electric glare.

But in those few passing seconds he thought very swiftly, and began to understand what was happening; in proof of which comprehension he stepped back, putting his shoulders to the closed door and tightening his grip upon the naked saber which he still carried.

"A trap!"

He ground the words bitterly between his teeth, looking about him dazedly, still unable to see clearly; but he heard a grim chuckle — the cold laugh of malicious satisfaction. And then, "Messieurs," said a voice that sounded reminiscently in his ears, "permit me to introduce the rat!"

O'Rourke looked directly toward the speaker; his gaze met eyes hard and without warmth — sneering eyes vitalized with hatred, small and black, set narrowly in a face pale and long — the face of Monsieur le Prince.

And as he watched, the thin lips twisted, while again the scornful laugh rang out.

"Messieurs," the prince repeated, "the rat!"

Some one laughed nervously.

O'Rourke recovered a bit of his lost composure. He addressed this new-sprung enemy. "I'm observing," he said coolly, "that here is not only the trap and the rat, but also the dog for the rat-killing — ye infamous whelp!"

He was looking into the barrel of a revolver, held in the prince's steady hand — looking, indeed, into death's very eye. And he knew it, yet turned a contemptuous shoulder

[232]

to Prince Georges, glancing around the room for others, seeking a friendly eye or a way of escepe.

The lodge — or that room of it wherein he stood — held five persons in addition to O'Rourke himself; respectively, Madame la Grande Duchesse, pale with rage, defiant of mien, helpless with the arms of Colonel Charles clipped tight about her; Chambret — at the sight of whom O'Rourke caught his breath with dismay — sitting helpless in a chair, his hands tied to the rungs thereof; Monsieur le Prince, Georges de Lützelburg, handsome and ironical of demeanor; and a fifth individual, in semi-uniform, whom O'Rourke guessed — and guessed rightly, it developed — for a surgeon of Lützelburg's army.

"Put down the saber," the Prince told him.

And O'Rourke let it fall from his hand, being in that case wherein discretion is the better part of valor. But though he was now unarmed ,the revolver continued to menace him.

"Let madame go," was the next command, directed to Colonel Charles, who promptly released the duchess.

"Messieurs," she cried, "I demand an explanation of this insolence."

Georges, from his chair, regarded her with lofty contempt. "It is strange," he mused aloud, "that a prince of Lützelburg should be addressed in such wise by a wench of the inns!"

"Ye contemptible scoundrel!" cried O'Rourke.

"Softly, monsieur, softly. I will attend to your case presently."

"At least ye will adopt a different tone to madame —" O'Rourke pursued undaunted.

"I shall order my conduct according unto my whim, monsieur. Another word out of you, and I'll settle you at once."

"Go to the devil!" cried O'Rourke defiantly, without looking again at the man. He turned to Chambret.

"A pretty mess we seem to have made of this business," said the Frenchman, interpreting his glance.

"Ye may well say that. What brought ye here, *mon ami?*"

Chambret shrugged his shoulders. "The patrol," he explained briefly. "My car broke down, and they caught up with me. What could I do?"

"True for ye there. And d'ye happen to know what's the program now?"

Chambret glanced toward madame, and shut his lips tightly. There was a moment of strained silence, which Monsieur le Prince took upon himself to break, with a sarcastical drawl addressing the woman.

"Permit me, dear sister," he said, "to offer humble apologies for my manner a moment gone; the confusion of identities, you understand — ah! And, more, dear sister, I have a favor to request of you."

She looked him coldly in the eye. "Well?" she said, paling with her disgust for the man.

"That you leave us alone for a few moments. We have business to transact with your friends. It will take but a minute, I assure you, and is a matter confidential —"

"I will not go!" she cried, grasping his meaning. "I will not go, to let you murder —"

"Ah!" he deprecated smiling. "Madame is pleased to be imaginative."

"I know you!" she told him. "I know you will stop at nothing. And I tell you I will not go!"

"And yet you will," he said with an air of finality.

"It would be best, madame — permit me to advise," O'Rourke put in deferentially. "Let me assure ye that in

[234]

this enlightened age, even a Georges de Lützelburg will not undertake a cold-blooded murder — before witnesses."

He stepped forward, opening the door against which he stood. Madame looked from his face to Chambret's, from Monsieur le Prince's back to O'Rourke's again. "I am afraid —" she faltered; then abruptly was resolved, and, holding her head high, passed out into the night.

"You will be kind enough to shoot the bolt," O'Rourke heard the voice of the prince. Unhesitatingly he complied, turning with a little sigh of relief to face whatever Fate might hold in store for him. At least the woman's eye was not to be offended by this princeling's brutality. As for himself, he, O'Rourke, could take what was to be his portion without complaining.

"And now —?" he suggested pleasantly.

"Monsieur is agreeable," commented the prince: "a becoming change. See here," he added, altering his manner, becoming exceedingly businesslike, "it is a plain proposition. The presence of yourself and of Monsieur Chambret in this duchy is distasteful to me. You seem, however, to consult your own inclinations, even at the risk of your necks. Frankly, you have annoyed me. I would have it ended once and for all. Legally, I have no right to prohibit your comings or your goings. Personally, I arrogate unto myself that right. If I request you to absent yourselves, you will courteously refuse. In such event, there is to my mind but one solution of the difficulty."

"And that is —?" inquired Chambret, suddenly brightening.

"Release monsieur," the prince commanded, and while Charles did his bidding, severing the cords which bound Chambret's hands to the chair, he pursued:

"And that is — a settlement of our differences by the sword. Candidly, messieurs, you know too much for my comfort. I would gladly be rid of you. By this method I propose to silence you forever."

"What!" cried O'Rourke. "You propose a duel?"

"What else?" Monsieur le Prince motioned toward a table which, standing near one wall of the room, bore a long, black rapier case.

"Faith, I'm agreeable," announced O'Rourke. "And you, *mon ami?*" to Chambret.

"It will be charming," returned that gentleman with a yawn. "It grows late, and I propose to sleep in a bed to-night, at the Grand Hôtel de Lützelburg. Decidedly, let us fight, and that swiftly."

"We are agreed, then, messieurs." The prince rose, went to the case, returned with four long, keen blades. One he selected and proceeded to test, bending it well-nigh double, and permitting it to spring back, shivering — a perfect rapier.

"Good!" he expressed his satisfaction, and threw the remaining three blades upon the floor, at O'Rourke's feet.

"Obviously, the Code is impossible in this emergency," he said with an assured air. "Our method of procedure will be simple indeed, but it will bear stating. Monsieur Chambret will second you, monsieur, in the first bout, Colonel Charles performing the like office for me. In the second assault, Monsieur Bosquet, surgeon of our army, will second me, Colonel Charles acting for Monsieur Chambret."

"But," objected O'Rourke, "providing that ye do not succeed in spitting me, O princeling?"

"In that case, Charles will first dispose of you, then of Monsieur Chambret. The rules hold good, either way. In any event, two of us leave the room feet first."

"I believe I can pick their names," laughed O'Rourke.

Georges glowered at him suspiciously. It may have crossed his mind that the Irishman was a man extremely con·fident for one who had, practically, one foot in the grave. But he made no reply.

Smiling his satisfaction — for indeed this was very much to his taste — O'Rourke stooped and possessed himself of a sword. He caused the yard of steel to sing through the air, bent it, threw it lightly up, and caught it by the hilt, laughing with pleasure.

Had he himself pulled the strings that were moving the puppets in this little drama, he was thinking, he could have devised no situation more thoroughly after his own heart.

Monsieur le Prince, he surmised, thought to administer to him first of all a speedy and sure *coup de grâce.* Having discovered that the Irishman was no match for him with the broadsword, doubtless the prince considered that proof of his own superiority with the rapier — a weapon naturally of a greater delicacy, requiring greater subtlety and more assured finesse in its handling than the saber.

Colonel Charles meanwhile advanced, picked up the two swords, offering one to Chambret, who accepted with a courteous bow, removing his coat and rolling up his cuffs ere putting himself on one side of the room, opposite Charles, leaving the center of the floor bare for the principals.

O'Rourke shed his jacket, bared his wrists, again seized the rapier. He brought his heels together smartly with a click, saluted gracefully, and lunged at the empty air.

Monsieur le Prince watched him with appreciation. "Very pretty," he conceded. "I am glad you have attended a fencing school, m'sieur. It is a matter for self-congratulation that I have not to slay an absolute novice."

O'Rourke affected an extreme air of surprise.

"Ye have scruples, then?" he gibed.

But already Georges' face had become masklike, expressionless — the face of a professional gambler about to fleece a dupe.

"'Twill be hard to rattle him, I'm thinking," said O'Rourke to himself. Aloud, "Since we waive code etiquette, monsieur," he announced, "I am ready."

Monsieur le Prince saluted silently, and put himself on guard simultaneously with the Irishman's guard.

Their blades slithered, clashed, striking a clear, bell-like note in the otherwise deathly silence that obtained within the lodge.

Chambret and Charles advanced cautiously from their walls, watching the crossed swords with an eternal vigilance, their own weapons alert to strike them up at the first suspicion of a foul on either side.

For a moment the two combatants remained almost motionless, endeavoring each to divine his antagonist's method, striving each to solve the secret of his opponent's maturing campaign.

Then, looking straight into the prince's eyes, "Come, come!" invited O'Rourke. "Have ye lost heart entirely, man? Don't keep me waiting all day."

Georges made no reply save by a lightning-like lunge, which O'Rourke parried imperturbably.

"Clever," he admitted cheerfully. "But too sudden, Monsieur le Prince. More carefully another time, if ye please."

Again he parried, riposting smartly; the point of his rapier rang loudly upon the guard of the prince's.

"Careful, careful," warned O'Rourke, gaining a step or two.

"Be the way," he suggested suddenly. "Faith, 'tis me-self that's growing forgetful, monsieur. Before I put ye out of your misery, tell me now, where is little Duke Jehan?"

"Be silent, dog!" snarled the prince.

"Be polite, ye scum of the earth!"

And O'Rourke, feinting, put his point within the prince's guard and ripped his shirt-sleeve to the shoulder.

"Just to show ye I could do it," he chuckled. "Another time, I'll not be so merciful. Tell me, now, where have ye put the child?"

He lunged thrice with bewildering rapidity. The prince gave way a half dozen feet of ground under the fury of the attack.

"Tell me!" thundered O'Rourke, "before I do ye a hurt, man!"

But the answer he got was a stubborn silence.

From that point he forced the fighting to the end. It was even as he had suspected: he was in no way inferior to Georges. Rather was the contrary the case, for the prince, marvelous swordsman though he was, fought by the rigid rules of a single school — the French, while O'Rourke fought with a composite knowledge, skilled in as many methods as there were flags under which he had served.

Slowly, carefully, and relentlessly he advanced, obliging Monsieur le Prince to concede foot after foot of ground. And the combat, which had begun in the center of the floor — and the room was both wide and deep — by gradual degrees was carried down its center to the wall farthest from the door.

And with every skilful thrust, he dinned into the ears of the other an insistent query:

"Where have ye put the child, monsieur?"

Presently Georges found himself fairly pinned to the wall.

He attempted an escape this way and that, to the one side or the other, but ever vainly; and ever, as he sought to make him a path with feint or thrust or tricky footwork, he found his path barred with a threatening point, like a spot of dancing fire engirdling him about.

For the Irishman seemed to wield a dozen swords, and as many menacing points enmeshed Georges de Lützelburg, denying him even hope.

O'Rourke's wrist was seemingly of steel, tempered like a fine spring; his sword gave nothing, took all ungratefully, and cried aloud for more and more of the prince's failing strength. The eye of the Irishman was clear and keen — now hard and ruthless of aspect.   And his defense was a wall impregnable.

"Tell me," he chanted monotonously, "what have ye done with the little duke?"

Slowly the prince conceded to himself defeat, and yet he sought about for a desperate expedient toward escape, be that however shameful, so long as it saved him his worthless life.

A hunted look crept into the man's eyes, and his breath came short and gaspingly, as he struggled to advance one foot, even, from the wall that so hampered him — and had his striving for his pains.

With the realization of his fate dancing before his weary eyes, yet he rallied and fought for a time insanely, sapping his vitality with useless feints and maddened lunges that came to naught but O'Rourke's furthered advantage.

And then, "It is over," he told himself.

O'Rourke's ceaseless inquiry rang in his ears like a clarion knell:

"Where is the Grand Duke of Lützelburg, dead man?"

Fencing desperately, "Will you give me my life if I tell?"

"That will I, though ye don't deserve it!"

"Hidden in my personal apartments at the castle," panted the man.

O'Rourke incautiously drew off, lowering his point a trifle. "Is that the truth?" he demanded fiercely.

"Truth, indeed," returned the duke.

At the moment a slight exclamation from Charles made the Irishman turn his head. For a passing second he was off his guard. That second Monsieur le Prince seized upon.

"The truth," he gasped, "but you'll never live to tell it!" And on the words he lunged.

Some instinct made O'Rourke jump. It saved his life. The blade passed through his sword arm cleanly, and was withdrawn. The pain of it brought a cry to his lips. "Ye contemptible coward!" he cried, turning upon the prince.

The treachery of it made his blood boil. A flush of rage colored his brain, so that he seemed to see the world darkly, through a mist of scarlet wherein only the face of his enemy was visible.

He turned upon the prince, shifting his rapier to his left hand. The very surprise of his movements proved the prince's undoing; O'Rourke's naked hand struck up his blade. He closed with Georges, his fingers clutching about the prince's throat — the fingers of the hand belonging to the wounded arm, at that. With incredible dexterity he shortened his grip of the rapier, grasping it half way down the blade, using it after the fashion of a poniard.

And what was mortal of Monsieur le Prince, Georges de Lützelburg collapsed upon the floor.

CHAPTER V

"Ye heard what he said? That the child is in his apartments in the castle?" O'Rourke asked Chambret.

The three men — Chambret, Charles, and Bosquet, the surgeon — were kneeling around the body of the prince. That man dead, his plan for the continuance of the duel was abandoned by mutual consent. Charles, for one, was ghastly, livid, plainly with neither heart nor stomach for another fight.

Chambret looked up from the face of the dying man.

"I heard," he said grimly.

O'Rourke stood above him, pulling down his cuffs composedly, and holding his coat and hat beneath his arm.

"What are ye going to do?" demanded Chambret.

"Go out for a breath of air, *mon ami*," replied the Irishman. "I'll carry the good news to madame, if ye've no objection."

"Ah, my friend, I thank you."

"Say no more about it, me boy."

He walked steadily to the door, pulled it open, after unbolting, and stepped out, closing it behind him. The duchess was instantly by his side, her hands stretched forth in an agony of supplication.

"Monsieur, monsieur!" she cried. ' You 'are not hurt?"

"Not a word for Chambret!" he thought "I must get out of this, and quickly." Aloud: "Not even scratched," he lied, to baffle commiseration, and kept his arm by his side.

Though he felt the blood trickling down within his sleeve, a hot stream, yet it was too dark for the woman to see.

"Georges is — dead," he told her, shortly; "and ye'll find your son, madame, hidden in his rooms in the castle."

"Thank God!" She was silent for a moment. "My little son!" she said softly. "Ah, monsieur, you have saved him from — who knows what? How can I show my gratitude?"

"By forgetting the O'Rourke, madame," he said almost roughly.

"What do you mean?" She caught him by the sleeve as he turned away. "You are not going, monsieur?"

"Instantly, madame."

"But why — why?"

"Madame, because me work is done here. Good night, madame."

"But, monsieur, monsieur! Ah, stay!"

He shook his arm free, with no effort to ameliorate his rudeness.

"Good night, madame," he repeated stiffly, with his heart in his throat; and was off, swinging down the forest path.

He had not taken a dozen paces, however, before she had caught up with him; and he felt her arms soft and clinging about his neck.

"Ah, monsieur, monsieur!" she cried; and her tone thrilled the ardent man through every fiber of him. "You have not deceived me as to your motive, O most gallant and loyal gentleman!"

She drew his head down, though he resisted, and kissed him once, full upon the lips. Then, wistfully, "*Au revoir, monsieur*," she said, and permitted him to leave her.

For the second time that night he dropped upon his knee

and carried her hand to his lips. When he arose, it was with an averted face; he dared not look again upon her.

"Farewell, madame," he said gently, and struck off briskly down the path. Nor did he pause to look back.

After some minutes he heard the voice of Chambret calling his name out frantically; and at that moment, discovering a by-path, O'Rourke took it, the better to elude pursuit. Presently, coming upon a purling little brook, deep in the silent, midnight heart of the forest, he sat him down upon the bank and there washed and bandaged his wound after a fashion. Then rising, he strode swiftly on, fagged with weariness and sick at his heart, but true to his code of honor; and to hold true to that, it seemed most essential that he should leave the eyes of Madame la Grand Duchesse de Lützelburg far behind him.

Late in the night he emerged from the forest and came upon a broad, inviting highroad, along which he settled down into a steady, league-consuming stride; and the continuous exercise began to send the blood tingling through his veins, making a brighter complexion for his thoughts. He kept his face towards the East — the mysterious East — and covered much ground.

It was a wonderful windy night of stars, bright, clear, bearing in upon the receptive mind of the imaginative Celt a sense of the vastness of the world. He lifted his head, sniffing eagerly at the free breezes, himself as free, and like the wind a vagrant, penniless. He was abroad in the open, foot-loose, homeless; the world lay wide before him, it seemed — the world of his choice, his birthright of the open road. And in his ears the Road was sounding its siren Call to the Wanderer.

And so he struck out, at first eastwards, but later verging

towards the south, his mind busied with thoughts of wars and rumors of wars, in the many-hued land south and east of the Mediterranean, where a free sword was respected, where honor and advancements and, above all, real fighting were to be had for the trouble of looking them up.

His thoughts reverted to Chambret and what talk had passed between the two of them, back in the Café de la Paix in Paris, bearing upon Madame la Princesse, Beatrix de Grandlieu, his heart's mistress. And because the events of the night were fresh in his memory, and because his transient weakness in the face of the charms of the Grande Duchesse had stirred the embers of his deep and abiding love for his princess, his mind dwelt upon her long and tenderly.

For a time it seemed as though she were with him in the spirit, during that long night walk, and that her lips were comforting him with words of cheer; bidding him hope and be of good heart.

And, if so, he reasoned, it must mean that he was to strike out for the East and the fortune that lay waiting for him to discover it — at the rainbow's end. So he came to a logical determination to follow its biddings, to dally no longer, to strike with all his strength for honor and fortune and the right to wed his love.

Danny, he understood, was in Alexandria. "And 'tis meself that misdoubts but that he's up to some manner of divvlemint there," considered O'Rourke. "'Tis me duty to look him up and attind to his morals. . . . I have neglicted the la-ad sadly: I have so. And sure and there's no doubt at all but that he'll be glad to see me! . . . Moreover, Alexandria's a great port. 'Twould be possible to take ship from there for almost anywhere on the face of the earth — including Egypt."

He nodded sagaciously. "Egypt!" he mused. "'Tis a fair land and troublous. I feel meself strangely drawn to Egyptland, where there is like to be much fighting. . . . Now, let us consider this proposition without prejudice. Whom would I be knowing in Egypt who'd be willing to give me a lift into the thick of a shindy?"

CHAPTER VI

THE GODDESS OF EGYPTIAN NIGHT

It was Danny who was frowning uneasily over the rather extensive consignment of wearing apparel which had just been delivered to Colonel O'Rourke upon that gentleman's order.

O'Rourke himself was standing with his hands in his pockets, indifferently whistling the while he gazed out of the window of his room in Shepheard's — a rather inferior room, giving upon the hotel's courtyard, wherein the rays of the Egyptian sun struck down like brickbats, driving all living things to shelter, with the exception of one solitary and disconsolate crane, tame and depressed, whose shadow lay like a pool of ink upon the flags.

The adventurer turned impatiently from staring at the bird, to inquire if Danny had not yet bestirred himself to finish the unpacking of the new clothes, which their owner desired to try on. The master caught the dubious smile on the man's lips, and the whistling stopped short.

Danny's uneasiness was a thing apparent, not to be overlooked — as the man had intended it should be; it was as near as he dared to an expression of disapproval of O'Rourke's judgment. For the rest, whatever his thoughts, Danny was keeping them to himself, with his tongue between his teeth — and that very prudently.

But, as for O'Rourke, a difference of opinion, even between master and man, was a thing to be settled promptly; and he went for Danny, speaking straight from the shoulder.

"For what are ye standing there grinning, like the red-headed gossoon ye are?" he cried. "What's on your mind — if ye've the impudence to boast such a thing, Danny?"

"Sure, now, sor," protested the red-headed one, "I was only thinkin' that there do be a terrible lot of thim clothes. Wouldn't they be costing a likely pot av money, now, sor?"

"True for ye, Danny; they would," complacently made answer O'Rourke, admiring in his mirror the effect of a new white pith helmet with several yards of beautiful green mosquito netting patriotically draped around and hanging down the back of it.

"That is," he amended, putting it aside in order to assume a fresh suit of immaculate white duck, "they would be expensive if me tailor's name did not happen to be O'Flaherty — a friend of me own, and, be that same token, glad of the chance to extend long credit to any son of the old country. Besides," he concluded, "what business is that of yours?"

O'Rourke sat him down on the edge of the bed and rammed his long legs into the trousers of a new suit of evening clothes; then he stood up and took joy because of their impeccable set, and the crease down the center of each leg as sharp as though it were sewn in place.

"Besides —" he added. "Hand me those suspenders, ye omadhaun, and don't stand staring as if ye never before saw dacint clothes on the back of a handsome man like meself! Besides, who's worrying about money?"

Danny hastened to disclaim any such reprehensible anxiety; but O'Rourke cut sharply into the man's excuses. "Danny," he asked severely, "now, how much was there in the treasury when we left Alexandria?"

"Wan hoondred an' foive pounds," without hesitation replied Daniel. "An' — an', askin' yer honor's pardon, sor —"

"Go on! Out with it, man!"

"How long will that be lastin', what with livin' six wakes at the foinest hotel in Cairo, yer honor, sor, an' two such batches av clothes already, sor?"

"Danny," said O'Rourke, "ye weary me inexpressibly. Give me the white trousies yonder, and likewise the old ones."

O'Rourke took his discarded trousers, ran his hand into the pockets, and produced, first a handful of gold and baser coin, which contemptuously he threw upon the bedspread, in turn exhibiting to Danny's astonished eyes an impressive roll of Bank of England notes.

"There!" complacently he exclaimed. "And what will ye find to say to that, now, I wonder?"

With his master's good humor, Danny's confidence returned; he grew emboldened, eying the money wistfully. "Not much to say," he conceded, "while ye're lookin', sor. But if yer honor will turn yer back for the laste parrt av a momint, 'tis meself that'll endeavor to hold converse wid th' roll."

"Umm," agreed O'Rourke. "I misdoubt ye've told the truth for the first time in your life, Danny."

Composedly he arrayed himself in the white duck suit, choosing and arranging his cravat with exquisite care. Presently he was satisfied. He turned and took possession of the scattered money, at the last moment flipping a sovereign to his servant.

"Take that," he said. "Be thankful, do not get immoderately drunk, and learn to trust your fortunes to the O'Rourke."

"But, sor," gasped the man, bewildered, "an' how did ye come by it all, sor, manin' no onrespect to yer honor?"

O'Rourke smiled retrospectively. "The Italian gentleman

[249]

who banks for the miniature Monte Carlo downstairs gave it to me last night," he returned, "as a tribute to me skill in picking the numbers on the wheel of fortune. He's hoping to see more of me."

"An' will ye be tryin' the roulette again, sor?"

"Divvle a bit," proclaimed O'Rourke impatiently. "Did I not tell ye to trust your fortunes with the O'Rourke, just now? Faith, for why should I be taking all this back to the man when I need it meself, ye lazy scut? Hand me me helmet; the O'Rourke is going to give the fair Cairenes a treat, Danny."

A moment later, when he stepped out upon the terrace in front of Shepheard's, his distinguished appearance caused a youthful American to point him out to his companions. "That's Donahue Pasha," he said; "the man who escaped from Omdurman —"

But O'Rourke did not hear the misstatement. He stood for a moment, casting about with his keen eyes as though for some friend in the throng about the tables. Apparently he did not find whom he sought.

"She's not here to-day," he admitted at length, reluctantly, walking to the edge of the terrace and seating himself at one of the tables overlooking the street. "Faith," he continued, with an inward grin, "if she only knew what she was missing, now —!"

He lit a cigar and sat puffing, looking out over the brilliant passing parade; as he watched, the tenor of his thoughts caused his eyes to lose their humorous light, and he began to chew nervously at the end of the cigar — in O'Rourke a sign that the man's mind was not at rest.

"Something *must* happen, before long," he was thinking. "Faith, 'tis impossible that things should go on this way, or me friend Satan will be cooking up some mischief for me idle hands — that's fair warning for ye, O'Rourke! . . . I can't," he went on, "keep hitting the wheel. 'Tis meself that has a presintiment that me luck's about to change; and, sure, I've been phenomenally fortunate these last few weeks. I can't sit forever waiting for Doone Pasha to find me a place in the Khedival army. And 'tis against nature that I should be under the fire of madame's eyes much longer without taking me fate in me hands and — raising trouble for meself.

"For the matter of that," he concluded, "'tis time I was on the wing. Me nest gets uncomfortable if I rest in it over-long. I've been here three weeks be the clock. Can I stand it much longer?"

A burst of laughter from a party at a neighboring table changed the current of his meditations.

"There's gaiety for ye!" he commented. "What does all this mean, can ye tell me? When has Shepheard's been so crowded in the middle of the hot months, as now? For why is everybody lingering in Cairo, if 'tis not for to see something drop? I wonder, now, if there's diplomatic troubles in the air? Will France and Turkey be making a little rough-house for England presently? Is that it? I've heard no word to that effect — nor to the contrary, for that matter. Is there to be a war, and *meself* not invited?"

He turned to survey the crowd with a speculative eye. But no, he concluded; it seemed no more than the usual gathering of Shepheard's guests — the ordinary aggregation of tourists, with a sprinkling of residents and native Egyptians, and a fair leavening of red-faced, pompous young sub-alterns of the Army of Occupation.

It was the fag end of an afternoon, painfully hot. Above O'Rourke's head a palm was stirring languidly in the least suspicion of a breeze that made life endurable on Shepheard's terrace. But in the street beyond only the camels seemed at ease.

At this season of the year Cairo is generally deserted by every soul who can get away — at least as far as to Alexandria, where the Mediterranean breezes are to be counted upon to temper the summer heat.

But still, the facts were undeniable; within his memory, O'Rourke had never seen the place so animated, even at the height of the winter tourist season, as now it was.

He swung around again to his cigar and his sherbet, shaking his head in wonderment. "Something's afoot," he muttered, "and the O'Rourke's an outsider!"

A bit later a carriage dashed up to the front of the hotel — a very handsome landau, evidently fresh from the afternoon parade on the Gizereh Drive.

As it stopped almost directly opposite O'Rourke, the man stiffened to a rigidity almost military — head up, shoulders back, eyes straight in front of him, and apparently seeing nothing at all. At the same time a slow flush mounted his lean, brown cheeks, till he had colored to the eyes.

"I will not look at her!" he was saying over and over to himself. "I will not look — 'tis as much as me soul is worth!"

Nevertheless, look he did — as though, in fact, his gaze was drawn whether he would or no.

A woman was alighting from the carriage — undoubtedly a very wonderful woman, worthy to rouse even the O'Rourke to an appreciation of her loveliness — O'Rourke, who had seen many beautiful women in his time, and found them all good to look upon.

She was, for one thing, exquisitely gowned, although that

was no more than in keeping with her superb grace of carriage; and though it all was forgotten when one — especially such an impressionable one as O'Rourke — looked upon her face.

She was very pale and very dark. "A goddess of Egyptian night," the Irishman had lightly termed her, at first sight. Her hair was of the blackness of jet, and of its high luster. And as for her eyes, to O'Rourke they were like nothing in the world but the soft, warm depths of the star-strewn Mediterranean — infinitely beautiful, infinitely dark, infinitely tempting. They drew his gaze as with a magnetic attraction; he looked, looked deep, and for the moment forgot — forgot Cairo, Shepheard's, Egypt — forgot even another woman beyond the seas to whom his troth was plighted, for whom he wandered in strange lands seeking his fugitive fortunes.

And then, in a moment, she was looking away, with her chin held a trifle higher, a bit more disdainfully than her wont, and, as she swept up the steps to the terrace, O'Rourke told himself that she colored faintly under her wonderful pallor — though, he admitted fairly, it might have been his own conceit that made him so fancy.

There followed her a man — a tall, clean-limbed young Egyptian, wearing the clothes of modern civilization and the inevitable tarboosh, bearing himself with some distinction of manner. But him O'Rourke honored with scarcely a glance. He was thinking only of the marvelous beauty of the woman, and, "Faith," he pondered, sighing, "there's the excuse for me, now!"

But who was she? The problem tormented the man; nor could all his inquiries about the hotel gain him an answer. Liberal bakshish distributed among the servants told him no more than already he knew — that she was accustomed to come to Shepheard's every evening, to dine there in the company of her Egyptian escort. Who either happened to be and whence they came, was a mystery apparently unsolvable.

For his own part, O'Rourke was now determined that the mystery should be probed. Hitherto he had hesitated; though always her eyes had sought his, and though always in their depth he had read something — an interest, a faint recognition — never until this day had she so compelled his gaze to hers, so given him a glimpse of her own soul through its windows.

"Sure," swore the Irishman, "'tis more than mortal man can stand — 'tis beyond endurance, beyond the limits of dacint flirtation — that look she gave me. I'll know her before another sun sets!"

To-day's was setting now; presently it would be night. O'Rourke bowed his head over his meditative cigar, deliberating ways and means to reach his end. The life on Shepheard's terrace quickened with the promise of the night's coolness; in the street the traffic moved at a more lively pace. And, presently, out of the gathering gloom, with a skirling of bagpipes and the clatter of side-arms, came marching a regiment of anomalies — kilted Scotchmen, bare knees moving to and fro in rhythmic regularity, in Egypt! — the Cameron Highlanders of the Army of Occupation.

CHAPTER VII

THE RUSS INCOGNITO

THE shadows lengthened; from the minarets of Cairo's mosques muezzins' calls to prayers rang out. O'Rourke, absorbed in musings, hardly heard them; and, indeed, so detached from his surroundings was he that a man sat himself down in the chair opposite O'Rourke's elbow and spoke twice before he roused him.

"Pardon," he said, in French; "Colonel O'Rourke, I believe?"

The Irishman came out of his abstraction with a start.

"Eh, I beg pardon?" he said. "I am Colonel O'Rourke," he admitted, after a careful scrutiny of the other's features, which were barely distinguishable in the fading light. "But monsieur has the advantage of me."

"Then, monsieur, I count myself fortunate," rejoined the stranger, with a careless laugh. "It is a brave man who gains an advantage over Colonel Terence O'Rourke."

He paused; but O'Rourke, with characteristic caution, was waiting for him to declare himself. In the meantime he continued his search of the stranger's lineaments, trying to discover therein some familiar feature. He saw a man of a distinguished type, in evening dress; with a high, pale forehead, rather narrow; eyes close set to the bridge of an aquiline nose; a pointed beard, exactly trimmed, and a mustache with upcurled tips, beneath which his lips showed rather full and red, of a cruel and sensual modeling.

"Never saw him in my life," declared O'Rourke to himself, watching the tip of the newcomer's cigarette alternately redden and pale as the man applied himself to it.

"You don't know me?" the Irishman heard him ask at last, with the same careless, self-satisfied chuckle.

"I confess —" O'Rourke bowed distantly.

"My card." He pushed a slip of pasteboard across the table; O'Rourke took it and struck a match, which he first applied to the end of his cigar ere holding the card to the light. He read, in fine script:

> "*M. Nicolas Kozakevitch,*
> "*St. Petersburg.*"

Below which, in pencil, and hastily, had been scribbled half a dozen words: "*Prince Vladislaus Viazma — incognito, if you please, mon ami.*"

"Yourself!" cried O'Rourke.

He put down the card; the man stretched forth his hand, took it up, and tore it into many infinitesimal fragments, keeping his dark eyes steadily to O'Rourke's.

"Myself," he admitted.

"But — but, Monsieur le Pri —" began O'Rourke.

"*S-sh!*"

The warning made the Irishman remember. "Oh, I beg pardon," he said, sitting back in his chair; then, "Well, I'm damned!" he announced. And, in a lower tone: "Faith, 'tis your beard, Monsieur Kozakevitch; it befooled me utterly."

"That is as it should be," returned the Russian, "when one travels incognito."

O'Rourke sucked strongly at his cigar, watching the smoke drift lazily upwards. "Ay!" he said aloud, but as though to himself; "I was sure of it; 'twas in the air, and I smelled it!"

"What, may I ask, monsieur?"

"Trouble," said the Irishman sententiously.

The Russian chuckled more grimly than before. He tossed his cigarette out into the street ere replying.

"Am I, then, a bird of ill-omen?"

"Ye are a diplomatist," returned O'Rourke cautiously.

The prince laughed again. He leaned forward, selecting another cigarette from a jeweled case. "And if so?" he asked guardedly. "And if, *mon ami*, it does mean — war?" He raised a cautioning finger. "Remember," he warned O'Rourke, "I speak in confidence."

"Surely, monsieur." The Irishman met his gaze directly until the other was fain to veil his eyes with their heavy lids.

"And if," he repeated softly, "it does mean — shall we call it a diplomatic crisis, monsieur?"

"Ye may, for all of me," permitted O'Rourke graciously. If he had any great respect for this man personally, he was not then showing it.

"Well," continued the Russian impatiently, "if this is so, what do you think?"

"*Eh-yah!*" yawned the Irishman. "I'm thinking that it all depends upon the outcome, what me opinion is to be. And now tell me, since ye are inclined to be so confidential, what is it all about?"

The prince bent his head to light his cigarette; the flame flared brightly, outlining his finely carven features; in particular, O'Rourke was impressed by the heavy brows of the man — a straight, black mark without break from temple to temple, giving to his face a somewhat sinister expression.

"Suppose," said the prince, glancing swiftly around to

reassure himself that the immediately adjacent tables were still unoccupied, and no listeners were nigh, "that two of the Powers are dissatisfied with affairs Egyptian — or, say, three?"

"Faith, 'twould not be difficult to name them."

"Yes?"

"France," said the Irishman, "Russia, Egypt. Have I guessed rightly?"

"You are very discerning, monsieur."

"Am I so? Thank ye. Let us proceed with your supposition."

"Suppose, then, that the three powers were to unite to drive the English out of Egypt. Eh? What do you think, *mon ami?*"

"Faith," laughed O'Rourke, his eyes brightening at the prospect, "I think there would be a most hell of a row — if ye desire me candid opinion."

"Yes, yes," returned the prince patiently; "but as to the outcome?"

"That is on the knees of the gods, Monsieur Nicolas Koz-and-so-forth."

"But in event of triumph for the three powers, monsieur, would it not be well with the man who fights with Egypt? In event of a new Dual Control, monsieur, would not the head of the Egyptian Army stand high in the favor of two world powers?"

"In that event — yes, 'tis likely he would. But, come, *mon ami*," — O'Rourke swung around in his chair and faced the man squarely — "ye've not told me all this without your purpose. And that is — ?"

The Russian carefully flicked the ash from the end of his cigarette. He took his time about replying; and when he did so, framed his thought in wary phrases.

"A skilful, efficient soldier is what the Khedive most needs," he announced slowly; "a man afraid of nothing — afraid not even of England — a soldier and a strategist to lead Egypt's armies to victory. Well, if His Majesty the Khedive's disinterested and loyal advisers suggest the proper man, it will be almost equivalent to an appointment."

"And —? Proceed, monsieur."

"May I venture to suggest that a certain Colonel Terence O'Rourke fills all the qualifications?"

"Ye do me great honor, monsieur."

For some minutes there was silence between the two. O'Rourke sat quietly smoking, his mind in a turmoil of thought; he saw a fair and newly prosperous country running with blood — as once India had run with blood, long years since. He saw brave men and true knifed, assassinated, stabbed in the back, that their places might be filled with others, their equals neither in morals nor in courage.

He saw — a number of things; and abruptly his mind was made up. He rose and bowed.

"It has been a very pleasant chat, monsieur," he said courteously. "Good night."

The prince got to his feet with a jerk, his eyes narrowing. "You are staying here?" he said. "Doubtless I shall have the pleasure of seeing you to-morrow."

"Unfortunately," O'Rourke told him, "I am leaving Cairo at daybreak."

He turned away, but the Russian's voice gave him pause. "I am to understand," said the prince, "that you refuse?"

"I can refuse nothing that has not been offered to me, monsieur."

"Be pleased, monsieur, to consider an offer made," suggested the diplomat silkily.

[259]

"Then, in that event," drawled O'Rourke, "and whatever it is, consider it refused, *sans* thanks, monsieur."

He started toward the hotel again; when a small, delicate yet heavy hand upon his sleeve constrained him to further attention.

"Let me suggest that you think twice."

"I have thought once, and that is sufficient." O'Rourke shook the hand from his arm roughly. "Let me tell ye, monsieur, me final word on the subject: I fight only for men who wear their shirts inside their trousers."

And still the diplomat restrained his rising anger.

"We will forget that — a childish quibble," he purred. "Think twice, monsieur, think twice! Remember, you Irish have no reason to love England."

"And damned little to fight her! We people of the Empire may have our private differences of opinion, but when it comes to outside interference, 'tis shoulder to shoulder we stand. Remember that. Remember also that, while me sword *is* for hire — and the more shame to me! — never yet has it been drawn in an evil cause. At least, it has fought for the right, Monsieur the Diplomatist. And that is the final word. I bid ye good evening."

This time there was no detaining him; the Russian recognized the fact, and had but one parting shot for O'Rourke.

"You will keep silence," he said.

O'Rourke halted and turned. "It is a matter of honor," he replied stiffly.

The prince laughed. "I did not ask, monsieur; I stated the fact — you *will* keep silence."

And O'Rourke went on to his room, pondering the hidden menace in the man's tone, and, "Danny," he told his man, "lay out me evening clothes; and, whilst I'm dining, pack our trunks. We leave for Port Said in the morning."

Danny's eyes shone with delight. "Sure, now, 'tis the good word for ears weary wid listenin'," he said; and got him to work immediately.

CHAPTER VIII

THE WORDS OF DELILAH

O'ROURKE dined alone. It was his custom, for his few friends in Cairo were, for the most part, out of town at the time. And yet, somehow, this evening he was resenting his loneliness, finding it depressive.

To his extreme disgust, too, he discovered that his interview with Prince Viazma had been of such length that, by the time he was suitably dressed for dining, his goddess of the Egyptian night had taken her departure; he was therefore deprived of what would have been some consolation to him in his gloom — the interchange of glances, stealthy and sweet, that had been theirs on other nights, lending a glamour to all the evening for O'Rourke.

He grumbled, eating slowly and considering.

"There's one thing certain," he told himself. "'Tis no place for the O'Rourke any more — Cairo. 'Tis very likely to become unhealthy to a person of me excitable disposition. I know too much, and there are entirely too many thugs in the city streets — Greeks and Armenians, for instance — that'd think of sticking a knife in me back as soon as they'd think of taking pay for the pleasure av doing it.

"Small wonder," he mused again, later, "that me friend, Doone Pasha, has been unable to get me a billet in the Khedival army! Oho! sure, 'tis like a searchlight on a dark night — this little proposal of me prince incognito. I begin to see various things. And the first and foremost av them is to stay quiet-like here in the hotel, I'm thinking, until Aurora's rosy fingers paint the dawn, and meself is on the train to Port Said. Faith, but 'tis meself that despises a Russian!"

He was, indeed, inclined to caution. If he remained at Shepheard's, without doubt he would keep himself within the bounds of safety. But if he chose to wander in the streets — well, there would undeniably be danger.

"And the worst of it is," he rebelled, "that 'tis all for a scruple. For why should I respect the man's confidence, when he forces it upon me?"

Honor is a subtle thing, of much seeming inconsistency at times; now it was keeping the man's lips sealed when he had cause to speak — grave cause, in point of fact.

But for his own skin he held such a profound respect that he found comfort in the weight of the revolver that was sagging his evening coat out of shape. There was little likelihood that he would be called upon to use it, in Shepheard's; and yet, your Russian is a strange man, with kinks in his brain that move his feet into devious ways, beyond the understanding of men who fight in the open. O'Rourke was taking no chances.

He spent the best part of the evening miserably enough; the music of the orchestra tired him; he strolled into the gaming rooms, but the rattle of coin and the whirring and the click of the roulette wheel had no fascination for the born gambler, that night; his brain teemed with other thoughts of a more absorbing interest.

Barring companionship of one of his own kind — which he craved — the next best thing seemed a solitude absolute. He paused in a doorway leading to the terrace.

Out there he might find what he desired; it was cool enough

—for the night breeze from off the desert held a nipping quality at times—to keep the tables from being crowded; at the same time, there were enough loitering guests and a sufficiency of light to insure against a stealthy attack.

O'Rourke ordered a drink and sought a secluded table, which he discovered in the shadow of a palm. Here he sat him down to soothe his soul with a smoke. Hardly had he settled comfortably, however, ere he had cause to regret his choice.

The night was yet young: as much as to say that it wanted little of midnight. But Cairo was alive; and momentarily carriages were driving up in front of the hotel, bearing returning pleasure seekers or taking guests to their homes.

From one presently alighted a man and a woman. O'Rourke, deep in thought of the Russian plot, gave them a transient inspection, noted something familiar in their aspect, and paid them no more attention until they took possession of the table immediately adjoining his own.

Thereupon, "Oh, the divvle!" exclaimed the Irishman. "Must I move to escape their infernal chatter? Faith, 'tis meself that may as well get me to bed."

He would have done wisely had he acted upon the impulse. Instead, the man lingered, reluctant to abandon his smoke; and a ray of light, sifting through the fronds of a waving palm, fell full upon the face of the woman.

The Irishman gripped the edges of his chair suddenly, feeling the blood hammering madly through his pulses. "Me goddess!" he said, under his breath. "Faith, but the beauty of her, each time, is like a blow in me face!"

For it was his divinity of the Egyptian night; and she was staring at him, frankly and without reserve, for the moment.

"Can it be that she knows me?" he asked himself. "Sure,

were she less beautiful her look would be bold, O'Rourke, me boy! Does she know who she's looking at? Dare I believe that?"

Abruptly she turned and said a low word or two to her companion. With a murmured reply, he rose — the tall Egyptian — and left her, passing on into the hotel.

"Faith," commented O'Rourke, "'twas a queer move to make." And he bent forward, feasting his eyes with her surpassing loveliness — more entrancing now than ever, when the soft, warm shadows of the night were a background to hair and eyes that seemed a part of that same night.

And suddenly it was plain to him that she was again regarding him, and again, with what he dared believe was no disfavor.

"No," he told himself stubbornly. "'Tis a fool ye are, O'Rourke, with your self-conceit! For what would she be lowering herself to speak with ye, penniless vagabond that ye are?"

And yet it was very true that she had spoken; for, upon the repetition of her address, the man could not deny the evidence of his hearing.

"Monsieur the Colonel O'Rourke, is it not?" she was saying — but rather timidly, as though she either feared the consequences of her act because of the audacity of the man, or was apprehensive of being overheard.

"Madame!" cried the Irishman rising. "Is it indeed meself that ye mean?"

He stood hesitant; truly, the man's awe of her was no pretense; O'Rourke's life — or a fair part of it — had been spent on his knees in worship of beauty such as was hers.

"If you are really Colonel O'Rourke?"

"I am that," he declared. "And at your service, madame."

She leaned easily back in her chair, but with a swift, frightened look around the terrace. It seemed that they were unremarked; the others who lingered thereabouts were preoccupied with their own affairs. And the fact encouraged her.

She faced him again, joining her hands before her on the table; and O'Rourke could see that she was trembling as with an excess of emotion — with fear, perhaps, or with some overpowering anxiety, or with a passion which he could not, in the nature of things, comprehend, but which had power to shake her like a reed in the wind.

"Monsieur —" she began again.

He approached more nearly, and bore himself with a deference which he hoped would be reassuring. "Madame," he questioned, "is there anything that I can do for ye?"

"Ah, monsieur, there is so much — if you can — if you only will!"

The hands were unclasped and extended in appeal; and they were very dainty and white, and moving with the helplessness they indicated. O'Rourke dared to catch one of them gently in his broad palm; with a quick movement he carried it to his lips, and released it.

"Monsieur!"

He was crushed by the reproach in her eyes. "But, madame," he pleaded humbly, "we are too deep in shadow to have been seen! And, sure, I couldn't help it — though, faith, ye must believe 'twas with all the respect in the world —"

She cut him short with an impatient movement. "I forgive," she told him. "I — I misunderstood. Pardon me, monsieur. But — I have so little time —"

"Then tell me quickly," he besought her, "in what I may serve ye."

"Ah, but do you mean it? I have such need of a friend, monsieur!"

"'Tis me hope, madame, that I may be made happy by being termed such."

"You don't know me, monsieur?" she doubted, with a pursing of her lips that nigh maddened the man.

For he had considered them rather in the way of perfection, as the lips of women go; and the heart of O'Rourke, though steadfast enough in the long run, was alarmingly tender towards beauty in distress. ·

"I have known ye long — in me dreams, madame."

"Ah!" she cried softly, as though his gallant words meant much to her — which, her eyes were telling him, was so. Nor was he loath to believe.

"I — I have noticed you, monsieur," she said at length, "many times. You may have guessed —"

"Faith, I laid it to me egotism, madame!"

"And all the time I was wishing that I might have a man such as you to lean upon in my trouble. Ah, monsieur! if I only had —"

"I'm here," he suggested simply.

At that moment she turned, with an apprehensive glance over her shoulder, and uttered a little cry of alarm. O'Rourke followed her gaze, and saw, stark and black in the doorway of Shepheard's, the slim figure of the returning Egyptian.

"Quick!" cried the woman. "Do not let him see —"

He lingered a perilous instant. "What am I to do?"

"Wait here, monsieur — to-night — I will let you know."

And, suddenly, O'Rourke was back in his chair, calmly enough watching the uptwisting smoke of his cigar.

[267]

For all that, the man's heart was rioting within him; her words, with their call upon his chivalric nature, her eyes, with their enchantment for his senses, the music of her voice — it was as though these had distilled into the man's veins some magic potion, filling them with a sweet madness.

"But 'tis meself that's the fool!" he repented bitterly, a second later. For madame's escort had approached, and, with a curt word to her, had offered his arm. She had taken it without reply; and now their carriage was gone into the mysterious night, leaving O'Rourke without so much as a backward glance, or a parting gesture of her free hand — leaving him half staggered by the unreality of the whole affair and more than half inclined to believe that he had dreamed it.

CHAPTER IX

THE PALACE OF DUST

SHORTLY after midnight a late moon rose behind the slim, white minarets of the Mehemet Ali Mosque, to sail peacefully over the quiet city, flooding Ismailieh's broad avenues and the tortuous byways of the native quarters with a silvery splendor that seemed well-nigh unearthly.

It grew more cool and yet more quiet. O'Rourke — stubbornly remaining in his chair on the terrace the while he wondered just precisely how many kinds of an ass he was making of himself — O'Rourke felt the chill of the desert breeze penetrating his thin evening clothes, and sent a servant for his inverness.

Danny brought it.

"Beggin' yer honor's pardon, sor," he said, "but yer honor will be comin' in 'now, will ye not?"

O'Rourke, though aware that the man was in the right, snapped at him angrily.

"Why?"

"Sure, now, sor, 'tis late, and 'tis mesilf that's bought seats on the first train for Port Said in the marnin', sor. We'll be startin' early, and 'tis yersilf that needs rest."

"Go to the divvle, Danny," said O'Rourke pleasantly, "if so be it ye do not want me to kick ye there. I may change me mind before the morning. Get out now!"

"Aw, wirra!" lamented Danny; but he wisely obeyed.

An hour dragged by with leaden feet; O'Rourke, shivering,

cursed his folly, and ordered brandy to keep his heart warm. Hardly had he swallowed it ere a shadow detached itself from the dense blackness on the farther side of the street and shambled uncertainly across to and up the terrace steps.

"Sure, 'tis a giant!" muttered O'Rourke.

It was almost that; a huge Nubian, black as a patent-leather shoe, his burly form enveloped in a Bedouin cloak. He made for O'Rourke with no hesitancy, as one who acts upon instructions to "seek out the man at such-and-such a table," and, without a word, handed him a little sealed note.

O'Rourke opened it, shifting his position to bring the sheet into the brilliant moonlight.

It was of light, flimsy paper, laden with an elusive perfume which went to O'Rourke's head — the identical indefinable fragrance that had mounted to his brain when he stooped over the hand of his Egyptian goddess.

With some difficulty, because of the uncertain light, he deciphered its few words:

"Come to me at once, *mon colonel*, if your words to me an hour gone were not mere gallantry."

It was unsigned. But O'Rourke was beyond doubting. He rose, wrapping his inverness about him and looking the Nubian over with a calculating eye.

"If ye are not trustworthy, boy," he said slowly, "I shall break your neck. Walk ahead of me — and go quickly, lest the toe of me boot assists ye."

The spherical black head seemed to split precisely in half as the man laughed silently.

"Yaas, sar," he said; and without another word turned and stalked away, O'Rourke following at his heels, his keen eyes searching every shadow that they encountered.

Their journey was long — unconscionably so, O'Rourke

complained. They walked swiftly, crossing the middle of the
Place Ezbekieh and making thereafter ever eastward, into
the narrow, crooked streets of the Arabian quarter, where the
reeking roadways, rough and ill-paved, were half white,
a-shimmer with moonlight, and half inky black in the shadow
of the overhanging upper stories of the native dwellings.

O'Rourke insisted they should keep on the lighted side —
insisted, to tell the truth, against the protests of the Nubian,
who seemed to have some strong and compelling reason for
exercising the utmost caution. And, indeed, when he announced that they were near upon the end of their journey,
the slave stopped stock-still and refused to budge another
inch unless O'Rourke would consent to creep along cautiously and as silently as possible on the shadowed side of
the way.

Reluctantly, O'Rourke agreed; it was not that he feared
the man himself, nor was he suspicious of the fellow's destination; but, if it so happened that a hired assassin from Prince
Viazma was dogging him, a path in the darkness would leave
him utterly defenseless against an attack from behind.

However, he would not have it said of O'Rourke that a
danger had ever daunted him. Too many times had he
taken his life in his hands for little or nothing, to draw back
now, at a time when, very likely, the most fearful of his dan-
gers sprang from his imagination alone.

Without argument, therefore, but with his fingers close
to the butt of his revolver, and a cautious glance now and
then over his shoulder, he followed the Nubian; in such order
they made silent progress for several minutes, eventually
turning a corner.

The black stopped, lifting a warning hand, and vanished
without a sound. O'Rourke tightened his hold upon his

revolver, half drew it from his pocket, and waited. And while waiting the man looked about him, and knew that he was, to all intents and purposes, lost; in the illuding moonlight, at least, the street in which he stood was totally unknown to him.

For some minutes he waited, with a growing impatience. The night lay about him beautiful and very quiet; far in the distance the faint jangle of some native stringed instrument stirred upon the breeze; and, farther yet, a pariah dog lifted his nose to heaven and poured out his soul's sorrow to the sympathetic moon; whereupon all his friends, neighbors, and relations in Cairo joined their wails of anguish unto his.

O'Rourke stood wrapped in the illusions of his imagination, fancying that the moon's rays, falling upon a distant wall of white, were like the glowing pallor of his goddess of the night; that the stark, black shadow of a far doorway, with a dim glimmer of reddish light from a native lamp in its center, was as the shadowed glory of madame's eyes . . .

A touch upon his arm made him wheel sharply about, alert, to find the Nubian by his side; he nerved himself against the slightest alarm and followed.

In a moment he had crossed a threshold, to stand in a room of Stygian darkness. A door was closed and bolted behind him. In another, the slave had caught him by the hand and drawn him forward — while he yielded with a strange reluctance. And in a third instant he had stumbled up a short, steep, narrow flight of stairs, passing through a second doorway; where the Nubian deserted him, stepping back and shutting the door softly.

The Irishman stood still, for a passing second somewhat confused — at a loss to imagine what would come next upon the program of this adventure that (he was thinking) might have been lifted bodily from the pages of the "Arabian Nights."

Before him there hung, swaying lightly, a curtain of thin, fine silk of a faded rose tint, faintly luminous; behind him was the door, and on either hand blank wooden walls. As he hesitated, he heard a voice, and his heart stood still — what power had a pretty woman's voice to stir the heart of this man!

"Enter, if you please, monsieur!"

He thrust the swinging drapery aside, and entered in one stride — to halt and stand, blinking, in the diffused, dim radiance of a single, shaded, hanging light.

His eyes sought the woman, but at first did not find her; and he mechanically inventoried his surroundings — obedient to the instinct that causes the adventurer to familiarize himself with the field against whatever emergency the future may bring to pass.

Apparently the apartment was one of those that had, at some former time, composed the harem in some wealthy Mohammedan prince's palace. Evidences of long neglect were crowded within its walls, however; the flimsy silken hangings that draped every inch of them were stained and frayed and torn, showing behind them glimpses of dark recesses. The mushrabeah lattice that gave upon the inner courtyard of the dwelling was fallen into decay; in one place it was quite broken away, revealing a portion of the court itself, dark, silent, patched with moonlight that fell through the trembling leaves of a giant acacia that overhung a lifeless fountain.

In the room, again, dust lay thick upon the furnishings; a tabouret that caught the Irishman's eye, because of the beauty of its inlaid design, could have been written upon with the tip of his finger; the coloring in the rug beneath his feet was half obliterated by a layer of dirt, that rose in little puffs when the man moved .

Pervading all, indeed, was that penetrating, insistent atmosphere of an abandoned dwelling, the indefinable musty, uninhabited odor that lingers within rooms that have once known, but, through the lapse of time, have well-nigh forgotten, the footsteps, the voices, the laughter and the burdens of men's lives — and women's.

And over all, too, brooded the compelling silence of dead homes — the stillness that abides in those tombs of human emotion, seeming fairly to shriek aloud its resentment of alien intrusion.

In it the sigh of the night wind through a distant window was loud and arresting; the rustle of the acacia's leaves shrilled high and clear; and to O'Rourke, upon whose optimistic, gregarious self the quietness jarred, the regular rise and fall of human respiration near to him was a distinct comfort.

He stood motionless for full a minute, from the first quite aware that the woman had secreted herself and was watching him from her retreat; he bore the scrutiny with the grace that was ever his — with an attitude of forbearing patience.

And then, as he had told himself it would befall, the draperies rustled and the woman stood before him.

Certain it is that she had never seemed so lovely to the man — even in his wildest dreams — nor so desirable; a breathing, pulsating incarnation of modern beauty in that rose-tinted boudoir of dead and forgotten loves.

She was still in her evening gown; her light cloak of black silk had slipped aside, exposing bare, gleaming arms and shoulders of a pellucid alabaster in their dark frame.

As for the eloquent face of her, it seemed more than ever

of a bewildering witchery. Her lips, half parted in her welcoming smile, flamed amazingly scarlet upon her intense pallor. And as for her eyes — even the florid Celtic imagery of O'Rourke's imagination had now no words to phrase their magnificence. He might but stand and look and rejoice in the seemingly aimless succession of events that had brought him into her presence, there to worship.

They were quite alone, he saw; his breath came hot and fast, his temples throbbed with the knowledge. He put his hand to his eyes, as if to shield them — in truth, to hide the look he knew had come into them.

"Pardon, madame," he stammered awkwardly.

She seemed puzzled. "The light, monsieur?" she asked, smiling.

"No, madame." He withdrew his hand and came a pace nearer to her; his gaze became steady, but his voice trembled. "No, madame; 'tis not the lights — not the lights, madame, that — Shall I be telling ye what it is that blinds me?"

It was impossible to misread the man's attitude. Her lashes lowered before his ardent gaze. She laughed a trifle nervously, and, "Not now, monsieur," she begged him hurriedly; "not now."

"Not now? D'ye mean that, a bit later, perhaps, ye will permit me to tell ye what is burning in me heart —"

But she checked him with an imperious gesture. "Monsieur!" she insisted, softening the rebuke with a dazzling smile. "Can you not wait?"

"Wait? Faith, not for long! 'Tis not in me to be waiting, when me —"

"This is not the time," she pronounced severely, "for — for folly, *mon colonel.* We have weightier business to pass upon."

He made a gesture expressive of his humorous resignation.

"Tell me," she continued in another tone, "were you followed?"

"To me knowledge? No, madame."

"You are not sure, then?"

"Madame, I am a soldier; a soldier is sure of nothing good until it is a proven fact. I was careful to watch, but saw not even a shadow move after us. Still —" He waved his hand with broad significance.

"Still," she amended, "one can trust for the best."

"One — or two, madame?"

She gave him a fleeting smile, then sat in silence for a space, which she terminated with a faint sigh of relief.

"Then," she remarked, as if to herself, "we dare hope that they do not know where you are."

"They —"

"Your enemies, monsieur."

"Ah, yes," said O'Rourke, scanning her face narrowly, "me enemies."

"And my friends," she added.

He opened his eyes very wide indeed. "Faith," he exclaimed, "madame, ye speak in riddles. I fail to comprehend. 'Tis meself that's the bad hand at riddles."

She did not reply directly, but contented herself with watching closely through her long and upcurled lashes the play of expression upon the Irishman's ingenuous and open features. She could have read therefrom naught in the world but bewilderment; for that was coming to be O'Rourke's sole emotion at such times as the strangeness of the affair made him forget to admire this woman.

Presently, growing restive under her long and silent critical appraisal, he took up his complaint.

"I'm fair dazed," he expostulated, with a halting laugh.
"Ye sent for me to do ye a service — and, sure now, me
heart's at your feet, madame. Say what ye wish of me, and
— 'tis done." He paused, knitting his brows over her
baffling secretiveness. Then, "I'm ready, madame," he
concluded.

"You promise largely, monsieur."

"Faith, 'tis me nature so to do. For how could I be an
Irishman were I of the breed to balk at obstacles?"

At this she laughed outright, and so sincerely that O'Rourke
was fain to join her. But, even in the height of her mirth, he
fancied he detected an undercurrent of anxiety.

Madame, he thought, seemed ever to be listening, to be
constantly upon her guard against the unforeseen, the unexpected. She seemed oppressed by a fear; and yet not to
know how to voice her apprehension to him upon whom she
had called to act as her protector.

So that her next words surprised him, though they sounded
as though she brought them out with some difficulty.

"It is very simple, monsieur," she began; and paused, as
one at loss for words.

"Simple?" he echoed.

"What I would have of you."

"Then, sure, 'tis me heart ye are thinking of," he protested.
"'Tis the simplest, most affectionate one in the world,
madame."

But she would not be turned aside from the trend of her
worriment. She cast upon him a look almost appealing in
its intensity; then hastily averted her face, arose, took a step
or two falteringly away, and finally paused with her back to
O'Rourke, her face to the lattice, looking out into the desolate court.

"It is a subject not too easy to approach," she confessed at length. "What service you may do me — it is a difficult thing to ask of you."

He marked her accent as of weariness.

"Ye have not asked it," he suggested gently. "Faith, I'm ready."

"You are a man, brave, straightforward, monsieur. I — I have a woman's love of the subtle. I — do not misunderstand my motive, I beg of you — I have coaxed you hither that you might escape a — a dreadful fate, monsieur. I — Ah! if only I knew what it were best to do!"

"Faith!" he muttered. "'Tis the O'Rourke who'd like to advise ye. But ye speak of matters quite too far removed from me knowledge."

She turned to face him abruptly, resolution large in her eyes.

"It is this, then," she said swiftly; "by chance I have learned that you are to be assassinated."

O'Rourke whistled softly.

"You will not be permitted to leave Cairo alive," she added.

O'Rourke sat down on the tabouret and eyed her with growing admiration.

"Had you remained at Shepheard's this night, monsieur, and either attempted to leave Cairo in the morning, or — or to communicate with the authorities — you would have died."

"Sure, now," O'Rourke admitted, "this is interesting. Yes."

He bent his gaze to the tip of his polished shoe, puckered his lips, whistled a little inaudible tune. The woman watched him impatiently, tapping the rug with the toe of her slipper. O'Rourke came out of his brown study with a suppressed chuckle. She started, looking her surprise.

"You laugh?" she questioned. "You do not believe me?"

"Indeed, and I do so. In fact, it but dovetails with me own suspicions. What I've been trying to figure out, madame, is how ye come to know so much. Another thing — ye did not bring me here to warn me of this; I could have taken such a warning as well at Shepheard's. . . . Well, madame?"

"No." She turned away again to the lattice; he divined that she did not wish him to read her face. "No, not alone to tell you that. I brought you here, monsieur — to save you."

"I — faith, I'm infinitely obliged, madame. But I confess that I fail to follow ye."

"In all Cairo" — her earnestness carried conviction — "you could nowhere be safe to-night save here."

"I'm not so sure of that as ye seem to be," he said to himself. "However" — aloud — "'tis very kind of ye; but why do ye take such trouble for a vagabond that's naught to ye, madame?"

"Have I said — *that*?"

Her answer was quick. But O'Rourke nodded sagaciously at her white shoulders. He was beginning to glimpse an illuminating light.

"Ye did **not**," he conceded. "For that matter, madame, ye have not told me how 'tis ye that are so authoritatively informed concerning the O'Rourke."

His tone apprised her of the fact that the blindfold had been lifted from his eyes. No longer the man was walking in darkness — as far as concerned herself, at least.

"I," she told him, "am acquainted with certain parties who — who —"

"Who are acquainted with me?"

"Yes, monsieur."

"For instance, if ye'll permit me, one Monsieur Nicolas Kozakevitch?" he suggested.

She nodded, almost timidly. O'Rourke caught her eye and grinned outright.

"That," he said, with a snap of his fingers, "for Monsieur le Prince. But, madame, as to yourself, ye are —"

"I am the daughter of Constantine Pasha," she declared outright.

"Yes," agreed O'Rourke musingly; "and the tall, brown, young man that dances attendance upon ye — he is Prince Aziz. I might have guessed it."

His mind worked rapidly. Madame of the wondrous eyes, then, was, in reality, a mademoiselle — daughter to Constantine Pasha, that wily Turkish diplomat who had been the power behind Arabi Pasha in the rebellion of '82·

Dimly he recalled having heard some boulevard rumor in Paris concering the wonderful, exotic beauty of this girl, daughter of the Turk by an Italian wife. He had heard, too, of her devotion to her father's memory, her outspoken declaration that she would carry on the work that his death had left unfinished. And he remembered having read in some newspaper a short paragraph announcing mademoiselle's betrothal to young Prince Aziz of the Khedival succession.

"Two and two," thought the Irishman, "make four. 'Tis four years since Arabi Pasha returned from exile in Ceylon. I've been told that he was living quietly here in Egypt; and 'tis surely so. A conspirator is always living quietly, for obvious reasons. Well, then, 'tis simple enough. Arabi is back; Viazma is here to represent Russia; mam'selle to honor her father's memory in oceans of English gore; Aziz playing

Abbas Himli's hand in the game; France wishing to see England turned out of control; Turkey, Russia, — Egypt herself, — quite willing — faith, here we have the ingredients of a first-class conspiracy, with the trimmings of battle, murder, and sudden death."

He smiled engagingly upon the woman. He had probed her secret; he now taxed her with his knowledge straightway.

"Ye are hand-in-glove, mam'selle, with the men who conspire against English occupation."

She mutely bowed assent; O'Rourke found it difficult to read what lay in her eyes — an art, too, wherein the man was somewhat skilled.

"Ye are with those," he went on, even a trifle bitterly, "who would raise again that old, deluding cry, 'Egypt for the Egyptians!'"

"I am!" she proclaimed passionately.

"I am not," he stated as quietly. "And ye brought me here, mam'selle. Faith, I begin to sense your motive. 'Twas not for me neck's sake ye did this. What is one man's life to ye more than another? Sure, if ye accomplish your purpose, the next Nile inundation will be out of all season, brought about by the oceans of English blood that'll sweep through the sands to swell the flood! Have ye thought on that, mam'selle? I see ye have — or believe ye have. What does a woman reck of war, and what stalks hand-in-hand with war? Faith, for ye 'tis all glitter and gold and glory — 'Egypt for the Egyptians!' (which means for the Russians and the Turkish and the French!), 'and divvle take the English!'"

He paused. The woman's eyes had widened; for the moment she was spellbound by his rude eloquence. Her breath came quickly, and she hung upon his words; though, in point of fact, the next were to sting her like the lash of a whip.

"And ye wanted O'Rourke to be with ye, to lead the massacre, whether he would or no! Faith, mam'selle, 'tis an
insult to your beauty that ye should make of it a snare for a
poor adventurer!"

She started toward him, blazing with anger; O'Rourke
sat awestruck with the flaming beauty of her. And then —
she stopped; the flush that had colored her cheeks with
shame evoked by his words ebbed, leaving her more pale,
it seemed, than before. She stood irresolute, her lips trembling.

What was she to say to him, who saw so clearly, who had
power to make her see more clearly than ever she had seen,
what the explosion would mean, once the spark touched the
powder?

What *could* she say? The phrases that she had thought
to use were become vapid, meaningless, since he had spoken
his mind — spoken it freely, boldly, forthright, like the man
he was. Her artillery was spiked, this Irishman triumphant.

He was right. She hated him for being right. She hated
him — or, did she? She had never loved; was this — the
dawn? Was this — love? Or fascination? What was
there about the man — the lean, bronzed face, the resolute
swing of his shoulders, the devil-may-care honesty of him —
that had printed his image on her mind, indelibly, it seemed,
since first she had met his look of almost boyish adoration?

But — she must not think of that. There was the Cause.
She was pledged to the Cause, whatever might befall.
And still, there was no heart in her for the alluring of
O'Rourke — the winning of him to the side of the Cause,
which she had pledged to her fellow conspirators.

What had she to say for herself?

The Palace of Dust

She looked up and deep into his face; read the trouble there, and the courage; divined how steadfast was his loyalty to his people — the English-speaking people — as well as how futile would be her most desperate blandishments directed against his simple honesty.

She put out her hands with a little, hopeless gesture — like a tired child.

"I am defeated," she admitted, smiling almost wanly. "What I have told you is true, monsieur. I learned that you were to die for Prince Vladislaus' indiscretion. He spoke more freely than he had warrant to speak. Granted, monsieur, that you pledged your word to silence. And yet —"

"A Russian judges all men by himself," laughed O'Rourke.

"Yes. So you were doomed. Yet, it was considered better that you should be won to our cause, if possible, rather than slain. I — I had marked your admiration of me, monsieur; I volunteered to — to bring you to the side of safety and of our cause. . . . Monsieur" — unconsciously she lowered her voice. O'Rourke drew nearer; he even dared possess himself of her hands, and to hold them firmly while he stood bending his head that he might catch what she was whispering.

"Monsieur," she said again; and hesitated for a long time; so long, indeed, that the silence began to seem strained and tense, and O'Rourke's ears were filled with the creak and the rustle of the stillness in this deserted palace.

"Monsieur," she whispered finally, "you have won. You are . . . right."

She lifted her eyes boldly to his; O'Rourke's breath came sharply.

"I am glad — very glad!" she declared aloud.

"Mam'selle will never regret having won me to her service," O'Rourke said clearly.

He bent and kissed her hands, while she gasped in sheer amazement.

"I am for mam'selle's cause!" he said. "The O'Rourke cannot fight against the side where his heart is, believe me!"

CHAPTER X

THE HAND

THE reason for O'Rourke's lightning change of front was not far to seek; indeed, when mam'selle raised her eyes, it was to see it and to comprehend.

While the Irishman had been standing before the woman, holding her hands and bending low his head that he might not miss one of her hardly uttered words, the stillness of the great, vacant palace struck sharply upon his sentience.

His ears were trained to a quickness; the creaking and the rustle in the adjacent rooms might well be those sounds which are never absent from an abandoned dwelling after nightfall.

But, O'Rourke, after learning that the woman was the daughter of the Turkish diplomat, Constantine Pasha, had not been slow to identify the building to which she had caused him to be led; plainly enough, it must be the former home of her late father, abandoned to decay and the dry rot of Egypt after its owner's death.

And he was by no means satisfied that, because the place was the property of mam'selle, she was alone in it, as appearances at first had seemed to indicate — that is, alone save for the Nubian slave.

He remembered having remarked the place in his wanderings about Cairo — a huge, rambling hotel of two stories, covering much ground, with the outward seeming of absolute desolation.

It came to him, then, that no fitter place in all Cairo, no

spot more secure from the surveillance of spies or the prying of eavesdroppers, could have been hit upon for a rendezvous for the conspirators than this same palace; and the fact that the woman was its owner rendered it available and doubly suitable.

Very likely, then, he deemed the possibility that there might be others — Aziz, perhaps, or even Viazma — waiting in a convenient room for the result of mam'selle's efforts for "the Cause."

So, when he caught a sound much resembling a man's footsteps in a distant room, O'Rourke did not lay it to nervous imaginings; neither did he connect them with the slave; in his own mind he felt quite assured that some one else was moving toward them.

Of one thing he could not be positive, however, and that was whether or not the sounds he heard were from an adjoining apartment or from one more distant. They were so slight that they might well be near at hand; at the same time, the contrary was possible.

It behooved him to maintain a lively watchfulness and an eye alert to see the first loophole for escape. He was very happy in the knowledge that his revolver lay snug in the pocket of his evening coat; but he dared not move his hand to it, under the circumstances. If the listener were, in fact, near enough to see, such action might prove disastrous; he might not be sure that an enemy was not at that very moment surveying him through almost any aperture in the torn and flimsy wall hangings.

Behind him was a door — a fact of which he had taken note by reason of the draft causing the portière that hid it to belly outward.

Likewise — and this proved O'Rourke's salvation — behind the woman of the night was a small glass, set into the wall: an old and tarnished mirror, which, nevertheless, had sufficient reflecting power to be of service.

Into it, then, from time to time, the man had been casting furtive glances with a care that mam'selle should not observe him.

The precaution had proven of great value; at the precise moment when the woman, herself with head lowered, had choked with tears, well-nigh, in the fulness of her emotion, O'Rourke heard a creak not thirty feet away — or so he could have sworn.

And then, while she groped in the maze of her thoughts for the words she desired, he saw the portière cautiously lifted to one side.

In the dark entry thus exposed stood the figure of a man; and that man he whom O'Rourke had most of all, just then, to fear — Prince Vladislaus Viazma.

He stood quietly regarding them, an attentive smile upon his face showing that he had not overheard what had passed between the two. There was an element of gratification in his expression that would not have been there had he dreamed that mam'selle had failed in subjugating the Irishman.

The prince was plainly prepared for such a failure, however; his arms were folded, the left above the right, and in the hollow of the left elbow rested the muzzle of a revolver, its body and the hand that held it being concealed by the folds of the sleeve.

From where the Russian stood he could, without moving, send a bullet into O'Rourke, — a tormenting contingency to the Irishman.

He — the prince — remained perfectly quiet while the woman did; but when she had ended her murmured confes-

sion with the honest assertion, "I am glad," an expression
of unholy joy had passed over the man's features. There
was, of course, but one way of interpreting the woman's
words to one who knew her heart and her purpose with
O'Rourke.

So O'Rourke had made quick use of his five wits; they had
stood him in good stead many a time in the past, nor did they
fail him now. His words were prompted by the desire to
stave off extermination until the last moment; delays would
be dangerous — to Prince Viazma.

And, somehow, the man knew that he had touched the
woman's heart, until then dormant, in this goddess of Egyptian night; he had beaten her fairly in argument; she had
acknowledged the justness of his stand, and had congratulated him on his courage in abiding by it.

He felt, intuitively — and in dealing with woman, man
must needs meet her with her own most effective weapon,
both of offense and defense, intuition — that he might throw
himself upon her generosity. Whether he had weakened
her in her devotion to the Cause or not was a matter aside
from the fact that her heart was softened toward him, that
she would aid him.

So he had declared, "I am for mam'selle's cause!" Which
was pure equivocation.

And the next instant, when he saw her look of supreme
astonishment as she raised her head and glanced over his
shoulder to the open doorway and to Monsieur the Diplomat,
he bent toward her and whispered hurriedly:

"My life is in the hollow of your palm, mam'selle. Do
with it as ye will. A word this way or that will save, or —
destroy me."

In this Viazma saw nothing but such gallantry as he knew

the man to be prone to; the effect of which was heightened by the fact that simultaneously the woman's face burned crimson.

"Poor Aziz!" thought Viazma.

And, "Monsieur O'Rourke, you make me very happy," said the woman. "I have not lived in vain, monsieur!"

The *double entente* touched the Irishman. "God bless ye!" he whispered hoarsely.

But the woman jerked away her hands quickly, as though confused.

"Monsieur le Prince!" she cried.

Viazma, assured that all was well, stepped into the room, dexterously dropping the revolver into the pocket of his dinner coat — keeping his hand upon it, however, ready to fire in event of any misunderstanding.

"Pardon," he purred, grimacing his approval; "I did not wish to intrude. Mam'selle, you have won our little bet. Colonel O'Rourke, permit me to congratulate you on your sound common sense. Believe me, sir, it is well to follow the example of Providence and fight on the side with the heaviest ordnance."

"But that," O'Rourke assured him, "is not me reason for abjuring me views of last evening, monsieur. I am, unfortunately, susceptible to the charms of the fair sex."

"There," O'Rourke muttered savagely to himself, "if that's not sufficiently crass to hoodwink ye, me diplomatist — well, I'm as big a fool as I hope ye think me."

But Viazma was already beyond suspecting. He regarded the conquest of O'Rourke as complete.

"Let us all," he suggested, "join the others and announce to hem our good fortune."

"The divvle!" thought O'Rourke dismayed. "Others! Faith, I *am* in for it!"

[289]

"If mam'selle will lead the way —" suggested the Russian. He bowed. The woman laughed lightly, and complied, sweeping out of the room.

"Monsieur le Colonel," suggested Viazma, "you will precede me. Oh, I insist. Or is it that you prefer your future title, 'O'Rourke Pasha'?"

O'Rourke gave in with what grace he could muster. "The little whelp!" he ground through his teeth — the while he smiled. "What's he afraid of, that he keeps his pistol in his fist? That I'll brain him? Faith, he may well be so!"

CHAPTER XI

THE palace of Constantine Pasha had been built with a truly Oriental eye toward the intricate and devious; to O'Rourke it seemed a maze, vast and well-nigh endless.

Following mam'selle, his goddess incarnate, and with Viazma close behind him, he passed through what seemed an interminable succession of empty, echoing rooms and long, re-sounding corridors — a honeycomb of desolation and of paled magnificence, dusty and grim; now in dense darkness, now spotted with the light of the moon, which by this time was riding high in the serene heavens.

There was little opportunity for conversation; indeed, not a word had been spoken. O'Rourke had ample food for hard thinking. What was in mam'selle's heart? What in Viazma's mind? Where were they leading him — or misleading him? What chance would he have to escape through this uncharted wilderness of rooms, should the coming events make flight advisable?

Abruptly, without warning, the woman drew aside a heavy curtain; a glare of light dazzled O'Rourke's eyes; almost blindly he strode on, into a great room, Viazma following.

As he paused, he heard the woman's voice.

"Messieurs," she announced clearly, "I bring you — victory! Messieurs, permit me to introduce to you Monsieur le Colonel O'Rourke, future Pasha of Egypt's victorious armies!"

"Is this acting?" dumbly wondered O'Rourke.

He looked around, engagingly smiling his embarrassment.

The center of the room was held by a table, spread as though for a feast; around it were ranged ten chairs — two unoccupied. Standing behind the others were eight men.

O'Rourke glanced from face to face, recognizing some, passing over others as unknown to him — seeing in all the head and forefront of the great conspiracy.

He saw Prince Aziz, tall and straight as an arrow, surveying him through keen, bead-like, black eyes.

He saw, slouching at the foot, or at the head, of the table — fat, gray; heavy of eye and heavily jowled, spineless and plump — a mass of flesh animated by notoriety: the man who had once brought disaster upon Alexandria, and death and defeat to thousands of patriotic Egyptians at Tel-el-Kebir, Ahmed Arabi Pasha.

He saw men high in the ministerial and executive councils of the land, and but two Europeans among the lot, barring himself — Viazma and a French consul-general.

As for the others, they were for the most part Egyptians, Arabs, men of Bedouin blood, with one great Greek cigarette manufacturer.

There was a murmur of complimentary applause. O'Rourke bowed. His gaze instinctively sought that of Prince Aziz, whose rival he was suddenly become; and he read therein a temperate hostility.

Arabi's eyes, too, met those of the Irishman. He nodded to him carelessly, in a negligent fashion that made O'Rourke's blood boil.

"We may welcome O'Rourke Pasha, indeed," said the intriguer. "Has he taken the oath, Monsieur le Prince?"

"Not yet," responded the Russian,

"There is yet time," said the woman. "Monsieur O'Rourke has pledged *me* his word. For the present it is sufficient."

"It is understood that he does not leave, of course, without taking the oath," Aziz insisted surlily.

"Oh, that is very true," some one agreed. "Let us return to the point at issue, messieurs."

"A place for O'Rourke Pasha," Viazma suggested.

"He is welcome to my chair, messieurs," said the woman. "I have important matters to look to, but will rejoin the council before long."

She threw O'Rourke a lightning glance; and he gathered, but with some distrust, that she was plotting an escape for him.

"But that chair is at the head of the table," interposed the Greek manufacturer, with a doubtful glance to Arabi Pasha.

"Precisely," assented O'Rourke promptly. With two steps, he advanced and took the chair in question. It was the one nearest the door. What matter if Arabi Pasha objected?

The rest were seating themselves. O'Rourke put himself into the chair weightily, his eye on the Greek merchant's greasy face.

"Where O'Rourke sits," he told him with meaning, "is the head of the table."

The remark passed unregarded, save by the Greek and Prince Viazma, who took the vacant place at O'Rourke's left. A buzz of discussion, in a babel of Arabic, Greek, and French, had started up; O'Rourke caught the name of Lord Cromer several times, but paid it little heed. He was occupied in furtively taking in the essential features of the scene. He must get away without compromising himself by an oath of allegiance to the conspiracy.

[293]

But that was not to be an easy matter, he plainly saw.

It was the last course of what had seemingly been a banquet. From the table the cloth had been removed. The majority of the conspirators were smoking. Glasses, brandy and champagne bottles ornamented the board, together with bottles of soda. What servants had attended the guests were withdrawn; at least, but two lingered in the room, and they at the farther end, behind Arabi Pasha's chair.

And that was all. The conspirators were nine to one, if O'Rourke should dare a hostile move. And should he succeed in making an escape from the apartment, he would be lost in the labyrinth that lay beyond.

Nevertheless, he evolved a scheme — desperate enough in all conscience, but offering some advantages, since escape was imperative, and he held no warrant for mam'selle's fidelity to himself.

"The fool that I was to have permitted meself to be drawn into this!" he swore inwardly.

The man at his right was absorbed in discussion; Viazma, on his left, was plying a busy champagne glass — making up for lost time. O'Rourke, for the moment, was observed of none.

It was an opportunity that might not again offer itself; it must be instantly improved, or let pass forever.

"God knows 'tis taking me life in me hands!" thought the Irishman. "But —"

He tipped back in his chair, his eyes fixed on the face of Arabi, who was leading the argument that centered about him, and carelessly crossed his arms; his hand slipped unobserved into the pocket of his dress coat, his fingers closing upon the butt of his revolver.

When he sat forward again — and, again, without attracting remark — the weapon was in his lap, firmly clutched and aimed for the heart of Viazma.

O'Rourke leaned forward and touched the Russian diplomatist on the shoulder, thus gaining his attention. The prince turned in his chair to face him; if O'Rourke had planned the maneuver, Viazma could have executed it in no more perfect accord with the Irishman's wishes.

"What is it, *mon ami?*" the Russian wished to know, pleasantly, smirking in his pointed beard.

"Viazma," said O'Rourke in a conversational undertone, "if ye say one word, upon me honor as a gintleman, I'll kill ye. Observe in me lap the revolver. Don't move, don't say a word above your usual tone."

The Russian became as pale as though already he were a dead man. At heart Viazma was a coward.

"What is it you wish?" he asked, controlling his voice only because he knew that it must be steady if he would live.

O'Rourke smiled upon him winningly, with the corner of his eye noting that the discussion was waxing fast and furious, and that they were noticed by none.

"Your revolver," he told Viazma; "ye will put your hand into your pocket, take the gun out be the muzzle, and pass it to me, butt first, under cover of the table."

Viazma laughed hollowly.

"This will cost you your life," he said, as who should say, "It is a pleasant evening, monsieur." "I can afford to humor you," he added.

"Ye can't afford to do anything else," assured him O'Rourke with force.

Again the Russian cackled feebly — acting for his life, and knowing it well. Obediently and unobtrusively his hand performed the actions dictated by the Irishman. In ten seconds the Russian's weapon lay upon O'Rourke's knee.

"And now what?" Viazma wished to know nervously.

"Sit around, face to the table. Say nothing to your friend on your left in a tone that I cannot hear. If ye do — well, a word to the Russ, me friend, should be sufficient."

Viazma slowly did as he was bid; but almost immediately afterwards the necessity of watching him was over and done with.

For out of the uproar of voices that of Prince Aziz rose dominant.

"Messieurs," he cried, standing and surveying the table, "silence, if you please." It was accorded him. "We are all agreed, I believe," he went on, "at least upon one point — the assassination of Lord Cromer is to be the signal for our uprising."

"That is so," a voice coincided.

"It remains, then, but to settle one thing — the date of the assassination. On the principle that the sooner the better, I appoint to-morrow evening, when the British representative takes his daily constitutional on the Gizereh Drive. Are we agreed?"

"We are," came from each individual sitter — save O'Rourke, upon whose silence none commented.

"I am the chosen instrument, as you all know," continued the Egyptian prince. "Messieurs, fill up your glasses. I give you a toast." He paused.

"A health," he cried, raising aloft his glass, "to the men who strike the first blows for Egypt! And — death to Lord Cromer!"

The conspirators arose, filling the room with loud manifestations of their approval.

Aziz tipped his glass to his lips. As he did so, O'Rourke, who had arisen with them, took his life in his hands and fired. The crack of the shot and the simultaneous crash of the wine-glass as it was shattered in the prince's fingers wrought an instantaneous silence where a moment before there had been loud acclamations.

In the momentary stupefaction that seized upon the conspirators, numbing them mind and body, for the instant, O'Rourke leaped to the doorway.

He held a revolver in each hand. Possibly to each of the nine about the table it seemed as though one muzzle was trained upon his head alone. They stood helpless for a space. O'Rourke, chancing to observe Arabi's face, could have laughed because of its whitish tinge.

"Ye will please not move, messieurs," he announced loudly. "I have the drop on ye all, and the man who thinks I cannot see him move will find out his mistake. Messieurs, allow me to give ye a bit of advice: Don't drink that health ye've left untasted. In the long run 'twill be the most unhealthy drink ye ever put in your bellies!"

His shoulders touched the jamb of the doorway.

"Messieurs," he said, "I wish ye the divvle of an uneasy night's rest!"

The Irishman, his eyes keenly alert, held the threshold. Once across that, it would be a flight for his life — hide and seek, he forecast it. "And 'tis the O'Rourke that'll be It, for once," he commented.

But he had reckoned without the spirit of one man — Prince Aziz, who seized upon what he thought was the Irishman's moment of relaxed vigilance.

O'Rourke, however, saw the Egyptian's hand go to his

breast pocket; he saw also the shimmer of the nickel-plated weapon as it flashed into sight.

At once, without hesitation, he shot him through the head.

"Let that warn ye!" he cried. "The man who pursues me will get the selfsame dose!"

And he was gone, with one backward jump that took him through the doorway and clear of the portière.

He faced around, dashing on to the spot where an oblong of grayish-black told him there should be a second door; he found it, gained through and collided with a man who had been running as hastily toward the banquet hall as O'Rourke was endeavoring to get away from it.

That man was the Nubian. He recoiled from O'Rourke; and the Irishman's eye, which seemed to have something of the faculty of a cat's in the dark in time of danger, caught the gleam of steel as the Nubian drew a dagger.

The inevitable followed. It seemed imperative. He pistoled the fellow ruthlessly.

The delay, infinitesimal as was the part of a second it had occupied, was more than serious. The dining hall was in chaos; the shrill, infuriated howls of the conspirators filled the building with an indescribably terrifying clamor.

O'Rourke glanced over his shoulder. The doorway was blocked with a struggling mass of men, fighting to be the first to get through and after him. He chuckled.

"Faith, so long as they keep that up," he said, "*I'm* satisfied!"

And he dashed on. The conspirators disentangled themselves and took up the chase. At first well bunched, it was no trouble at all for the Irishman to locate them, and to double away.

But, as he blundered headlong through empty suite after

suite of rooms, he became naturally confused; door after door invited him to safety, and he tore through, only to find that he was apparently no nearer the end than at first. In no place did he seem able to discover a passage or a door leading to the outer air.

Once, indeed, he dashed through an arched opening into the court. But a dark figure crouching in the shadow of the acacia fired upon him, and incontinently O'Rourke turned tail and took up the thread of his endless weaving in and out through the echoing rooms of the palace of Constantine Pasha.

The conspirators scattered; and then it was more troublesome to divine each man's whereabouts, and to avoid him. But for the circumstance that they, too, were confused and led astray by the sound of their own comrades' flying footsteps, O'Rourke might easily enough have been run to earth.

He heard, once, a shot and a reply, and smiled grimly to think that two had mistaken one another for himself. He hoped their aim had been more accurate than that of the man beneath the acacia.

But, at last, they began to close in upon him; up to a certain point he had endeavored to keep to the ground floor, knowing beyond doubt that all doors leading to the street would be found there. But gradually they forced him from one room to another, until at last he was obliged to put the butt of his weapon into the face of a too-fortunate pursuer — thereby rendering him speechless with a broken jaw — and to take a staircase to the upper story in four jumps.

And then, again, began the gradual closing-in process. Once above the ground floor O'Rourke confined his efforts to an attempt to regain the room wherein he had been received by the goddess of Eygptian night, knowing that from there led a staircase to the lower private entry, where a door would give him exit to the street.

For all he could determine to the contrary, however, that room had never existed, save in his fancy; suite after suite he tried, desperately, only to find one passage after another closed to him; until, at last, he stood cornered, choking for breath and disheartened, in an open closet.

On either side he could hear the trampling feet of the conspirators, as they searched and prodded each several recess to poke him forth from hiding. He dared not move a pace out of his refuge; and if he remained he was foredoomed to discovery.

And then — well, then there would be trouble, indeed. "A shindy," he called it, with a rousing of his blood at the thought of battle. He was, for a little space, debating the advisability of sallying out and changing rôles with his enemies, becoming the hunter instead of the hunted.

It seemed at the time quite feasible, when all else seemed hopeless. He wetted his dry lips with the tip of his tongue. "It might be done," he whispered encouragement to himself. "It might be done."

He had nine bullets left; there were eight pursuers; he dared not miss one single shot. Beyond doubt, the others were all well armed — some, doubtless, with two revolvers, even.

No; it would be madness, folly! But, then, everything he had done that night had been madness and folly; not a single action that he could recall had been of a nature that could be characterized as anything but insane.

And the chase was fearfully near at hand. He drew himself together. It was now too late to take the initiative; they were in the next room.

He poised one revolver. The first to pass across the

moonlit lattice by the door was to die. It might keep the
rest back for a little time; and — anything might happen
in a little time.

He held the gun ready — and heard, leading the others,
the rustle of the woman's skirts.

Mam'selle passed across the luminous lattice and came
straight toward him. Afterward he wondered if she had
really seen him from the first, or in some other way been
made acquainted with his hiding place.

For she passed almost directly to the recess — the sole
place in the room admitting of even a temporary concealment — put out her hand and touched his face, drew it back
without a sound, and turned her back to him.

"The next room, perhaps, messieurs!" she cried breathlessly. "Hasten! Ah, hasten!"

O'Rourke did not stir. He waited patiently — though
patience was no virtue; there was no alternative in his case.
He waited. Mam'selle had gone on with the others, yet
presently he heard — as he had known he would presently
hear — the *tap-tap* of her little slippers and the soft *frou-
frou* of her garments.

She entered through the door by which she had left,
stood for an instant looking out through the lattice, drawing her skirts tightly about her with one hand, the other
being pressed to her lips, as though she feared to give
them play for utterance. Without glancing in his direction,
she whispered hoarsely: "Monsieur!"

"Mam'selle!" he responded, advancing.

"Quick!" she cried. "The next room but one. I will
follow. They have gone through to the other wing. For
two seconds, only, we are safe."

Without demur the man obeyed.

[301]

Tiptoeing lightly, he gained the farther room that she had indicated; and she moved as lightly behind him, almost without a sound. And, then, in silence, she drew him by the hand to the rear wall, where she pushed aside some rotting draperies and disclosed the door that he had sought and, even in this very room, had missed.

In deference to her silent command, he stepped boldly down into darkness, upon a winding staircase of wrought iron; as he descended, he heard her shut the door behind them and shoot home a bolt.

Below, still mutely, she guided him through total darkness to a second door; it likewise was bolted, and the bolts had rusted into a firm resistance.

But O'Rourke's strong fingers forced them back; he found a latch, lifted it, and the door swung open, the blessed moonlight flooding the little entry.

O'Rourke drank in the good, clean air in great gulps. For the first time, the woman spoke.

"It is a secret entry," she said. "The door above is bolted, and there is no door upon this floor. You are safe to rest yourself for a moment, O *mon colonel;* but do not endanger yourself further by lingering."

Her tone was cold, her words seemed forced and stilted. And she stood in shadow, where he might not see her.

"I go," he responded softly, "in one moment. I have something to say, mam'selle."

"Say it," she said brusquely, "and go, monsieur — go!"

"Very well. I'm returning to Shepheard's. To-morrow I shall stay in me room, armed, all the day. I shall eat nothing that me body-servant does not himself prepare."

There was a pause while he hesitated.

"That were wise," the woman approved listlessly.

"In the evening," he continued, ' I shall send word of what I have to-night learned to the authorities."

She did not reply.

"I tell ye this, mam'selle, in gratitude. If it were possible for me to keep silence and retain me honor; if it were possible for me to keep silence and do me duty by me fellow men — believe me, mam'selle, I would do that. It is not possible. This monstrous crime that is here plotted must be crushed. . . . And so I give ye time, mam'selle, to get ye to safety."

"My thanks, monsieur," she returned, without emotion. Still the man lingered.

"I — I killed Prince Aziz, I fear," he said. "I could not help it. It was his life or mine."

"I fear . . . you did . . . not," she replied, faltering. "He may live . . . I am betrothed to him and — and I do not love him, monsieur!"

O'Rourke hesitated; there seemed to be nothing more to be said, and yet he felt that there was, to the contrary, much that might be said, were he but able to find the words to say it in. At length, diffidently, he put out a hand, caught the woman's, and bent to kiss it. She stood passive; her fingers rested unresisting on his broad palm. The clear moonlight fell softly upon the dazzling whiteness of her countenance; her eyes were fixed upon him steadfastly, with a regard inscrutable, profound, bewildering; even in the deep shadows that lay beneath her brows, he could see that they burned with a curious, almost an uncanny glow. He felt oddly drawn towards her, irresistibly tempted to clasp her in his arms . . . With an effort he recollected himself.

The woman saw his lips move mutely; they framed a word she did not hear, nor would have recognized had she heard. "Sure," O'Rourke comforted himself, "'tis a most potent

talisman and powerful to make me immune to strange beauties." And he repeated inwardly the syllables of the name
of her to whom he had sworn loyalty. "Beatrix! . . . Beatrix! . . . Beatrix!"

And suddenly he found himself stumbling off down the
rough-cobbled thoroughfare, his brain all a-whirl and the
heart of him like a live coal burning in his breast. After a few
yards he came to the entrance to a tortuous, reeking alleyway,
leading off towards the European quarters; and it seemed
best that he should trust himself to its dark mercies rather
than stick to the beaten ways and run the chance of being
overtaken by the conspirators. "'Tis no use," he philos-
ophized benevolently, "killing the lot of them outright. 'Tis
no butcher ye are, Terence."

In a shadow he halted, turned and looked back at the high,
blind yellow walls of the Palace Constantine — unmarred
in all their visible extent by balcony or window or other opening save that little postern door whence he had escaped.
And now even that was closed.

Dawn was breaking when he reached Shepheard's, unde-
terred. He roused Danny and stirred him to action, with
liberal profanity. "'Tis in Alexandria we must be be noon,"
he informed the bewildered red-headed one. "I'll wire
Doone Pasha of this business from there. 'Tis a sight
easier than 'twould be to keep a whole skin in Cairo! . . . A
prince of Egypt, shot down be me own hand, d'ye understand, me bye? Faith, 'twill be many a long day ere Egypt
is favored with the prisince of the O'Rourke again, let me
tell ye!"

CHAPTER XII

THE CONSUL-GENERAL

BILLY SENET's observations were always illuminating and sometimes very instructive. For instance, shortly after his installation in the Tangiers consulate, he wrote home to his sister:

This is a great place. You ought to see it. The city itself is the most beautiful spot on the footstool, I bet a red apple. It looks like a week's washing spread out to dry on a green, grassy bank — white and dazzling, you know; and it smells the worst ever; and it's as full as it can stick of the very purest, old-vatted Original Sin. It gets me, both going and coming. Tell the truth, I'd have trouble morning, noon and night, if it wasn't for a queer chap I've run across at the *Hôtel d'Angleterre*.

His name is O'Rourke — Colonel Terence O'Rourke — and he's the goods for mine. He's six foot or more of lean strength, straight as an Indian, brown as a berry, minds his own business, and, if half the yarns they spin about him are true, fears neither God, man, nor devil. I've taken the biggest kind of a shine to him, and he tolerates me, and helps me along with advice. Inasmuch as he's been all over, he's qualified to dispense the same to yours truly,

WILLIAM EVERETT SENET, C.-G.

Senet was the very latest specimen of a Consul-General sent by the United States of America to Morocco, and he was young — excessively so — for a consul-general: a well-built man, with steady, brown eyes, an open-air look, and a faith in his fellow man that had been badly shaken since his arrival at Tangiers.

For Senet was born honest — which, though he himself
had no suspicion of the fact, was the precise reason why he
had been chosen for the post he then filled. His immediate
predecessor had been a man of placid instincts, untroubled
by any manner of scruples whatsoever, and had grown rich
by selling protection papers to any one who came along with
cash-on-the-nail purchase money.

All of which, of course, had been exceedingly detrimental
to the moral tone of the United States Consular Service in
Morocco.

And so a paternal government had selected Mr. William
Everett Senet to adorn the vacant consulship at Tangiers,
and to prove to the honest Moor that there really were
honest Americans, after all.

Senet had accepted with considerable relief; he happened
to be wanting to get away from home for reasons of his very
own, and he fancied that a residence in a strange, semi-
barbaric land like Morocco would fill his life with new interests, and help him to forget certain matters which he
earnestly desired to forget.

Item: One American girl, who had married a German
title. *Item:* Her eyes, which haunted the young man. *Item:*
A nasty rumor which he had heard from some gossipy Americans returning from a residence in Berlin, and which had
been confirmed by discreetly vague paragraphs in the New
York papers. And there were other items, all disturbing.

But once in Morocco, Senet found work sufficiently en-
grossing to send him to bed at bedtime so tired that he went
promptly and sweetly to sleep and forgot to lie awake and
watch for the coming of the eyes, with their distractingly
beautiful, serious, and troubled expression that so nearly
maddened the young American.

But then, too, he found a great many things to bother him — little reminiscences of his predecessor's reign that just naturally cropped up in the day's work — and sickened Senet.

He voiced his resentment of such a state of affairs one night on the terrace of the *Hôtel d'Angleterre*, where he sat enjoying the coolness, and the view, and a Scotch whiskey-and-soda, with Colonel Terence O'Rourke.

O'Rourke himself was sojourning in Tangiers under protest, and, by that token, not enjoying his stay to any overwhelming extent. For which reason, if for no other, he had interested himself in the fledgling Consul-General, who seemed to be trying so hard to do the decent thing in a land where everybody else seemed to be striving equally as hard with a totally contrary end in view.

And the Irishman was by way of liking young Senet rather thoroughly, both because the American was distinctly likable, and because we are always inclined to like those whom it has cost us some effort to favor.

When Senet had maintained a meditative silence unbroken for several minutes, O'Rourke turned to him, grinning in friendly wise.

"What's troubling ye now?" he inquired, with emphasis on the "now." "That is," he stipulated, "if 'tis not poking the nose of me into your private affairs."

"Oh, not at all, sir," replied Senet respectfully, sitting up. "It's nothing new — same old story. About a week ago," he added with a queer little laugh, "I granted protection papers to a fellow who had a right to them — a petty leather merchant over Ceuta-way. To his infinite surprise, I wouldn't take a cent, although he assured me that it was customary, and all that.

"Now, to-day stalks into the consulate this chap's caid —

really a very impressive and distinguished-looking old Moor — and offers me one hundred pounds if I'll remove the protection. I explained that I wasn't doing business on that basis; and he gradually bid me up to five hundred pounds — finally flung out in a towering rage because I wouldn't do t'other chap dirt. Said that my predecessor would have jumped at one hundred pounds. As near as I can figure it out, the caid and the bashaw between them have a grouch against my leather merchant, and want to chuck him into prison, bastinado him, and confiscate his property. They don't dare touch him while he has my protection, and it's worth twenty-five hundred dollars to them to have it removed. I told the caid that sort of thing was what lost the other consul his job, but he didn't or couldn't understand, and was pleased to take it as a personal affront."

Again Senet laughed — compassionately and wonderingly. "Now, what are you going to do with people that behave that way?" he asked.

O'Rourke chuckled grimly. "Ye've a lot to learn, me boy," he told him; and sat quiet for a space, looking rather wistfully out to sea.

From the terrace of the *Hôtel d'Angleterre*, pretty much all Tangiers slopes down steeply to the harbor. In the moonlight the low, white houses shone brightly in a way resembling a glacier seamed with narrow purple rifts, and crevasses, and ravines — which are the streets of Tangiers.

Down on the harbor front the electric arcs were blazing fitfully; by the wharves and at anchor in the roadstead, slant lateen sails of feluccas gleamed weirdly in the moon's soft radiance, and a mail steamer just in from Gibraltar looked like some monstrous crawling white bug studded with many-colored eyes.

The Straits were very calm that night; they seemed a sheet of clear, black glass, star strewn; far out rested a blur of faintly luminous haze, behind which Gibraltar itself loomed dark and menacing. The night was bland and silky, very warm and still with a sort of a sibilant silence, disturbed only by the long soughing of the surf, or by the distant tinkling of mule bells as some belated caravan approached along the Tetuan road, or, again, by the rattle of chips and the busy *whirr* of the roulette wheels in the *salon* of the *Hôtel d'Angleterre*.

It was all very mysterious — Oriental and fascinating; and especially so to O'Rourke, who was never really content unless in a tropic land. He sat there and drank in the atmosphere with appreciation before he answered Senet. And when he did again open his lips, it was to sigh before he paraphrased himself.

"'Tis the divvle of a deal ye have to learn, lad," he said, with some envy in his tone. "One of these days ye'll wake up to the fact that ye have acquired the least suspicion of an insight into Moorish character. But 'tis a far day from this, now I'm telling ye. . . . I know ye'll not be taking this amiss, me son, but," he pronounced, authoritatively, "at present ye are as innocent as — as — well, more innocent than anything I call to mind this side of Gibraltar. Be thankful 'tis so; innocence is a gloss that too soon wears off."

Young Senet bagan to wag his head argumentatively. "Well," he began, "of course, I *know* I'm new —"

"Ye are," O'Rourke affirmed solemnly, his twinkling eyes robbing his words of all suspicion of offensiveness. "Green — that's the word. Me boy, ye're no better than a salad. 'Tis truth for ye — and all for no reason in the world but that ye're dacint and a gentleman. Now, I mean ye no harm by saying this; but what ye know about the Moors and the rest of us here in Tangiers I could put in me eye without so much as winking. '*Um-m*, now, don't be getting wrathy with me; 'tis for your own good that I'm putting ye wise. Observe."

He waved a hand gracefully toward the Rock, that seemed a low-lying, threatening thunder cloud on the horizon.

"That," he laid down the law, "is the home of the nearest respectable white man I call to mind, barring the two of us, Mr. Senet. This side of the Straits we're all tarred with the same feather, speaking generally; every last one of us is a swindler, or otherwise *déclassé*, according to the sex. 'Tis not for the beautiful climate and the outrageous smells of Tangiers that we're squatting here, but because Morocco has neglected — very thoughtfully — to make extradition treaties with other countries. So we can't be haled away to suffer for our naughtiness. Take meself, even — I'm bold enough to hold meself a little better than the general run, but I'd hate to meet up with certain persons on European soil, just now."

"I don't believe it!" cried Senet, promptly loyal to his new-found friend.

"'Tis so. Not that 'twas me own fault, I admit. I was dragged, in a way of speaking, into a little shindy in Cairo. A herd of one-horse conspirators were planning to indulge Egypt in a second edition of the Indian Mutiny, a while back. I refused to mix with them, and wan of them jumped me. 'Twas his life or mine, and — I plugged him. Misfortunately, he happened to be a prince of the Khedival household. So 'tis meself that's wanted; and 'tis here I must be waiting till I have a chance to sneak through Suez, quietlike and unbeknownst to the Cairenes that are thirsting for me blood."

Senet sat up, his face shining. "You don't mean to say,"

he cried excitedly, "that you're the man who defeated the Egyptian conspiracy"?

"The same," placidly affirmed O'Rourke.

"But England should be grateful —"

"Perhaps England is," allowed O'Rourke with caution. "But faith, Egypt is not! In Cairo or Alexandria, sure and me life would not be worth the ice in me glass here."

"I'm glad I know you, sir," said Senet warmly; adding, after a moment: "But why did you not go east, in the first place, when you had to fly?"

O'Rourke looked away — out to sea again. He answered in a tone more sober, from which the raillery was gone.

"There was a woman in the case, Senet," he explained softly. "She — well, she took passage on the Eastern-bound steamer. So, faith, the O'Rourke came west!"

He shook his head and called to the waiter to replenish their glasses. "But," he added, "I'm not the only one. Far be it from me to say wrong of any woman, Senet; but there's not one in Tangiers that I care to see ye dancing attendance upon, as ye did on that handsome Mrs. Challoner at the hop night before last. Did ye know that she's wanted in England for blackmail, lad?"

"I did not," said Senet gravely.

"'Tis true. Steer clear of them all. I mind —" He paused and ran his hand across his eyes, as though collecting his thoughts. "Ye were not down to the landing when the steamer came in, this afternoon?"

"No; I had to go over towards Ceuta, and got back just in time for dinner."

"Then ye did not see her. Faith, boy, a woman came in on that boat whose beauty would pay any man for his hereafter — as young and fresh and innocent-looking as a rosebud, Senet, and the fear of God-knows-what so tight about her heart she could scarcely breathe."

"How do you know that?" demanded Senet contentiously. "I'm not questioning your word about these others, Colonel O'Rourke, but it seems to me you're going out of your way to condemn a woman you've never laid eyes on before."

"But I have, sir," O'Rourke told him, with a tolerant chuckle. "I saw her year before last, in Berlin. Now, she's here under an alias. Does that speak well for her?"

"An assumed name?"

"Just that. She's registered —" O'Rourke broke off motioning quietly toward the piazza of the hotel, whereon a woman's figure stood clearly silhouetted against the lights of the main entrance. "If I mistake not, there she is now," he said.

Senet looked. The woman's features were indistinguishable, because of the obscurity; but there was that about her form and the carriage of her head, instinct with a supreme grace, that set the younger man's heart to going like a trip-hammer.

He put his hand across the table and clutched O'Rourke's imperatively. His glass fell over and spilled its contents unheeded.

"What name?" Senet demanded hoarsely. "Under what name did she register? And who is she?"

O'Rourke elevated his brows in surprise. "Faith, what's this?" he wondered. "She's on the register," he proceeded, watching Senet's face narrowly, "as Mrs. Ellen Dean and maid, U. S. A."

O'Rourke sat without remonstrance while the younger man's finger nails dug into his hand. "I've touched a live nerve," he commented to himself.

"But — but her title?"

"Did I mention a title, lad? 'Tis true — she owns one. She is the Countess of Seyn-Altberg."

His words fell upon unheeding ears, for the woman had taken a forward step, and now stood in the full glare of the moonlight; her head was held high, so that every perfect feature was clearly outlined in the mellow light — and the youthful consul-general needed no other identification.

He sat very still, almost holding his breath, for a little while; then, abruptly, as though he had just recollected, he took his hand from O'Rourke's and sat bolt upright, breathing hard and trembling in every muscle.

The woman turned her profile to those whom she had not noticed; she seemed to be waiting, listening as if for some dreaded footstep. Senet got to his feet, somehow, and stumbled toward her. O'Rourke heard him grind a word or two between his teeth, chokingly.

"Oh, my God!" cried Senet.

And O'Rourke, listening, nodded his head in sage sympathy. "There," he muttered to his cigar, "goes a man whose heart has been broken — and 'tis not be way of being mended, I'm thinking."

The adventurer shifted uneasily in his seat, watching the retreating form of the consul-general as he almost haltingly progressed across the lawn to the hotel steps whereon stood the Countess of Seyn-Altberg.

Senet had come up to the steps and put a hand for support on one of the newel posts ere the woman relaxed from her expectant attitude and turned toward him; so that his coming was entirely without warning, so far as she was concerned.

"Nellie!" said Senet pleadingly.

She started and seemed to shrink away from him.

[313]

Because of the stillness of the night their voices came very clearly to O'Rourke, who squirmed because he was unintentionally eavesdropping, and could see no way to withdraw without attracting attention to himself.

"Nellie!" said young Senet again; he stretched forth his arms toward her, forgetting the time and place — forgetting everything in the gladness of his heart because this woman stood before him.

The woman stepped back into the shadow; which, however, might not hide the lines that dismay and some emotion nearly akin to terror had graven upon her face. Her eyes stared at the young man as though he had been an apparition — as, indeed, each was to the other — a ghost risen out of the dead days of their youth.

And then, suddenly, and still without speaking, she came forward and clasped Senet's extended hand in both her own.

"Oh!" she cried in a tone that was half a sob. ' You—' you startled me so, Will — Mr. Senet!"

"Will," Senet insisted gravely.

"But — but," she floundered on, desperately, "it's — it's such a time since we have seen each other — isn't it, Will? You — you must come and see me, some other time. I — I shall be awfully glad, you know, to talk over the old times — the good times we used to have together, Will —"

"Nellie," interrupted the consul-general gently, "you're in some trouble, dear —"

"Bless the boy!" thought O'Rourke. "He'd have choked if he'd kept that 'dear' down another minute!"

"Oh, no — no, not at all, Will. I'm simply not very well — I'm here for my health, you know — and your appearing so suddenly startled me."

"Tell me what it is," persisted Senet, "and if I can do

[314]

anything — anything in all the world, Nellie — you know I'll do it."

"I know — I know, Will." The woman glanced around apprehensively, as though she feared a listener. O'Rourke slouched in his chair, motionless and very miserable because he couldn't get away decently.

"I know; but there is no trouble, Will — really, there isn't. You'll come to-morrow — call to-morrow afternoon, won't you, and we can have a nice, long, comfortable talk, Will?"

"Why, yes; but you're not expecting anybody now?"

"No — no — but I'm very tired, and — and I must go to bed, now. You'll come to-morrow? Yes? And you'll go now, won't you, like a dear boy?"

Senet gazed full in her face.

"I'll go — yes," he conceded, "because you want to get rid of me, Nellie. I — I haven't any right to resent it, I suppose. Good night."

He wheeled abruptly and went directly down the walk to the street, without once looking back or even casting a side-long glance at O'Rourke. The woman stood swaying for a moment, then darted into the hotel.

O'Rourke turned his eyes to the seas again; the mist was spreading, he observed — spreading and rising in silvery coils; Gibraltar was no longer visible. Only the footsteps of a man scrambing along the narrow street at the foot of the terrace broke the silence.

"There," said the Irishman to himself, "is a woman whose pardon I should ask. She is suffering, yes — but for another's sin, not her own. She's a good woman, if ever I knew one."

He swallowed the drink at his elbow. "Poor Senet!" he muttered, rising and going into the gambling *salon* of the *Hôtel d'Angleterre*.

CHAPTER XIII

THE VOICES OF THE NIGHT

THE tables were fairly well filled; the European element in Tangiers was amusing itself in the only way it knew. For there is nothing in particular to do in Tangiers, after the mail boat has come in and the home newspapers have been hungrily devoured — every blessed line of them, even to the advertisements.

There are, of course, pig-stickings and picnics; but after a while these pall upon one; and the small talk of the exiles is not exhilarating after one has learned all the noisome details that led up to this or that person's selection of Tangiers as a permanent residence.

And when one is tired, the tables are always open in the big, gilded *salon* — open and dispensing their opiate of feverish excitement that deadens one's sense of degradation and one's heartache.

O'Rourke strolled among the tables, watching the play, but without any great interest; his mind was filled with speculation about the Consul-General and the Countess of Seyn-Altberg; he was recalling the little scene out there on the piazza, and wondering what it all meant.

One thing was very evident to him, — that Senet was desperately and hopelessly in love with the Countess. But the whole affair was something of an enigma, and O'Rourke found himself vainly racking his brains to recall something that he had once heard, and forgotten, in reference to the countess — some bit of rumor, not entirely creditable to the woman's husband.

What was it? Faith, he couldn't nail it down, at all, at all; it was right there, on the tip of his tongue, so to speak, but it wouldn't form itself into coherency; something —

Impatient with himself for bothering his head over other people's business, O'Rourke sat him down in a big armchair, placed comfortably between two of the long French windows that opened out upon the piazza. He started a fresh cigar, and tried to put young Senet and his hopeless love affair out of his mind.

But he was not to be permitted to forget. For a gambling room, this *salon* was rather quiet; the patrons at the tables were mostly hardened *habitués*, who placed their stakes and accepted losses and gains with silent aplomb. Only the croaking of the croupier and the chatter of the chips sounded loudly.

So that it was an easy matter to accustom one's ears to outside noises. O'Rourke found himself attentive to the measured tread of a couple who were promenading the veranda — listening to their footsteps die out in the distance, and then gradually come to a crescendo as they approached and passed his windows.

They were a man and a woman — he knew that from the rustle of the woman's skirts and the heavy, steady tread of the man. And quite suddenly he knew the woman from her voice, when she spoke in passing.

It was the Countess of Seyn-Altberg.

And the man? O'Rourke grew impatient for their return, that he might place the fellow by his voice. When they did come back, however, he was disappointed; he did not recognize those guttural accents.

· But the words of the man startled him. They were speak-ing in German, to which O'Rourke was no stranger. And —·

"Frankly, countess," he heard the man's voice, "it is the money that is of moment with me —"

The tone was insolent to an extreme — a triumphant sneer O'Rourke analyzed it. Unconsciously he held his breath when they again approached.

This time it was the woman who was speaking.

"But you have taken everything — everything!" she was saying drearily. "I have nothing left —"

"Five thousand pounds, English — or exposure!" inter-rupted the man.

They passed and returned.

"I am tired, tired!" cried the woman passionately. "I do not care —"

"Ah, countess; but think of the shame —"

"Don't — ah, don't!" she wailed.

"This," muttered O'Rourke, "begins to smell most dam-nably like blackmail—and the dirtiest kind, at that! Faith, 'tis hardly honorable, but 'tis meself that will listen — for Senet's sake," he soothed his conscience.

Again they passed.

"That," said the man, in accents of finality, "or marriage!"

"But — but I cannot marry you, Herr Captain!"

"Captain, eh?" said O'Rourke.

"Europe need never know that your husband lives, countess."

The woman stopped, and the man halted with her O'Rourke could hear the hurried, desperate sound of her breathing. He fancied that he could see her, pale with rage and dread, as she faced the oppressor.

"I will not! I will not!" cried the woman. "You have gone too far, — too far, Herr Captain! I warn you —"

"Countess," mocked the man, "pardon — a thousand pardons!" He laughed harshly. "I give you until to-morrow evening, my countess!" he said.

"Now to interfere," thought O'Rourke.

As his shadow fell across the light oblong cast by the French window, the man turned; their eyes met.

O'Rourke knew him instantly. "Ah!" he said, bowing mockingly. "Good evening, Captain von Wever!"

The German looked him up and down, twirling his mustaches.

"Good evening," he returned curtly, with a slight inclination of his head; and showed his back to O'Rourke.

The Irishman was no wise disconcerted. He remained standing in the window, inhaling the night air. For a moment the tableau held; then the woman took the initiative.

"Then," she said with a courteous little laugh, — the perfection of dramatic art, — extending her hand, "I may drop you a line to-morrow, Captain von Wever."

The German bent low as he took his dismissal. "I shall be desolated if I do not hear from you — by evening, Mrs. Dean," he said. "Good night." And he stalked down the steps and out to the street.

As for the woman, she hurried into the hotel. O'Rourke remained where he was, simulating admiration for the beauty of the night, but, in reality, busily trying to build a working hypothesis of the case out of the fragments he had overheard.

It was, admittedly, none of his affair. But the hunted look in the woman's eyes, as she had confronted her persecutor, had gone straight to O'Rourke's heart. She was a regally beautiful woman, worthily the bearer of her title; and she was in sore distress. As to that, there could be no doubt.

That fellow — this cashiered captain of the German army

[319]

— had some strong hold upon her. O'Rourke remembered him well — remembered his dishonorable discharge, two years previous, from the German army, on secret charges. He recalled having seen the fellow in the *sok*, or slave market, at Tetuan, shortly after his arrival in Morocco, and that he had heard an unpleasant rumor concerning the man's almost inconceivable brutality to the slaves he had purchased there.

That the woman whom young, clean-minded, gentlemanly Senet adored should be in the power of such a despicable character — the thought was insupportable to O'Rourke (though, indeed, such would have been the case with any other woman).

But, again, it was none of his business. If he should attempt to stir a finger into the unsavory mess it was more than likely that he would receive a rebuff for his pains.

He turned, with a sigh of regret, and made his way to the least frequented roulette table, determined to banish the whole unpleasant affair from his mind.

It was an hour later that he looked up from his somewhat listless and abstracted attention to the vagaries of the wheel and the ivory ball, and discovered the countess standing on the threshold of the *salon*. She seemed irresolute, undecided; twice she swayed forward as if to enter, and twice drew back, hesitant. But at length she got the bit of her determination between her teeth, and plunged boldly into the room, making for that table at which O'Rourke was seated.

At first the Irishman fancied that she recognized him; but later on he understood that, had she done so, she would have avoided him — that her reason for selecting his table was that it was the least crowded of any in the *salon*.

Into a vacant chair by the center, near the wheel, she slid, and resolutely opened her pocketbook. O'Rourke watched her narrowly out of the corner of his eye. She was plainly no novice at the game; and yet she conducted herself with that cautiousness which told him that she was unaccustomed to the atmosphere.

She was, for instance, of a vacillating mind in regard to which number she first should play. When finally she decided and placed a sovereign boldly on the 25, O'Rourke hid a smile.

"Twenty-five years of age, eh?" he commented inwardly. "Faith, madam, 'tis not yourself that looks it!"

For the next few minutes he rather neglected the game, the countess absorbing his entire regard. For, by hapchance, the 25 won for her; and, as she took the thirty-five sovereigns, the woman's color deepened, her lips parted, her eyes glowed, and for the moment she looked radiantly happy.

Nevertheless, "No, madam," the O'Rourke remarked silently; "'tis not the gambling fever that brings ye here — that makes ye glad to win. 'Tis the need of money, madam; and let me advise ye, 'tis to the most unlikely place in the world ye have come for it."

The woman had repeated her stake — a sovereign on the 25. It lost. She bit her lip nervously, and glanced guiltily about her at her fellow-players to find if one observed her. None did, it seemed; even O'Rourke was at that instant apparently drunk with the intoxication of chance-worship.

At first her luck held, however; for several turns she won, until her winnings attracted the attention of the croupier. He eyed this too fortunate madam with disfavor, and thereafter his keen, hawklike eyes paid her the honor of a constant regard.

Thereafter, also, the woman lost; luck, the fickle goddess, had deserted her. She played steadily, without display of emotion other than an occasional deep intake of her breath — an astonishingly pretty and delicate woman aping the stolidity of a hardened gambler.

O'Rourke smiled and shook his head sorrowfully. "Ah, madam!" he whispered, "had I but the right to advise ye!" But he had not; therefore, he, too, scrutinized madam's play with a respectful pertinacity. She was losing without a break; O'Rourke contented himself with an occasional small bet on the color that madam's coin did not cover — and, as a rule, he won.

Strangely enough, the coincidence angered him; his face hardened, his eyes acquiring a steely glitter, and the muscles on either side of his jawbone coming out into undue prominence as he set his teeth and bided his time.

For an hour he continued this careless system; it was growing late, and the frequenters of the tables were, one by one, forsaking their places. Eventually but half a dozen remained — O'Rourke and the countess having their table entirely to themselves.

The woman was still consistently losing. She had gone quite pale — almost haggard. Her lips, that had been full and red, had become a firm, set line, well-nigh white; her eyes were filled with anxiety; and the short, sharp gasps with which she bade farewell to hope, as each coin was ruthlessly gathered in by the croupier's rake, showed how hard she was taking her ill fortune.

At length the end was very near; for the tenth time, perhaps, she had reopened her pocketbook; and by now its once plump sides were limp and flabby. Her slender, tapering fingers trembled nervously as she felt in the bare depths of the receptacle — searched tremulously, and found little.

She produced a solitary sovereign; intuitively, as well as

by process of deduction, O'Rourke knew it to be her last. She had staked all — lost all. A wave of pity and compassion swept upon the man as he noted the nervous agitation of her hand, the dryness of her lips, the agony of suspense with which she awaited the verdict of the wheel. It was the last chance; should she win, it would mean a respite, a breathing space with the possibility of further winnings; it would mean that she might possibly recoup.

At least, thought the sympathetic Celt, it would mean that to her. As for himself, the world-worn and worldly wise, he thought he knew exceedingly well how matters were to turn out.

The countess had staked upon the 25 again — at the last as well as at first. She bent forward eagerly, perhaps breathing a little prayer as the croupier twirled the wheel and set the little pellet of fate whirling in its race.

As for the croupier — a faded Frenchman, on whose weary, seamed physiognomy was written large the history of dissipated days — he glanced at the clock, and delicately concealed a yawn with his white, elegant fingers. Then, as the wheel began to slacken in its revolutions, he made a careful mental note of madam's stake.

It was late — very. *Monsieur le croupier* was weary and quite agreeable that the play should have an early end. If madam lost, there would remain only the Irishman. And the tables are not kept open for one lone player.

The wheel gradually stopped; for an instant the ball was sliding smoothly in its ebony run; another, and it rattled madly over the compartments.

The countess's eyes refused to leave the ivory arbiter of her fate; she hung upon its maneuvers, fascinated. To all appearances O'Rourke was in like suspense; yet the Irishman's swift glance did not fail to record the fact that one of the croupier's hands had sunk beneath the level of the table.

Abruptly the ball hesitated; it seemed about to fall into the 25. Indeed, for the fraction of an instant it was in that compartment; and then it recoiled, slid gracefully out in a slight arc, and settled in the double zero.

Impassively the croupier took up his rake, announcing the result with merciless clearness. He glanced at the two stakes — madam's on the 25, black; O'Rourke's modest bet upon the red — and reached forth with the rake like a hungry, clutching claw.

Madame sank back with a half-suppressed cry.

O'Rourke put out his hand, and deflected the rake. "One moment," he said calmly.

"Monsieur!" expostulated the scandalized croupier.

"Oh, come now!" remonstrated O'Rourke pleasantly. "Ye're not meaning to do anything like *that*, now, are ye?"

"What does m'sieur mean?"

"M'sieur means," mimicked O'Rourke, still good-naturedly, "that ye're a trifle barefaced in your swindling, me lad. Steady, now! Don't shout! Ye'll only attract undesirable notoriety."

The croupier paused, his mouth open, his eyes glaring undying hate into O'Rourke's. The Irishman dropped his hand nonchalantly into the side pocket of his coat, and turned to the woman — but without taking his gaze from the gambler.

"One moment, if ye please, madam," he begged her, as, frightened and apprehensive, she was about to rise and take her leave. "There has been a trifle of a mistake here. This gentleman is about to make amends."

From the gentleman's expression, one would have said,

rather, that he contemplated springing at O'Rourke's throat. Doubtless, in point of fact, nothing kept him from such an assault but that hand which remained negligently concealed in the coat pocket.

O'Rourke followed his glance, and nodded meaningly. "I should not hesitate," he assured the fellow, twisting the revolver upward so that its muzzle showed sharply through the cloth. "Be very careful that I do not forget meself."

The croupier's voice rattled huskily in his throat. "What does m'sieur mean?" he would know. "I do not understand —"

"Oh, yes, ye do!" contradicted O'Rourke. "But, as for that, I mean this."

He bent forward, very quickly, and seized the wheel by the cross, attempting to lift it; and it failed to budge to his strength.

"Ye see, madam," explained O'Rourke, "the wheel is fixed — likewise the game. Monsieur has cheated ye shamelessly. He will make restitution."

He nodded brusquely to the man. "Quick, monsieur," he warned him, sharply. "Repay madam what she has lost or — do ye wish all Tangiers to know your methods?"

So far the altercation had been conducted in tones discreetly modulated; the others in the *salon* were unaware that aught was amiss. The croupier assured himself of this fact with a hasty glance. Then —

"You will not tell, m'sieur?" he pleaded.

"Not if ye repay madam's wagers, and that quickly."

"Nor madame?"

She shook her head in negation; not a word had she uttered from first to last of the little scene. Only her gaze, at first bewildered, then with dawning understanding, and later instinct with the light of gratitude, had searched O'Rourke's face.

"Very well, m'sieur," submitted the croupier meekly. "How much, madame?"

She stated the amount in a small, tremulous voice: "One hundred pounds." And, counting out the notes with care, the man handed them over.

"And now, madam," suggested O'Rourke, "if ye will be kind enough to leave us, I have a word or two to whisper in this gentleman's ear."

She rose. "I — I — " she faltered, at a loss for fitting phrases wherein to frame her gratitude.

"Later, if ye insist, madam," said O'Rourke. "'Tis but the bit of a minute."

She bowed slightly, and swept out of the *salon*. O'Rourke wheeled about, his eyes blazing, his anger at last out of leash.

"One word of this, ye scut!" he snapped, "and ye'll regret it to your dying day! Do ye understand me clearly?"

The man backed hastily away. "Yes, yes, m'sieur!" he implored. "I — I shall be discreet."

"See that ye are. And — mark me words! — if an attempt is made to do me an injury while I am in 'Tangiers, your life shall be the forfeit. Don't forget that!"

Contemptuously he turned his back and left the room. In the hall he found the woman waiting for him, and forestalled her protestations.

"'Tis nothing!" he told her lightly. "Madam, I beg of ye! The thanks are due from me; 'tis meself that has been waiting for that opportunity for several days. And will ye permit me to give ye a word of counsel? Then, don't ye risk another sou in Tangiers; there's not a table in the place that is run on the level."

"But, sir," she insisted, "I must, must thank you. You — you cannot know what service you have done me! I —"

"Faith, madam, and I'd do the double of it in the twinkling of an eye if ye would do me the honor of asking me. 'Tis only to ask me, to tell me in what manner I may serve ye — and, I promise ye, 'twill be done!"

His offer was not made lightly, but in all earnestness; his tone was weighty with a meaning that brought home to the woman how greatly she stood in need of one who could do that which the Irishman boasted his ability to accomplish. She stepped back a pace, a flutter of hope in her eyes, a tremor shaking her. For a passing instant she even contemplated taking advantage of his offer. Perhaps she had a glorious glimpse of a vista of unharassed days stretching before her — of peace and quiet, and the liberty to live out her own life as she willed.

He bulked so big, so masterful, this Irishman who seemed to mean every word that he uttered; his bearing was so assured, his control of himself, as well as of others, so indisputable, that it seemed feasible for her to confide in him, to trust in him to rid her of the abiding horror of her days.

His silent sympathy, so evident, tempted her mightily; and yet she paused to think — when, all at once, hope was crushed, blotted out, buried in the depths of her heart.

The man was an utter stranger to her. She did not even know his name; what right had she to give into his hands the weapon which von Wever held threateningly over her poor, distraught head — to confide in this stranger, when she dared not even breathe her secret to Senet, who, she knew, would give his life for her?

"No," she gasped, stepped back from him, as though the man personified the most alluring temptation of which her mind could conceive; "no, no, sir — I — I — you are very kind, indeed — but — I am so excited, nervous — you see — I will be able to thank you properly to-morrow."

He bowed gravely; she recovered her control sufficiently to smile ravishingly upon the Irishman; and then, "Good night, monsieur," she told him, and was gone — all but stumbling in her haste to be up the staircase, to be alone in the seclusion of her room and free to lie awake, to plot, to plan, to scheme her endless futile schemes to rid herself of her crushing incubus.

O'Rourke, when she was out of sight, shrugged his shoulders with a whimsical smile. "'Tis yourself that would be the squire of dames, is it, O'Rourke?" he said. "Faith, but it seems that ye will not. Let us go out and think about this thing — for, if ever a woman stood in need of a man's strong arm, a man's honest generosity, 'tis this countess, and upon this very night — I'm thinking."

He wandered abstractedly out upon the veranda. "Seyn-Altberg, Seyn-Altberg!" he prodded his memory. "Now, what is it that I misremember? And what is the rôle of Herr Captain von Wever in this little drama? Let me think. What's that, eh?" He gazed up into the cloudless Mediterranean sky, brilliant with an infinity of stars that paled before the serenity of the high-sailing moon. Von Wever's words came back to him like an echo:

"Europe need never know your husband lives, countess!"

"And," added O'Rourke seriously, "'tis true that I have no overpowering love for this von Wever in me heart! Faith, *now* I begin to see a light!"

CHAPTER XIV

THE CAPTAIN OF VILLAINY

DANNY, the careworn, the solicitous of his master's fortunes — he of the brilliant head of hair — who slumbered
peacefully on the foot of O'Rourke's bed, was roused by the
application of the toe of O'Rourke's boot.

He looked up, yawning and digging clenched fists into his
sleep-laden eyes. O'Rourke stood over him, ejecting the
cartridges from the cylinder of his revolver and reloading the
weapon with a scrupulous care.

Without even a sidelong glance at his body servant, the
Irishman absentmindedly, carelessly, kicked him a second
time. "Get up, ye lazy gossoon!" he murmured softly.
"Who d'ye think ye are, to be wallowing there and making
the night hideous with the snoring of ye? Get up — and
that at once, Danny!"

Grumbling a remonstrance, Danny got to his feet and
stretched himself; he looked at the clock. "Three, is it?"
he cried. "Sure, now, sor, 'tis yersilf that's the late one to
bed! Sit down, sor, and I'll be taking aff the boots av ye."

"Ye'll be doing naught of the sort, Danny," remarked
O'Rourke pleasantly. "'Tis yourself, on the contrary,
who'll be putting a hat over that fiery crop of ye, and coming
along with me."

"Sure, now, sor, 'tis yer honor's joking," expostulated
Danny.

"Um-m," agreed O'Rourke. "But 'tis not the time for

the laugh yet, Danny. Ye stick that other gun in your pocket, now. Is it loaded? Good! And remember that the O'Rourke is a great man, and ye have only to stick by him, and your fortune's as good as made."

He twirled the cylinder; it worked smoothly, easily. "Is it not so?" asked O'Rourke.

Danny dodged a third well-aimed kick. "Sure, an' 'tis the living truth!" he hastened to agree. "Phwat is yer honor going to do, if I may make so bold as to ask?"

"Faith, Danny, I'm going to solve a puzzle. Come on with ye, now, and no hanging back at all, as ye value your peace of mind, Danny."

Quickly and quietly they left O'Rourke's apartments and the grounds of the *Hôtel d'Angleterre;* in two minutes they were in the street, climbing up the hillside toward the dazzling white citadel that crowns Tangiers.

As they proceeded, O'Rourke enlivened the tedium of a walk at an hour so unholy with a running fire of comment and instruction.

"There will be two ways of solving a puzzle, Danny," he said. "One is to take hold of the clue the maker of it puts in your hand, and run around like a chicken with its head off, wondering what 'tis all about. The other and most approved method is to get right at the black heart of the mystery and butt your way out to daylight. Ye follow me?"

"Yis, sor," assented Danny, gaping at the O'Rourke's display of erudition.

"I misdoubt that ye are lying, Danny. At the same time, it is indisputable that a gun in the hand is worth two in the *Hôtel d'Angleterre.* And 'tis a long worm that has no turning. I'm convinced that the Herr Captain von Wever has reached the end of his rope. Do ye not hold with me there,

Danny? Sure ye do. If ye stumble again and yelp I'll break the thick head of ye. Now listen to what I'm expounding. Ye see this letter?" He displayed an old envelope which he had taken from his pocket. "Ye do? 'Tis the penetrating mind ye have, Danny. Take it in your hand. Ye observe 'tis addressed to me. No matter.

"Presently we'll be standing in front of the house of Captain von Wever — a God-forsaken Dutchman, Danny. I will knock at the door, and stay in the shadow of it. Ye will stand in the street, and when the Herr Captain puts his head out of the window, Danny, ye'll tell him ye are a boy from the *Hôtel d'Angleterre* with a note for him from a lady. When he comes down to open the door, I'll attend to the captain, Daniel."

"And phwat will I do then, sor?"

"Ye will trot yer damnedest to Mr. Senet's residence, Danny — 'tis but the bit of a walk from here — tell Mr. Senet what I have done and where to find me, and that he's to come to me."

"And if he says 'Why?' sor?"

"Tell the man that 'tis in the name of the Countess of Seyn-Altberg. I'm convinced that will fetch him, hotfoot."

By then the two had gained the crown of the hill and passed on out into the suburbs of Tangiers. Presently they halted before a detached residence that lay dark and silent in the moonlight — a building of the old Mooresque type, with a high, blank wall fronting upon the street and broken only by an overhanging latticed balcony on the second story and by the main doorway.

This was a low, arched postern, deep set in the stone walls. Without further words O'Rourke motioned his man to the center of the street, where the moon glare showed him clearly while O'Rourke flattened himself in the embrasure of the doorway.

He hammered a thunderous alarm upon the panels; at first getting no response. But, as he continued to bruise his knuckles upon the hard wood, a stir was audible within, and a moment later a harsh, angry voice could be heard from the balcony.

"What the devil is this?" stormed Captain von Wever. "What the devil do you want — you out there in the moonlight?"

"Will that be Captain von Wever?" Danny pretended to consult the address on the envelope.

"I am Captain von Wever. Well?" angrily demanded the German.

"'Tis a note that I have, sor, from a lady at the hotel, sor. She said ye must have ut at once, sor, and gave me a dollar for the bringin' of ut."

"Good boy!" commended O'Rourke in an undertone.

There was moment's pause; and then the German laughed — laughed exultantly. "So soon!" he cried. "Very well — I'll come down and get it, boy."

He retired from the lattice, still chuckling. O'Rourke ground his teeth with resentment; under the circumstances, it seemed a particularly nasty laugh.

"'Twill be from the other side of your mouth that ye'll be laughing next, Herr Captain!" he threatened.

He waved a hand to Danny. "Be off!" he whispered, and his body-servant stole silently away toward the city.

There was a rattle of chain bolts within, and the rasping squeak of a rusty lock. O'Rourke put his shoulder to the door, on the side of the lock, and as the German turned the handle, pushed with all his strength, driving it inward with

[332]

a crash. In an instant he had stepped within, closed and locked the door behind him.

"'Tis a fine morning, Captain von Wéver," he remarked briskly. "The top of it to ye, sir."

The surprise was a complete success. The German stood stolidly staring at O'Rourke, to all appearances absolutely benumbed with astonishment. His small, round eyes were open to their fullest extent, giving his heavy-jowled face, with its bristling mustache, an expression of childish stupidity.

He stood in his pajamas, his toes thrust into loose, heelless slippers. Through the folds of the night garments his heavily builded figure shaped impressively — well set up and soldierly. In one hand he held a candle, whose flame flickered and smoked in the draft.

For a moment he maintained this attitude of bewilderment; and then rage began to gather at the back of his eyes. His thick lips settled into a cruel line, as he placed the candle on a convenient little table and stepped forward.

"What does this mean, sir?" he shouted furiously. "By what right —"

"Softly, softly," O'Rourke deprecated. "Don't ye attempt to strike me, sir, or, be the Eternal, I'll knock ye to the end of the passage! Besides," he added, seeing that the fellow was unawed by his threat, "I've a gun in me pocket. Is it that ye're wanting me to stick it under the pink nose of ye?"

Von Wever restrained himself. He eyed the Irishman as though now, for the first time, he was recognizing him. "O'Rourke," he said slowly, "are you going to this insolent intrusion explain?"

"All in me own good time," the Irishman airily assured him. "'Tis the bit of a confabulation I'd be having with ye. I take it ye have a convenient room where we can sit down and discuss things at ease?"

"Yes," grunted the German. "But —-"

"Then suppose we go there, and ye'll not be catching your death of cold standing here in your nighties."

With an inarticulate growl, von Wever wheeled about and pushed aside a portière. "I've no doubt you will some explanation make," he said surlily. "Enter, if you please."

"Oh, after yourself, sir!" protested O'Rourke with exaggerated courtesy. "And — light a lamp before ye sit down, captain, dear."

Again the mystified German obeyed, O'Rourke remaining on guard at the entrance, while the captain's slippered feet paddled around into the darkness of the apartment. A match was struck, and a hanging lamp of Moorish design ignited. O'Rourke removed his hand from the butt of his weapon, and entered.

The room was the reception room of the house, as was evident from its furnishings. A smell of stale tobacco smoke pervaded it, and on a little stand by a divan were bottles and glasses.

Von Wever sulkily threw himself on the divan, motioned O'Rourke to an armchair, and, with another wave of his hand, signified that the whiskey was at his unwelcome guest's disposal.

"Thank ye," said O'Rourke drily. "I'm not drinking this night."

Von Wever was; he poured himself a stiff dose and downed it, then looked expectantly at the Irishman. "Well?" he said.

"'Tis to refresh me memory that I'm knocking ye up at this early hour," O'Rourke began. "Ye'll pardon me, I'm sure, when I state me case."

"I'm waiting," growled von Wever non-committally.

"I suspected as much. To get on: 'Twas the matter of two years ago, I believe, Herr Captain, that ye came to Tangiers?"

"What business is that of yours?"

"'Tis coming to that I am. Yes or no?"

"Well,—yes."

"D'ye happen to call to mind visiting the slave market at Tetuan shortly after setting up this pretty little home, captain, dear?"

"What's that to you?"

"I was there — that's all. I seem to remember observing ye, while ye purchased a naygur or two — a likely-looking girl from the Soudan, was it not? And a light man into the bargain?"

Von Wever sat up, his little eyes glinting vindictively.

"If you think for an instant that I'm going to submit to your cross-examination," he snarled, "you mistaken are! Do you wish me the door to show you?"

"Aisy, aisy, captain, dear," laughed O'Rourke. "For what end? I'm not ready to go, and 'tis yourself that's going to sit on that couch until I permit ye to get up. I've warned ye that I am armed. Is not a word in your ear as good as a bullet through your head?"

"What's your game?"

"Answer me question." O'Rourke twirled his weapon giddily on his forefinger.

"Yes."

"Ye bought the girl?"

"Yes."

"And the man?"

"Yes."

"A very light man, for a slave — eh, captain, dear? Almost as white as a white man, wasn't he, now?"

"Many of the Fazzi are, I am told," muttered the German. The muzzle of that revolver was bulking very large upon his range of vision; it seemed to fascinate him.

At that moment a knock resounded upon the outer door.

"A friend of mine," explained O'Rourke, in a matter-of-course tone. "Get up, captain, dear, and open the door to him."

"I — I —"

Von Wever rose, shaking his fist at O'Rourke — a huge, heavy fist that trembled with passion. "You'll pay for this!" he declared.

"One of us will, that's sure," assented O'Rourke. "For the present, ye'll pay attention to what I tell ye. Open that door, ye swindler!" he thundered, with an abrupt change of manner.

The German hastily obliged, O'Rourke following him out into the hall with a quiet suggestion that von Wever would do wisely to "try no funny business."

Senet was admitted. "Captain von Wever?" he said. "I'm told you wish to see me."

"'Twas meself that sent for ye, Senet, lad," spoke up O'Rourke, over the German's shoulder. "Come on in."

He waited silently until both had entered the reception room, then followed them. "Be seated, gentlemen," he said, waving the dumbfounded Senet into a chair. "'Tis a little reminiscence that Captain von Wever is regaling me with. I thought ye'd be interested. Sit tight, me boy, and ye'll understand why before long."

Continuing in his standing position, he addressed the German.

"Now," he said sharply, "we'll come down to business, with no frills, sir! Ye bought this slave—this white slave?"

"Yes." The revolver forced the monosyllable from the German.

"What have ye done with him?"

"None of your cursed business!"

"Answer me!"

Men, by the regiment, had heeded O'Rourke's commanding voice. The German, a craven at heart, weakened, cowering.

"The slave is in his quarters," he admitted sullenly.

"Call him, then — or, better still, take us to him."

"I — he cannot be seen."

"Why?"

"The man is dying."

"Ah!" O'Rourke's eyes were informed with a hard light. "Ah!" he repeated. "Dying?"

Still with an eye for the German, he began to talk rapidly to Senet.

"I'm going to tell ye a little story, Mr. Senet," he said. "Be good enough not to interrupt me. The captain here isn't going to speak unless I give him permission.

"Part of this I read in a scandal-mongering newspaper in Paris, and forgot. Part of it I heard from another man when first I came here, and noticed this von Wever buying slaves in the *sok* at Tetuan; and that, too, I forgot. Part of it is pure deduction; but we shall see if Herr Captain von Wever dares to deny it.

"To begin at the beginning, a girl named Ellen Dean, of the States —"

Senet started up from his chair, but O'Rourke silenced him with a gesture. The German looked around him furtively, with something of the expression of a trapped animal.

But O'Rourke was too vigilant for him; there was no possibility of escape.

" — of the States," he continued in an even tone, "married herself and her papa's money to a German count — the
Count of Seyn-Altberg, we'll call him, because that's his title.
He was a young chap, good-natured, weak, and a little lively
— a captain in a crack infantry regiment of the German army,
whose brother officers were a bad lot — such as von Wever
here. One night, shortly after his marriage, he played cards
with them. Someone — an officer who had fallen in love
with the count's wife — accused the count of cheating. In
fact, he proved it — found the cards up his sleeve, I believe.
Eh, captain, dear?"

The German made no sign, and O'Rourke continued:

"Naturally, the others present were scandalized. They
got together and agreed to keep silence, for the honor of
their regiment, on one condition — the Count of Seyn-
Altberg was to kill himself. He pledged his word to do so;
and the others kept their words — all but one.

"This poor divvle of a count was frightened when he felt
the touch of his razor on his throat. He weakened, and —
fled here to Tangiers, without saying a word to a living
soul save one — Captain von Wever! The count fell in bad
ways. He was *incognito*, of course, and nobody gave a damn
for him, and he gave a damn for nobody on earth but his wife,
whom he looked upon as a memory. *He* never troubled the
poor girl. But he went downhill faster than the pigs possessed by the devils that the priests will be telling ye about;
he sunk lower and lower, and finally took to living in the
native quarters — and the worst of them. And in the end,
one bright and beautiful morning, the Count of Seyn-Altberg
turned up missing.

[338]

"About that same time, one Captain von Wever was cashiered for conduct unbecoming the officer and the gentleman he pretended to be. *He* came to Tangiers, and, though he had no visible means of support, lived on the fat of the land. He bought him slaves, the dirty dog — slaves to wait on *him;* and one of those slaves was a man nearly white, corresponding in every particular to the man who had once been the Count of Seyn-Altberg. Now — this is the tough part of me story, Senet; sit still and wait till I'm through with it — the money that kept Captain von Wever going came from — can ye not guess where and whom? It came from Germany, from the poor, terrorized, little Countess of Seyn-Altberg that once was an American girl.

"Mr. Senet — I'm not quite finished, sir! That's better.

"And she sent it to Captain von Wever, not because she loved the dog, but because he threatened to take back to Europe this miserable, degraded, semi-idiotic, hashish-crazed Thing who had at one time answered to the name of the Count of Seyn-Altberg — threatened to carry him home, and expose him, and bring shame and humiliation on the girl. He bled her; she sent him every cent she had in the world, and still the infamous whelp snarled for more. And when he found that she was at last at the end of her resources, he made her come here to meet him and told her — I heard him this night, Senet — that she must give him five thousand pounds or else marry him — marry him while her own husband was yet living, and while both knew it!"

O'Rourke paused and glanced swiftly at Senet. The younger man was clutching the arms of his chair as though by main strength alone he kept himself seated. His face had become fairly livid — as white, well-nigh, as his collar; and his eyes burned like live coals.

"Von Wever," O'Rourke cried in a tone that brought the wretch's eyes obedient to his gaze, "tell Mr. Senet if this be true."

The German answered without premeditation, for O'Rourke had recounted his narrative with such a wealth of circumstance — and it was all so true — that he was appalled.

"The countess told you!" he snarled.

"Ah! but she did not," remarked O'Rourke. "Then it *is* true?"

"True?" The sound of his own voice carried a flush of returning courage to the man's heart. "True?" he raged. "Well, then, what if it is true? What are you going to do about it, eh? By God! O'Rourke, I'll make you suffer for this outrage! There's one thing that you've got to learn about Morocco, and that is that every man is a law unto himself here."

He was telling the plain, unvarnished truth; and because that was so, confidence was returning to him.

"You can't touch me!" he screamed. "Yes, you dogs, I've done all you accuse me of; but *you — can't — touch — me!*"

"No?" interrupted O'Rourke, with polite surprise. "Faith then, I'm deceiving meself wofully, Herr Captain. Let me tell ye one thing, blackmailer — no matter where ye go, sir, no matter how greatly ye esteem your liberty or how secure ye feel in your arrogance, there's this one thing ye'll answer to — the judgment of decent men, who weigh ye in the scales of decent living! Senet," he concluded, changing abruptly, "this is your affair. If ye want help I'll be outside the door, and ready and willing. I notice a rawhide dog whip in the corner there — ye may find it useful."

Senet leaped from his chair; he was across the room in a trice; he faced about with the whip in his hand.

"Thank you, O'Rourke!" he panted gratefully.

And as the portière dropped behind him, the Irishman heard the crash and the clash of shattered glass as the table was overturned; a second later he heard the first shriek of von Wever's agony.

CHAPTER XV

IT was the middle of the following afternoon, and there was quiet in the premises of the *Hôtel d'Angleterre*. Its guests languished, napping through the heat of the day in their rooms; and only in O'Rourke's quarters were any evidences of activity to be found. But there confusion reigned — such confusion as might be expected to attend a sudden and unexpected departure from a place wherein one has believed oneself established for an indeterminate if lengthy period of time.

Danny, his face as red as his hair, perspiring and profane, stood in the middle of the floor, ankle-deep in a litter of wearing apparel, saddles, belts, holsters, and all the variegated paraphernalia which O'Rourke had seen fit to attach unto himself in the course of a short but active campaign for fortune — upon which in this one instance, contrarily enough to prove her sex, Fortune had smiled. The acquisitiveness of an Irishman with a pocketful of money is proverbial; of late nothing had been too good for O'Rourke, too cumbersome, or too expensive. He had been prospering, and the shopkeepers of the Mediterranean ports were bearing in fond remembrance his extravagances.

And Danny, wild-eyed and desperate, was endeavoring to pack all this resultant accumulation of rubbish into one small trunk and a smaller leathern suit-case, in time to get them off, together with himself and his master, upon the mail boat scheduled to touch and leave Tangiers at five that afternoon.

The reason for this activity was not far to seek. It lay before O'Rourke in the shape of a letter on the top of a little rickety table, whereat the Irishman himself was sitting and writhing in the agonies of epistolary composition.

O'Rourke's color was scarcely less vivid than Danny's; and his perturbation of mind was apparent, even to the body-servant, — who therefore, and sagaciously, was at pains to make no unnecessary disturbance which would tend to distract his master's trend of thoughts, and who kept the corner of an eye warily alert for flying boots and other missiles, which were to be apprehended as signals that O'Rourke was annoyed by his follower.

But, for all that, Danny was trembling with joy; and even the eye of O'Rourke was alight with satisfaction as he conned and reconned the information contained in the brief, legal-looking scrawl which had arrived per the east-bound mail packet, that very morning.

The adventurer divided his attention between that communication and another which he was setting himself determinedly to compose, pending his early departure. He dug fingers into his dark hair and ground his teeth with despair as the pen sputtered and tracked an irregular way across the many sheets of hotel writing-paper which he had requisitioned for his purpose.

At length, with an exclamation which caused Danny to retreat with rapidity to a fine strategic position near the door, whence a further retreat to the outer hallway would be feasible if necessary, O'Rourke thrust aside the page he had just blackened and took up another. With the fire of grim purpose in his glance he settled himself to a fresh start.

"My dear Chambret " (he wrote):

"'Tis no manner of use. I am not a polite letter writer. This I tell you frankly, having no intent to deceive. The truth is that this will be about the 'steenth start I have made to this note — and so far, praises be! the most promising. Being in a hurry to get this off within the next two hours, which I am, this must serve — or nothing will. At the same time, I'm appreciative of the fact that 'tis the deuce of a poor hand I am to write letters, and I'm sorry for yourself, who'll have to wade through it all.

"Nevertheless, I feel expansive, and it's myself who will be opening my mind and heart to you, and probably at length — since I am unskilled in the pruning of my thoughts to fit in a certain number of words. Faith! telegrams were always an uncommon expense to me!

"I am here in Tangiers — a fact of which you will be suspicious the minute you lay eyes on the note-paper and the postmark. No matter. When you receive it, it is myself who will be in a neater, cleaner land than this — and glad am I of the prospect. I leave this night for the old country. And you will please to address your answer to The O'Rourke himself (who is now me), Castle O'Rourke, County Galway, Ireland, U. K.

"It's the matter of a year, more or less, since I left ye in Lützelburg, and by that same token it's the divvle of a long time, and it's much we'll have to tell one another, I'm hopeful, when next we meet. During that time, it's not a word you have sent me of yourself nor your affairs; though I understand from other sources that all's well with you and Madame la Grande Duchesse — to whom you will kindly convey my respects and best wishes. You are a fortunate man. Faith, I wish I could say as much for myself!

"Not that I would blame you for the neglect. 'Tis as much my own fault as yours. I despise letter writing, as I've said before. And what with wandering up and down upon the face of the earth, seeking what I might devour, like the Old Gentleman in the Good Book — may he fly away with himself!—and going hungry a good part of the time at that, and bearing with Danny — whom I picked up in Alexandria, by the way — and having a good time, truth to tell, and doing not so badly in a money way, though my income has been, as usual, casual, and what with the news that's come to me now, this very bright and beautiful morning, of my poor old Uncle Peter, one of the best men who ever lived, who's finally had the decency and courtesy to die — God rest his soul! — which rest he will be needing in the Hereafter, I'm convinced; for a meaner old skinflint and curmudgeon never trod the old sod and refused to accommodate his affectionate nephew with enough money to pay even a part of his debts, thus forcing the tender lad to go out into the cold and heartless world and seek his fortune, which he has been a long time finding — my dear Uncle Peter, I was saying, has died and left me — because he could not help it and for no other reason, the mean old miser, himself having no nearer of kin — a pile of gray rock and green moss called Castle O'Rourke, together with two hundred acres of peat bog and a few shillings that should have been mine long ago if I'd had my rights, to say nothing of several expensive suits in litigation of which I know nothing at all and care less, but which my solicitors advise me he willed to me especially in a damnable codicil, whatever that may be —

"But wherever at all I am in that sentence I shall never tell you, my dear man, for I don't know. What I'm trying to tell you is this: that the O'Rourke is at last come into his own, praises be and no thanks to Uncle Peter, whom I verily believe lived ten years longer than he really wanted to, just to keep me out of my due!

"And now I am resolved to settle down and lead a quiet and peaceful life for the rest of my days. I'll never again lift a hand against any man either in anger or for the love of the fight. And if you dare laugh, or even so much as chuckle, at me for saying that, I give you my word that I'll call you out and run you through, friendship or no friendship, Chambret!

"Now, the meat of all this lies in the fact that, so soon as I can settle my affairs I will be strolling over to Paris, and I shall count upon your meeting me, if you still love me, with word of the whereabouts of the one woman in all the world for whom I give the snap of my fingers. There's no need naming names, but in case there should exist in your mind any confusion as to the identity of the particular lady in question, I'll just whisper to you that she's Madame la Princesse, Beatrix de Grandlieu.

"Where is she, Chambret? Don't be telling me she's married, for myself wont believe a word of it. Faith, she promised to wait for me, and now 'tis no penniless Irish adventurer who is languishing for her, but The O'Rourke — you have my permission to inform her — landed proprietor himself and as good a man as ever walked in shoe leather.

"Is she happy? Does she talk of me? Would she, do you think, be glad to see me? Where can I find her, Chambret? And when? In a single word — Speak out, man! Don't you know I'm faint with longing for her? — in a word does she still love the O'Rourke? I can't live without her, old friend, now that I'm rich enough to support a wife, and the man that tries to win her from me will be sorry for the rest of his life!

"Tell her from me, that I have on my watch chain the half of a sovereign that —"

"Yer honor!"

"Go to thunder!"

"But yer honor —"

"I'll 'honor' ye, ye omadhaun! Get the deuce out av here, before I —"

Danny, who had quietly finished his task of packing and had slipped away, leaving O'Rourke in the heat of composition and dead to the world, on returning had merely ventured to stick the tip of his snub nose and the corner of one eye around the edge of the door. From this vantage point he dared persist, emboldened by necessity.

"Yer honor, 'tis —"

"D'ye want me to flay ye alive?"

"The min f'r th' troonks!" shouted Danny defiantly.

"What's that?"

O'Rourke paused and put down his pen with a sigh.

"'Tis the stheamer that will be in in half an hour, yer honor —"

"Very well, then. I'm coming," said O'Rourke pacifically.

But it was with regret that he added a hastily scrawled signature to his letter to Chambret, then sealed and addressed it. Calling Danny, he handed him the missive, with strict injunctions to let nothing deter him from posting it without the least delay; and, rising, O'Rourke left the *Hôtel d'Angleterre* and strolled down to the water-front deliberately, watching the mail-boat steam slowly into the roadstead — the vessel that was to bear him away from Tangiers, away from the East, away from Romance. He found himself almost sorry that he was to know no more this life that he had chosen

— and yet the memory of the princess of his dreams lured him northwards irresistibly.

As he waited, upon a pier-head, for the boat which was to bear him and Danny and their luggage to the steamer, a man came bounding hurriedly through the precipitous streets of Tangiers, and caught him almost at the last moment, — a young man, with a glowing, happy face, breathing heavily because of his haste.

"I have come to bid you God-speed, O'Rourke," said William Everett Senet, Consul-General, grasping the adventurer's ready hand. "And — and I suppose I am wrong to feel this way, but I have good news — of a sort."

O'Rourke lifted his brows. "The Count of Seyn-Altberg?" he asked.

Senet nodded. "Von Wever confessed — you know. We found the poor fellow — the count — But there's no profit going over that. He — it was terrible; he was beyond aid. Died this morning, early. Von Wever's gone inland . . . hunting!"

"And yourself?"

"Oh, I've sent in my resignation," said young Senet. "I'm going to take Nellie home — the countess, I mean —" he blushed furiously — "just as soon as my successor arrives."

"That's right," said O'Rourke. "Me boy, 'tis no place for the likes of ye — this Tangiers. May ye both be happy!"

CHAPTER XVI

THE TWO MESSAGES

(COPY of cablegram received by O'Rourke upon his arrival in Ireland.)

Madame has need of you. Come. Imperative.

A. CHAMBRET.

It was a cold night and a wet one in Paris when O'Rourke arrived at the Gare du Nord; it was, in point of exactness, nearly two o'clock, on a moist and chilly December morning.

The Irishman, haggard and worn with the hardship of continuous traveling, by night and day, from County Galway to Paris posthaste, darted out of the railway terminal as impatiently as if he had just been fresh from a long night's sleep in his bed, with Danny tagging disconsolately in his master's wake, and, since he dared not swear at O'Rourke, melodiously cursing the luggage which had fallen to his care.

 The two of them piled into a *fiacre* and were whirled rapidly across Paris to Chambret's residence in the Rue Royale; which turned out to be nothing more nor less than that happily married gentleman's one-time bachelor apartments.

Despite the lateness of the hour, O'Rourke's determined and thunderous assaults upon the door finally were rewarded by a vision of a red night-capped *concierge*, from whom the information was finally extracted, with much difficulty, that Monsieur Chambret was from home — that he had left two

·days since for the provinces, or for Italy, or for Germany, or perhaps for a trip around the world. The *concierge* did not know and doggedly asserted that he did not care — that is to say, his demeanor continued surly enough and altogether annoying until O'Rourke happened to mention his own name.

Thereupon a distinct change was noticeable in the demeanor of that *concierge*. He prefaced all things by demanding mysteriously the name of O'Rourke's valet, and the color of that person's hair, which having been pronounced respectively to be Danny and red, the *concierge* with alacrity invited O'Rourke to ascend to Monsieur Chambret's apartments, at the same time declaring himself to be possessed of a letter intrusted to him for delivery to O'Rourke upon his arrival in Paris.

Accordingly, O'Rourke and Danny mounted five flights of steps and were admitted to the apartments, and, the gas having been lighted by the *concierge*, O'Rourke was permitted to peruse the communication. Being translated, it ran somewhat to the following effect:

MY DEAR COLONEL: Nothing could have been more opportune than the receipt of your note. Only the previous day I had received a call from a trusted servant of madame's, who gave me a message which madame had not deemed wise to trust to paper; together with the little packet, herewith inclosed, which I was requested to forward to you. I did not then know your whereabouts. To me there is something wonderful in the fact that I now do know.

This will be left with the *concierge*, who has instructions not to deliver it into any hands save those of Colonel Terence O'Rourke, whose valet is a red-headed Irishman named Danny. I take these precautions for reasons which you will readily understand, as you read on.

By the time this is handed you, I shall be at Montbar, whither I trust you will follow me at your earliest convenience. Nay, I know that you will arrive there without a minute's delay — else you are not the impetuous lover that once you were.

Madame is at Montbar — I believe. Three days ago she was in Paris. Since then — since communicating with me, that is — she has mysteriously disappeared. But I happen to be cognizant of the fact that, within the week, an announcement will be published in the Parisian newspapers of her contract to marry Duke Victor, of Grandlieu, brother of that Prince Felix whom I had the good fortune to exterminate during the Lemercier-Saharan affair, thus making madame a widow.

Duke Victor is a worthy brother to Felix. I scarce need elaborate. Probably you are aware of his reputation; since the death of Felix he hàs come to be regarded as the most notorious *roué* of all Europe, as well as the most conscienceless and skilful duelist.

Of course, you understand that nothing but the most persistent and the strongest pressure in addition to your continued silence could ever have induced madame to consent to marry this man. Victor himself is a man of undoubted charm; he has fascinations at his command which are not to be regarded lightly — even by The O'Rourke of Castle O'Rourke. His personality is at once magnetic and repellent. In other words, he is a man calculated to entrance a woman's fancy.

Moreover, I repeat, you were not upon the ground.

Notwithstanding all this, however — notwithstanding the fact that madame has agreed to put her name to the marriage contract, your influence is feared. To prevent her meeting you, madame has been spirited away to Montbar. Of this there can be little doubt; her servant confided to me madame's fear that something of the sort might take place, that she might be kept in seclusion until the marriage was an accomplished fact.

For all of which you are entitled to feel complimented.

I am going to Montbar — which, as you are doubtless aware, is the capital city of the principality of Grandlieu — at once, to be upon the ground, ready to render whatever service I may. I shall lodge at the *Hôtel des Étrangers* under my own name. I should advise you, however, to come to Grandlieu *incognito* – as an English milord. I should also counsel you to come at once, and shall look for you hourly. Possibly I may have good news for you, monsieur; for, if I can pick a quarrel with Duke Victor, he will be as good as a dead man from the moment.

I am, devotedly,

ADOLPH CHAMBRET.

O'Rourke replaced the letter in its envelope, frowning thoughtfully.

"Faith," he said aloud, "'tis something to have made a friend like Chambret — the saints presarve him!"

And eagerly he opened the little packet which Chambret had mentioned as an enclosure. All during his reading of the letter it had lain squeezed tight in the palm of O'Rourke's clenched fist. Now he regarded it tenderly ere breaking the seals — a round, small package, no broader than a silver dollar, though twice as thick, wrapped in heavy, opaque paper and protected by many seals of violet-hued wax, bearing above the arms of Grandlieu the initial "B." It was entirely unaddressed.

"Beatrix!" whispered O'Rourke softly. He glanced hastily around the apartment, discovering that Danny had fallen asleep in a chair; he was practically alone, and he raised the packet to his lips and kissed the seals. "Beatrix!" he breathed.

He opened the small blade of his penknife and ran it under the edge of the wrapper, so preserving the seals intact; for had she not impressed them with those hands for whose caress the heart of O'Rourke was fairly faint?

Something fell into his hand — the half of a golden coin — a broken English sovereign, in fact. O'Rourke's eyes glowed as he fitted it to the other half, which hung dependent from his watch guard.

"Sweetheart!" he said. "Ye promised me ye'd send it — when ye needed me sword! Please God, I'll not be too late to save ye from that black-hearted scoundrel, Victor!"

But there was something else, and it was with a rapidly beating heart that O'Rourke removed it from the wrapper and held it to the light. This was a tiny miniature, no larger than a man's thumb nail, wrought with marvelous skill by some painter who had seen beneath the face, deep into the soul, of his subject.

For the face that looked out from the dark background was very lovely — the features of a most wonderfully beautiful woman.

But it was her eyes which held him as one bewitched. Large eyes they were, and dark, and gently smiling beneath their deep fringe of dark lashes. And out of their depths the woman's soul flamed to greet O'Rourke; the love that she bore him gleamed and glowed therein, — even as he had seen it glow when he had loved her, long years past, undying and undoubting, faithful unto the end, whatever that might be when it should come.

"This," he said, awed, "is a miracle — a miracle, sweetheart — this portrait of ye. Faith, 'tis beyond belief, so real it makes your presence seem, dearest. And d'ye think — or does Chambret think — that I can look into those eyes and believe that ye are marrying this fellow, Duke Victor, of your own choosing? Faith, no! The sovereign — that is to tell me ye need me. But this — this is to tell me ye love me still, sweetheart! Sure, and wild horses wouldn't be keeping me from ye now!"

For a long time he stood, gazing upon the miniature with a kindling eye.

It was with a start that he was roused by the footsteps of the *concierge* on the stairway; and it was with smoldering resentment that he realized that unsentimental Danny was snoring peacefully in Chambret's armchair.

"Call another *fiacre!*" he instructed the *concierge*. "And then come back and lock up these rooms. 'Tis ourselves that won't be troubling ye ten minutes longer. Yes — run along.

"And, Danny!" He stepped across the room and stirred with the toe of his shoe his servant's recumbent form.. "Danny, ye lazy gossoon, wake up, before I take strenuous means to wake ye. Come, ye scut, move!"

Already his plans were formulated and solidifying into determinations. He communicated them to Danny, as the *fiacre* conveyed them rapidly to the Gare de l'Est. And Danny, with an eye toward his personal comfort, was swift to subscribe unto them.

CHAPTER XVII

THE ROAD TO PARADISE

ALONE in his compartment, the adventurer slept fitfully throughout the morning run, and, indeed, for the better part of the following day, while the train drummed swiftly over the plains of old Champagne, Burgundy, and Franche-Comté.

At eleven o'clock that night he was roused from a nap by a hand that clapped him heartily upon his shoulder. He sat up, blinking, yawning, stretching himself, and shivering; for they were then in the mountains, and the night air is chill and penetrating in those high altitudes.

"Well?" he demanded sourly. "What is it now?"

The train had come to a halt. Through the open door of the compartment naught was visible save the blank darkness of a winter's night, under a sky shrouded with a pall of lowering clouds. Near at hand a small hand lantern swung a foot or more above the ground, its rays lighting up a patch of sodden earth perhaps a yard in diameter, and silhouetting the boots and gaiters of a man, the upper half of whose body was invisible.

Bending over O'Rourke were two others — the guard and a uniformed stranger, whose hand still lay heavy upon the Irishman's shoulder as he continued to peer intently into his face.

"'Tis to be hoped," growled O'Rourke, "that ye will know me the next time we meet, me friend."

But he spoke in English, which the man failed to comprehend. The look of suspicion upon his face, however, was intensified by the ring of the unfamiliar accents.

"What language is it you speak, m'sieur?" he asked peremptorily.

"English," responded O'Rourke in execrable French — French positively mutilated by a strong British accent. "And what's that to ye?" he desired further to know.

"This is the frontier, m'sieur — the frontier of Grandlieu. M'sieur will be pleased to exhibit his passport."

"M'sieur will be pleased to do nothing of the sort." O'Rourke lolled back in his chair and pulled his broad-brimmed, soft hat well down over his eyes. "If ye want to see me passport," he grunted, "ask me courier for it. He has both his own and mine. Now, get out."

But the officer of Grandlieu's frontier guard lingered.

"And m'sieur's courier?" he asked. "Where is he?"

"How the divvle would I be knowing? In the third-class carriage — I know no more than that. Ask for the courier for Lord Delisle, and he will declare himself, probably. A small, quick-looking fellow he will be, with black hair and black eyes."

"Many thanks, milord. Pardon, milord, for the unfortunate but necessary intrusion. Good night, milord."

O'Rourke snorted and snuggled himself within his greatcoat, pretending to woo sleep a second time. The guard and the customs officer sidled respectfully from the compartment and closed the door. O'Rourke did not move. To all appearances he was sound asleep when they returned, chattering excitedly.

"But, milord!" expostulated the man of Grandlieu, jerking open the door and a second time letting in a gust of icy wind.

O'Rourke brought his feet down upon the floor with a bang. He opened his eyes, and they were shining with anger. He opened his mouth, and, with a care to lose nothing of his English accent, cursed the train, France, Grandlieu and the customs official, respectively and comprehensively.

"Milord!" he snorted. "Milord, milord! What the divvle milord is it now? Cannot an Englishman have peace and privacy in a compartment which he has reserved for himself? What is it now?"

"Pardon, milord." The customs official was deferential but determined. "Milord's courier is not on this train."

O'Rourke flew into a veritable transport of passion. He grew red in the face with rage. He waved frantic fists above his head, declaiming with vigor and rhetorical fluency — in English. The two men were visibly awed and impressed. Such profanity — at least, it sounded like profanity — had never been heard either in France or Grandlieu. It was wonderful, inspiring and typically British — to their comprehensions, at least, who were accustomed to regard every traveling boor as an Englishman.

"My courier not on this train?" he concluded. "What divvle's work is this? Why is he not upon this train? What does it mean?"

"Perhaps," insinuated the guard, "milord's courier has made off with milord's luggage."

It was so. O'Rourke, otherwise Lord Delisle, had suspected as much from the first. The man had proven what he had appeared, an untrustworthy scamp. He had decamped with his employer's valuables, to say nothing of his clothing and his passport. O'Rourke's rage knew no bounds; and the men were correspondingly overawed.

It was truly unfortunate. But, after all, although there was an order about something which they concluded not to enlarge upon, but which evidently had to do with Englishmen purposing to enter Grandlieu, the milord would not be subjected to further discomfort. It was not necessary. One single infraction of the rule would do no harm. No. The milord could proceed to Montbar, from which place it would be possible for him to set forward inquiries after the missing courier.

And again O'Rourke found himself alone in the compartment, with the train crawling slowly on and up a steep mountain side. He was in Grandlieu at last, and at that, despite the order which Duke Victor had evidently issued calling for O'Rourke's detention at the frontier — just as O'Rourke had suspected he would.

O'Rourke hugged himself in the grateful warmth of his overcoat, chuckling inwardly at the deception he had practised upon the two men. It had been well planned. Beyond doubt the order for his apprehension had spoken of an Irishman using most excellent French, and accompanied by a red-headed Irish servant. O'Rourke congratulated himself upon the foresight which had led him to leave Danny in Paris.

He was, in point of fact, just entering upon the danger zone. From that moment on his life was in peril — or at least his liberty and his heart's desire were hanging in the balance. And so — he was comfortable and well pleased, as was strictly in keeping with the disposition of the man.

But it is conceivable that, could he have known of the mark which the customs official had unobtrusively chalked upon the door of the compartment, O'Rourke would not have felt so assured of the man's stupidity, nor so sure that in the end he would win to the side of Madame la Princesse, Beatrix de Grandlieu.

An hour later the Irishman left his compartment and stepped out upon the platform of the railway station at Montbar.

The midnight wind that rushed, shrieking, between the mountainous walls of the narrow, level valley which constitutes the major part of the principality of Grandlieu — an independent state with a total area of some sixty-nine square miles — was bitter cold and searching. The faces of the porters and railway officers, who were forced to attend to outdoor duties, were blue and immobile in its ice-laden breath; and upon the lighted windows of the station itself frost had formed, thick and white.

O'Rourke, noting these things, thought of the warmth of a bed in the *Hôtel des Étrangers*, and the comfort of a meal, with warm drinks, in the supper room of that hostelry, and was glad that he journeyed no farther that night.

Runners for the three most prominent hotels in the city besieged him with advice bearing upon the surpassing merits of their respective houses. O'Rourke listened to all alike stolidly, and apparently at random indicated him who represented the *Hôtel des Étrangers*, so avoiding all suspicion of having chosen Chambret's place of shelter with purpose aforethought.

Priding himself upon the neatness of this little strategy, he climbed into a hack and settled himself for what he was assured would be no more than a ten minutes' drive.

His eyes closed and he nodded, thinking dreamily of the fair face pictured in that miniature which rested above his heart. The hack plunged on through the night, rattling and bouncing over a road broad and well macadamized. At intervals electric lights illuminated the vehicle's interior with a bluish and frosty radiance. Buildings, stark and drear, unlighted, loomed on the roadside.

Time dragged. It began to seem a long ten minutes. O'Rourke had understood that the railway station was situated something like a mile beyond the limits of the city of Montbar, but still — a glance out of the window showed him that the bordering line of houses was no longer on either side of the road. The electric lights, also, seemed more infrequently spaced; the intervals of blank obscurity were longer; and when the illumination did come, it showed nothing but frozen fields stretching off into the darkness.

Moreover, the carriage appeared to be ascending a steep grade. O'Rourke puckered his brows, puzzled. Had he mistaken the hotel runner? Or had the uncouth French which he had affected conveyed the wrong meaning to his hearers' comprehensions?

He leaned forward and rapped smartly on the window pane. Promptly the vehicle slowed its speed, and presently it came to a halt. O'Rourke heard the driver climbing down from the box, and the rattle of a carriage lamp as it was detached from its place.

"Curse the fool!" grumbled the Irishman. "All I wanted was a word with him."

A glow of light filled the interior of the vehicle from the right-hand window. Simultaneously the left-hand door was jerked open and a man stepped in.

O'Rourke sat still, looking into the mouth of a revolver. To sit still was the course of prudence. He could do nothing else. His own revolvers were in the hand bag on the floor of the vehicle. But he was biting his lip with vexation, at the thought that he had blundered so blindly into a trap so self-evident.

The intruder was a man larger in every way than was the Irishman himself; and with the odds of the revolver in his favor, he had O'Rourke entirely at his mercy. He was prompt to press the muzzle of it, a ring of frozen steel, against the Irishman's forehead.

"Monsieur is armed?" he inquired brusquely.

"No," returned O'Rourke sullenly.

"Monsieur will not be angry with me for assuring myself of that fact, I am positive. Will monsieur be kind enough to remove his hands from his pockets, unbutton his overcoat and then hold his hands above his head?"

O'Rourke had no choice. He did precisely as he was bid, unwillingly but with alacrity. Still holding the gun to his head, the man patted each of the Irishman's pockets, with painstaking thoroughness, and found nothing in the shape of a weapon to reward his search.

"That is very good," he announced. "Monsieur will now be kind enough to rebutton his coat and to sit very still for the rest of the journey. The coachman will presently remove the light, but monsieur will be so good as to believe that I can see in the dark, and that any rash move on his part will be rewarded with a bullet through his head. François" — this to the driver — "go ahead."

The light was replaced, and in a moment or two the horses were hammering steadily up the mountain road. O'Rourke obeyed orders agreeably enough, debating ways and means whereby he might surprise and overcome his captor. The thing was, possibly, feasible. In the long patches of darkness between the lights, he might spring unexpectedly, dash aside the revolver and throttle the man. On the other hand,

[361]

he might not succeed. The game was not exactly worth the candle. It was better to wait, to see what opportunity the future might offer. When no other chance remained, it was all very well to stake everything on a single throw; but until that time, O'Rourke, for all his daring, was the man to weigh thoroughly the advisability of each least action.

"May I inquire," he said at length, in his execrable French — it was painful even to O'Rourke to assume such an accent — "what is meant by this outrageous treatment of an Englishman?"

The man, sitting opposite him in the gloom, laughed softly.

"Monsieur the Colonel doubtless is aware of our intentions," he suggested.

"Monsieur the Colonel?" repeated O'Rourke. "I assure ye that there is some mistake here, monsieur —"

"Pray spare yourself the trouble, Colonel O'Rourke. You did very well. Permit me to congratulate you upon confusing our man at the frontier; but still the odds were all against you. We have been expecting you daily, ever since Monsieur Chambret cabled you. Our agents in Paris watched you last night, and saw you take the train for Montbar. Even your — pardon me — your infernal French, could not prevail against such information. Monsieur the Colonel is bold, but I trust he will not be angry if I venture to observe that in this instance he has acted somewhat thoughtlessly. But, perhaps, monsieur, you did not think that we would be so vigilant."

O'Rourke did not reply. He was caught; there was no disguising that unpalatable fact. Anything that he might say would do no good; moreover, he feared to speak lest the anger in his voice should betray his deep chagrin.

"No? You refuse to answer me, monsieur? Believe

me, I should be desolated" — the man mocked — "to be lost to your good graces, Colonel O'Rourke, merely because we have succeeded in outwitting you. In all fairness, that was our business. Could you have expected us to act otherwise?"

"No," admitted O'Rourke, caught by the fellow's tone of good-natured raillery; "but surely ye don't expect me to be pleased with meself, monsieur? Faith!" And he laughed bitterly.

"So, then, I have made no mistake, after all? You admit that you are Colonel Terence O'Rourke?"

"Admit it, me friend? Sure, and ye did not expect me to deny it? Whilst there's a fighting chance, monsieur, I am prepared to lie with the best of ye; but when ye have me, body, soul and breeches — I'll throw up me hands, just as I did when ye asked me to, so politely. But," he continued, talking to make time, and to throw the fellow off his guard if possible, "could ye favor me with a bit of a word as to me probable fate, monsieur? Sure, and 'tis no crime for a man, even an Irishman, to journey into Grandlieu?"

"No — no crime, monsieur. But, perhaps, an indiscretion. Shall we call it a breach of international etiquette, monsieur — taking into consideration all the circumstances?"

"Faith, would ye make me out a Power, together with that precious duke of yours?" O'Rourke laughed.

"The comparison is not unapt, monsieur." His captor bowed — and maintained the muzzle of the revolver within a foot of O'Rourke's heart. "Not unapt," he repeated; "which you are to consider as the reason why I am taking such care of you, monsieur."

"I would ye were less careful. Is there anything now, monsieur, which might tempt ye to carelessness — for one little moment?"

[363]

There was an instant's silence. Then the man chuckled disagreeably. "We are arrived," he announced briefly, glancing out of the window for the fraction of a second, and immediately resuming his vigilance.

The carriage stopped. There were the sounds of voices, of rapid footsteps, of the jingling of bits and the pawing of hoofs, clear upon the frosty air. After what seemed an interminable wait, something clanged loudly metallic, and a face appeared at the window. The door was opened with a jerk, and a man's voice invited "Monsieur the Colonel O'Rourke" to be pleased to alight.

He was *not* pleased; but an instant's consideration of the menacing weapon constrained him to give in with what grace he had to command, and, rising, he jumped lightly to the frozen ground. At once he was seized from behind, his arms twisted into his sides, a rope passed about them and drawn tight.

"The divvle!" swore O'Rourke — but under his breath; outwardly he maintained an impassive aspect.

Before him loomed the steep, rock wall of a castle. He had heard somewhat of this castle from the lips of Madame la Princesse herself, in former, happier days. They called it Castle Grandlieu. It was centuries old — a grim reminder of the days when from this rocky aerie the lords of Grandlieu held the countryside in meek subjection, harrying the lowlands of France and taking toll of all unfortunate passers-by.

It had been the whim of the princes of Grandlieu to live in this castle, keeping it with all its medieval atmosphere — its moat and drawbridge, its portcullis and battlements and towers, all as they had stood frowning down upon the valley when first erected back in the darkness of the Middle Ages.

Something in its bleak and austere showing sent a chill to

the marrow of the Irishman. It bulked as grim and forbidding as a tomb. It — who knew? — might be his tomb.
It was said, indeed, that Duke Victor was a famous duelist
and one invincible. If he offered O'Rourke the chance to
fight, there would be an instant acceptance; of that one might
feel assured. And who should prophesy the outcome?

Not the O'Rourke of Castle O'Rourke, be certain. There
was a legend in his family that a penniless O'Rourke was
unconquerable; and vice versa.

Was this, then, to be the end of his epic?

CHAPTER XVIII

THE DEVIL IN THE DUKE

UNDER the sharp-toothed portcullis they passed; and behind them, to the rattling of chains and the creaking of rusty windlasses, the drawbridge rose. O'Rourke, as he was hurried across a courtyard, tried to smile at this grim travesty; but deep in his heart lurked an uneasiness.

He had not in the least anticipated all this. Otherwise, he had chanced a quick death at the hands of the man in the carriage. But now, evidently, he was to die; and all possibility of escape had been cut off by the raising of that draw. He stood, for all he knew to the contrary, without a friend in that huge pile of masonry set upon a cliff on a mountain side, concerning any portion of which he knew not the least thing in the world.

Well, his part was to hold up his head and take what had been prepared for him with the easiest grace he could assume. Time out of number he had laughed back into the jaws of death; and, after all, it was childish of him to assume that Duke Victor would dare a murder in order to remove from his path so insignificant a stumbling block as the O'Rourke — the empty-handed Irish adventurer.

But assuredly he might confidently count upon a fighting chance, in the end. Or — and this occurred to him for the first time — he was merely to be kept a prisoner until after the duke's marriage to Madame la Princesse had been consummated.

That, doubtless, was the real explanation of it all. Somehow, the Irishman's heart lightened in his breast.

A short wait had to be endured, while his captor entered the castle proper. O'Rourke was left in the charge of three men, who paid scant heed to what he said, but, on the other hand, watched him with a catlike interest, which O'Rourke appreciated as highly complimentary to his reputation.

But, ere long, he was conducted into the building, through a maze of echoing passages of stone, into what appeared to be the more modern part of the castle — that portion, evidently, wherein the princes of Grandlieu were accustomed to live, in the infrequent periods of their sojourns at Montbar.

Here the walls were paneled with a dark wood, and hung with rich tapestries; the floors were of hard wood, painstakingly polished to a rare brilliancy, and strewn with heavy, soft rugs of somber designs. The air was warm — warm with the comfort of open fires.

His captor halted him on the threshold of a heavy door of oak, upon which he knocked thrice.

"Enter, messieurs." A clear, even voice sounded from the further side; and O'Rourke was ushered across the threshold into a great apartment that, very likely, had been the dining hall two centuries back — high-ceiled, so that the rays of the electric lights, set in lieu of torches in the sconces upon the walls, hardly penetrated the shadows above them; and long and deep, with a huge fireplace built in one end, and the other shadowed by an overhanging balcony draped with tapestry.

The center of this room was occupied by a long table strewn with books and papers and bearing a reading-lamp. The walls were lined with racks of arms, collected with the care of a lover of weapons, and representing all ages and climes. In front of the fireplace a canvas had been stretched across the parquetry flooring, to serve for fencing bouts.

It was an immense room, and deeply interesting; O'Rourke's eyes lit up as he glanced down the racks of arms, but he had little time to feast his martial spirit with the sight of them.

For, standing with his back to the fire, teetering gently upon his toes, with hands clasped idly at his back, was a man whom O'Rourke found little difficulty in identifying as the Duke Victor himself, from his resemblance to his dead brother, and from a certain air of domineering confidence in himself as well.

Whether or no he was a young man would have been hard to say; at least, he had the air and the look of youth — the hue of rich blood in his cheeks and the lines of youth in his figure, that was as straight and supple as any stripling's. He was something above middle height, and as good a man to look upon as ever O'Rourke had seen — save, perhaps, for a lack of breadth between his eyes: a sure index to a nature at least untrustworthy, if not positively treacherous.

O'Rourke's captor halted at the door and saluted with a military air. For the first time O'Rourke was able to have a good look at him. Now that he had thrown aside his cloak, a uniform of light gray adorned with a sufficiency of gold lace and insignia was revealed. From the straps on his shoulders O'Rourke calculated that he was a captain in the standing army of Grandlieu — which, in all, numbered eighty men and officers; or so the Irishman had heard.

For the rest of him, he was of a Gallic type — a large man, blond, well-proportioned, heavier and taller than O'Rourke, and as well set up. He was smiling slightly, with an ironic air, as he endured the Irishman's gaze, and stood at ease with one hand upon the hilt of a saber which he had assumed since entering the castle.

Duke Victor was the first to speak.

"Colonel O'Rourke, I believe?" he said pleasantly enough — with the air of one greeting an unexpected guest. "Captain de Brissac!"

"Your highness?"

"I observe that Colonel O'Rourke's hands are bound behind him. Surely that is unnecessary, in addition to being an indignity. Loose him at once."

The captain untied the ropes. O'Rourke moistened his lips nervously, looking the duke up and down, for once in his career at a loss for words. But the duke saved him the trouble of speaking.

"Colonel," he said familiarly, resuming his nonchalant teetering in front of the great fireplace, "you will no doubt have complaint to make in regard to our method of welcoming you to Grandlieu!"

"Faith, I have that!" O'Rourke assured him earnestly.

"So I surmised." The duke smiled. "As to why we have acted in this manner — why, monsieur, it's hardly necessary to discuss our reasons. I fancy they're evident and well understood by you and myself."

"Faith, yes," O'Rourke agreed. "I'm not the man to deny that. But I dispute your right, monsieur."

"Oh —!" And the duke waved a slender, white hand airily. "There's no need of going into that, either, my colonel. You dispute the right — I arrogate it unto myself and shall consistently maintain it. No gain to either of us — to fight over that. The point of the whole matter is —" He paused thoughtfully.

"Now," assumed O'Rourke, "ye seem to be getting down to business."

"Precisely, my friend," laughed the duke amusedly. "And it's simple enough, Colonel O'Rourke. You were, to use the legal term, accessory before the fact of my brother's — Prince Felix's — death. Naturally, for that I hold you in no very great good will. And I understand that both before and after the mur —"

"Monsieur!"

"Oh, very well! Before and after, — shall we say? — the unfortunate accident, you made love to the wife of my brother — *my* promised wife of to-day."

"Ye may understand what ye will," said O'Rourke. "But I'll tell ye this, monsieur the duke, that when ye say that madame promised to marry ye, ye lie!"

"Strong language, Colonel O'Rourke! Upon what do you base such an assertion?"

The duke was holding himself well under control; but he had flushed darkly on hearing the epithet which O'Rourke had flung in his teeth with intent to provoke. Indeed, at present all that the Irishman was hoping for was to madden the duke into accepting or issuing a challenge to a duel. Then — well, the best man would win.

"I know that ye lie," continued O'Rourke evenly, ' from the fact that within the week madame has sent for me."

"Which means — what, monsieur, may I ask?"

"It means that madame once promised to be me wife, Monsieur the Duke; and that she is standing ready to redeem her pledge. Is it conceivable that she'd be promising her hand to ye at the same time? I think not."

"Your judgment may be prejudiced, colonel. Madame may have changed her mind, may have wished to see you in order that she might inform you of that fact — which, by the way, happens to be the case."

It was a view of it that never before had presented itself to O'Rourke. For an instant, so confidently did the duke advance it, he was shaken by a suspicion that this might be the truth.

And then he remembered her word-of-mouth message to Chambret — that she needed O'Rourke — and the miniature that she had sent him, that intimate portrait of her whose eyes had spoken to him so eloquently of her steadfast love. And, more than all else, the remembrance of that strengthened O'Rourke and heartened him.

"That," he said coolly, "is he number two, Monsieur the Duke. Faith, if it were truth, why did ye find it necessary to spirit madame away?"

"And have we done so?" For affected surprise, the duke's was almost convincing.

"Beyond doubt, ye did."

"Ah, Monsieur the Colonel deceives himself. To be frank with you, madame is at this moment in Paris, for all I know to the contrary."

"Which I'll take the liberty of branding as lie number three. If *that* were truth, ye would not have troubled to capture me before I could find it out for meself."

"Very well, monsieur. Have it your own way." Assuredly the duke had his temper well in hand. He bowed his head forward, caressing his chin with his strong, slender fingers, and seemed to ponder O'Rourke deeply.

Under this meditative yet insolent regard, the Irishman grew restive.

"The divvle!" he cried impatiently. "Will ye be kind enough to signify your intentions with regard to me?"

"Exactly what I was about to do, monsieur. I have brought you here by force, for one reason because I well knew that you would not come of your own free will. For another, I wish to negotiate with you. I admit that you have a claim upon madame's hand — a claim which, perhaps, she might feel called upon to acknowledge, to be just, howsoever much such a course might prove distasteful to her. So — Monsieur the Colonel O'Rourke, what will buy you off?"

O'Rourke drew himself up, and his hands clenched. For a moment he seemed about to spring at the duke's throat. Captain de Brissac started forward, and even the duke betrayed signs of uneasiness. But O'Rourke contained himself.

"Did ye bring me here to insult me, ye scum o' the earth?" he demanded tensely. "Faith, if it's to fight ye wish, I'll accommodate ye. *I* could not insult *you* by branding ye a liar to your face, but, monsieur the duke, ye have managed mortally to affront *me!* Did ye mean it, dog?"

The duke's face was quite livid with rage. But his voice was steady and even as he replied:

"It is not to fight that I wish, Colonel O'Rourke. I am quite well aware that nothing could please you better than to murder me, by foul means, as you did my brother. I understand you have your fellow, Chambret, in the town below here, and I've no doubt the two of you could put a period to the Grandlieu line, between you. No, Colonel O'Rourke. I have asked you in all earnestness, and I ask you again, knowing as I do that you adventurers all have your price: For what will you consent to relinquish your claim upon madame's hand?"

De Brissac's hand moved toward his revolver, whose butt

was visible above the line of his belt. O'Rourke marked the gesture, and the true significance of the scene was quite abruptly apparent to him.

He had been brought here to be baited like an animal, to the point where, goaded to desperation by the duke's taunts, he would lose his temper and throw himself at the man's throat; when it would be justifiable to shoot him down, just as one would a maddened animal, in self-defense.

If that, then, was their scheme, he was determined to frustrate it. And quickly he swung about upon his heel, facing the door.

"Monsieur the Duke," he said, "'tis your privilege to consider yourself challenged. If ye refuse to meet me, ye prove yourself a coward. If ye consent to meet me, ye are this minute as good as a dead man. But, meanwhile, I am in your power. And the divvle another word will ye get out of me till I'm free!"

There was a moment's silence. Then the voice of the duke, quivering as though with amusement:

"You refuse any and all propositions, then, I am to understand?"

O'Rourke nodded his head.

The duke sighed. "I am sorry, Monsieur the Colonel; we might have made an offer which you would have been glad to accept, had you met our advances in a different spirit. As it is, I must bid you good night. Captain de Brissac, be kind enough to escort Colonel O'Rourke to his hotel. Messieurs, good evening."

Something sinister in the duke's tone — O'Rourke could not see his face — robbed his words of their surprise for the Irishman. He uttered not one syllable, however; and waited patiently until De Brissac, with a laugh, touched him on the arm.

"This way," he said softly.

And O'Rourke stepped forward and out of the great room, into the hallways of the Castle de Grandlieu — of which, as has been said, he knew nothing at all.

CHAPTER XIX

THE DOOR TO ETERNITY

For some minutes the two strode on in silence, De Brissac in the advance, O'Rourke watching his huge shoulders with a calculating glance, debating whether or no, upon necessity, he could overcome this man in a struggle hand to hand. He shook his head dubiously, much impressed by De Brissac's evidently ponderous muscular development.

From the inhabited portion of the castle they passed back into the more bleak and uninviting section, where the air hung heavy, chill, and damp, and great gusts of wind eddied through silent, echoing hallways. And they followed, in the main — or, at least, so far as O'Rourke could determine — the course by which they had entered.

At length De Brissac paused before a heavy door, set deep in the walls of stone.

"Colonel O'Rourke," he said, "I regret that our carriage is no longer at your disposal. Had you been otherwise minded, it might have been a different matter. As it is, we have no choice but to consider you a determined enemy, to afford whom food, aid or comfort would be treason." He laughed sardonically. "This door," he continued, "opens upon the road. There is a little bridge over the moat, which you'll find it no trouble to negotiate. After that, the road is lighted all the way to Montbar. It is a short journey at the worst. You will reach the *Hôtel des Étrangers* within the hour. Good night."

He swung open the door. O'Rourke looked into his eyes, and smiled contemptuously. "A small lot," he commented: "a petty revenge. I'm pleased to be able to breathe air unpolluted by ye, monsieur. Good night."

He turned and confronted the black, vacant oblong made by the open door. The frost-laden wind slapped his cheeks and pinched his nose. Without, there was unrelieved night. O'Rourke negatived the proposition, mentally. He did not know what lurked out there, in the blackness. He would have much preferred to leave the castle and come out at once upon the lighted road. And he stepped back toward De Brissac.

"If 'tis not too great a strain upon your courtesy," he suggested, "I'd prefer to leave be the way I entered, monsieur."

Abruptly he became aware that De Brissac was making for him with outstretched, clutching hands, and the apparent intention of seizing O'Rourke and casting him forth bodily into the outer darkness.

The Irishman did not precisely comprehend; but he was quick to step to one side and to meet De Brissac's rush, with a blow from the shoulder, delivered with all the strength that was in him. It struck the man's chest, glancing, and staggered him for the moment; and that instant O'Rourke improved by grappling with him.

Neither spoke. O'Rourke was bewildered, but in some vague way aware that he was fighting for his very existence. De Brissac was straining, with set teeth, to break the Irishman's hold upon him. For many minutes they swayed back and forth and from side to side, there in the narrow, stone-walled passage in the old castle.

At length, De Brissac stumbled and went to his knees. He was up again in a trice, but in the struggle to regain his standing his sword became in some way detached from the belt, scabbard and all, and fell clanking to the floor.

O'Rourke noticed and desired it greatly. It is a fine thing to have the hilt of a good saber in your hand, with the knowledge that you have the skill and prowess to wield it. It seemed to O'Rourke that, could he but get the weapon in his grasp, all would be well with him, despite the fact that he was in a castle infested with the creatures of Duke Victor.

Gradually, at the expense of furious effort, he swung the other in front of him, with his back to the open doorway. De Brissac seemed to sense his intention and to strive against it with a desperate ferocity, his eyes protruding from his head, staring as if with terror, his panting as loud in O'Rourke's hearing as the exhaust of an engine. He dug his feet into the crevices of that floor of solid rock and fought as one fights on the grave's edge.

O'Rourke conceived that De Brissac supposed he could be cut down instantly, once his antagonist managed to possess himself of the saber. And he thought grimly that De Brissac was not so far wrong.

Chance aided him — or the luck of the O'Rourkes. For an instant De Brissac managed to break away; but as he did so, O'Rourke's fingers brushed the hilt of his revolver in the man's belt, and closed upon it, withdrawing the weapon.

De Brissac spat an oath between his teeth, and sprang. O'Rourke was too quick for him. There was no time to aim, or even to fire. There was time only sufficient for him to dash the hand that held the revolver into the man's face; and O'Rourke did that with all his heart.

The man reeled, staggering, caught his heel upon the threshold of the door, and fell backward, grabbing frantically at the empty air. He shrieked once, and disappeared utterly, with the instantaneous effect of the vanishing of a kineto-scopic picture.

For a moment O'Rourke waited, holding the revolver ready, expecting any moment to see De Brissac rise from the ground and attempt a re-entrance to the hall.

Nothing of the sort happened, however. The silence and quiet without continued unbroken, save for the sighing of the wind. It struck O'Rourke as a curious fact that he had not heard the sound of the fall. A dread thought entered his brain, and took possession of his imagination, and he paled with the horror of it.

Slowly he picked up the sword, and he cautiously advanced again to the threshold of the door. Then he unsheathed the weapon and poked about in the blackness with the scabbard, holding the revolver poised to repel an attack, should one come — as he half hoped.

None came. Abruptly O'Rourke threw the empty scabbard into the darkness, listening to catch the clank of it upon the bridge of which De Brissac had spoken.

There was no sound.

The Irishman's heart seemed to cease its pulsations for a full minute; and then, far, far below him, he heard a faint, ringing clash.

So! *That,* then, had been the fate prepared for him by Duke Victor and De Brissac — that sudden plunge into a fathomless void, with a sure, swift death waiting at the end of his flight!

Faint and sick with disgust, trembling as with a vertigo, reeling and swaying like a drunkard, O'Rourke managed to close the door, and stagger a dozen yards or so away; and then, for a long time, he stood with one forearm to the wall, supporting his brow, the while he shuddered with sympathy

for the man who had sought his life by a means so foul —
and found therein only death for himself.

.   .   .   .

It was with an effort as of rousing from a stupor that
O'Rourke found himself again before the door of that room
wherein he had met and left Monsieur le Duc, Victor de
Grandlieu.

How he had managed to find it he did not know. His
mind was obsessed with a vision of De Brissac as he had last
seen him — toppling backward to his death. He seemed to
have been thinking of nothing else for a very long period of
time. And it was surprising, to say the least, to realize that,
during that train of thought, he had unconsciously threaded
his way back through the halls of Castle Grandlieu to this
particular room.

He paused, leaning dazedly against the wall, and passed
his hand across his eyes in an endeavor to collect his thoughts,
to marshal them into some form at least resembling coherency.

After a bit he discovered that he was listening — listening
intently for some sound within that silent hall. There was
none, except perhaps the crackling of the logs in the great
fireplace, as they spat, and sputtered, and crumbled to ash
in the flames.

Why was he there? Why was he not attempting to force
his way out of the castle? Or why was he not thinking of
Madame la Princesse?

At once he understood that there was an account to be
balanced with Monsieur the Duke — an account, it was true,
of short standing, but none the less demanding an immediate
settlement.

He turned the knob, pushed open the door and quietly
entered.

Duke Victor was sitting before the fire, gazing placidly into the dancing flames. His face was half averted; and he did not trouble to look around upon O'Rourke's entrance.

The Irishman waited, his shoulders against the panels of the closed door — waiting, he scarcely knew why, if it were not for monsieur the duke to assume the initiative. Meanwhile, his eyes roved the hall; and they brightened as they fell upon a rack of sabers at his side. Thoughtfully he removed one from its scabbard, and, resting it upon his arm, hilt outward, together with the sword he had taken from De Brissac, O'Rourke walked down the hall toward the duke.

The latter raised his head languidly, at the sound of approaching footsteps. With a half-interested, affected air, he pretended to be examining his nails, spreading his fingers out to the firelight and scrutinizing each with an excess of care.

"Well, my captain?" he inquired, drawling in a tone well-nigh of raillery. "Well, Captain de Brissac, has Monsieur the Colonel O'Rourke started upon his long journey — eh?"

"No, Monsieur the Duke," responded O'Rourke. "Ye will be surprised to learn that Monsieur the Colonel O'Rourke objected to being pushed into oblivion; and ye will, I doubt not, regret to hear that Monsieur the Captain de Brissac has — shall I say? — walked the plank in the O'Rourke's stead!"

At the first syllable, the duke turned. Before O'Rourke had made an end, the other was on his feet, every line in his face expressing the most complete stupefaction. Gradually, however, he regained his poise; by degrees he comprehended what must have been to him, with his unshakable faith in the might of De Brissac, quite incomprehensible.

"So?" he asked at length. "So you have conquered, Irishman?"

"The O'Rourke was not made to be thrust over the edge of a cliff by a mercenary murderer, Monsieur the Duke."

"It is apparent." The duke's nerve was admirable; he turned away again, and resumed his inspection of his finger nails. "And — and," he asked after a slight pause, "what do you intend to do about it, Colonel O'Rourke?"

"I propose, Monsieur the Duke, to give ye an opportunity to prove your right to live," returned O'Rourke calmly.

"What does that mean, monsieur?" The duke swung about quickly.

Bowing courteously, the Irishman proffered the weapons over his arm.

"It is your choice, monsieur the *canaille*," he said gently. "Choose quickly, monsieur, and defend yourself; for, if ye refuse, by the Eternal, I'll cut ye down as ye stand!"

The duke threw back his head and laughed joyously — a boyish laugh, ringing with superb self-confidence, that might well have sent a shiver quivering down O'Rourke's spine.

With a graceful gesture, the man seized the first hilt that came to his hand and led the way to the padded fencing floor.

"This," he said mirthfully, "is the apogee of chivalry, Colonel O'Rourke. You escape from one death and willingly offer yourself upon the altar of another. It is sad — nay, touching, Colonel O'Rourke. For — well, it would not be fair to myself to permit you to live, you understand. Moreover, it would be a weary disappointment to madame, should I fall. So, then, I grant you two minutes to make your peace with God, O'Rourke!"

"Guard!" cried O'Rourke briefly.

"You have no sins, then," asked the duke, with evident surprise, "for which to crave forgiveness ere you die?"

"Monsieur," returned the Irishman, "if ye are not on guard at once — your blood be upon your own head!"

He threw himself into position, facing his antagonist, and saluted. The duke laughed evilly, and carelessly touched O'Rourke's blade with his own.

A second later he was retreating swiftly down the hall — falling back under an onslaught the like of which he had seldom experienced, in point of sheer audacity and cunning.

But he parried with amazing ease, giving ground until he had recovered from his surprise, and permitting the impetuous Irishman to tire himself to the fill of his satisfaction.

"This is not so bad," he jeered. "It is, in fact, somewhat a pleasure to cross swords with a man who knows his weapon."

"The pleasure will be short-lived, I promise ye!" retorted O'Rourke.

The firelight flickered like lightning upon the crossed blades. The stamping of their feet was like dull thunder upon the padded fencing place.

The duke did not attempt again to speak. There was an anxious look in his eyes; he was trying to fathom the school by whose precepts O'Rourke fought — and trying in vain; for O'Rourke fought with the cunning and the technique of all schools, or, when occasion demanded, audaciously, according to his own inspiration of the moment. Possibly he was the most dangerous broadswordsman in the world; certainly his equal was not to be found in all Europe — not even at Castle Grandlieu in the person of the redoubtable Duke Victor himself.

And the duke was realizing that fact. He was tacitly

admitting, by the conservatism of his sword-play, that he was encountering, for once, his master. He was making no effort to attack, but contenting himself with desperate parry after parry, and, it may be, congratulating himself that he was able to parry an attack so artful and so infernally persistent.

Mere skill would serve him not at all. If he was to escape a crippling wound, if not death itself, he must rely upon his luck, upon chance, upon the turn of fortune's wheel. And he kept himself most vigilant to seize upon whatsoëver opening the Irishman might carelessly offer.

But O'Rourke was not careless. He underestimated his antagonist's abilities not in the least, and he knew assuredly that one false move, one attack too strong to permit of the speediest of recoveries, would prove fatal to him. It was in his mind to wear the duke down and administer the *coup de grâce* when the man was too weary and fagged to resist.

But that was not to be. The duke had not the slightest notion of permitting himself to be worn down. Recognizing O'Rourke's superior strength and endurance, he foresaw the ultimate outcome of the combat, if it continued for long.

And he laid his plans accordingly.

Step by step, inch by inch, he gave way, retreating to the paneled wall behind him. In time he felt its unyielding surface at the back of his shoulders.

Abruptly his sword arm dropped as though wearied. O'Rourke seized the opportunity, swung his saber high and brought it down with irresistible violence. Had the duke remained where he had been standing, he would have been split to the chin.

But he had dropped like a shot, thrusting upward, but, fortunately for O'Rourke, thrusting short. The Irishman's

point sank deep into the panel, and the blade snapped halfway down to the hilt.

Agile, and merciless as a cat, the duke was again instantly
upon his feet. O'Rourke, defenseless save for the hilt in his
hand, leaped backwards, a dozen feet, in the twinkling of an
eyelash. The duke hurled himself after him, like an avenging whirlwind, slipped upon the polished flooring, and
sprawled headlong.

His saber blade fell at O'Rourke's feet, and the adventurer promptly put one heel upon it while the other, without
compunction, he brought down heavily upon the duke's
fingers. The man swore with the pain and relaxed his
hold upon the hilt; O'Rourke stooped and tore the sword
from him.

Disarmed, the duke rose, his death clear to his eyes; the
polish of the nineteenth century dropped from him, like a
mummer's cloak; he stood, raging like a rat in a corner, showing himself for what he was — a primitive savage, raw, blood-
thirsty, unprincipled, untouched by the monitions of a conscience. Fear was in his eyes, for he expected his just due
— death; but rage was in his heart — rage, because he had
fought and lost and must pay the penalty.

He threw his arms wide with a passionate gesture, inviting the down sweep of the saber, bowing his head to its cleav-
ing stroke. And when that did not come, he raised his gaze
again to the face of the adventurer, puzzled, wondering; and
saw O'Rourke standing at ease, regarding him with pity, but
without hatred. He recognized that the Irishman was of a
fiber finer than his own, that he could spare the life even of
an antagonist who had but the moment gone tried to take his
own by cowardly assault. And the knowledge was insupportable; it was intolerable to contemplate an existence

owed to the mercy of a man to whom one had shown no mercy.

He stepped back a pace, his features distorted with hate and cunning. O'Rourke made no move, but continued — the saber swinging idly in his hand — to regard the vanquished man, reflectively, as though he were wondering what was to be the outcome, what portion — barring death — he should mete out to him to whose honor he might not trust.

The duke sidled away, his eyes fixed upon the adventurer's, and informed with an implacable, unreasoning hatred. Abruptly, when he had contrived to put a sufficient distance between them, he turned and began to run down the length of the great hall, swiftly, with an eye ever glancing over his shoulder, watching to see whether or no the Irishman would follow.

But O'Rourke did not. Somewhat puzzled, he waited, confident in his own prowess, now that he was armed, in his ability to cope with any device of the duke's, however infernally inspired.

At the center table, Monsieur the Duke stopped and fumbled with the lock of a certain drawer, a slight, crafty sneer of triumph and contempt admixed with the fear and hatred in his expression. He jerked open the drawer; it slipped from its runners, crashed loudly upon the floor, and the duke knelt by it, watching O'Rourke always, with cat-like vigilance, and groped an instant among the papers it contained.

Abruptly he started to his feet, holding a small, shining object that fitted snugly in his grip. There was a flash, a crack, and a bullet sang past O'Rourke and splattered upon the stones of the chimney-place.

With a roar of honest rage, O'Rourke started for him, swinging the saber above his head; it was to that alone that he must trust — to the edge against the lead: to the straightforward sword against the subtle bullet.

Yet there were many feet between him and the revolver — perhaps ten yards. He had been criminally negligent in thus permitting the man a chance to redeem his life. He had trusted his life to the honor of one without honor, and he was to pay the price of his folly.

He had scarce moved before the revolver spoke again; and again the duke missed. He had, however, four bullets left, and remembering this, the man calmed himself, steadied his hand, took time for a more accurate aim. His next bullet ploughed through the adventurer's shoulder.

It was like being pierced by a rod of fire; for an instant O'Rourke was staggered; and then the burning agony maddened him. He felt that he was to pay the price of his own life for the duke's, yet felt that he would gladly do so if only he might pass the threshold of Eternity in company with the soul of Monsieur le Duc, Victor le Grandlieu.

Half blind with wrath, he threw himself towards the man, like an avenging angel with flaming sword. There sounded one more shot: fortunately the revolver was of small caliber — no larger than a .38; though the bullet again took effect and found lodgment in the Irishman's side, yet the impact of it was not sufficient to stop him. He whirled on, swinging the broadsword high above his head.

Cold fear tightened about the heart of Monsieur the Duke. His fingers trembled. He fired again, futilely, then, in a gust of abject terror, dropped his weapon and leaped back, cowering his arms wavering above his head, a weak barrier against the gleaming yard of steel.

His heel caught, somehow, upon a rug, and he fell, but not more swiftly than the saber. The blade smashed through his guarding arms, lopping off neatly one hand, crashed through his skull as though it had been brittle cardboard, cleft his head from crown to chin, and stopped, almost inextricably imbedded in the man's chest.

O'Rourke tugged once, without reason, at the weapon, then released his grip. He stepped back, and the pain of his wounds bore upon him like a crushing weight. He clapped a hand to his side, and felt the hot gush of his life's blood.

For a space he stood reeling, a red mist swimming before his eyes, trying to think what now to do. He must escape — get away somehow — win from out that castle that, for all he knew, fairly teemed with the armed and faithful retainers of the dead man.

Already the succession of shots had roused them; already O'Rourke could hear, faintly through the thundering in his ears, shrieks of alarm, shouts, cries, the drumming of men's footsteps as they ran hither and yon, searching out the cause of the disturbance. . . . And he was powerless!

He staggered forward and slumped into a nearby chair. He could no more: he trembled with pain and exhaustion like a thoroughbred horse than has been run until it falls.

Unconsciously he flung out an arm upon the table. His head fell forward upon him. . . . The pain subsided; languor, invincible, insidious, ran in his veins. . . . And he fancied, dimly, deliriously, that the figure of his princess hovered near him, that her face, tender, passionate and compassionate, hung over him.

His lips moved. "Beatrix!" he muttered. "Beatrix! . . . Faith, 'tis . . . worth while . . . even to die for ye . . . heart's dearest . . ."

CHAPTER XX

THE END OF THE QUEST

HE came to his wits, strangling, his throat burned by a stinging dose of brandy, and sat up, coughing, conscious that the pain in his shoulder and his side was growing yet more agonizing with each passing instant.

Blinded with it, he was yet aware that he was not alone. Realizing this he strove to force himself into clear sentience.

As though from a distance of many leagues a voice thrilled in his ears — a voice to whose sweet accents he had not listened for long years.

"...*Terence!*..." it whispered, "...*Terence, beloved!*..."

"'Tis not so," he muttered thickly. "'Tis ... not so!..."

A hand, soft, cool, light as the leaf of a rose, was upon his forehead; there was a shiver of breath upon his cheek; and the whispered appeal: "*Terence, Terence, my beloved!*"

Through all the pain and nausea, through the deadening lethargy that seemed to be numbing him thoroughly, penetrated the knowledge that he had won — somehow — to the presence of his heart's mistress. With a magnificent effort, drunkenly, he straightened up in his chair, erected his head, opened his eyes, even found strength to bring himself abruptly, with a mechanical movement, to his feet.

"*Princesse!*" he said clearly. "I am come ... to die for ye ... as I promised ..."

The filmy mists of weakness that had lain, tremulously, before his eyes, seemed to tremble and fall apart — as the mists of morning before the rays of the sun. He saw, and saw, it seemed, more distinctly than ever he had been able to observe, his princess, and the beauty that was hers, — her face close to his, her eyes upon his own, glorious with the light of the love that she bore him.

"Terence!" she whispered again; and he felt her arms close about him, lending him strength to support himself. "Terence, sweetheart! Ah, but you are —"

"Dying, madame," he breathed hoarsely. "'Tis me fate . . . and me desire . . . to die for ye . . ."

He heard her sob softly. "But you will not — must not die, sweetheart. You — ah, but I thought you had come back to claim me — at last, Terence, at last! . . . And I had waited so long, so long, my beloved!"

He passed a hand across his eyes, with the other gripped the back of a chair.

"D'ye mean it?" he cried. "That ye want me, after all, my princess? . . ."

"Want you, dearest? Ah, but that I might die in your place."

He seemed to concentrate himself as by a powerful putting forth of his will. The veins upon his forehead stood out darkly; the muscles of his jaw were like huge knots beneath his skin. He forced speech between his clenched teeth.

"Is there . . . chance of escape? . . ."

"I have locked the doors," she told him. "None can enter. We are alone, and there is a secret way out of the castle."

"Then," he interrupted tensely, "give me brandy . . . 'Twas that ye gave me the minute gone? . . ."

She pressed the edge of a goblet against his lips. He gripped its stem, threw back his head and swallowed, gulp after gulp. Sound and in his right mind, the quantity would have well-nigh killed him. At the moment it lent him, temporarily, fictive but necessary strength. He showed it at once in his manner.

"Time?" he demanded.

"They are battering upon the doors; they may break in."

"I can't go this way."

It was true that the people of the castle were assaulting the doors of the great hall; the thundering blows upon the stout oaken panels were rapid and constantly increasing in force. Yet the doors were strong, and would hold yet a little while.

"The way out?" he asked.

She seemed to glide across the floor, swiftly, to one wall, where, beneath a hanging tapestry, she discovered to him a sliding panel. "Here?" she announced, waiting expectantly, quivering with anxiety and pity.

"Turn your back," he commanded roughly, "and stay so for — till I speak."

She obeyed. Despite the exquisite pain he endured, the man nerved himself to manage to remove his coat. With his knife he slit away one sleeve and the side of his shirt — grinding his teeth with mortal anguish. Then, swiftly tearing the linen into strips, he moistened them with water from a silver pitcher on the table and plastered them upon his wounds. "They be not wide, nor deep," he said to himself. "'Tis not worthy the name of O'Rourke I am if I cannot overcome them — win out of here — mend. . . ."

Somehow — it seemed by hours of painful struggling, he got the coat on again and buttoned it tight about him. Then, with his one sound arm pressing the other against his side, tightly, to hold the bandages — such as they were — in place, he turned, gathered himself together for a supreme

[390]

effort, and with a tolerably firm step moved across the floor and joined the woman.

He noted that she was attired as though for traveling. The circumstance puzzled him, yet at the moment he could spare no strength for words.

"Ready, madame," he announced with difficulty.

The woman stepped through the opened panel into stark blackness, which lay beyond. He followed; and she turned and slid the panel back into position. A furious crash told him that the doors to the hall — one or both of them — had given away.

Summoning the utmost of his iron resolution, the Irishman permitted the woman to take the lead, stumbling after her, guiding himself through the impenetrable darkness by the sounds of her passage — the rustle of her skirts and the light, almost inaudible tap of her footsteps.

"Faith, 'tis a woman after me own heart, she is!" he thought. "To lead on so, without weakness or faltering, in a time like this — without stopping to comfort me, or to mourn!"

He felt himself stronger with each instant. The liquor was acting upon him oddly, seeming to flood his being with great, recurring waves of power. This effect, he knew, was but transient; yet it would serve.

It seemed that they trod miles of dense darkness; they descended steps, climbed again, felt their way down narrow and tortuous passages, cold as the heart of death itself. It was a progress interminable to the wounded man: hours seemed to elapse.

"Surely," he thought, "'tis morning be now."

Yet when they unexpectedly emerged, it was into the open air of the mountainside, and the winter's night still held over the land. Above hung sable and opaque skies, cloud cloaked; below the mountainside sloped to the clustered, twinkling lights of Montbar, the city, to which the road wound down the mountain, a serpentine course outlined by threads of electric light.

Behind him — apparently the eighth of a mile distant — the stark and ugly battlements of the Castle of Grandlieu reared their blunt heads to Heaven. Before them, immediately at hand, lay the road, and upon it squatted, huge and monstrous, an automobile, purring huskily, diffusing a taint of petrol upon the cold night air, illuminating the highway with huge, glaring head lamps.

The woman paused and caught O'Rourke in her arms again. "My beloved!" she said. And then, turning, called aloud: "Monsieur Chambret!"

A man clambered hastily out of the tonneau of the car and came running towards them. With a few brief words the woman explained the situation. O'Rourke said nothing. He could not. It was all he could encompass to keep his feet. Chambret sprang to his side, silently, and gave him aid to the automobile. Somehow the Irishman was got in upon the rear seat. The princesse entered with him. Chambret buried them both under a mountain of fur robes.

O'Rourke closed his eyes, his head resting upon the woman's shoulder, her lips — he never forgot the cool, firm touch of them — upon his forehead. He heard the motor cough raucously and was conscious of a thunderous vibration, together with a sweep of nipping air against his face.

The freshness of it and the crashing of the car through the night kept him conscious for a space. He whispered now and again with the woman of his heart — little, intimate phrases that epitomized the undying passion that was theirs.

The End of the Quest

Once she told him: "The frontier is not far, sweetheart. Once over that, beyond immediate pursuit, we will stop at an inn and summon a surgeon. Can you bear, O my dearest, to wait so long?"

"I — Ah, faith! I could endure a thousand deaths — and yet live on — in your arms . . ."

And again he asked: "'Tis miraculous — this escape! Tell me how it was contrived."

"Through Monsieur Chambret," she replied: "Monsieur Chambret, to whom we owe all. He communicated with me through my maid, by means of that secret passage, of which you know. And, not knowing when you would arrive, dear heart — Ah, but you were long! — we laid our plans for an escape whether or not you came . . . I had sworn that I would marry no man but you! . . . It was schemed for this very morning; the automobile was to be in waiting on that by-path. I was in the act of leaving the castle when I heard the shots . . . I ran, was the first to enter the hall."

"And so . . . Ah, sweetheart, sweetheart! If the O'Rourke dies, 'twill be of sheer happiness!"

She caught him more closely to her. The pain in his wounds seemed to be lessening; a delicious and dreamy languor crept over him, and he lay very still, content in her arms, feeling himself slip gradually into slumber from which he could not be sure that he should ever waken: while the motor car crashed and roared on through the dawn — the bright dawn of many confident to-morrows.

CHECKERS

A Hard Luck Story

By HENRY M. BLOSSOM, Jr.

Author of "The Documents in Evidence"

Abounds in the most racy and picturesque slang.—*N. Y. Recorder.*

"Checkers" is an interesting and entertaining chap, a distinct type, with a separate tongue and a way of saying things that is oddly humorous.—*Chicago Record.*

If I had to ride from New York to Chicago on a slow train, I should like a half-dozen books as gladsome as "Checkers" and I could laugh at the trip.—*N. Y. Commercial Advertiser.*

"Checkers" himself is as distinct a creation as Chimmie Fadden and his racy slang expresses a livelier wit. The racing part is clever reporting and as horsey and "up-to-date" as any one could ask. The slang of the race-course is caught with skill and is vivid and picturesque, and students of the byways of language may find some new gems of colloquial speach to add to their lexicons.—*Springfield Republican.*

A new popular edition just issued, in attractive cloth binding, small 12mo in size. Price, 75 cents, postpaid.

GROSSET & DUNLAP

52 Duane Street,   ::   ::   ::   New York

BREWSTER'S MILLIONS

BY
GEORGE BARR McCUTCHEON

The hero is a young New Yorker of good parts who, to save an inheritance of seven millions, starts out to spend a fortune of one million within a year. An eccentric uncle, ignorant of the earlier legacy, leaves him seven millions to be delivered at the expiration of a year, on the condition that at that time he is penniless, and has proven himself a capable business man, able to manage his own affairs. The problem that confronts Brewster is to spend his legacy without proving himself either reckless or dissipated. He has ideas about the disposition of the seven millions which are not those of the uncle when he tried to supply an alternative in case the nephew failed him. His adventures in pursuit of poverty are decidedly of an unusual kind, and his disappointments are funny in quite a new way. The situation is developed with an immense amount of humor.

OTHER BOOKS BY THE SAME AUTHOR:

GRAUSTARK, The Story of a Love behind a Throne.
CASTLE CRANEYCROW.   THE SHERRODS.

Handsome cloth bound volumes, 75 cents each.

At all Booksellers, or sent postpaid on receipt of price by the Publishers.

GROSSET & DUNLAP :: NEW YORK

Lightning Source UK Ltd.
Milton Keynes UK
UKHW020749180219
337443UK00007B/689/P